Peter Tonkin was born in Northern Ireland, the eldest son of a forces family, and was raised in the UK, Holland, Germany and the Persian Gulf. He is married and is the Head of English and Director of Post-16 Provision at the Wildernesse School in Sevenoaks. He has written five previous novels, including three Richard Mariner adventures.

Praise for Peter Tonkin and his adventure-thrillers:

'A master of sea-going adventure. Enough taut suspense to satisfy any reader' Clive Cussler

'Good technical detail, plus an exciting climax, makes this entertaining reading' *Publishing News*

'In the rattling good yarn mould, this story . . . never flags and has the virtue of being well written' *Yorkshire Evening Post*

'Edge-of-the-seat terror on the high seas' *Daily Post*

The Bomb Ship

Peter Tonkin

HEADLINE
FEATURE

First published in 1993
by HEADLINE BOOK PUBLISHING PLC

First published in paperback in 1993
by HEADLINE BOOK PUBLISHING

A HEADLINE FEATURE paperback

10 9 8 7 6 5 4 3 2 1

ISBN 0 7472 4031 0

Phototypeset by Intype, London

Printed and bound in Great Britain by
HarperCollins Manufacturing, Glasgow

HEADLINE BOOK PUBLISHING
A division of Hodder Headline PLC
Headline House
79 Great Titchfield Street
London W1P 7FN

For Cham and Guy

BOMB SHIP: 'A ship loaded with mortars or bombs.'
First used 1704.

Oxford English Dictionary

For there is no friend like a sister
In calm or stormy weather;
To cheer one on the tedious way,
To fetch one if one goes astray,
To lift one if one totters down,
To strengthen whilst one stands.

Christina Rossetti, *Goblin Fair*

PART ONE

The Bombs

CHAPTER ONE

Naming Day

Tuesday, 16 February   04:00

The black waters parted and a black-wrapped bundle rose all but invisibly to the surface. It was rounded but not round, as though a square object had been wrapped in some protective material and then swathed in black plastic. It was about the same size as a backpack and roughly the same shape, though the way it sat on the water made it seem that something larger and more buoyant was supporting it from just beneath the inky waves.

A westerly squall gusted across the lough, spraying chill rain like handfuls of gravel, setting the surface to dancing and foaming, and sending all the flotsam bobbing eastward with the choppy wavelets it created. The black bundle moved determinedly westwards into the teeth of the wind, shorewards towards the sickly yellow of the security lighting and the twinkling city beyond.

A second squall roared over the mountain and across the sleeping streets and on down to set the water rearing into more ugly wavelets, giving the first bundle a brief bow wave just as a second one broke water beside it. The foul weather continued to beat against them as they pushed forwards, like two slightly misshapen naval mines, towards the shore. As they neared the tide line, so the heads and air tanks of the divers pushing them broke the surface in turn and the steady beating of their diving fins disturbed the wave pattern behind. The nearer the tide line they came, the slower the divers swam, so that at last, just as the two black bundles began to grind up a solid slope, all forward motion stopped and the glass of two face plates reflected the security lighting as the divers looked up and around themselves.

Beyond the bulk of the bundle, each saw first the slope of a concrete slipway, slick and glossy with rain, ribboned with steel rails like giant railway tracks. At the crest of the slope, on the runways waiting to be launched, sat two ships side by side. The ships were facing inland, and the perspective combined with massive size and impenetrable shadows to make it impossible for the divers to comprehend everything at once. All they could clearly make out as they hung immobile in the freezing water, waiting until their first visual check of this end of the shipyard was complete, was the massive brass propeller sitting beneath the overhanging stern of each of the ships.

Each propeller had three blades and each blade shone, bright new metal reflecting the security lighting almost as clearly as the glass in the face plates. Each blade was as tall as the first storey of a house front and almost as wide. With the huge conical boss round which the blades were hinged, each of the propellers would have obscured the front of any of the modest two-storey terraced houses in the city beyond the shipyard. There was about them an air of massive weight and solidity, an impression which was deepened by the hulls of the ships beyond.

The divers floated for an instant side by side, a tall,

muscular figure beside a shorter, slighter one. For all their physical difference it was clear that the shorter of the two was the dominant one the instant they were in action. There was no signal apparent between them but they were in motion at exactly the same moment, pushing their burdens forward up the slipway to reveal black rafts on which the bundles sat. The wind thundered around them as they rose out of the water like black seals. The rain spattered and hissed on the concrete as they slipped off their air tanks and face masks, then crouched to remove their flippers and to release the bundles from the rafts. The foul weather cocooned them as they sprinted forward into the outwash of the security lighting, each now burdened with his black-wrapped parcel, heading with one accord for darkness and quiet.

But not warmth: there was no heat available to the two divers within or without. All they could hope for was some shelter from the stormy wind and the driving rain, some opportunity to catch their breath, chafe their shaking hands, and endeavour to massage some feeling back into their numbed fingers. So cold were they that the rain felt warm against their lips and chins before the wind-chill factor cooled the wet skin to freezing. Bare feet as senseless as fingers stumbled and stubbed as the two black-clad figures ran up the slipway and into the darkness between the two ships. The closer they came to the pair of vessels, the greater their size seemed to grow. The thrust of massive steering gear became obvious behind the great propellers. Smaller, manoeuvring propellers behind the main ones were dwarfed by the sheer scale of the shafts thrusting out to the main propellers. The hulls of the ship towered over the two scurrying figures and the bundles they were carrying.

Between the parallel keels was a tunnel of darkness five

hundred feet long and into this the two divers plunged
side by side. Moments later they emerged, every bit as
hesitantly as they had come out of the water, into the light
between the steel-clad cliffs of the bows. Immediately
beyond the dizzy reach of the shear cutwaters stood a
grandstand constructed of steel girders dressed in bright
canvas. The gaudy colours seemed to be bleached and
running under the twin effects of yellow light and driving
rain. The bunting seemed to be light and sere under the
influence of the stormy wind. Beneath the canvas covers,
however, there was relative calm and apparent warmth, if
not much reduction in noise, and the two figures crouched
side by side again, like children sheltering in a massive
tent. The canvas was heavy enough to cut off most of the
light and so the first thing taken from each of the bundles
was a torch. Two beams swept around the forest of tubular
steel supports and the wooden sky of seats rising into
impenetrable shadow, step by step as the grandstand fell
back. But the divers were not interested in the further
reaches. They unpacked their bundles and retraced their
steps to that part of the grandstand which stood nearest to
the twin hulls of the ships. Here they shone their torch
beams along one steel strut after another, bright pools of
light lingering especially on the joints, until one thick
reinforcement tube answered the yellow brightness with a
small red mark.

The taller diver held the beam on the marked member
while the other carefully unscrewed it. The wind gusted
with a sound like an avalanche outside and all the girders
flexed and creaked. Both divers looked around apprehen-
sively, but the joint they were uncoupling remained firm.
The sleeve which they were unscrewing slid down to reveal
the gape of open tubes. While everything else around then

flexed and groaned, these tubes remained firm. It was the work of a very few minutes to pack the contents of the black bundles into the hollow tubes. Twenty pounds of doughy Semtex explosive oozed stiffly into the metal members, turning the grandstand's false supports into a lethally powerful bomb. A timer, itself tubular, fitted exactly between the ends of the tubes within the joint. A white finger pushed a button and a pre-set display flashed into life. The finger was chalk-white because it was chilled to the bone and what should have been a simple, accurate, single stab of action, became a clumsy, shaking one. The display flashed into life, died, lit up again. The pre-set figures jumped forward, adding ten minutes to the countdown.

The two divers looked at each other, frozen with shock. Then the slighter one, who had mis-set the timer, gave a peculiar, almost French shrug. 'C'est la vie', it seemed to say. Clearly it would be impossible to reset the digital display through twenty-three hours and fifty minutes if the simple act of switching it on could go so disastrously wrong. Hurriedly now, as though unnerved by the bad luck that had rendered their actions less than perfect, the first diver lifted the joint sleeve and screwed it back into place so that its extra thickness perfectly concealed the explosive and the timer. Then the two of them stumbled back to the little pile of rubbish which was all that remained of their two bundles. Carefully they cleared up any trace of themselves and then they ran back out into the stormy night. Under the restless canvas, all that remained of their presence was a twin set of wet footprints which were almost instantly concealed by the drizzle forcing its way through the wooden seats above.

At the water's edge, they fought their way back into

their compressed air tanks and their flippers. They carried the rubbish with them back out into the water until they could leave it floating safely, anonymously, lost for ever among the flotsam. Then they turned to look back one last time and the taller one hit the other on the shoulder in exuberant relief. 'Well done!' the friendly blow seemed to say. The smaller figure reacted unexpectedly. Turning towards the tall diver, it reached up for him, face plate dangling from one slim wrist. He lowered his head and, waist deep in the black water, the two divers kissed long and deeply.

Then the slighter figure put her mouthpiece where his lips had been and turned away. He stood for a moment longer looking back at the pale wash of the security lighting, the dark loom of the sister ships and the two bright brass stars of the propellers. The glass of his face plate reflected the dockyard and the lights of the city beyond, creeping up the black shoulder of the mountain behind. Then he gave a fatalistic, almost hopeless shrug and followed his companion eastwards into the first steely promise of the stormy dawn.

CHAPTER TWO

Naming Day

Tuesday, 16 February   08:00

Robin Mariner turned away from the shaving mirror above the washbasin and padded across the bathroom. She had used a flannel to wipe away the condensation from her bath, but it kept returning to make the little glass useless as a make-up mirror. As she passed the bathroom chair, she caught up her towelling dressing gown and used it to clear the condensation off the full-length bathroom mirror instead. When she had done so, she stood back and moodily surveyed her naked body in it. She did not much like what she saw.

Since her teens she had taken a sort of thoughtless pride in her girlish figure and her ability to keep it. Her busy, physically demanding work had seen to that. Slim muscularity and complete fitness had been something she had taken for granted. But during the last eighteen months, motherhood had changed all that. It had added an unwelcome softness to her breasts, inches and stretch marks to her waist and hips, an all too apparent weightiness to her thighs and bottom. She felt fat.

An explosion of hilarity came from beyond the bathroom door as the twins pulled their father into one of their games. Robin's mouth twitched into an automatic smile which only served to show the wrinkles around her eyes. Really, this mirror was merciless! She padded closer and concentrated on her face. Too many windswept, blistering days at sea had undermined the natural creaminess of her complexion and all the oils and unguents money could buy did nothing to smooth the lines at the corners of her eyes and lips. At least the gold of her short-cropped curls concealed the increasing number of silver hairs among them. Even so, she felt old.

The noise from the bedroom reached a kind of hysterical climax and then stopped abruptly. Robin knew what that meant: Nurse Janet had entered and the three of them were in trouble. She shook her head, still lost in thought. Where did Richard get his energy from? Janet had been hired to help him convalesce after the Gulf War and had stayed on to act as a nanny to William and Mary and yet of all of the family, it seemed that Robin had the least energy, the lowest resilience.

The twins had been up all night, unsettled by yesterday's journey and the strangeness of their surroundings; no one in the hotel suite, probably no one in the hotel itself, had got any sleep at all. She leaned forward until her breath clouded on the water-streaked glass. She rarely bothered with much make-up but she would have to do something about those dark rings round her eyes. There were bound to be photographs when she launched the sister ships and she didn't want to see herself looking like a panda in all the papers. Or on television either, for that matter.

And cameras added pounds to even the slimmest of figures. Oh, why had she agreed to do it? she asked herself pettishly, though she knew the answer well enough. The sister ships were important to the company which Richard and she ran.

Heritage Mariner was just about the last independent shipping company in Britain. The oil-shipping trade, the backbone of their business, was on its uppers these days. What little demand there had been was all but killed by the Gulf War. At the moment, all attempts to broaden their base into commodity shipping had been crippled by the IRA's recent attack on the Baltic Exchange, which had also destroyed the original offices of Crewfinders, Richard's first company, and had blown out all the windows in Heritage House, their current headquarters. Heritage Mariner's more recent venture into leisure boats had been hampered by the recession in Europe and America.

The sister ships waiting to be launched later this morning represented Heritage Mariner's move into the only growth area in modern shipping: the safe transport of military and industrial waste – if the term 'safe' could ever be applied to the chemical and nuclear filth the two ships were designed to carry across the wild North Atlantic.

Her watch alarm began to sound, jerking her back to reality. She glanced at the multi-function diving chronometer on her left wrist, though she knew what the time was well enough. Eight fifteen. She had better get a move on. The long fingers of her right hand ran through the damp curls of her hair. She never normally bothered with a hair dryer, but today was different. She returned across the room, reached for the portable, battery-powered one Richard had bought her especially for this trip and turned it on the mirror above the washbasin, clearing away the condensation which had crept back while she was lost in thought. Perhaps this one would be kinder than the full-length one, she thought.

Twenty minutes later she was just putting the finishing

touches to an unaccustomedly thorough make-up when the bathroom door opened.

'Nurse Janet and I have given the monsters their breakfast,' said Richard. 'I have the porridge on my dressing gown to prove it. God, you look wonderful.' He wrapped his arms round her waist and lifted her off the floor until the bristles on his chin were scraping softly against the junction of her neck and shoulder. The sensation made her shiver with lust.

Even reflected in the little mirror they made a striking couple. Her blonde ringlets curled against the solid plane of his cheek, setting off its steel-blue lines. The grey concealed within them was more obvious against the black of his temples, a salt and pepper effect she loved. The peaches and cream complexion she felt she was beginning to lose remained enough in evidence to show off the weathered tan of his high forehead and sharp cheekbones. The deep grey of her eyes set off the light blue in his. Where her nose almost turned up, his plunged in that patrician way, broken slightly out of line by some adventure in his youth. God, how she loved him, she thought.

'Put me down, darling,' she ordered, but her voice lacked conviction. Then she felt the chilly patches which told her he had not been exaggerating about the porridge on his dressing gown. She thought about going through the next few hours with cold porridge drying in her back. 'Put me down at once!' she said again and this time he did not hesitate.

'May I shave now?'

'Yes. I haven't much more to do.' She ran her fingers through her hair again in case his clumsy playfulness had disturbed it. Her mood began to darken once more. She crossed back to the full-length glass and leaned closer to it as Richard's hot shaving water splashed into the basin. At once, her mirror began to fog up again.

Dan Williams met them in the hotel lobby. He was a huge Canadian with a wise, wizened Celtic Welsh face perched atop a Viking giant's body. His clothes were conservative and businesslike – a dark suit, a pale shirt and a silk tie – but they were unmistakably American and seemed ill-suited to his massive frame. At first glance it was hard to sum him up; he could have been anything from a lawyer to a lumberjack. He was in fact a shipping man. A Canadian version of Richard Mariner, running an independent shipping fleet in a depressed market in a shrinking world. He, unlike Richard, ran a one-man show, but he had used the extra years he had over his English associate to broaden his base: he was a partner in the Sept Isles Waste Disposal Company and he was the man who had part-funded the ships they were here to launch. He owned one of them outright, although Robin would have the honour of naming both. He would run his ship out of Sept Isles where his headquarters was. Richard and Dan had great plans – and a great deal of money bound up in them. But he might just as well have been here to amuse the twins. As soon as they saw him, they ran across the lobby, screaming with glee, to be swept up against the barrel of his chest, one in each arm, for a bear hug.

As far as the twins were concerned, the limousine was their greatest adventure so far, even better than yesterday's jet. The sheer size of the car was a source of excitement – even for toddlers used to riding in their parents' Range Rover and their grandfather's Bentley. The rear-facing seats in the back proved a source of amusement which Dan Williams compounded and even the disapproval of Nurse

Janet could not dim. They crawled all over the seats and
tottered dangerously from door to door as the motorcade
swept down the North Circular Road round the foot of the
mountain and into the outskirts of Belfast itself.

Robin watched them with a jaundiced eye. Her outfit,
carefully chosen from among her favourites pre-pregnancy,
felt restrictively tight. She was sure she would present a
laughable figure in the news photographs, all horizontal
wrinkles and straining seams, like a mother dressed in
her daughter's clothes. Perhaps she should have chosen
something more flowing and matronly. But she didn't feel
like a matron, so why should she dress like one? Nurse
Janet leaned forward to collect young William just as he
began to explore an ashtray beside his father's elbow.
Richard was oblivious, locked in deep discussion with
Dan.

'So, this is it, everything ready to go.'

'I guess so. It's exciting, Richard, but sometimes I think
maybe I'm getting too old for this stuff, you know?'

'Anything in particular?'

'I need to go through the crewing lists again. I brought
them with me to check through on the plane, but I'll have
to take another look when I get back home next week. The
captain . . .' The Canadian's voice drifted off uncertainly.

'That's the price of running a one-man show, Dan,' said
Richard sympathetically. 'I did it for long enough before
I joined the Heritage Mariner team. Thank God it's not
like that now. I've Bill Heritage, looking after things in
London at the moment – he knows the shipping better
than any of us. Helen Dufour's sorting out the Russian
end . . .' He too broke off. Voicing sympathy with his
friend and associate was one thing, making a list of his
own relative strengths was too much like boasting. Silence

fell for a second; an unnatural state which the twins were
happy to dispel.

Nurse Janet was slim and calm and blonde and
especially slim, thought Robin. She would look much
better in all the photographs and television news bulletins.
Robin stopped Mary from following her brother's example
and handed the squirming toddler to Richard, interrupting
his tête-à-tête. At least it didn't matter how creased
Richard's clothes were, she thought maliciously; it was
Dan and she who were on the firing line today.

As the limousine swung into the Crumlin Road, it
became part of a motorcade and suddenly the twins were
straining to watch what was going on around them, as
though they had suddenly joined a circus parade. William
stood on Janet's lap, his button nose pressed up against
the car window, and Mary jiggled up and down on her
father's knees, equally entranced. Even Robin was momentarily distracted by their innocent excitement, though she
was all too vividly aware of the importance of the other
vehicles in front and behind them. She glanced across at
Richard and found that he had been looking at her. The
shock of his ice-blue gaze shivered down her spine as it
always did and she smiled, relieved to know that he shared
some of her concerns.

The Secretary of State's motorcade joined in behind
theirs as they swept past the end of Corporation Street
and into Albert Square.

It had been a gloomy day so far. The mountain behind
the hotel had loomed darkly all the way down to the North
Circular Road and the clouds above it had hardly been
any lighter. Now, as they came out of Albert Square,
past the Custom House and onto Queen Elizabeth Bridge,
another squall swept across the city and seemed to follow

the river down towards the sea, doing its level best to take the two motorcades along with it. Robin felt the limousine lift off the bridge and she clutched Richard automatically with her left hand, and felt him clutching at Mary as she reached for William with her right. Only Dan Williams sat still, apparently unconcerned, as though his massiveness would hold the car safe in spite of all the wind could do. The car settled back onto the road. The twins screamed with delight. Robin let go of her husband and her son. She met the mocking smile in Dan's dark eyes and blushed, feeling faintly foolish.

They turned left out of Queen's Quay and into Queen's Road, the backbone of the dockyards. Down the centre of Queen's Island they sped, with the river on their left, invisible behind the buildings, until they reached the great gates surmounted with the legend 'Harland and Wolff'. As though by magic, the gates opened and the two motorcades swung in. There was a kind of bedlam as the security vehicles pulled up in one spot and the limousines parked in another. Then Robin was out in the blustery morning, with a solicitous official holding an umbrella over her, and Richard was there beside her, steadying the umbrella with his iron grip as the wind threatened to tear it away. Neither he nor Dan actually seemed to fit beneath the straining umbrellas, but both of them treated the squall with disdain in any case. They had no need to worry about hair-dos and outfits and looking as though they had just stepped out of *Vogue* magazine. Another set of gates stood in front of them, opening onto a bunting-dressed grandstand, but between the guests and their seats stood eager ranks of photographers and news reporters.

Both Robin and Richard had enjoyed a fairly positive relationship with the press over the years. Not for many a day had they featured regularly in the gossip columns, though their appearances on the society pages in *Tatler* and *Hello* had been frequent enough. They were not really of any interest to the paparazzi; and the financial correspondents who were the other news people interested in their doings rarely went too far in their search for information. Only Richard's involvement in the Gulf War had pulled them out of the comfortable relationship they enjoyed with the press, and that affected nothing here.

Indeed, as Richard and Robin approached the press, they smiled at familiar faces and accepted smiles in return with very much more confidence and aplomb than did their old friend the Secretary of State beside them. It was to Sir Jeffrey that the press spoke first, of course, shaking hands with the plump little politician in the over-cheerful pantomime of a photo opportunity. At once the welcoming committee from the great shipbuilding firm joined them and the ritual was repeated against the bright background of the straining golf umbrellas. At the earliest opportunity the news reporters surged forward for comment and question. Here the Secretary of State came into his own, smoothly answering the questions of cub reporters from the local papers and the older hands from the nationals with courteous vagueness. To all of the TV cameras he gave equally bland sound bites. But then the weather took a hand, turning the biggest of the umbrellas inside out, and they were hurried on through, only five minutes behind schedule.

The press people were all British, with one exception. Richard was surprised to see the familiar face of an old American friend among them. Ann Cable was now established as an investigative journalist with a considerable international reputation, but when Richard had first met her she had been a stringer for Reuters working out of Naples and an active member of Greenpeace. They had sailed together on a battered old freighter called *Napoli* and her fate had at one stroke established Ann's reputation and Richard's desire to ensure that the transport of toxic waste was as well controlled as possible. It was his power and influence that had resulted in the ships Robin was about to name. Richard met Ann Cable's eager, intelligent gaze. The tall American brunette's bright blue eyes crinkled in the ghost of a smile. Her full lips lifted ever so slightly at the corners. All her Italian blood shone through the minuscule facial expressions. Only the Neapolitan Nico Niccolo, destined to be first officer of one of these ships and long-time lover of Ann, could say more with less expression. Richard found himself giving the ghost of a shrug and she gave the hint of a nod: they would get together later. For the moment, the ceremony must proceed.

Richard glanced round. The momentary communication with Ann had put him out of step with the rest of his group: Robin was gone with Dan Williams, the Secretary of State and the shipyard and company representatives. Janet seemed to have the twins well in hand. Richard moved forward to join the minor VIPs and climbed onto the brightly dressed grandstand from where he could look down with justifiable pride upon the sister ships he had caused to be built and on his wife who was about to name them.

Robin's speech was brief and to the point. Any temptation she might have felt to talk at length was curtailed by the persistent rain and the stormy west wind. Even with the aid of the microphone, much of what she said was all but lost beneath the roaring of the squalls and the explo-

sive flapping of the canvas, the creaking of the grandstand's tubular steel structure and the hiss of the stormy
surf pushed high up the slipway by the tide.

She told the story of *Napoli*, the battered old freighter
laden with atomic and chemical waste. She explained how
she had been trapped at home, heavily pregnant, while
Richard had been trapped aboard, hopelessly trying to get
the cargo to Canada while the chemicals ate away at the
ship and at the protective covering around the atomic
waste. Richard had been lucky to survive the loss of the
Napoli and was still involved in a court case arising from
the incident. That being said, his shock at discovering the
state in which such dangerous cargoes could be shipped
had strengthened his resolve to see that it was done safely.
Heritage Mariner had, in conjunction with the Sept Isles
Waste Disposal Company of Sept Isles in Canada and
the Williams Shipping Company with which they were
associated, set up a route between northern Europe and
North America along which toxic waste could be trans-
ported safely, at each end of which were facilities which
guaranteed equal safety in the disposal of the waste. And
these ships were the backbone of that plan. They would
be named for two of the Greek Fates, in the hope that a
third would be ordered in due course; a hope which in
turn rested upon Heritage Mariner's bid to become
involved with the transport for disposal of the massive
stockpiles of Soviet nuclear hardware. Hence the ships
had been designed with strengthened bows, to function as
icebreakers, and the routes to be explored would run as far
north as the North Atlantic would allow. Ultimately, should
the Fates for whom the sister ships were to be named
prove kind, the routes would stretch from the St Lawrence
Seaway to Murmansk and even Archangel. In the

meantime, the sisters would have to be content with sailing between Sept Isles in Canada and Sellafield in Cumbria.

'I name these ships *Atropos* and *Clotho*.' Robin raised her voice so that the names of the Fates rang around the shipyard and, as she did so, she pressed a button upon the console in front of her which released a bottle of champagne to explode in white foam across the bows of the great ships. In turn, their launch separated by the pause Robin placed between her ringing declamation of the two names, the ships began to move. 'May God bless them and all who sail in them.'

Robin paused for an instant to watch the majestic sight of the ships sliding towards the grey, stormy waters of Belfast Lough. The thunder of applause joined the jarring rumble of the sisters inching down the slipway. Then Robin turned and began to make her way towards her husband at the back of the VIP box. The Secretary of State turned at her side and two of his bodyguards automatically closed in behind, but Dan Williams shouldered his way in front of them, wanting to compliment Robin on her speech. The marine architect who had designed the great ships and the shipyard foreman who had built them lingered a little, watching as they gathered way, then they too turned to follow Robin, Sir Jeffrey and the huge Canadian. The completion of the ceremony was exactly ten minutes behind schedule.

The front of the grandstand blew out in a great cloud of canvas ripped into blazing shreds which whirled around the bows of the sister ships and away down the wind. The two massive vessels seemed to flinch and all the glass at the front of their bridges exploded inwards in seeming sympathy. Several shipyard workers standing on the slipway itself simply ceased to exist: the first of many, many casualties.

The pipe in which the twenty pounds of Semtex had been packed was not a load-bearing member. When it turned into a cloud of shrapnel, its destruction did not immediately undermine the strength of the tubular steel construction. But the force it unleashed certainly did. The nearest poles were shattered as the original one had been. Further away, they broke. Beyond that, they bent outwards like grass stalks in a storm, flattening and twisting. The wooden sections on top of them came tumbling to the ground. The section Robin had been standing on while she made her speech became a geyser of splinters, black specks hurled skywards like a flock of deadly starlings. The two men who had paused upon it to take one last look at their handiwork became indistinguishable from it: just so many more black splinters rising skywards.

Most of the power of the explosion went outwards, towards the ships, but much of it also went upwards. Beyond the seat of its power, where everything became atoms, shards and splinters, it still had sufficient power to tear and scorch. The wooden sections became flying boards and the security men upon them became human rockets blazing in the lower air. Hungrily, the lethal power flashed wider and collected the massive form of Dan Williams. By chance, he had stepped onto the third series of boards, and as the section beneath his feet rose in a solid piece, his tree-trunk legs and huge back presented a brief wall against the deadly force of the explosion. A wall of fragile cloth and soft flesh. A wall destroyed by the force unleashed by the motion of the blast and the inertia of the Canadian himself. A wall which, in a millionth of a second, was stripped and scoured and seared to the bone. A wall in the shadow of which stood Robin Mariner. But then the blast took the Canadian. His front remained miraculously unscathed but his back from scalp to heels became an oozing red-and-black anatomy lesson. As the power of it hurled him over Robin's head, the shock of it stopped his heart.

Robin never really distinguished the sound of the explosion from the sound of the ships thundering down the slipway. She simply became aware of a force which took her and the Secretary of State and hurled them up the slope of the grandstand atop the tumbling pile of bodies there. But the Secretary of State flew higher than she did and she wondered why that should be so.

Only Richard seemed to stand firm on the heaving, tearing storm waves of wood. He saw what was happening and – which was more than most did – he understood it. Robin was hurled towards him as the wooden section she was standing on slammed bodily into the air and the one beyond it broke apart and simply flew away. It was impossible that he could catch her or protect her from the unimaginable forces released around her, but he had to try. Such was the nature of his love for her that it never occurred to him to worry about the twins until he knew that she was safe. He knew this was almost stupid: the twins were so helpless and she was quite the opposite, but he had adored her so much for so long that even proud fatherhood could not rival what he felt for her. So absolute was his concentration upon her that he never even saw what happened to Dan Williams or to the Secretary of State.

He did not consciously follow the flight of her body but some atavistic ability, far deeper and more powerful than generations of civilisation, took him to where she lay almost as soon as she fell on the jumble of stunned and stricken people there. Like a wild man he leaped across the heaving structure until he could fall to his knees by her side and roll her tenderly onto her back. Her skin was white and cold. She was covered in blood. He could smell the odour of burning about her but neither her hair nor her clothing seemed to be alight. He knew the risk he was running in moving her, but he had little choice in the matter.

His ears were not what they once had been: explosive decompression had done them no good at all as he fought free of the sunken *Napoli*, nor had the Gulf War, and this blast now had set them to ringing again as though he had a carillon of bells in his dizzy head. Even so, the sounds he could hear from below the sliding wooden sections warned him that the whole grandstand might well be coming down. He had to get her clear of it as quickly as he could. Desperately, he began to look for help.

He did not look in vain. He was by no means alone in his quick reaction to the unexpected blast. The security men were already in action and the soldiers who had been in the security vehicles were forming quickly into rescue squads to get the wounded away. But it was Ann Cable who got to him first. He saw her forcing her way towards him through the flood of people going the other way. No, she was not hurrying towards him, he realised, but towards the Secretary of State sitting dazedly a few feet away, watching smoke curling up from the rags of clothing on his arms.

Some sort of order was beginning to form now. The people on the upper sections of the grandstand were streaming towards safety. They were quiet, shocked no doubt; there was no sign of panic except where one or two knots of horrified people had gathered around the corpses blasted up there in bits and pieces. Richard, Robin

and Sir Jeffrey were among the hurt and unconscious in
the middle section of the great construction. Behind them
was the great gaping hole above the heart of the blast.
Below this hole, in a twisted jungle of ruined metal, the
first rescue workers were looking for any life amid the
obviously dead who had been blown straight up and who
had rained back down.

But the middle section where so many helpless people
were sitting or lying was in immediate danger of collapse.
Clearly, it was imperative to get people up to the safer
section as soon as possible. Richard looked around for
Dan Williams but could see no sign of the big Canadian.

'Jeffrey!' called Richard, putting as much force into his
voice as he could, and the Secretary of State jerked awake
as though he were on the foredeck of one of Richard's
ships. 'You've got to lead the people up off here,' said
Richard urgently. 'It's going to collapse.'

The wooden sections heaved as he spoke and Sir Jeffrey
was on his feet at once, his familiar, distinguished profile
pulling the gaze of even the most dazed people nearby, in
spite of the fact that his hair had gone, just as though it
had been a wig blown off by the blast. He had no idea
that he was all but naked from the nape of his neck to
the backs of his heels.

'UP!' cried the politician as forcefully as his friend, and
people around them began to respond.

The first ripple of reaction was encouraged by Ann
Cable and her video cameraman. While he filmed, she
began to direct the survivors up the safer slopes. 'Richard,'
she called as she worked just above him, 'Nurse Janet got
the twins clear. They're fine.'

It came as a shock to him to realise how little he had
thought about them, how utterly he had been concerned

with Robin. And even as he thought this, he felt her stir. He looked down and found her looking up at him, her grey eyes clear and unclouded. 'Can you stand?' he asked.

'I think so. Richard! The children.'

'Safe and sound with Nurse Janet. Now I want you to get up there beside Ann.'

She was still shocked or she might have argued, but he was using his quarterdeck voice which brooked no disobedience, much as she had used hers this morning when she had ordered him to put her down. She got up with his hand solicitously at her elbow and stood, wavering for a second.

She thought it was simple dizziness which made it so hard to stand. She thought the roaring in her ears was faintness. She stepped up onto the solid third section of the grandstand and just as she did so, the weakened section collapsed onto the ruins of the other sections, twenty feet below.

Sir Jeffrey was a half-step behind her and Richard was still pulling himself to his feet. Both men went down with the wreckage, falling into a wilderness of twisted girders and shattered planking.

Robin stepped forward unsteadily. She took another step and found herself at Ann Cable's side. She felt a little disorientated and the overwhelming roaring in her ears didn't help matters. The blast must have affected her hearing, she supposed, for she could see that the American was saying something quite urgently but she couldn't hear a word. She looked over her shoulder to ask Richard if he could hear what Ann was saying but Richard wasn't there. The whole section of the grandstand she had just stepped off had simply disappeared. And so had Jeffrey and Richard.

Reality and horror hit her together. The dreamlike state
of shock which had cocooned her since the explosion fell
away. It was as though she had been hit in the stomach.
Hard.

When she went down on her knees, Ann Cable reached
for her, thinking she had fallen and was going to faint.
But no. Robin was a full ship's captain and had faced
many an emergency almost as stunning as this. She didn't
hesitate, recriminate or ask questions. She was in action,
recognising the situation and moving to remedy it at once.
Her knees hit the wood at the edge of the firm section
and she craned over the precipice, looking down to see if
she could make out where Richard might be lying. The
gusty rain proved a blessing at last: there was no dust to
obscure her vision and soon her sharp eyes made out the
pale star of Richard's left hand, easily recognisable to her
because of the battered old steel Rolex which never left
its wrist. The hand was protruding from beneath a square
section of wooden planking and lying on another. Dull
steel members like broken bones stood out all around it.
Of Sir Jeffrey there was no sign at all. And Robin suddenly
realised that she hadn't seen Dan Williams either since
she woke up.

A movement at her side made her look up. Ann Cable
had moved back to allow a young army lieutenant a view
of things. 'That's a hell of a mess,' he said, his voice awed.

'And the Secretary of State is underneath it,' Ann
supplied.

Robin's mouth fixed in a pale straight line.

'That's what, ten feet?' said the lieutenant, though it
was by no means clear who he was talking to.

'Ten feet down to the top of the pile and another ten
to the ground,' said Robin. 'It'll take the rescue team down

there a long time to work their way up.'

'Especially as I think some of them were underneath when the whole lot went down,' Ann added.

'Well, I suppose we'll have to send some people down from up here,' mused the lieutenant. 'Shouldn't be too difficult to climb down the scaffolding here. Have to be careful where one stands at the bottom, of course.'

'If I were you,' said Robin quietly, 'I'd get some ropes and some stretchers up here, then you can lift anyone who can be moved.'

'Good idea, ma'am.' The lieutenant sounded distracted. He was looking around as though surprised to find himself without his men up here. Apart from Robin, Ann and her cameraman, the stands were empty at last. 'Rope,' he said to himself, clearly thinking aloud.

'The bunting,' snapped Robin. 'All those pretty little flags are tied to metres of the stuff.'

'Right-ho.' His young face cleared. 'Better go and get it organised.' He got up to go, but turned back. 'You ladies need any help?'

'No,' said Robin. 'Just get the stretchers up here PDQ.'

As the lieutenant hurried off, Robin sat on one hip, swung her legs out and let them dangle over the edge. She was in her stockings – what was left of them; the blast had removed her shoes. Now she rocked forward and took hold of the hem of her skirt. A brief, furious jerk broke the stitches at the seam and another tore the skirt wide almost to the waist. She swung round until her foot reached the first strut down. Automatically, Ann reached out to steady her. Robin looked up at the American woman. 'You game?'

Ann shrugged. 'Sure.' She kicked off her own shoes and rolled up the cuffs of her jeans to stop them catching.

Swinging down beside Robin, she looked up at her cameraman. 'You'd better get some damn good pictures of this, you useless son of a bitch,' she growled.

'Pictures and every word you say, boss,' he answered. 'Just don't expect me to come down there after you.'

It was an easy climb. The cross-pieces made an effective ladder and each woman was well over five feet tall so that they only had to negotiate some four feet down to the top of the pile. Robin hesitated as soon as her foot touched wood and swung round to try and see what to do first. The new angle made it difficult to see Richard's hand but she had taken a bearing on a couple of spectacularly marked uprights and even from here she knew where he must be lying. The piece of planking on top of him was unexpectedly large, however, and for the first time it occurred to her that he might in fact be seriously injured, perhaps even dead.

The thought threatened to incapacitate her and so she thrust it fiercely away, filling her mind instead with plans for the removal of the wood. But it was difficult to see what they could do from their current position. They needed rope and preferably some muscles up there beside the cameraman. Where was that bloody lieutenant? She stretched out her leg like a ballet dancer and stepped down beyond the edge of the planking onto the jumble of struts beneath it. She tested the first strut gingerly and it held her weight. As slowly as an actor performing an improvisation exercise, she detached herself from the makeshift ladder and began to work her way from one strut to the next round the edge. Ann saw what she was doing and began to reflect the move on the far side.

They were crouching side by side at the outer edge of the platform on either side of the jumble of struts with

Robin gently searching for a pulse on Richard's cold wrist beside the Rolex's steel strap when the lieutenant returned. 'I say!' he called in genuine surprise and shock. 'What are you ladies doing down there? It's extremely dangerous, you know!'

Robin really didn't have the patience for this. 'Have you brought some help and some rope?' she snapped.

'Well, yes, but—'

'I want the end of a strong piece down here at once. Clear?'

'Well, certainly, but—'

'*Now*, Lieutenant! Jump to it!'

'Sergeant McAdam!' called the lieutenant, and he handed over to the NCO with every evidence of relief.

McAdam squatted on the edge of the wooden platform. He was a square, solid man who wore an air of worldly-wise cynicism as inevitably as he wore his regulation straight beret. Robin recognised the type at once and relief swept over her. 'What do you have in mind, ma'am?' asked the sergeant.

'Look, Sergeant, I'm a ship's captain. I haven't the papers on me at the moment but I do assure you I know what I am doing. Get me some rope down here. I want to tie these struts together so you can raise them a little. They cross at this point and I'm sure they make a rough "A" frame under the wood. Lift the top of the "A" and the whole lot should come up.'

The sergeant watched her calculatingly for an instant and then he gave a minuscule nod. Just as she had recognised a rock-solid NCO, so – by some near miracle, given the state of her appearance – he had recognised an utterly competent officer. 'Aye, Captain. I think we can manage that for you. Corporal! Over here . . .'

The rope came down a moment later and Robin's strong, capable hands lashed the heavy woven polyester cable into a safe, tight knot. 'Move back,' she advised Ann Cable quietly. Then, 'Lift, please, Sergeant,' she called.

The rope seemed to stretch under the strain and then the struts stirred. There was a tearing wrench and then a kind of grating roar as the great square of planking began to lift. As soon as there was room, Robin wriggled forward and underneath. It was dark, but there was no need for her to see anything at first as she followed the muscular line of Richard's arm until she felt the barrel of his chest and – tears flooded her eyes most unexpectedly – she felt the ribs rise convulsively as her beloved husband breathed.

Light and Ann Cable followed her in almost at once and the women were soon able to make out the figures of both the men lying side by side, their bodies all but lost among the jumble of metal struts. 'Richard's breathing,' called Robin. 'Can you check Jeffrey?'

'There's no pulse here,' the American whispered after a moment. There was a brief silence, then, 'No. I'm sorry. This guy's dead and gone.'

As Ann spoke, the 'A' frame came upright above them and the great square of wood fell back with an incredible roar to sit firmly against the ladder of struts the women had climbed down.

The dull Ulster daylight revealed the pile of jumbled metal lying across the late Secretary's flattened torso and the twisted wreckage of Richard Mariner's legs.

Robin's cry of agonised distress echoed among the screams of the panicked sea gulls, across the grey reaches of Belfast Lough where the sister ships *Atropos* and *Clotho* rode side by side on the sullen swell. The blank stare of their shattered bridge windows gave clear testimony to the blast damage from the terrorist bomb. The structural damage done to one set of bows was far less easy to detect.

CHAPTER THREE

Day One

Wednesday, 19 May   16:00

The A595 trunk road running down from the reprocessing plant at Sellafield to the new dock at Seascale nearby on the coast was full of chanting people. The hard core of protesters who had been around the nuclear facility for the last few weeks had been supplemented by more brought out by the bright spring weather. Had Richard not been driving the big Range Rover Discovery, they would never have got through. Even so, he had to keep in the lowest forward gear and ease through the tight-packed bodies with a gentle insistence. His face was familiar to the crowd but few of them could actually have put a name to it, even though it was a scant three months since it had been in all the newspapers and on television screens across the country, twisted with agony and anger.

It was lined with discomfort now – the effort of keeping the big green vehicle moving at such a sluggish pace was playing havoc with his slowly-mending knee joints. His face was also lined with unaccustomed frustration: the interview with the shipping manager at the British Nuclear

Fuels plant had not been at all satisfactory. With the constant demonstrations going on outside Sellafield and around the dock, the shipping in of waste for reprocessing had been slowed to a trickle. There had been no chance of meeting the date for delivery of *Clotho*'s first cargo for some time and now they had reluctantly agreed that she would have to sail unladen: she was expected in Sept Isles soon. *Atropos* would be setting out on her reciprocal course from Canada later that day. The whole system would only function properly if the ships worked to the agreed schedules, whether they sailed with a cargo or not. Heritage Mariner were reluctant to keep footing the bills to have a brand new ship sitting idly off the Cumbrian coast, even manned with the smallest of harbour watches and a very necessary security team, and British Nuclear Fuels as part charterer for the voyage were not happy to pay full rates for an unladen crossing. But the death of Dan Williams had thrown the Canadian side of the deal into confusion too: the people in Sept Isles insisted that all they could do under the circumstances was stick to the agreed schedules and wait to see what happened. They had all come to an agreement, therefore, each reluctantly making the best of a bad job.

On the other hand, thought Richard grimly, if many more such bargains had to be struck, then the sister ships would drag Heritage Mariner into the bankruptcy courts. But it was unfair to blame the ships for the actions of a nameless group of terrorists and a few thousand protesters. His hand jerked towards the horn yet again, only to slam painfully against the steering wheel's rim as he overcame the automatic gesture. The people in front of them knew well enough that the Range Rover was there. Blasting the horn at them would only sour the boisterous good nature

of the demonstration and with Robin beside him and the
twins behind, Richard didn't want to risk that. It wasn't
much further now.

'You'd think they'd realise,' said Robin, bitterly.

Richard shrugged stoically. 'There's nothing we can do,
so there's no point in getting upset.'

'But I mean to say, the proper, careful shipping and
handling of the stuff is the only way forward. If they stop
Clotho from sailing fully laden and disposing of the waste
properly, they're only making certain some cowboy outfit
like Disposoco dump it in the sea or on some deserted
Third World beach. It's criminally shortsighted!' Her voice
rose with simple rage and he was tempted to take her in
his arms – to look across towards her at the very least –
but he could not do so without running the risk of killing
someone in the road ahead. His heart was wrenched by
the imminence of their separation and his inability to
comfort her. It was so sad, he thought. The dazzling girl
he had loved so much for so long seemed to have gone
away for a while. The new Robin seemed to be so much
less confident and cheerful. Her overpowering enthusiasm
and lust for life were diminished, almost exhausted. She
had started to look upon the dark side automatically,
always expecting the worst, as though simply waiting for
the next blow thrown at them by a bitter Fate.

He glanced across at her, brooding silently beside him,
then away right as he swung off the A595 and into the
little B5344 leading down to the coast. The cottages of
Gosforth village where the two roads joined had never
seen so many people in the centuries of their existence,
he mused. Then his mind turned back to his own concerns.
They had been so lucky, he thought. He had been more
than lucky to survive the loss of the *Napoli* with little

more damage than a ruptured eardrum and a bad case of the bends. He spread his right hand and looked at his shortened middle finger, the top of it lost in the Gulf War. He had been lucky to live through that war, even though he had watched most of it from the sidelines. Behind him, the twins were doing their best to imitate the chant of the people outside. They were lucky to have the twins. So lucky still to have the children and each other after the bomb in Belfast. Their good fortune seemed incredible to him. But at the moment Robin seemed incapable of seeing it. All the blessings Richard could think of seemed to be the opposite to her. They had talked it all through often enough for him to know her thinking perfectly well.

Why had he got involved with *Napoli* at all? Why was he still involved with those sharks who had owned her? Why had he got involved in the Gulf War? It had damaged him far beyond anything she could bear. How could the twins be such a blessing (she asked this only in her darkest moods) when they had almost cost too much? How could he look at his survival in the Harland and Wolff shipyards as such a miracle when it had cost him two close friends, several respected colleagues and so much pain and grief? How could he love *Clotho* and *Atropos* so much when the sister ships stood a very good chance of destroying the great company her father, he and she had worked so hard to establish? And when *Clotho* was about to pull them apart again just when they needed so badly to stay together?

Even as he thought of *Clotho*, the Range Rover breasted a low rise and the bay of the anchorage at Seascale opened out in front of them. The coast here was low and shelved gently out to sea. Further north, the river estuaries were so wide and shallow that the incoming tide could travel

across the sands faster than a horse at full gallop and
many an unwary traveller had been swept away by the
terrifying inward rush. Here the bay had been artificially
deepened so that the big ocean-going freighters like *Clotho*
and *Atropos* could come close to the dock and load directly
from the shore.

But *Clotho* was riding high and unladen. She looked
arrogantly massive towering above the docking facilities
around her, casting the power of her presence across the
security fencing and over the protesters gathered at the
wire-mesh gates. There was no singing here, only a silent
stillness like the utter hush before a thunderclap. The
Range Rover grumbled forward and the crowd fell apart.
When the bumper touched the wire mesh, a line of uniformed security men appeared from a guard hut nearby.
At once a sigh passed through the waiting mob and
Richard's mouth suddenly went dry. The prospect of just
such a confrontation was what he feared most.

Even as he gathered himself to jump from the vehicle
and dismiss the guards at once, another line of uniformed
men appeared: the crew of *Clotho* herself, come to welcome their new captain. Through the wire diamonds,
behind the mob of cheerful sailors, he could see the square
figure of Nico Niccolo, the first officer, sending the security guards away. Richard looked across at Robin and he
saw that she too was watching the stocky Neapolitan with
every sign of approval on her thoughtful countenance. But
her glance rested on the officers and crew for only a
moment before it was pulled up and away inevitably by
the powerful magnetism of *Clotho* herself.

They hadn't seen much of the ships since the launching.
In the interim, all the bomb damage had been repaired or
hidden; the ships had been refitted and repainted in the

house colours of Heritage Mariner, with that great eye instead of a figurehead on her forecastle. The only other ships in the world which looked like her were the massive supertankers of the Heritage Mariner shipping fleet and *Clotho* seemed to gain scale from the association though she was only one-tenth of their deadweight tonnage. But she was by no means merely a tenth of their size; she was more than five hundred feet from stem to stern and nearly a hundred wide from outside rail to the rail of her bridge wings. She was more than forty feet deep from deck plates to keel and nearly fifty feet high from main deck to radio mast. Her bridgehouse sat three-quarters of her length back from her forecastle head. Halfway down her deck sat a mobile gantry capable of moving on its rails from one end of the main deck to the other, carrying containers of pre-packed waste for lowering into her holds. On the top of the gantry, atop two great struts folded shut like an elbow, the control cabin could be extended out over the side to act as a dockside crane. But, from where they were looking, the crane, the gantry, the effulgent white of the accommodation and navigation decks were almost obscured by the high flare of her super-strengthened ice-breaker's bow.

The gate in front of them opened and two white-over-alled figures came towards the Range Rover. Neither wore any badges of rank, though they both had the air of men used to command. The way they moved, the unhurried calm of their steps and the air of authority they exuded made the the crowd fall back for a moment and Richard let the Discovery roll forward almost silently. The two men, First Officer Nico Niccolo and Chief Engineer Andrew McTavish, turned and fell in beside them, escorting the Mariners through the gate and across the dock to the foot of their gangplank. Only when the gates were closed did the people outside begin to call out and chant their protests into the faces of *Clotho*'s crew who proved cheerfully ready to reply.

As Andrew courteously handed Robin out and then turned to help her and Nurse Janet with the twins, Nico aided Richard in his rather more laborious descent, then handed him his walking stick and slammed the door. 'The dunnage is in the back, Nico,' said Richard, easing himself gingerly onto his stiff joints. He usually needed two walking sticks – he was using one at the moment out of sheer bravado. He looked up the slope of the gangplank and poignantly regretted the decision.

Janet and the twins went first – they unstoppably and she hurriedly. Robin and Andrew McTavish followed, deep in conversation – the chief engineer had been a fast friend for all of fifteen years. Last came Richard and Nico Niccolo. 'Have you heard from Ann?' asked Richard courteously, but his eyes, and his mind, were busy about the ship.

'Yes,' said the Italian. 'She went aboard *Atropos* yesterday and came through on the radio last night. Very cagey about first impressions. She feels a bit isolated.' He gave one of his minuscule, eloquent, Neapolitan shrugs.

Ann Cable was coming across with the Canadians aboard *Clotho*'s sister ship, hoping to write a sequel to her best-selling book on the loss of *Napoli*. It was hardly surprising she felt isolated, thought Richard grimly. The sister ships were crewed and owned by different partners in the consortium. A fierce rivalry was developing between them, and there was Ann, all but engaged to Nico, first officer of the rival ship, close friends with the Mariners, masters and owners of the rival ship, and an investigative journalist apparently – and actually – looking for every failure of procedure and flaw of routine. She must be about as welcome as the plague aboard *Atropos*. No wonder Nico sounded concerned.

As Richard reached the deck, all thought of Ann Cable left his mind. It was mid-afternoon now and the sun was beginning to creep down towards the western horizon. It was the first really warm day of spring and the whole of the Irish Sea seemed calm and turquoise under the pale blue sky. Only the shadowed faces of the larger waves took a really green tinge and their crests were a cheerful riot of silver and gold as far as the eye could see. There was little discernible pattern, but the waves roared against the dockside in steady series and there was a swell just regular enough to make *Clotho* stir at her moorings. The Point of Ayre, the northernmost point of the Isle of Man, lay just below the horizon, and beyond that lay Ulster. Richard's knees gave a twinge at the thought of it and he returned his mind to the ship.

Robin and Andrew McTavish were halfway to the bridgehouse, in the shadow of that massive central gantry, and the twins had already vanished into it. Richard turned and followed, with Nico still by his side. 'What do you think of her?' asked Richard.

'She's very pretty,' said the first officer but Richard seemed to hear something below the bland answer. Some criticism or reservation implied. He frowned.

'Everything up to scratch?' he probed.

'You'll go all over her. You'll see. I never been on a ship fitted like this one. She's like a palace. A very practical palace.'

Again, just a shade of reservation, like one of his tiny, telling shrugs.

'So there's nothing wrong?'

'*Niente*. Nothing.' But the double negative was just not quite satisfactory.

Richard thought about Nico Niccolo – the typical Neapolitan, cool, worldly-wise, cynical, a shade sarcastic and utterly superstitious.

'You think she's bad luck?'

Nico held the A deck door open for him. 'Are you mad to say such a thing, Capitan?' he asked quietly as Richard stepped past him into the bridgehouse. And it was not until they were in the lift, purring up towards the bridge deck, that Richard realised that there was more than one way to take that remark.

The wheelhouse and navigation bridge were sparse but not spartan. The equipment stands seemed barely adequate for the safe navigation and control of such a vessel, and yet closer inspection showed how well-equipped *Clotho* actually was.

There was a complete communications stand, quite apart from the radio equipment. The bridge could at any time be in communication with head office through the fax machine. At the same time it could be in communication with one of the low-flying weather satellites, receiving detailed weather information for their immediate area. The collision alarm radar had three settings, at radiuses of five, ten and twenty miles, as well as a 'big picture' facility. It was specially enhanced to see almost as far both beneath the water and in the upper air. And it was super-sensitive, to pick up the slightest trace of ice at the earliest moment.

Below the broad, angled clearview, in the centre of the forward bank of instruments, stood not one steering control system but three: one to control the rudder and the pitch of the great single screw at the stern; another to control the smaller manoeuvring screws beside it and at the bow; a third to control the extra thrusters on the sides. Even the binoculars which sat so snugly in their pouch by the comfortable black leather of the watchkeeper's chair on the port side of the bridge had electronic rangefinding facilities and image intensification systems for enhanced watchkeeping in poor light.

The whole ship was the same: all glittering, spacious work areas whose size was emphasised by the miniaturisation of the high-tech work aids. The engine control room seemed to have nothing more than a couple of computer screens in it. Yet those screens could call up a graphical representation of every working part of the engine, together with a readout of its efficiency, past, present and projected. And within the invisibly mounted but massively powerful computers, all such monitoring went on constantly so that any failure likely to occur could be foreseen and an automatic warning given before anything actually went wrong.

While the twins ran riot around them, Richard and Robin went with Nico and Andrew all over their ship. They examined everything from the exquisitely fitted galley to the massively strengthened bow, from the spare propeller clutched in its clamps behind the forecastle head to the weight-training facilities and the sauna in the gymnasium which overlooked the swimming pool area currently covered over aft of the bridgehouse. As the inspection proceeded, Nico and Andrew fell back and allowed them to walk together side by side. After a while, Robin slid her arm round Richard's slim waist and took a little of his weight on her shoulder – she too had been worried about the bravado which had left his second walking stick behind. And he was glad to wrap his arm round her shoulders and hold her close.

At last he slowly turned their steps through the now familiar passageways back towards the main deck and the companionway. It was time for *Clotho* to set sail.

'All ashore who are going ashore,' he said quietly, and Robin's eyes caught Nurse Janet's. The nanny hustled the twins away towards the dockside and the Range Rover.

They stepped out onto the main deck and into the first truly beautiful sunset of the year. There was not a cloud to spoil it; simply the dying fire of the westering sun half drowned in the vivid waves. Far to the east, immediately above the sullen crags of the Lake District, stood the evening star like a lighthouse on a distant shore, casting its steady gleam across a sea of shadows. The evening wind stirred against them as they walked across the deck together, still with their arms wrapped round each other, and their quiet words were all but lost beneath the low rumble of the surf and the high, sad keening of the black-backs and the herring gulls.

At the top of the companionway they stood alone, lost in the sadness of their parting.

'I love you, Richard,' whispered Robin, her grey eyes like still pools, brimming.

'I'll miss you, darling, more than I can say.'

'The case . . .' she was reluctant even to name the *Napoli* and the vicious court case Heritage Mariner was so deeply embroiled in over her loss. It was yet one more thing which she feared would go wrong and do them irreparable damage.

'Sir William and Sir Harcourt have it all sewn up, don't worry,' he said quietly.

They exchanged one last, crushing embrace before surrendering to the demands of time, tide and duty.

Then Captain Mariner came up to full height and turned away to stride back across the deck towards the bridge-house and the navigation bridge. Already, family was being thrust aside by thoughts of the North Channel, the Western Ocean and the St Lawrence Seaway.

But when the tears on her cheeks called her back to the present for a moment, she turned and looked at Richard still standing at the head of the companionway, watching her walk away. 'Don't forget to kiss the twins "Good night" from me every night,' she said.

It was her first command as master of *Clotho*.

The control room of the gantry, nestled on its folded arm nearly fifty feet above the main deck, was exactly that: a room. It had a wide window through which could be seen the wheeling horizon and the sun setting beyond it. Below the window was a complex control console, the controls idle and useless now because the ship was sailing unladen, but vibrating slightly with latent power as the ship got under way. Behind the console was a bench seat long enough to accommodate four people easily. On the padded seat lay a sleeping bag, unrolled and unzipped. Behind the seat, hidden from the eyes of all except the circling, incurious gulls, was a small work area. Here was set up a kind of camp: a small primus stove surrounded by pans of food and water. There were tins and packages of all kinds. They looked plentiful but in fact they would have fitted comfortably in a well-filled backpack, leaving plenty of room for the sleeping bag and the plastic containers full of Semtex high explosive neatly piled beneath the bench with the detonators and timer in a little Tupperware box beside them. The detonators and the timer took up hardly any room at all. There had even been room for the stowaway to bring aboard a book with her when she had climbed, unobserved, up from the seaward side while all that excitement on the dock had been going on. She got it out now and began to read, contentedly. It was Victor Hugo's *Les Travailleurs de la Mer*, and it was in the original French.

After a few moments, however, she set the novel down and pulled out some blank paper and a pencil. 'My darling,' she wrote in French, 'I know that you will never read these words because they must never fall into the captain's hands and so I must destroy them almost as soon as I have written them, but it will be so lonely here without you that I must write them down or I shall go insane.

'Simply to think of you so far away makes my heart ache. But when I think that you are coming ever closer to me, and that soon I too will be coming towards you, I can feel such a passion building in me that I find it hard to breathe. I have never known anyone like you and only a mission such as this could ever separate us. Oh, my love, do you remember that first night we were together on Avalon and we swam in the sea at high tide? How the whole of that coast of Newfoundland out to the Grand Banks themselves seemed to be alive with those tiny fish that night so that we, swimming naked like seals, were caressed by them in their millions? You were so angry because of the danger. So many fish, you said, would bring whales and sharks, and so they did. But not to us. Not to us, my beloved, because we are beloved of Nature. Gaia is our goddess and she keeps us safe from harm as she did that night when the silver fish cooled our burning flesh with their teeming numbers but lit other hotter fires within. Who would have thought that a life such as mine, of killing and maiming, could have come to such a fruition

as this? Did you know that all those tiny fish had come
there to give birth and to die? Do you know that we, too,
will give birth soon? I found out just after you had
returned to Canada and I cannot wait to tell you. How
soon will I see you? Let me count the days until we meet
at Farewell . . .

'I must break off soon because it is growing dark and
I cannot risk a light. Tomorrow I will reconnoitre and soon
I will set the bomb. Our friends covered things well at
Seascale and I was able to bring aboard even more than
we managed to set in Belfast. When *Clotho* goes up, it
will destroy Sept Isles and stop this foul traffic. And when
I set the charges you have aboard with you, *Atropos* will
close things down in England.

'Our friends in London and New York will send the
publicity material within the week and Heritage Mariner
will feel the weight of our wrath.

'We cannot allow these beings to pollute our beautiful
world. We cannot rest from trying to destroy these people
who have already put our magic Avalon at risk with the
filth on *Napoli*.

'But the thought of you so far away hurts me more than
I can say. Tonight I will dream of your hands and your
lips upon me. It is all that stops me going mad. We will
be together in six short nights. Six short nights and no
longer. Then the two of us will go back to Avalon until
we are no longer two, but three.'

CHAPTER FOUR

Day Three

Friday, 21 May   16:00

The seventh tee at Brampton golf course, halfway between
Cold Fell and Carlisle in Cumbria, was called Cardiac Hill.
Neither of the two men currently considering it needed to
worry about its reputation. They were both slim men, light
but strong, and they were both fit; they carried the weight
of their responsibilities well, no matter what the burden
of their years.

Sir William Heritage, Robin Mariner's father and chairman of Heritage Mariner, was coming up for his middle
eighties but he was wiry and strong enough to be pulling
his own golf clubs. Sir Harcourt Gibbons hoped that in
ten years' time he would be as hale and hearty as his
friend – and as able to slam more than two hundred yards
out of his drives with such consistency.

But the slope of this hole was a challenge to intellect
as much as to technique. It was Harcourt's honour, though
he would gladly have traded the privilege to see what club
Sir William chose. He squinted up the hill and wondered.
At last he pulled a number two wood out of his bag and

began to set himself up to drive off. He was acutely aware that this was his friend's local course and he was very much the stranger here. It seemed to him that distance would be preferable to height at this stage.

The conversation between the two men had been going on since Harcourt arrived at Cold Fell just before luncheon. He had caught the train up early on Friday morning and had been ensconced snugly in one of Sir William's guest rooms at Cold Fell by drinks time at noon. But the topic of conversation had been of such importance that it had interrupted the social chit-chat at lunch and undermined the sporting talk over pudding. And this afternoon, between the comments about what wood and what iron, it had dominated the golfing conversation, too.

'Look, Bill,' said Harcourt as he bent and drove his tee deep into the ground. 'The law is like the Savoy Hotel. It's open to anyone.' He balanced his ball on top of the tee and straightened, looking up the hill in front of him. 'Anyone who can afford it,' he added, pleased to have found a use for the famous old saying.

He took his number two wood and patted the grass behind the tee with its varnished head, glancing up speculatively. At the last two holes he had taken practice swings and then sliced both drives. Perhaps he would do better just to let rip. With no further comment, he swung back and hit the ball. The hole was three hundred and eighty yards. The first three hundred yards went uphill steeply and the last eighty fell away sharply. His drive did not gain the height he had hoped and thumped rather hard into the left of the fairway. At least it didn't vanish into the rough.

Sir William took his number three wood and sat his ball on a high tee. 'It's not just a question of money,' he observed as he, like Harcourt, settled the rough grass behind the little plastic pin by patting it with his club head. 'We have insurance, as you know, and we could under normal circumstances afford a couple of comparable hulls. I am worried, however, that there may be more to this thing than meets the eye.'

He stopped talking and squared up properly for his shot. The conversation was important, but there was no sense in losing the match because of it. His tee shot lifted far higher than Harcourt's had, very nearly reaching the crest. He watched the white dot bounce and rest. Neat little five iron down to the green from there, he thought. He would win this hole too if the weather held.

'As we've stated in the submissions already before the court, the case against Heritage Mariner is quite simple,' said Harcourt, not for the first time, as they rocked their clubs up onto the trollies and began to pull them onwards and upwards. 'The Italian company, CZP, owned the ship. Richard does not dispute that he was on board CZP's ship, nor that he was notionally in charge of her. He agrees that, just before the ship sank, he was actively engaged in setting explosive charges with the expressed intention of sinking the ship. But he maintains that the ship went down in the final analysis because of the action of the cargo, which effectively ate its way through the sides. His defence is simply that he was prevented from scuttling the ship by the fact that she sank herself. That's all there is to it. I must say, these are late days to be having second thoughts, old chap. I mean, we have agreed the pleadings before the judge already; there's only the final liability to settle now. You should have brought up any worries weeks ago, before I took it to the judge in his chambers.'

They came up to Harcourt's ball at this point and he

squinted up the hill, which looked much steeper from this
vantage point. It had hit the ground so hard that it had
bounced and was sitting on top of a clump of grass just
at the edge of the fairway. Harcourt reckoned he could
risk a three wood from here. Certainly it looked as though
they had better finish the hole as quickly as possible – it
might be their last. Although this was a late weekend in
May, the weather was still behaving as though it was an
early weekend in March. There were tall black clouds
sweeping down over the Borders towards them.

Bill waited until Harcourt had bashed his ball up over
the ridge before he asked, 'You're sure about the case? If
it's just a question of buying CZP a new hull, we can
probably stretch to it. But after the bomb in Belfast, we
have all the spare cash we possess tied up in refitting
and reinsuring.'

'All the spare cash,' echoed Harcourt speculatively.

'We've signed away all the family possessions – houses,
cars; unlimited liability. We're counting on you. If it's just
the hull of *Napoli* then our insurance will cover it. Costs
enough, God knows. But if there's anything further, we
could be stretched too far.'

They were up with Sir William's ball now and he didn't
even pause before pulling out his number five iron. He
was so caught up in what he was saying to his barrister
– his silk, as the jargon had it – that he didn't even
calculate his shot. The five iron whispered through the
grass with a sound like a headsman's axe and the ball
went flying up over the ridge.

'No,' said Harcourt firmly. 'You have nothing to worry
about. I have it all worked out and, but for the final aspects
to be dealt with in open court, it's all settled. You can rely
on me, old chap.'

He strode on up to the top of the hill and looked
down onto the green. Sir William's ball was still running,
so the barrister had no trouble in seeing that his own ball
lay a two-inch putt from the hole. A sense of achieve-
ment welled up inside him. The game was turning his
way.

As the thought came, so did the first of the rain.

Sir William paused, lost in thought, part-way through
the action of putting his number five iron back into his
golf bag. Was there anything more he wanted to check
with Harcourt? The case came to court in less than two
weeks and, as he had said, mistakes were likely to come
very expensive. But no. There was nothing else he needed
to know – beyond the fact that he trusted his barrister
with the absolute confidence of long association. And he
needed to. One mistake here and Heritage Mariner would
go to the wall with a vengeance.

He settled the club in the golf bag and turned, just as
the first great raindrops spattered into his face. At the top
of the rise, Harcourt was just putting up his umbrella.
Wise man, thought Sir William, and considered following
suit. But just at the moment he turned, a column of light
seemed to leap between the sky and his friend's umbrella.
As long as he lived, he would never be able to say whether
the light went up from the umbrella or came down from
the sky. But in the second it took him to settle his club
and turn, a massive power of light connected Sir Harcourt
Gibbons to the sky. It persisted, crackling like crisp cello-
phane and smelling like a distant barbecue borne on a
fresh sea breeze, then it was gone. Sir William didn't stand
still to watch it but when he went to run forward he found
he was falling down.

When he pulled himself, shakily, to his feet, his old

friend Harcourt was lying curled up on the crest of the hill and his umbrella was on fire.

CHAPTER FIVE

Day Four

Saturday, 22 May   06:00

Ann Cable had never felt so isolated in all her life. Alone
in her cabin, unable to sleep, disturbed by the constant
background throbbing of the ship's generators, she would
try to lighten her thoughts in the loneliest hours of the
dead watch by making ridiculous comparisons. She felt
like the first black householder in an all white neighbour-
hood, she would tell herself. Like the first Chinese to open
a restaurant in Paris. Like the first gay footballer out of
the closet. Like a lone female reporter on an all male ship
which had something to hide.

She felt more than isolated, she felt threatened. Anything seemed possible. Just the way most of the crew men
looked at her made her flesh crawl with its combination
of lust and financial speculation: she was good-looking
and rich – would it be possible to get into her pants and
her purse, her bed and her bank balance? She knew the
answer most of them would make: she was a woman, only
good for one thing; and it would be a nice change if they
made money out of the deal rather than being parted from

it, which was what most of them were used to. But the sexual threat – only implied, so far – was less disturbing than the other.

She did not know all that much about ship handling, in spite of the fact that she had made her name and fortune writing about the loss of the *Napoli*. She had only ever been aboard one ship for any length of time – *Napoli* herself – and it was now becoming obvious that the way that the ship had been run, under a Heritage Mariner captain, was very different from the way *Atropos* was being run. *Napoli* had been an old rust bucket rapidly rotting away, crewed by a polyglot collection of southern European ruffians, but there had been an air of common purpose and mutual respect aboard. *Atropos* was brand spanking new, equipped like a space shuttle and crewed by men hand-picked by the owners in Sept Isles, but there were undercurrents of mystery aboard which had set her short hairs to prickling as though the ship were full of ghosts. She was burning to investigate. But in those dark hours of the dead watches, sitting in her bunk in the darkness feeling *Atropos* buck and shoulder north-west-wards through the St Lawrence, it was all too easy to imagine that if she actually discovered anything, then she would end up lost at sea. Just another maritime mystery; just another *Mary Celeste*. And there was no one she could call on for help. Or no one less than three thousand miles away.

She was very strongly tempted just to lock herself safely in her cabin and stay there right through the voyage. That would be the sensible thing to do.

Her day began at six. This was the fourth aboard, though only the second afloat, really. They had sailed more than twenty-four hours behind schedule because of some panic of the captain's, and because of the grannies demonstrating at the dockside. She knew she would begin to tell the time by bells and changing watches soon, but for now she relied on her watch and was up by six. The cooks and the deck officer on watch were the only other people up at that time, she had discovered; and that fact was important. She loved to exercise but had brought with her only a tight grey body stocking and a high-cut one-piece exercise suit. Her first attempt to run down to the weights room had drawn so many eyes that it had also drawn an acid reprimand from the skeletal Captain Black. If she wished to flaunt herself – he hadn't quite used the words but his meaning had been clear enough – she should do so when none of his men could be distracted by her. So now she only exercised when she would be alone. And that meant between six and seven in the morning.

Her cabin was on C deck, one level below the navigation bridge. She shared the deck of four cabins with day rooms and showers *en suite* with only the captain and the chief engineer, who seemed to hate each other. Neither of them ever appeared before late breakfast at nine. Nevertheless, she found herself behaving as though she were the victim of a voyeur. She had always slept naked; now she wore briefs and a T-shirt. She stripped and dressed with the cabin lights off. She looked each way along the corridor before exiting. Like a child about some mischief, she tiptoed along the corridor, used the stairs rather than risk any noise from the lift, and gasped with fright when the sole of her trainer squealed against the linoleum of the top stair. Three decks down, in the great lateral A deck corridor, she hesitated. There was an internal route to the gym but it would take her past the ship's galley, past the only other people aboard awake. Under the eyes of the men. It would be better to run round outside, unless it was raining.

The bulkhead door at the end of the corridor swung open silently and Ann stepped out into the early morning. The icy wind made her catch her breath but the clean cut of it in her lungs was heavenly. It was just getting light, and she found herself looking across a steel-grey vista of sharp waves, all seeming to run the same way as *Atropos* was heading, as though the ship were grinding down the back of some huge flat file. She stood, legs a little spread, hands on hips, breathing deeply, drinking in the vista. Behind the water rose a rugged grey coastline, dark slate where the water was light steel, almost black at the edges of the snowfields which clung to the hilltops sawing at the white sky. She was on the port side of the ship, looking northwards towards the coast of Labrador, but had she been on the starboard looking south, the view would not have been very different: *Atropos* was pounding slowly through the Strait of Belle Isle between the mainland of Canada and the island of Newfoundland.

Abruptly, her steady progress faltered, as though the five-hundred-foot vessel had stumbled. Ann staggered sideways and forward, her movements dictated by the movement of the ship. The deck heaved upwards slightly towards the bow, then settled back. Ann knew the motions *Atropos* made when she pitched over waves now and this had been something new. She continued to move towards the rail and looked down into the hissing, foam-streaked water just in time to see a large lump of ice heave by. It looked too small to be a floe. What did they call them? Growlers. Yes, it was a growler. Half a growler, by the look of things, already turning turtle, readjusting to its new state having been chopped in two by *Atropos*' ice-breaking bow. It was surprisingly white and its sides, moving through the water, showed shades of luminous blue which settled back to steadfast grey as the ice settled, only to be whirled into the ship's pale wake to clash against its other half as though trying to heal the breach.

Still watching the restless ice and trying not to think about *Titanic*, Ann pounded back along the deck just inside the rail. She considered going round the deck a few times but decided against it after twenty or so steps — the icy air was just too cold. She was a health nut, not a masochist.

The outer door to the gym extended a great long window overlooking the swimming pool area on the after deck. The pool had facilities to be heated and covered so that it could be used in most weathers, but Captain Black had ordered it to be battened down for the duration of the voyage. He seemed to look upon all provision for the welfare of his men as a waste of time and a dangerous temptation towards idleness and slackness. 'I run a tight ship!' The arcane phrase had been the first she had heard him use and it had not taken her long to learn that the crew, officers and men alike, called him 'Tightship' behind his back. The fact that they often changed the last letter, replacing the 'p' with a 't', made her suspect that this was not a mark of respect or affection. But, in spite of having lived in Italy for many years, she was not an expert on men's games and macho, so the nickname could have held some grudging appreciation, for all she knew. There was no doubt about First Officer Timmins, however. Everyone definitely despised him.

She swung the door to the gym open and crossed to the nearest of the two multi-gyms standing at the back of the big room, behind the basketball court. Between the multi-gyms was an exercise mat. Still lost in thought about the officers of *Atropos* and how she was going to describe them in print without spending the rest of her life fighting libel suits, she stood on the mat and began the routine she always used to loosen her muscles prior to putting them to serious work. It was a routine she had learned in ballet class at acting school when she had harboured dreams of dancing. She stood erect, then spread her legs until the muscles in her groin began to pull. She leaned forward from the hips and let her body relax so that the backs of her hands brushed the floor between her ankles. Eyes closed, concentrating with every fibre of her being, she pulled herself erect, allowing her arms to flow up above her head, stretching ever upwards as though attached by tightening lines to the ceiling. Then she flopped forward until she could feel the fibres down the backs of her thighs stretching, and began again.

The first officer was called Yasser Timmins. At first she had thought his given name denoted an Arabic mother – the scrawny little man was so wizened and weathered that it was impossible to tell what mixture of races his forebears might have sprung from. But no. Soon enough she discovered that 'Yasser' was another nickname and had nothing to do with race. It was a mocking echo of the words he used most often, especially when talking to Captain Tightship: 'Yes, sir!'

Yasser seemed to have little or no character, motivation or understanding of his own. He existed to obey orders and to ensure that the orders he passed on were equally well obeyed by those unfortunate enough to be beneath him. While he grovelled before his captain, he lorded it over the others, enforcing his demands with petty, sadistic punishments. It was a miracle that he had ever risen to any kind of rank at all and the thought of him going further and actually gaining command of a ship simply made her blood run cold.

She stood up and began a series of exercises designed to loosen the muscles of her torso and lower back. These, too, were her own variations on ballet exercises. She put her hands on her hips and began to swing her torso from side to side, eyes closed as she concentrated on stretching the muscles in her sides and buttocks.

Next under Yasser was Hogg, and Fate had given him his nickname for real. All Hogg seemed to think about was food, though Ann suspected he might indulge in other fleshly delights too whenever he got the chance. He was not the youngest of the officers, but he seemed the most juvenile, with his childlike over-indulgence at meals and his legendary Dagwood multilayer sandwiches in between. There was something soft and faintly repulsive about his roly-poly, odorous, dough-boy body, and Ann had no trouble at all in imagining him spending all his nights between his watches abusing himself in his cabin poring over the porno mags the Wide Boy had brought aboard to hire out among his shipmates.

Ann went into her last set of loosening-up exercises and thought about the Wide Boy. She sat with her back straight and spread her legs as far apart as they would go. Then she lowered her head until it all but touched her right knee. Extending her hands down her calf, she pulled gently, feeling the long muscles of her back stretching, all the way down to her bottom, while every tendon and fibre in her leg pulled, from toe-tip to the top of her thigh. After three on each leg, she rolled onto her back and pulled her legs, toes pointed, down towards her nose.

His name was Reynolds and he was third officer, but everyone called him the Wide Boy. He might have had a given name but she had never heard it. If he wasn't called the Wide Boy, then it was Butch. Butch Reynolds. He was like a caricature from a gangster film, posing like Pacino or Mickey Rourke as though always ready to pull a comb out of his back pocket – a comb or a blade, or a gun. There seemed to be nothing he could not supply. Ann had seen enough war movies where some member of the command, some supply sergeant or junior officer, was always able to get his hands on anything. These fictional characters seemed to be pleasant enough, and useful, too. But not the Wide Boy. Reynolds was bad. And the stuff he could always get his hands on was not the kind of stuff they supplied in innocent old war movies. He was the one with the funny smokes, the pills, the little plastic packages and God alone knew what else. Of all the men aboard, Wide Boy Reynolds was the one, perhaps, who frightened her the most.

She sat up, pushed herself erect and crossed to the nearest machine. She was going to start on the peck pumper. It had two hinged pads which were pulled in from their positions either side of the ears to meet in front of the nose. The multi-gyms worked by a series of pulleys so that the pads and bars raised an adjustable column of weights varying from five kilos to fifty. She adjusted the weights carefully. She wanted light work which would build stamina not muscle bulk.

She moved to the padded seat between the peck pump pads and sat with her back to the machine. She shook her head to ensure her long dark hair would not get caught up in the machinery. Her mind still involved with the list of deck officers, she reached back to grip the pads. The position thrust out her breasts to straining fullness against the stretch top of her exercise suit and her reverie was interrupted by a series of catcalls and wolf whistles. All along the gym window stood a line of early-bird seamen who had clearly discovered a new and popular spectator sport. She looked at them, stunned by the simple rage this puerile invasion of her privacy ignited inside her. Her Italian blood commanded that she rise up and scream at them at once. Explain to them in some detail what pathetic excuses for men they really were and speculate individually, collectively and loudly upon their parentage and personal habits.

She was up out of the machine and halfway across the basketball court before she realised it and only the arrival of Yasser Timmins stopped her. He shoved past the end of the line of men and slammed in through the door. 'What kind of an exhibition is this, Ms Cable?' He had a high, whining voice which she found she disliked as much as everything else about him.

'An exhibition of pre-historic chauvinism!' she spat.

'I thought the captain had forbidden you to wear that outfit around the ship,' he persisted.

'It's the only exercise outfit I've got. It's six thirty in the morning, for heaven's sake!'

'You will just have to take some other form of exercise. I can't have my men distracted by . . .' he paused. His words were identical to Captain Black's words yesterday and he couldn't remember what came next.

'What other form of exercise?'

'Screwing!' came a call from outside. She recognised the New York Irish voice of crewman Sean O'Brien.

Timmins was shaking with rage now, and all of it was directed at her. 'You see?' he hissed. 'You see what your *exercise* is inciting? I forbid you to come here again, no matter what the time!'

'None of the idle slobs you call crew seem to use these facilities in any case. How dare you forbid me to use them!'

Timmins drew himself up to his full height, which was a mistake. His balding scalp almost drew level with her eyes. She could see the dandruff in the oily black wool round it. 'I will not allow the crew of this ship to stand watching through these windows while you put on a pornographic . . .' He faltered as she took one step towards him, a right hook in the making.

A roar of sound stopped her. Over the scrawny officer's shaking shoulder, she saw the huge metal storm shutter rattling down the outside of the window to cut out all the daylight and every crewman's gaze. The lights flickered on to reveal a tall, powerful-looking man in an exercise vest and tracksuit pants. 'Hey, Yasser, what are your work team doing hanging around out there?' he asked with quiet amiability. 'O'Brien got nothing better to do than leer? I think Symes is actually drooling. You waiting for old Tightship to get up and tell you what to do next?'

'They were watching our *guest* here doing her *exercises*.' He spat out the word 'exercises', making it sound dirty.

'They've never seen anyone aboard do any real exercise before, I guess,' said the tall man. 'I sure as hell never have.' He crossed to the exercise machine Ann had been using, saw the way it had been set with one flick of his bright blue eyes, and walked to the other one. 'Certainly never seen any officers do any exercise. Tightship's too old, you're too scrawny, Hogg's too fat, and the Wide Boy's got other fish to fry. None of you're much when it comes to exercising. But you'd think one of you would know how to run a ship, how to command a crew. And you'd think a first officer would know that the best way to stop a bunch of idle, dirty-minded, shit-for-brains layabouts from looking through a window at people taking a little exercise is to pull down the shutters.'

He sat down on his chosen machine and took hold of a crossbar immediately above his head. With all the power of a trained body-builder, he pulled the bar down until it was level with his short ribs. His eyes rested on Timmins, brows slightly raised. 'You still here?' he asked, mildly surprised. He pulled down again, muscles expanding with the effort. The bar was almost touching his massive thighs and Ann suddenly realised he hadn't bothered to adjust it: he was pulling fifty kilos and he wasn't even straining. 'I tell you what, Yasser. Till old Tightship gets up and tells you what to do, *I'll* tell you: take your men and give them some breakfast.'

He released the crossbar and the weights slammed down like a guillotine. Timmins jumped and automatically turned to obey. He was out on the deck before he realised what the big man had made him do but by then it was too late to do anything about it except to slam the door behind him.

Ann sat down on the exercise machine and waited for her breathing to slow. Silence filled the room, emphasised by the distant throbbing of the generators and the almost subliminal rumble of the ship's hull through the water. At last she looked across at him. He was sitting with his arms up, still holding the rubberised handles of the steel crosspiece above his head. The blue eyes were distant, but even in profile she could see the slightly amused look in the nearest one. The laugh lines at the corners were crinkled in wry amusement; the long valley down his lean cheek from sharp cheekbone to square jaw was pulled back from the vertical by the ghost of a grin which stretched the moustache on his upper lip and revealed a gleam of square white teeth. The fluorescent lighting was bright enough to show a gleam of stubble on his chin, as though the tanned flesh had been brushed with gold dust.

'I'm Ann Cable, the writer,' she said, 'and I'd like to thank you for what you just did.'

He turned fractionally towards her and the smile widened. 'I'm Henri LeFever, scientific officer, in charge of the cargo,' he answered. 'And what I just did was to strain every single muscle in my body.'

CHAPTER SIX

Day Four

Saturday, 22 May   21:30

The couple entering the exclusive little restaurant over-looking the River Thames were arresting enough to turn a number of heads, even among the bustle of a busy Saturday evening. The man was tall and slim. His height and apparent frailty were emphasised by the way in which he leaned on a walking stick, causing him to stoop slightly; and the angle of his shoulders made the beautifully tailored suit jacket hang loosely on his frame. Only the youthful power of his face gave the lie to the first impact. From the blue-black waves of the hair, dusted with grey at the temples, to the blue-grey thrust of his jaw, it was a face full of intelligence and life. The eyes burned brightly, like flares behind blue glass. The lines at their corners were deep, but from the steadfast examination of far horizons, not from the weight of age or illness, and the high, tanned forehead was smooth. And if the body moved carefully, there was nothing slow about the change of expressions which fled across that visage like cloud shadows over the face of the ocean.

The woman was in many ways a perfect match for him. She was well above medium height but beside him she looked almost petite. She walked with the hint of a dance in her step, emphasised perhaps by the length of her ballerina's legs. Her short back was ramrod straight and she held her shoulders back and her head high. The oiled abundance of her hair was, if anything, darker than his but it contained no hint of blue. It curled like smoke down onto the breadth of one shoulder, lying languidly on the emerald silk there, stirring slightly with her movement as though it was alive. The high arch of her brows lent an air of artistry to her carefully made-up face. But the make-up was calculatedly understated, almost subliminally drawing attention to the massive black-brown almond eyes, the long, straight nose flaring into broad nostrils, the wide, deep, deep brown lips. Her jaw line, ebony where his was steely and rounded where his was square, was every bit as determined as her escort's. And the authority of the intelligence sweeping through her lively expression was every bit as powerful as his.

The *maître* was expecting them and welcomed them as old friends. He showed them to a reserved table at the back in the shadows beside a massive picture window looking over the gleaming water down towards the Pool of London. There was no real impression of over-service, but the chief cellarman came to discuss their choice of a single bottle of wine and the chef himself came to guide their selection from his menu.

Other patrons soon became bored with watching the pair who were immediately locked deep in discussion, but a couple of newspaper gossip columnists, never off duty, kept an eye on that shady, exclusive corner, for they recognised the man as Richard Mariner and they knew that his wife was away. The woman was familiar, too, but more difficult to put a name to.

Magdalena DaSilva leaned forward and continued her animated conversation. 'It's a question of money,' she was saying.

'Only money? Nothing more?' Richard's tone was lightly ironic but there was a trace of shock there too.

'Primarily money. It's what you can afford and how long you can afford it for and there's nothing guaranteed. Except me, of course. I'm guaranteed.'

'But you're the most expensive item.'

'For you, yes, I am. But I'm also the best in the circumstances.'

'Which is why I came to you.'

'You've got to be certain about this. You're running quite a risk. You know there are alternatives.'

'But it's not a situation that will just go away, is it?'

'No. You're right. It won't go away on its own.'

'Then you must take care of it for me, Maggie, however much it costs.'

One of the reporters on the far side of the restaurant slapped the table in front of him as the penny dropped. 'I know who that is with Richard Mariner,' he said, his voice a mixture of triumph and disappointment.

'Oh? Who?' asked his companion, fastidiously steadying the chiming glasses and quietening the tinkling silverware.

'It's Magdalena DaSilva. She's his silk.'

'Right,' continued Maggie. 'Let's take it from the top. It's a civil suit, served against Heritage Mariner and yourself, here in London, although CZP, the company serving it, is registered abroad, the ship was registered in Panama

and she was lost in the North Atlantic. It's for the full
cost of a replacement hull. Millions of pounds. You have
insurance but you're worried. You're over-stretched. If anything else goes badly wrong, then there's an outside chance
that Heritage Mariner goes down. Folds. Calls in the
receivers.'

'That's it exactly. And Sir William, Robin and I lose
everything, quite apart from all our employees being
thrown out of work and all our ships going under the
hammer. We have every spare penny we possess tied up
in *Clotho* and *Atropos* and the insurance on them since
the bomb attack is simply crippling.'

'Could you give me enough background to make some
sense of this or shall I go to your solicitors for the details?
I assume the papers were with them when Sir Harcourt
died?'

The case had been outstanding against Heritage Mariner
for nearly two years now, ever since the leper ship *Napoli*
had sunk. For nine months, Richard, his solicitor Brian
Chambers and their barrister Sir Harcourt Gibbons had
been putting together the most careful of defences. And
yesterday, a mere five days before they were due in court,
Sir Harcourt had been killed on the golf course at
Brampton. Feeling as though he had himself been struck
by lightning, Richard had spoken at length to Brian Chambers and he had recommended the replacement barrister.
'I know you've met her socially, Richard, but don't let that
slow you down,' Brian had told him. 'Get onto Maggie
DaSilva and promise her anything she wants. Word is that
she's the rising star of the maritime sets.'

'I can fill you in on what happened,' Richard said. 'Then
if you can't see the way they've put their action at law
together, I suppose you'll have to talk to Brian Chambers

tomorrow. Does this mean you're definitely going to proceed with us?'

'I'll be seeing Brian anyway. I'll make up my mind after
I've talked to him and looked at what he and Harcourt
Gibbons have put together. You just tell me what you can.'

'The ship was called the *Napoli*. She was an old freighter originally built in Gdansk. Her cargo was chemical and
nuclear waste which had been loaded aboard under some
pressure in the Lebanon.'

'Yeah, I read about that bit. The captain was killed.
Heritage Mariner supplied the replacement.'

'Our Crewfinders section did. Captain John Higgins.
Yes. But it was more complicated—'

'Complications later, unless you think they change anything about their case against you.'

'Not really. There were full discussions all along the
line, renegotiated at Naples and then again at Liverpool.'

'When all the ports refused her entry because her cargo
was so dangerous.'

'Yes. But they're not disputing any of this. It's the ship's
loss which is the basis of their case.'

'Because your man John Higgins was in command when
she went down.'

'And because I was also aboard, yes.'

'Seems pretty thin.'

'And because we were actively trying to sink her at
the time.'

There was a brief silence, which was extended by the
arrival of the langoustines and the *pouilly fumée*.

Maggie's fingers were as long and finely shaped as her
legs and were tipped with nails which were also long, and
sharp and painted red. They pulled the huge prawns apart
with feline grace and enjoyment although her mind was

clearly elsewhere. Waiters hovered. Richard sniffed the familiar bouquet of the wine and nodded. Two glasses were poured and they were alone again. He poured himself some Malvern water and sipped it.

'Tell me what you were doing first,' she said. '*Why* comes in a moment.'

'We had explosives aboard. We put them at the bow and at the stern. We wanted to blow a hole in each end and send her down as quickly as we could.'

'Isn't it normal practice just to open the seacocks and wait?'

'The seacocks wouldn't work. Neither did the pumps, for that matter. The leaking chemical had destroyed them.'

'So, you considered several alternative ways of sinking the *Napoli* before you started playing around with explosives?'

'We thought of every way we could. We were forced to take what we knew to be a very dangerous course of action because there was absolutely no alternative at all.'

'Now, *why*?'

'There was chemical waste on her deck and nuclear waste in her holds. The chemicals were leaking and dissolving the protective covering around the nuclear waste. It was already beginning to overheat. We had to stop the process at once or the whole lot was going to melt down and blow up. A full-scale nuclear explosion. Just off the eastern seaboard of America.' The thought robbed him of his appetite. He pushed his first course aside.

'Witnesses?'

'Any number. Me, John, the crew.'

'Expert witnesses?'

'Ann Cable, the reporter. She was working for Greenpeace at the time. She was on board to keep an eye on the cargo.'

'And she'll support what you say?'

'We acted on her expert advice.'

Maggie sipped her wine and looked longingly over the wreckage on her plate to his untouched food. This had not begun to affect her appetite. Yet. The vividly pink point of her tongue flicked along the perfectly sculpted edge of her upper lip. Richard gave the slightest of smiles. They were old friends, though she had never represented Heritage Mariner before. If she did so this time, it would only be on her own terms. He pushed his plate towards her and in an instant hers was in front of him.

'So. You sank the ship on purpose.'

'That is what her owners, CZP, say. That is why they are suing us for the hull.'

'No doubt their insurance doesn't cover deliberate scuttling.'

'No doubt – if they have regular insurance, which I also doubt. And whatever insurance they do have is unlikely to cover loss of the vessel because the hull was eaten away by the cargo.'

'But you said you sank her.'

'No. I said I was trying to sink her and I said the owners are accusing me of sinking her. But I didn't. We were still placing the explosives when she went down under her own steam.'

The waiter arrived then and the chef was close behind, particularly pleased to observe that Richard had so much enjoyed the langoustines. The smile that Richard gave Maggie then was deeper and more genuine than any smile for many a day. They suspended their conversation until, with due ceremony, the grilled turbot with green peppercorn butter and the lobster thermidor arrived.

Maggie started doing to the big crustacean exactly what she had done to the small ones. Richard peeled back the crisp black skin and took a forkful of firm white flesh. It tasted sublime. He began to eat more seriously, but he still paid close attention to her.

'Let me get this absolutely clear. You contend that while you were engaged in trying to sink this ship she just happened to go down anyway.'

'That's about it.'

'Before you could actually carry out your own plans?'

'That's it exactly. Sir Harcourt and Clive Standing, CZP's silk, have been before the judge already, putting all their submissions. As I understand it, the case in open court will simply come down to this: they say I sank their ship and I say I didn't.'

'And that's all there is to it? I mean, I'd have thought it was worth CZP's time trying for the further contention in the lawsuit that if you actually sank the ship then you are responsible for putting a considerable environmental and ecological hazard on the floor of the ocean off the east coast of America.'

'If I sank the ship, then I'm responsible for putting the cargo where it is.'

'Which is what CZP allege.'

'But if the ship sank under me because the cargo had damaged the hull, then whoever shipped the cargo is responsible for the loss of *Napoli* and the final resting place of whatever was in her holds.'

'Which would be your defence. But you say that no one has made any allegations of further responsibility.' Her eyebrows rose, and her long almond eyes gleamed with disbelief.

'No,' he said firmly. Then he frowned. 'That is . . .'

'What?'

'The owners of the cargo, Disposoco, are a pretty shady

outfit. I haven't heard much from them except that they will be supporting CZP in this case. But if what you say is true and there is a case to answer for the cargo, then they would be in deep trouble because it was their cargo.'

'Unless the high court says it was you who put the cargo where it is.'

'So this case could be about much more than just the *Napoli*. And if I lose it, then it could be only the beginning.'

'And that is where I come in. If I come in.'

They ate in silence for a while, then Richard continued, 'It's potentially ruinous. Heritage Mariner could stump up the cash for a new hull if push came to shove. And, of course, Crewfinders carries insurance against the loss of ships under their personnel. But if CZP prove liability against us for the criminal placing of the cargo, then the matter rapidly seems to go out of control. I wouldn't be surprised if there are already lawsuits in the offing from American environmental agencies, fisheries, individuals. Whoever ends up with the legal responsibility for having put that cargo where it is could well be facing lawsuits from anyone on the eastern seaboard who contracts cancer.'

'That's overstating the case, I think.'

'Look what happened to Pan Am when a case was made against them over Lockerbie.'

'Well, let's look at another aspect. What sort of people are CZP?'

'Sharks. Desperate ones, by the look of it. But they're not as bad as Disposoco.'

'Let me get this clear. CZP owned *Napoli* and chartered her to Disposoco, who were responsible for moving the cargo.'

'That's correct. It was Disposoco's captain, a man called Fittipaldi, who was replaced by John Higgins. Fittipaldi was killed in the Lebanon while the ship was being loaded. He was the lucky one, as it turned out. The rest of the crew they had hired were trapped aboard by trick contracts. Couldn't get off no matter what.'

'Is that legal?'

'Not what you'd call ethical, certainly.'

'Are you being coy?'

'Yes, I am. If my experience with them so far is anything to go by, they make the Mafia look like a benevolent society.'

'And you say Disposoco will be supporting CZP in their lawsuit against you?'

'Count on it. They'll be working hand in glove. Whatever it takes. Whatever it costs.'

She pushed aside her thermidor, not quite finished. 'All right. So we're looking here at a suit against you presented by CZP, owners of the ship, but supported by Disposoco, owners of the cargo. This suit charges that you personally and Heritage Mariner are responsible for the sinking of *Napoli* and are therefore liable for the cost of replacing the hull. But my bet is that somewhere behind all this there is a further suit which says that by criminally sinking the vessel, you are directly responsible for the placing of the cargo in its present position. And that consequently you must indemnify them and also bear responsibility for any other suit arising from the placing of the cargo in the place where it presently lies.'

'My God, do you think Sir Harcourt thought of any of this? Or Brian Chambers?'

'I doubt it. Look, they're lovely men, both, but whose men are they? Sir William's, I'll bet. Even if they've arrived in the twentieth century, they'll still think the British Empire's in place. New York simply won't have entered their thinking. Especially if they've been fiddling around with pre-trial hearings in front of the judge. They won't have had leisure to look at the big picture at all. You do realise that in theory the American government might require whoever is proved to be responsible to get the whole lot up and to dispose of it correctly?'

'I hadn't thought of that.'

'It might be a cheaper alternative, especially if you lose.'

'I don't think so, Maggie.'

'Why?' she asked, surprised by the bitterness in his tone. 'Where is it?'

'It's right on top of the *Titanic*.'

They were still deep in conversation when the plates were cleared. They had eschewed pudding, but their communion, interrupted only by a final word with the chef, took them through several cups of coffee and it was not until nearly midnight that they finally called for the bill.

At the same time as Richard reached for his wallet, Maggie took out her purse. 'No,' she said decisively, 'I'll get this. You're a friend and I'm not your silk yet. I don't want to get hauled in front of the Council for touting. But if anything goes wrong with this case, you'll need every penny you can lay your hands on.'

The purse was in her handbag, and as she was taking care of things, the spine of a book caught his eye. It was such an unusual thing to see in an evening handbag that he looked at it more closely. It was called *The Leper Ship* and he knew it well. It was Ann Cable's best-selling account of the final voyage of *Napoli*.

When Maggie looked up again, his eyes were still on

the book. 'So,' he said, 'you came prepared.'

'I haven't read it yet. I wanted to hear your version of events before I read hers. Then I wanted to think whether there's a case for either side before seeing Brian Chambers.'

'And will you?'

'Go to see Brian Chambers? Yes, I shall. That I can promise.'

'And will you get involved?'

'Ah, well, that's quite another question.'

CHAPTER SEVEN

Day Six

Monday, 24 May   08:00

The largest feature of the North Atlantic is the Gulf Stream. Fuelled by the westward pressure of the North Equatorial Current, it spews endlessly up out of the Gulf of Mexico and pushes north. Moving millions and millions of gallons of warm water at a mile or two a day, it flows up the east coast of Florida, past Georgia and the Carolinas before turning eastwards to slide over Bermuda and away towards northern Europe.

Along a front perhaps a thousand miles wide, it washes the western coasts of Cornwall and South Wales, of Ireland from Fastnet to the Bloody Foreland, of Scotland from Kintyre to the Shetlands past the Hebrides and the Orkneys and the Summer Isles. By the time it sweeps past the Faroes and away along Norway towards Russia, it has changed its name but not its nature. It has become the North Atlantic Current but it still carries with it mists and warmth, fecundity and the occasional tropical fish.

As it reaches the outer edge of the European Continental shelf, where the abyssal depths of the Atlantic climb precipitously upwards towards the shallows of the North Sea, the Gulf Stream splits and sends a wayward tentacle due north. This never-ending river of warmth pushes up into the coldest arctic seas, washing up past Iceland, through the terrible Denmark Strait and into the frozen Norwegian Sea, washing back to the west of Greenland through the Labrador Sea into the icefields of the Davis Strait and Baffin Bay. And, according to the simple laws of physics, as the warm currents push northwards towards the Pole, taking the occasional lost garfish, shrimp or snapper, so the cold currents come back southwards, bringing ice.

The Gulf Stream was pulled northwards that year. It seemed to want to follow the sun which was just beginning to bring spring to the tundra and light to the far north. But this apparent beneficence was double-edged, for the extra flow of warm water gave added strength to the currents flowing north and this broke up the icefields more quickly. And as the flow into the Norwegian Sea and Baffin Bay was stronger, so the cold currents coming south also moved with more force and they brought a lot more ice. This situation was further complicated by a series of particularly destructive storms which swept along the old tracks, as predictable as freight cars, from Hudson Bay to Murmansk. Until, during that week late in May, a ridge of high pressure – a wall of solid air – spilled south off the polar icecap to stand along the icecap over Greenland. It stopped the storms dead in their tracks so that they piled up one on top of the other, each one fiercer than the last.

Atropos and *Clotho* were sailing the same course between Canada and Cumbria, one going eastwards and one going westwards. The course was far north of the normal shipping lanes because of the potential danger of the cargo. All things being equal, the two ships would have met just south of Kap Farvel at the southern tip of Greenland, which the old charts called Cape Farewell. But things were not equal. The disturbing Gulf Stream was running further north than usual and the Denmark Strait was spewing out ice on the back of the Greenland Current. But it was doing so under clear heavens and light airs.

Clotho was sailing calmly westwards through still seas made strange by the unusual conditions. The Davis Strait was haemorrhaging floes and bergs in the freezing grasp of the Labrador Current under black skies and increasingly frenzied winds, and *Atropos* was pushing doggedly eastwards into the teeth of a south-easterly storm, with every sense alert for disaster.

They had both been at sea for six days now, and in fact they were less than a hundred miles apart. But they were still separated by the wall of heavy air standing over the Greenland icecap and they might as well have been on different planets.

'Sound "abandon ship",' ordered the captain.

Nico Niccolo was just handing over the watch to Johnny Sullivan, but the Neapolitan first officer was still technically in charge of the bridge so it was he who obeyed, crossing to the console under the broad, angled clearview window and hitting a button beside the microphone there. He turned back and the captain handed him a stopwatch and a walkie-talkie radio. He nodded once to show he understood what was required; speech would have been wasted for it was nearly impossible to hear. *Clotho*'s emergency siren bellowed through the ship's tannoy system, through all the navigation, storage, accommodation and work areas and out across the quiet ocean.

Clotho was on automatic, following a parallel course to
the optimum course in her computers, a little under twenty
miles south of where she should have been. For days now,
five miles to the north of her had stood a grey wall of
fog where the icy, ice-laden current coming down from
the north met the warm water running up beneath them
from the south. But at dawn this morning, Nico, the watchkeeper, had woken Robin to report that the mist wall had
turned south to cut across their course. Now it was 08:00
local time and the day around them – as far as the edge
of the fog – was bright and calm and utterly clear. Forward
for five miles or so, and astern and on their port beam,
the air was so limpid it seemed as though mere eyes could
see as far as the instruments on the bridge. It was warm
enough for the bridge wing doors to be standing open.
The gentle breeze brought in only the occasional rumble
born of their progress through the sea to mix with the
throbbing of their massive engine. And, once in a while,
from beyond that impenetrable mist wall to the north, it
brought the eerie howling and groaning that ice makes.

In the engine room, all the systems were on automatic
and none of Andrew McTavish's engineers had come on
duty yet, so there was no one to obey the urgent summons
to abandon ship. In the crew's quarters, the cabins all
stood empty: the crew were up and the stewards were not
yet at work. In the officers' quarters it was the same story,
though the bunk of Rupert Biggs, the young third officer,
was still warm – he had enjoyed a mere four hours' sleep
since handing the watch to Niccolo. Only in the galley
and the mess rooms was there any reaction as *Clotho*'s
complement threw down their knives, forks and spoons,
their pots, pans and ladles, and abandoned their breakfast
to take part in the practice. Last man out was the cook

who made sure all the ranges were switched off.

This was the second practice they had had so far and it passed off as smoothly as the first one had done: it was a new crew with a new captain aboard a new vessel, but everyone belonged to the Heritage Mariner fleet and was used to doing things the Heritage Mariner way. That didn't stop the complaints, though.

There were four big lifeboats, each designed to take up to twenty in an emergency, ten under normal circumstances. They hung in pairs on either side of the bridge-house, suspended on davits in the shelter of the overhanging bridge wings, ready to be swung out and lowered into the ocean at a moment's notice. The captain was in charge of the forward boat on the starboard side with the third officer in charge of the one behind it. The first officer was in charge of the port-side boat, level with the captain's, and the second officer's was just behind that. The engineers went with their corresponding deck officers, the chief with the captain and so forth. Also with the captain went the ship's cadet Jamie Curtis and the radio officer William Christian.

In fact, it was Jamie who was detailed to take charge of the second lifeboat on the port side because the second officer, Sullivan, held the watch and would only abandon the bridge in a real emergency.

Under the watchful eyes of the captain and the first officer, each of whom held a stopwatch in one hand and a walkie-talkie in the other, the boats' crews lined up beneath their pendant keels and waited to be dismissed. They were ready to abandon in a matter of minutes and felt that the next natural step should be the stowing of the boats and the completion of breakfast.

Why she let the exercise run on she would never know.

Perhaps the crew were too confident. Perhaps she felt the whole Heritage Mariner atmosphere was too cosy. Perhaps it was because the crystal stillness of the morning was perfect for the full practice – and they could do with a full practice. Perhaps it was because of that sinister mist wall closing from dead ahead, warning so vividly of a terrible change in the weather and sea conditions to come. Perhaps she had an inkling of what was to come.

When stillness settled on the scene and silence fell, apart from the throbbing of the huge engine and the whisper of the wake as *Clotho* surged onwards to the south of Kap Farvel, Robin's eyes flicked up to glance along the line of rigid profiles under number one boat. She glanced across to Nico Niccolo whose position matched hers exactly and saw that he was waiting too. 'Proceed, Mr Niccolo,' she said.

The groan came from the davits as they swung full out to suspend their burdens over the sea, but it might just as well have come from the throats of forty hungry sailormen seeing their breakfast disappear. At once the scene closed down. Up until this point the captain had overseen the whole. Now the officer commanding each boat took his responsibility for its correct launching and for the safety of all within it.

Robin strode forward and stood by the radio officer, Bill Christian. Beyond him, Andrew McTavish was keeping a wary eye on the group of GP seamen who made up the rest of the lifeboat's complement. Robin knew three of them – old hands all: Sam Larkman, his narrow face set hard as stone and his thin lips tight closed on some blistering thoughts about officers in general and captains in particular – female ones being the worst of all; gentle Joe Edwards echoing Sam's every movement, though probably none of his thoughts; big Errol Jones, the only black person aboard in spite of Heritage Mariner's positive policies with regard to race, sex and background. The others were not so familiar, but they seemed to know what they were doing well enough. While Joe Edwards and Errol Jones held the falls and lowered the boat until it was level with the safety rail, the others crowded forward and stripped the canvas covering away to reveal the neatly disposed contents.

Once again they paused, and this time Sam Larkman actually glanced up at her, though she realised later it was a simple glance of enquiry and probably held no thought of a complaint at all. Her eyes met Sam's for a moment and she felt her eyebrows rising. Her own lips set to a thin, pale line. She switched her gaze to Christian's and gave a brief nod. The radio officer swung the lifeboat's radio out of the doorway and onto the first thwart with a convulsive movement. Then he was in after it. 'Look to the falls,' snapped Robin and two of the nameless seamen joined Joe and Errol while everyone else climbed in.

'Lower away!' She called it loudly enough to carry to all the boats so that the other officers would know how far the practice was proceeding and how fast her crew were working. She stayed on the deck and noted the time when number one lifeboat's keel kissed the water – though she did not stop the watch until the second starboard boat was in the water too. Then, with a curt 'Stay there, please' to the teams on the falls, she crossed to the port side.

Here, too, the boats were in the water and beginning to trail behind the ship. Nico stood above the fourth one, obviously surprised that young Jamie Curtis had got his into the water as quickly as everyone else. Jamie, too, was jubilant and he stood in the bow of his command, his left

hand holding the double fall above his head, and waved
up at his captain with youthful glee. She gave him the
same curt nod she had given Christian, though in fact her
mood was quite light. She turned and met Nico's watchful
gaze and at last allowed herself to thaw a little. A glimmer
of a smile crinkled the corners of her eyes and stirred the
corners of her lips. 'Well done, Nico. Bring them in,'
she said.

Being a Neapolitan, he appreciated that tiny smile as
much as if she had laughed aloud. Being an officer, he
was pleased at last to see some of his captain's gloom
beginning to lift. And being a man, he considered basking
a little in the sunshine of her approval. He got less than a
second to indulge these feelings before young Curtis went
overboard into the water.

It was an easy enough mistake to make. The cadet had
stood up on the whaleback covered bow of his boat without noticing that there was a loose loop of rope from the
fall beneath his feet. As soon as the men aboard *Clotho*
tightened their grip, ready to lift the lifeboat back aboard,
the loop jerked up tight, caught his foot and catapulted
him overboard. The second engineer, now in charge of the
boat, was caught completely by surprise and the seamen
crewing her weren't too quick on the uptake either. Nico
thrust past Robin who had her back to the incident and
crossed to the rail. 'Let go the falls,' snapped the first
officer, but the men on the deck, thinking to help, simply
let go of the ropes instead of releasing them correctly. The
pull of the lifeboat was enough to whip the ropes through
the block and snarl them hopelessly. Nico swung back,
suddenly infuriated, and opened his mouth to bellow a
string of orders only to find his captain standing calmly
just behind him.

'Over you go, please, Nico. Take your boat and go after him. I'll be on the bridge and I'll bring her round at once.'

Nico was in action as soon as she finished speaking.

'You men,' said Robin in the sort of tone she might have used to discuss pruning roses with her gardener, 'cut the falls below that mess, but don't let the boat break free.'

Down the side of the ship from the main deck to Nico's lifeboat was a Jacob's ladder. Nico swarmed down it as fast as he could, almost shocked by the calm firmness with which Robin was handling the emergency. This was certainly the way to be proceeding: exactly by the book. She should be pounding up the companionway towards the bridge about now, walkie-talkie to her lips, commanding Sullivan to bring *Clotho* round in a Williamson turn and to sound 'man overboard'. She could rely on Biggs and McTavish to get the other two boats up with a minimum of fuss.

The Neapolitan stepped down into his boat. 'Let go, all,' he called to his men. Then he looked down to the second engineer crouching over the motor, ready to go. 'Full ahead,' he ordered, and caught up a yellow life preserver as he spoke.

Jamie Curtis exploded wildly to the surface and forced himself to calm down, lie still and float quietly, all too aware of the fact that he should have been wearing a life jacket, but he had been too excited to go to the bother of putting one on. It required an enormous effort of will to remain calm, which it never occurred to him was actually almost heroism. He had never realised that the sea could seem so big. That a ship as large as *Clotho* could become so small so quickly. That she could sail away so fast.

He hung motionless in the water, looking after her,

fighting to believe that this was actually happening. He
gasped in a breath, knowing that his face would go under
the water again during the next few seconds. He closed
his eyes and went into convulsive movement once more.
Three seconds later, he had kicked off his shoes and was
hanging in the water again, waiting for his heart to slow.
The next thing he should do, according to the theory, was
to take off his trousers, tie knots in the legs and inflate
them. But he was wearing a white boiler suit and a cursory
experiment soon revealed that his water-clumsy fingertips
couldn't undo any of the buttons or even loosen the belt
buckle. Any thought of taking it off and inflating it was
out of the question. Thank God. Getting out of his shoes
had been bad enough and they had been loose slip-ons.

He was young for his eighteen years and this was his
first long period away from home. His parents lived in
Portsmouth and he had gone to school and college there.
His cadetship with Heritage Mariner had begun with the
year and *Clotho* was his first posting after four months of
further training ashore. He was a quiet, sensible, reliable
young man and was already establishing himself as a
popular shipmate and something of a ship's mascot. He
was unaware of the way his shipmates viewed him, however, and his first thought after the initial panic had washed
over him was anger at the stupid bravado which had made
him do such a silly thing – and without a lifebelt, too!
God alone knew what the captain would say when she got
him back aboard. The fact that she was a woman only
made things worse. Jamie's father was a small, quiet
businessman who rather tended to indulge his intelligent,
clear-minded son, so Jamie's mother had been left to exercise discipline in the Curtis household. It did not seem
likely to Jamie, therefore, that his captain's femininity
would make her a soft touch.

These thoughts all raced through his head in a very little time and many of them were barely conscious in any case. They hardly impinged on the enormity of what was happening to him; what he could see, hear, taste and feel was so overwhelming that it made what he was thinking seem utterly insignificant.

He was looking after the *Clotho*, along the line of her wake, so he was facing the set of the sea. The surface of the water was just below his chin and he could only see beyond the face of the next wave during those few seconds when he was held up by each round, green crest. At these moments, he could see a seemingly endless series of turquoise waves washing up towards him from a horizon which was only a mile or two away – a horizon below which *Clotho* was already hull down and vanishing fast. Apart from her darkly silhouetted upper works, there was nothing else to see except for the endless ocean.

From nowhere, a picture of the chart leaped into his mind. He saw it as he had seen it at seven thirty this morning when Nico Niccolo had showed it to him before breakfast. The tiny mark *Clotho* had been, one hundred and fifty-six hours out of Seascale, just over a hundred miles due south of Kap Farvel in Greenland. Cape Farewell indeed, he thought. Farewell Jamie Curtis.

At least the water wasn't too cold. That was a relief, and something of a surprise. But then he remembered what Nico had told him about the Gulf Stream and why the weather here was clear and so foggy so close to their starboard beam. A wavelet slapped him in the face and he tasted salt and choked, but it cleared his mind a little and it finally occurred to him to stop floating and to start swimming. If he followed *Clotho*'s course, he reasoned, then he would bring himself closer to the rescuers who must be coming back after him.

As he took his first clumsy breaststroke, panic washed over him again. The ocean was so unimaginably enormous. So unutterably deep. Angling his body as though he were in his local swimming pool suddenly made him think that there wasn't fourteen feet of water beneath him but more like two thousand metres down to the Eirik Ridge. That was more than a thousand fathoms; more than six thousand feet. The weight of these terrible figures all but pulled him under the surface.

The Williamson emergency turn was something of a turning point for Robin herself. She stood on her bridge, calmly quiet, eyes everywhere, but implicitly trusting Johnny Sullivan who held the watch and Sam Larkman who held the wheel to know what to do. The practice had gone well enough and even Jamie Curtis's accident could not undermine that. In fact, it was the sort of thing that could happen all too easily and there was no sense in getting upset. If they got the snagged lifeboat up safely, if they got Nico's boat back and, most importantly, if they got the cadet safely out of the water, then it would have been quite a satisfactory morning's work. They would have proved themselves to be just the sort of crew she would be happy to lead through that mist wall into the ice-bound maelstrom of the Labrador Sea. For the first time since coming aboard, Robin got the impression of her command working under her quietly but efficiently, like the movement of Richard's old steel Rolex watch.

The thought of Richard caught her with unexpected force and she suddenly found herself trembling with desire for him. Literally knocked breathless by an overpowering need to feel his hands upon her. It was a feeling which was by no means new to her, but not since pregnancy had rearranged her hormone doses had she felt overpowering lust for him like this. It was most distracting.

They had been in contact at least once a day and he had updated her on Harcourt Gibbons' death and the fact that he had approached Maggie DaSilva. She knew and liked the young woman barrister, but the sudden, tragic death of her father's old friend had only served to darken her view of the current situation further.

Her contact with *Atropos* and its headquarters at Sept Isles had been hardly more satisfactory. The Canadian vessel had set sail late and then fallen further and further behind schedule as the weather closed in. The organisation in the small Canadian city seemed to be an utter shambles, one which had lasted far longer than it should have done, even after Dan Williams' death. As for herself, she knew she had had an easy ride of it so far; she was well aware that things between here and her destination would all too likely be the exact opposite.

Bill Christian stuck his head through from the radio shack and called her back to the present. 'No ships near enough to help with the man overboard,' he reported. 'And *Atropos*'s eight o'clock report has still not come in. But the weather report has. That high pressure ridge over Greenland has a bitch of a storm trapped right over their heads. They're in deep shit over there. And we'll be in it with them in four or five hours' time. Ah. Sorry about the language, Captain.'

'Okay, Bill, thanks.' She was back to the present but still too distracted to be irritated by his embarrassment over his mild swearing – one of the few aspects of sexism currently extant aboard. She would check on *Atropos*'s situation when they had Jamie back aboard. She thumbed the SEND button on her walkie-talkie. 'Nico?'

'Here, Captain. No sign.'

'I have a clear trace from the first officer's boat, Captain,' said Rupert Biggs from his position beside the collision alarm radar. It would be too much to expect him to see Jamie too, though the equipment was almost magically powerful.

'Keep feeding bearings to the helmsman until it's dead ahead,' she ordered, and crossed to the watchkeeper's chair. There was nothing she could do until Nico found Jamie and *Atropos* found Nico. She settled back into the black leather executive chair and let her mind drift a little.

For the first time in two years she didn't feel fat and dumpy. She hadn't dictated any special diet, indeed she was eating like a pig. She hadn't lost any weight. Her body hadn't changed at all. She had simply ceased worrying – indeed, thinking – about it. She had had six nights of uninterrupted sleep – again, for the first time in two years. Although Nurse Janet slept on one side of the nursery, Richard and Robin slept on the other side and it was a rare event for the twins to sleep through. Or, once they were up, that they would be satisfied with anything less than being carried through to their parents' bed. Only on the nights before the most important meetings did Richard and she let Janet try to handle the monsters on her own.

And there had been quite a few important meetings for Robin as Richard seemed to have been convalescent in one way or another for the last eighteen months. Her father, Sir William Heritage, and the chief executive, Helen Dufour, had kept Heritage Mariner well on track, but times had been hard in the City and it could not have happened more unfortunately that both Richard and she had been pulled away from the office. Neither of them had been on a Heritage Mariner vessel for far too long. Richard had

been ashore since the Gulf War and she had been beached
since her involvement in the recovery of the Heritage
Mariner flagship supertanker *Prometheus* more than two
years ago. And, for the first time since then, it seemed,
she felt wide awake, fit and confident. A different person
to the woman who had examined herself so glumly in that
mirror in a Belfast hotel bedroom three months ago, and
yet the change had started in less than a week.

It was simply wonderful to be back at sea.

To be *free*.

The walkie-talkie squawked. 'Yes, Nico?'

'I think we have him . . . I think . . . What *is* that?'

A distant voice behind Nico's came over the walkie-
talkie faintly, but the words, and the tone in which they
were said, were clear enough: '*It's a shark*!'

At first Nico couldn't believe it. A shark seemed so
unlikely in these waters that he was about to dismiss the
triangular fin as belonging to a dolphin or a small whale
when he saw the telltale second point which told of a
vertical fish's tail. The tails of all whales and their cousins
lie horizontal. This certainly was a shark.

'What sort of sharks are there in these waters?' he asked
his crew. 'Basking sharks? Whale sharks?' Neither would
harm the boy; they were both toothless and fed on krill
or plankton.

'That's a tiger shark,' said the man who had first seen it.

And even as he spoke, one of the other lookouts called,
'There he is, sir!'

The only thing they could do was to go for Jamie as
quickly as possible, taking care to keep the lifeboat
between the man in the water and the shark. The man-
eater's senses were not so easily fooled, however, and it

began to make a race of it, clearly attracted by the signals given out by Jamie's attempts to swim. The boy was practically asleep by the look of things. His body appeared and disappeared up and down the backs of the rolling green waves, and it continued a slow, automatic breaststroke and gave no reaction at all to the chorus of shouts and warnings which all aboard the lifeboat were giving.

Nico began to look around for a way to scare the fish off. 'What the hell is a tiger shark doing this far north?' he muttered as he worked, pulling out all the survival gear, looking for the packet of distress flares which were all he could think of that might help. But he wasn't really asking, for he knew the answer well enough: it was the Gulf Stream. The shark had simply cruised up out of its normal home waters and been pulled north by the warm current. And that current was the only reason Jamie was still alive. He had been in the water for nearly ten minutes now and if he had been swimming ten miles north of here, in the waters of the Greenland Current, he would have been dead for some time.

They were still twenty feet away when the shark began its first charge. It had been swimming parallel to the lifeboat and gaining on it slowly but surely, when it turned abruptly and cut across the bows, going straight for Jamie. The change of course was so sudden it took them all by surprise, but Nico was quickest on the uptake.

'Full ahead,' he yelled at the top of his voice. The lifeboat gathered way, its engine screaming. 'Come left, left,' he bellowed, waving his left arm wildly. The boat came round onto a convergent track, its sharp bow cutting towards the striped brown flank.

The shark disregarded it utterly. It was homing in on Jamie and was even beginning to roll, its vicious mouth agape.

Nico forgot all about looking for the flares and leaned as far out on the whaleback bow as he dared, using his weight to force the wooden blade down deeper into the water. So that when they came together, the lifeboat actually hit the thing right on the head, immediately behind the tooth-packed maw. The boat bounced up, and Nico was lucky not to be thrown into the water himself. The keel grazed the fish's flank and there was a kind of thudding shock as the propeller bit into one of its fins. Then they were past it and looking back, praying one and all that the impact had been enough to scare it off. With a pettish flick, sending up a wall of water like an irritated child splashing in its bath, the fish turned away.

Moments later, the fainting body of the cadet was safely aboard and the lifeboat was heading back towards *Clotho* as she pulled herself up over the low horizon.

Nico was on his knees in the bottom, his face folded into a frown of confusion. He was the man in charge of the provisioning of these vessels, and he had checked this one, checked them all, less than two days ago. But someone else had been through these carefully filled lockers in the meantime, and they had taken a whole range of stuff.

Who?

Why?

'*Abandon ship*! We got to sound "abandon ship".'

'Don't be such an asshole, Yasser. How the fuck are we going to abandon ship in this crap? The lifeboat wouldn't last a second even if those morons below could get them out in the first place.'

Another massive sea threw *Atropos* up into the air and Ann only stayed standing because of the grip she had on the edge of the chart table.

'We got to do *something*! We'll die.'

'We won't die, you schmuck, unless you fuck this up.
Now shut the hell up and let me drive this son of a bitch!'

It was eight o'clock in the morning and First Officer
Timmins was trying to relieve Third Officer Reynolds.
And Ann, for one, didn't want him to. Reynolds was a
sexist little shit, a porn merchant and a drug dealer. She
had been in his cabin on one occasion only – in the spirit
of accurate research – and she had seen the kind of pin-
ups he favoured. Only those over the vile O'Brien's bunk
in the crew's quarters were more explicit. And, during that
visit, the cocky little officer had taken the opportunity to
say that he could 'fix her up', though the precise meaning
of the offer was something Ann had been happy not to
think about. But still and all, from what Ann had seen,
Reynolds was actually the closest thing they had to a
genuine sailor aboard and she really did not want anyone
else in charge of the wheelhouse just at the moment.

Eight o'clock. It might as well have been midnight.
There was nothing to see beyond the bridge windows, only
the reflected brightness and their shadowy figures within
them. They couldn't even see the waves which were chuck-
ing their bows up at the skies every few minutes, or the
troughs which pulled them halfway to hell in between.
Hogg was leaning over the radar bowl and Ann hoped it
was as robust as it looked because he kept throwing up
into it – though, for the first time in years by the look of
things, his belly seemed to be empty now so at least there
wasn't enough vomit to obscure his electronic view of the
icy seas around.

And ice was all there was to see; the ocean was otherwise absolutely empty. Empty of shipping, certainly. Every
other vessel – every vessel blessed with even a half-sane
captain – had run for port. Nobody in anything like his

right mind wanted to get his ship stuck in a south-easterly gale six days out in the Labrador Sea with nothing to the lee downwind except millions of tons of ice. Ann understood little enough about ship handling, but the only good thing that seemed to have happened recently was that Reynolds had finally turned almost due south and tried to run out of the danger area. The black walls of water which had been thumping into their starboard quarter, forcing them north towards the ice and the forbidding, glacier-bound cliffs of the Greenland coast, were now punching the port, forcing them west back towards their all too distant home. And at last they were heading south towards safety.

So Timmins wanted to abandon ship.

'Get that goddamned woman off my bridge!' said a cold voice, quivering with outrage. Captain Black had arrived.

Ann stared at him. 'Captain—'

'Reynolds, your watch is over. Get her out of here.' He stood just inside the chart room door, tall but tubercular, a grey vision in an old uniform, refusing to acknowledge that she even existed, except as a thing he wanted removed from his bridge.

For a moment, Ann thought the Wide Boy was going to stand up to him, but that was never really going to happen.

'Yes, Captain,' answered Reynolds and crossed towards her. She met his eyes and shrugged. They both knew when they were beaten.

As they exited through the door into the bridge deck corridor, a lull in the banshee screaming of the wind allowed them to hear Tightship say to Timmins, 'Now, how's she heading?'

The next few seconds of conversation vanished under the sound of the next squall, but there was no mistaking

the captain's scream of 'Reynolds!' a moment later. The
third officer gave Ann a weary shrug and went back into
the wheelhouse.

Ann was a reporter. She stood outside the door and
spied. There was nothing to hear because of the wind, but
there was no mistaking the fury in Captain Black's gestures
as he berated the young officer. This was the sort of thing
Ann had come to expect. Her experiences in the gym four
long, dark days ago had showed her the kind of people
she was dealing with, but it had come as something of a
shock to discover that they all treated each other with the
same lack of respect, trust and courtesy with which they
treated her. She had fondly imagined a ship's crew to be
like a team led by an echelon of officers who were a unit
almost combat-hardened by their experiences of the sea.
What *Atropos* had was a group of self-important, arrogant
individuals who tried with a marked lack of success to
disguise their own shortcomings by picking on everyone
else's. So Reynolds' bold attempt to get the ship out of
trouble had had to be done without the captain's knowledge, for it contravened the captain's orders.

As Reynolds came back across the wheelhouse towards
her, she turned away and walked to the head of the internal
companionway. Halfway across the corridor she felt the
movement of the deck beneath her feet begin to change
as *Atropos* came round onto her original course due east
towards Kap Farvel.

She had seen Reynolds take a dressing down from the
captain before and shrug it off easily enough, but now his
mood was as foul as the weather. They ran down the stairs
side by side until she could take his thunderous silence
no more. 'What is it?' she asked, betrayed by concern for
him because he was young and good-looking and because

he had seemed to be doing the right thing when he changed onto the safer course.

'I got to check the fucking cargo,' he spat.

'What? Why?'

'Because old Tightshit up there says I might have shifted the fucking filth when I came round onto the new heading! Bastard son of a bitch knows better than that. He's just rubbing my nose in it.'

'Are you going out onto the deck?' On *Napoli*, this had been the only way to check the holds to see if the cargo might have shifted.

'Are you out of your mind? Out on the deck in this? Not even for the best lay in Las Vagas, honey.'

She hated it when he did that. He thought it was smart and it set her teeth on edge almost more than she could stand. It was little enough among everything else that was going on around her, but he just kept on and on and it was sending her insane – not for the best ass in Albuquerque, the best tits in Toledo, the best tail in Tallahassee.

'So, how do you do it?'

'There's an inspection tunnel. Under the weather deck. I'll get that idle son of a bitch LeFever and we'll go in from the engineering section. Sure as hell be no fucking engineers down there.'

'Can I come?'

That stopped him dead in his tracks. 'Well, I don't know. Ain't no fucking picnic down there. Though if the cargo's broken open it might just be a barbecue!' He thought that was extremely funny.

The idea of being roasted alive by nuclear radiation did not amuse her, but she had been closer to the reality of it than most.

'Come on, Reynolds, I won't tell.'

'It'll be like screwing in a coal sack on a roller coaster.'
He was weakening. Her carefully chosen phrase had
reminded him how much it would upset the captain if he
let her come.

LeFever was in his cabin, and when he saw who had come
calling, his long face crinkled into an engaging grin which
seemed to touch something rather too deep within her for
comfort. He had no station to be at in an emergency and
until Yasser Timmins actually convinced Tightship to
sound 'abandon' there was nowhere else he had to be. He
took surprisingly little convincing to come with them. 'I
didn't know whether to die of boredom or have a nervous
breakdown,' he cheerfully informed Ann. 'It's too rough
to read – can't hold a book steady. Can't even write a
letter. I have to tell you, Reynolds, I don't like the way
you've got your boat here going up and down!'

'Hey, me neither. And you can lay your *linguini* on that.'

If anything, the dipping and swooping was getting
worse. The three of them were bouncing off the stairwell
walls with bruising force as they stumbled down into the
engineering areas. As Reynolds had surmised, they were
deserted. The engine was set on automatic. Chief
Lethbridge and his men would be here from nine to five,
as per contract, but it was nowhere near nine yet, so, as
the cook had announced there would be no hot meals
until the storm calmed, the engineers were either eating
bread and butter or they were doing whatever idle engineers did for fun. Ann hadn't got to know them as quickly
as she had got to know the deck officers. She just knew
that one set seemed to loathe and despise the other. It
never ceased to amaze her how hard the men of this crew
worked against each other.

At least Reynolds and LeFever seemed able to co-oper-
ate. And they needed to. A big bulkhead door at the front
of the first engineering deck opened into a short tunnel
which ended in another heavy door. It really required two
to open this door, and the reason it had been sealed so
carefully was apparent as soon as it was open and the first
set of lights was switched on. It led onto a walkway
suspended from the ceiling of the first cargo hold, illuminated from high on the port side by the harsh glare of
practical, low-maintenance, shatter-proof lighting. Wedged
into the angle of the deck above and the starboard side
on their right, the walkway was like an enormously long
gallery with a see-through grating for a floor, opening on
the left over a safety rail to a view across the tops of the
cargo containers which nearly filled the hold. Walking
along here would have been a cramped, uncomfortable
affair in a dead calm with nothing so potentially dangerous
just beneath their feet. As it was, Reynolds was quite
right: this was no picnic. The gallery was too low for
them to walk upright. This fact was further emphasised
by the sharp-edged cable conduit which stuck out of the
angle where the deck met the wall – perfectly designed to
brain the unwary. There was nothing on the cold metal
to protect their heads and bodies as *Atropos* pitched and
heaved. There was nothing to hold on to with the right
hand and the waist-high railing on the left seemed more
interested in breaking their ribs than in protecting them.

Immediately inside the door, above the light switch, a
Geiger counter had been clipped to the wall. After he and
LeFever had closed the door behind them, Reynolds made
things worse for himself by carrying this forward and
checking the cargo as he had been ordered. LeFever had
brought his own and he checked the third officer's

readings. They communicated satisfaction with the results in a kind of pantomime, for the sound of the sea on the side of the ship by their head and the weather deck immediately above them was overpowering. Ann shoved her lips to LeFever's ear and yelled, 'Isn't there an automatic system to check this?'

'Sure... Captain... Reynolds... Checking the system...' was all she got by way of reply.

At the far end of the gallery was a solid steel wall stretching from side to side and deck to keel, with a heavy door in it leading through to the next hold.

The two men wrestled with this door, which seemed, if anything, more securely fastened than the first. A particularly foul sea threw Ann up onto LeFever's back, as though she were playing leapfrog with him. Only the unforgiving steel of the conduit beneath the roof stopped her going right over him – at the cost of a dizzying headache.

And all for nothing, it seemed. Or nearly so. The only thing they found amiss was a section of that lethal, sharp-edged conduit partially adrift. It was a pathetically little thing to have come all this way to fix, which was why the two men almost fought each other for the privilege of doing it, Ann supposed.

From hold to hold they went, along the length of the ship. And not a container had shifted. The needles of the counters remained safely in the green. The captain's petty punishment gained its point from being pointless. But then, back in the first hold, in the very spot where Ann and LeFever had had their brief conversation, they stopped again and this time there was something to look at, some point to their being here after all. From beneath the edge of the hatch above their heads a waterfall of water was cascading into the hold. It hadn't been there when they came through this way the first time.

So far, Ann had been subconsciously impressed by the dryness of the holds; by the reassuringly waterproof nature of the good ship *Atropos*. She looked at the leaking water with something akin to horror, mesmerised by the unsteady fall of it swinging left and right according to the pitch and heave. She was fascinated by the apparent silence of its impact exploding balletically into misty rebound against the drenched tops of the containers and vanishing like quicksilver into the cracks between them. Then she shook herself free of the hypnotic power of it and turned to look at LeFever. His normally open countenance was scored with frown lines. Reynolds looked furious and his lips were moving. Ann was very glad indeed that she could not hear what he was saying.

She heard soon enough as they climbed out into the relative quiet of the engineering areas, however.

'. . . out onto the fucking deck and batten it down!' he was yelling at LeFever.

'Why you? Report it to the captain. He'll send a work crew.'

'The hell he will. He'll send me. Only by that time it'll have opened up some more and it'll be *really* fucking dangerous.'

'Take an engineer.'

'I wouldn't trust Lethbridge's lot to piss in a pot.'

'You can't go alone.'

'It's the nearest hatch cover. I rigged good safety lines. I'm a first-class fucking deck officer and that is no damn shit.'

Ann felt like screaming at him, 'Can't you even be brave without all this foul-mouthing?'

'Okay,' said LeFever, 'I'll come and watch your back.'

'In and out. Quick.'

'Quick,' said LeFever emphatically and Ann found she was suddenly feeling sick.

They seemed to have forgotten all about her. She followed doggedly as they fought their way back up towards the weather deck. The three of them paused inside the huge bulkhead door at the starboard end of the long, lateral, A deck corridor. Inside it, there was a pile of safety harnesses and the two men caught them up and buckled them on as they waited for a lull in the wind long enough to let them swing the heavy portal open. Numbly, Ann found herself mimicking their action, as though she, who had followed this far, was also going out onto the deck. LeFever saw what she was doing and caught Reynold's gaze. All at once Ann found the third officer's face thrust into her own. His dark, Latin eyes were almost black. 'When we open the door, clip on to the safety line, but stay inside,' he bellowed at her.

'I—'

He shook his head. He didn't have time for this. 'If we don't come back in in three minutes, you go tell the captain. It's important. *Vital*. We're relying on you, Gottit?'

'Yes!' she screamed. And her scream was suddenly loud. The wind had died.

The two men threw themselves at the door and it burst open to slam back and catch on a hook against the outer wall of the bridgehouse. They paused in the doorway for an instant, hands busy, then they were gone.

Ann stepped unsteadily forward and fastened the quick-release of her harness where the others had snapped theirs on, then she wedged herself in the doorway as best she could with spread legs and crucified arms. She was not a moment too soon, for the icy fury of the wind returned and all but tore her free. The freezing cold of it blinded her with tears but she would hardly have had leisure to look around during those first few moments in any case. It took all of her concentration and will simply to stand up in the face of it. Then it moderated for a moment and she could blink the hot tears away to roll freezing down her cheeks and look out into the dark heart of it. There was just enough light to see the flat coal-faced clouds seemingly as near her head as the deck had been on the walkway. The waves loomed, every bit as dark as the clouds, like a range of obsidian mountains rushing in towards her. *Atropos* reared back, almost as though her bows would pierce the scurrying whirl of the clouds, and white water boiled past the doorway to cascade in over Ann's feet, shockingly cold. Then the long ship threw herself forward, seeming to twist her right shoulder down into the massive seas.

A towering wave washed past, much taller than the tall bridgehouse on whose ground floor she was standing. It was so close she could see into the glassy heart of it. The angle of the ship as the wave rolled by brought the quivering curve of water almost to the rail a metre or two in front of her. She even heard the hissing whisper it made against the side of the ship and the distant thunder of its crest against the bridge wing five storeys above her head.

And, that close, *that close*, she found herself looking into a face. She stood, crucified in the door, looking out across little more than a metre of quiet air at a cliff of water sliding past her, seemingly as solid as an iceberg. And standing in the wave, exactly level with her, staring out through it, as clear as a reflection in a looking glass, stood a man. Suspended, frozen, like a fly in amber.

It was Reynolds.

She never knew whether he saw her when their eyes met. Or if he was capable of understanding what he saw. He seemed to know her when he saw her looking at him, but that must have been a trick of that frozen stare. He must have been dead already, she thought; please God let him be dead already.

She screamed with all the strength in her lungs. Then he was gone.

LeFever came in through the door in an avalanche of foam with so much power that their safety lines snapped off. Writhing together like lovers *in flagrante*, they were washed along the corridor floor, choking and drowning, in a deep river of salt water. The stern of the ship swung round viciously and the whole hull seemed to plunge backwards as though *Atropos* had reversed off a cliff.

The movement threw Ann and LeFever down the stairwell into the engineering section where the water, at least, washed away.

But the movement was short and came to an abrupt cataclysmic halt. The stern of the ship slammed into something solid with almost unimaginable force. The two bruised bodies found themselves hurled across the corridor towards the engine room. The sound of the engines – and it had been there, in among the cacophony of the storm – stopped. The ship hesitated in her forward passage and slid back again. The second impact made the first one seem like nothing at all.

Ann was in deep shock. She was badly bruised and mildly concussed. She was almost insensible, but the words that the young third engineer yelled as he ran past them to alert the crew cut through the icy fog in her head. His face was almost as white as Reynolds's face had been in the heart of the wave. His eyes had the same glassy stare of shock. And his words were babbling out of him, almost beyond his control, nearly drowned by the terrible noise going on around them. But what he said brought her out of her shock more quickly than anything else could have done.

'The propeller's gone!' he screamed. 'We've hit hard ice and the propeller's gone!'

CHAPTER EIGHT

Day Six

Monday, 24 May 11:00

The solicitors' chambers were on the second floor of Viscount Astor's tiny Gothic gem of a building at No. 2, Temple Place, and Brian Chambers' office occupied a corner. One window looked south over the Embankment and across the Thames. Another looked eastwards over a tiny car park full of Jaguars, Porsches and Mercedes Benzes toward the red-brick façade of Queen Elizabeth Buildings in the Middle Temple, where the maritime sets of barristers worked. Richard stood moodily at the second window looking towards the Temple as though if he looked hard enough he could see into Magdalena DaSilva's office. Brian's phone jangled. In this as in so much, Brian was militantly old-fashioned. Until Maggie made the point at dinner, Richard had never noticed. Brian lifted the black Bakelite handset and listened for a second or two before hanging up.

'We're off,' he said crisply and stood up. His military bearing, emphasised by a clipped salt and pepper moustache and a short back and sides haircut, gave added inches to his slim, bantam-weight frame. Even when he came very close to Richard, he was not dwarfed by the size of his client, and would not have cared a damn if he had been.

Coming out onto the street, they turned left and went through the gate and across the car park. The door into Queen Elizabeth Buildings gave on to a narrow, slightly dingy corridor with stairs rising on their left and a wall on the right covered with lists of names. These were the names of the barristers practising in each set of chambers in the building.

'Look at that,' said Brian in disgust as they passed. His finger traced a line of fresh paint where a name had been painted out. 'They used to end these lists with the names of the judges associated with each practice. They've had to paint them all out. Security. Bloody terrorists everywhere.'

For once, Richard was not concerned about terrorists. Magdalena DaSilva had only agreed to take the case if she could apply for an adjournment. Even if she worked every waking hour, she felt that she would not do justice to such a potentially complicated action in the time she had left to prepare for it – particularly as Sir Harcourt's agreed submissions had already tied her hands to such a great extent. They were going up to the law courts to apply for that adjournment now.

As they climbed the dark stairs towards the second floor, Richard actually found he had his fingers crossed. How he wished he had Robin here. She would tell him not to worry and he would listen to her. He had forgotten how heavy it could all seem, running Heritage Mariner without her indomitable optimism to rely on. But that optimism had been in short supply lately. God, he hoped she was all right. He had missed her 8:00 broadcast – it was due in at this very moment, as a matter of fact, for London time was three hours ahead. She had been tired and some-how guarded the last time they talked. He knew she felt guilty for enjoying her holiday from the twins but at the same time she said she felt out of touch where she was. Harcourt's death had worried her; she knew how much it would have affected her father.

They arrived at Maggie's chambers. They reported to the clerk's office and were shown through at once. The atmosphere of the place was one of ancient and hallowed halls, but the building was in fact quite new, having been built since the Second World War and dedicated to Queen Elizabeth the Queen Mother. And the same atmosphere pervaded Maggie's office, with its wall of leather-bound volumes and its long, dark refectory table piled with briefs, each substantial pile of paper bound with a simple pink ribbon – the famous red tape. Richard looked at it almost superstitiously. He hoped they wouldn't get bound up in any red tape today. But then Brian gestured towards one of the bound bundles. Richard could see the names on the plain white typed cover sheet: *CZP vs Heritage Mariner*. His pious hope had come too late. There they all were, bound up in red tape after all; and no way out, as Maggie had said, except time and money. Neither of which he had.

Maggie entered carrying a substantial robing bag. In court she wore the special black frogged jacket and waist-coat with the white legal collar and stock of a woman barrister, and the bag contained the costume. The only real concessions to her dashing sartorial reputation were the tightness of her tailored court-length skirt and the fact that her shoes had something of a heel. Her junior fol-lowed, also lugging wig and gown. Richard had met the junior counsel before, a quiet, intelligent young woman of Indian extraction called Lata Patel, and he nodded and

gave her a tight smile. There was no hanging around with
Maggie. As soon as she entered the room she was in
action; her meter was running and she wanted to give
value for money. 'Right,' she said, rapping out her words
with all the military curtness which Brian Chambers used.
'The judge has squeezed us in. We'll be putting our case
for an adjournment to him in his court – that's court
thirteen – while he's got a few minutes between two other
cases on his calendar. He's busy and we'll have to be
brief. If we manage to convince him, then he'll move us
to September or October: new term, new court. But if we
fail to convince him, we'll be back in court thirteen next
week. Let's go. We don't want to keep him waiting.'

The four of them were off at once, Maggie in the lead,
sweeping past the clerk's office and leaving Lata Patel to
pop her head round the door and make sure the clerks
knew what was going on. With the men in tow, Maggie
thundered down the stairs and strode out onto the pavement overlooked by Brian's office, just behind the car
park. It was a bright, warm afternoon with more than a
promise of summer in it, but Richard noticed nothing of
the weather. He strove to keep pace with his impulsive
barrister and Brian almost danced at her far side. 'I shall
be pleading Sir Harcourt's death, of course, and trying
to convince His Lordship that it would be unacceptably to
your detriment if he proceeds according to his calendar.
Whether he listens or not could depend upon almost anything. Whether I make a good case. Whether he is in a
position to listen to it. Whether CZP's silk makes a good
case for proceeding – he will, I'm sure; Clive Standing is
an excellent man – and whether His Lordship is inclined
to listen to that. Pleas like this have been known to be
settled on the fact that the judge has a particularly good

spot on a salmon river in Scotland for a particular week in October. That sort of thing doesn't happen too much nowadays, but it can all still turn on luck, if the balance of arguments is really fine.'

They bounded up the steps into Middle Temple Gardens. 'This is where the two sides in the Wars of the Roses chose their roses,' Maggie announced suddenly. 'Lords Suffolk and Somerset chose the red rose. Warwick and York chose the white. And so the Wars of the Roses began. Right here. Shakespeare says it, so it must be true.'

Richard was silent. I hope we have a less destructive outcome, he thought. The Wars of the Roses lasted nearly twenty years, if his memory served.

Maggie fell silent as they went on up past Fountain Court and Middle Temple Hall into the Elizabethan red brick of the 1500s, not the 1950s. Richard was in no mood to appreciate the architecture or the history with which they were surrounded. He accorded the Round of the Temple, the church erected by the Knights Templar in 1185, only the briefest of glances, then he plunged on after Maggie and Brian into the narrow thoroughfare leading to the Middle Temple gate.

The four of them came out into the bustle of Fleet Street, crossed the busy thoroughfare at once and plunged left into a throng of people. Conversation here was impossible. The noise of traffic – mostly big red buses, black cabs and motorcycle delivery men – was compounded by the bustle of early tourists brought out by the sun.

The pace did not slacken and the silence between them remained unbroken until the cathedral silence of the main chamber of the Royal Courts of Justice claimed them. They went through the security gate in single file. Lata completed some hurried business with an official and the two women disappeared to the robing room while Richard and Brian Chambers were off again up the stairs to the courtrooms on the upper levels. Richard had never been here before – like many who lived in London, he did little sightseeing in his own city, and he had never been forced to face litigation before. Apart from an incongruous impression that he was, in fact, in Westminster Abbey, the building made little impression on him that day and he was content to study the patterns on the black and white flags of the floor. And, all too soon for his taste, the ornate wooden door, with *Court Thirteen* written in copperplate handwriting on a white board on the wall beside it, opened.

The courtroom made little more impression on him than the building itself had. He was an observant man and an active one, used to using his eyes, used to moments of crisis. But being so helpless in this place, and relying on someone else under such circumstances, his mind concentrated upon the matter in hand rather than the location. It was a small room with a bank of seats stepping up like those in a cinema balcony or theatre. It reminded him of the lecture theatres of his university days, except that there was an undeniable air of pomp and power here. Maggie plunged down to the front bench. Lata went in behind her and Brian went behind Lata. Richard sat further up the slope of seats, towards the back. No sooner had he sat down than the opposition bustled in. Maggie looked across the courtroom and nodded coldly at CZP's barrister, who deigned to grace her with the very slightest, curtest of responses. His name was Clive Standing, Richard recalled.

The clerk of the court glanced around and went up a set of steps to vanish through a door behind the judge's bench. In an instant she was back, pausing at the end of the long wooden dais to intone, 'Please be upstanding in court . . .' and the judge swept in.

In the centre of the bench he turned to face them, then, fastidiously arranging his scarlet robes about himself, he bowed to the court and sat. They all bowed and sat in a courteous mirror-image. The judge was a thin, grey-faced man, whose pallor was accentuated by his grey wig and the grey eyebrows which sat beneath it. And, indeed, by the thin gold frames of the half-glasses he settled on his nose, an action which served to frame his face with the deep, pale grey cuffs of his robe.

'Now,' he said, drawing the word out and giving himself an air of deep deliberation, 'we have an application for adjournment of this case, which is on my diary to begin one week today.'

He spoke, apparently, to nobody at all, but Maggie was on her feet immediately. 'That is so, my lord. As I am sure Your Lordship is aware, this case has been in the hands of my learned friend Sir Harcourt Gibbons for the nine months since the suit was first brought.' She paused for an instant. 'I am also sure that you are aware of the tragic accident which befell Sir Harcourt last Friday at Brampton golf course in Cumbria.' Again she paused, and this time the judge filled the brief silence with his thin, deliberate voice.

'And your contention, Ms DaSilva, is that you would not be able to pick up where Sir Harcourt, ah, left off, so to speak, at such short notice.'

'Precisely so, my lord.'

'And when would you have gathered together all the pieces to your own satisfaction, do you think?'

'A further six weeks might—'

The judge was gently shaking his head and actually clucking his tongue.

'My lord?' she asked when he had stopped.

'Six weeks is a long time, Ms DaSilva. I am sure that you are as well aware as I am myself just how busy the courts will be in June. My calendar will be particularly full then, I know. Effectively, you are asking for a post-ponement until next term, are you not? Realistically, until the middle of October, perhaps even until November. Thus, Ms DaSilva, does your six weeks become six months. As I'm sure you have calculated.' He shook his head again, then looked to his left. 'Mr Standing, what do you think of this idea?'

CZP's barrister rose slowly, portentously, to his feet. 'I believe it to be an utterly unwarranted delay, my lord. Particularly as so much work has been done in the prelimi-nary hearings before Your Lordship, and so little work is actually left to do. While I regret the tragic circumstances which have transferred this brief into my learned friend's most capable hands, I cannot but deplore this brazen attempt to make the suit collapse through unwarranted delay. May I remind Your Lordship that it has been two years already since the loss of the ship which is the cause of this action. And, indeed, I understand that there may be other actions, in other courts, which hinge upon the deliberations of this court. I ask, therefore, that there be no delay.'

Richard sat up at that, for these words were unexpected, and confirmed his darkest fears. There was the slightest hiss upon the air and he did not know whether he or one of his legal team had caught their breath with surprise.

Standing rolled smoothly on. 'As you are all too well aware, my lord, what we have here is a very simple situ-ation. My client, the firm CZP, is a shipping company in a small way of business in a shrinking market. I am sure I need not explain to Your Lordship the sad facts underpinning the circumstances of commercial shipping nowadays. This small firm, on the verge of bankruptcy, has a suit against one of the largest independent shipping companies in Europe over the matter of a hull. One small, battered, fairly elderly ship. Heritage Mariner could easily afford half a dozen such ships and in any case carries full insurance to indemnify such payments should the case against them be found. And yet, instead of coming to court so that the case may be heard and such payment awarded or negotiated, they linger and delay, knowing that it is only a matter of time – a very short time – before my client goes bankrupt and his threatened suit collapses.'

'You are saying, in short, that Heritage Mariner are callously using the death of Sir Harcourt as a tactic to delay the hearing of this case until such time as your client is bankrupt and no longer a threat?'

'Exactly so, my lord.'

'Ms DaSilva?'

'This is, of course, a complete fabrication, my lord. My learned friend has interpreted the circumstances with extreme partiality. And if there is callousness being used in this courtroom, it is not I who am using it. The fact is, my lord, the case is complex. I would no more be able to do it justice in seven days than seventy-two hours. To prepare this defence adequately under the circumstances, I must beg the court for more time.'

'Mr Standing, you see the matter as being much simpler than does Ms DaSilva. Does this view stretch to an esti-mate of how much time it will take to hear the case?'

'My lord, as you are aware from the ground we have already covered, the final section of my case will rest on the submissions of a very few witnesses. As it will be heard in front of yourself, without the time-consuming necessities of selecting a jury and directing them as to law, I would be surprised if the whole process took more than a day or two of your time.'

'Ms DaSilva?'

'I am not sure that I can concur, my lord. My reading of the relevant documents so far has convinced me that the case as it stands needs more support. I would in all probability be asking for leave to present a broad spectrum of defence witnesses, whose testimony would be both expert and eyewitness.'

'I see,' said the judge. 'So, Ms DaSilva, you have had the opportunity to go through the relevant papers.'

'Briefly, my lord, in preparation for this submission.'

'Quite, but sufficiently to see that Sir Harcourt's notion of a defence was actually inadequate—'

'My lord—'

'So that you actually require the extra time to undo all the work which we have already done in chambers and start a completely new defence. To summon extra witnesses, to gather more testimony, and to turn this simple little matter into a protracted bear garden for your friends in the gutter press.'

'My lord! I must protest!'

'Well, Ms DaSilva, I will not allow it. Sir Harcourt was one of the oldest and most respected gentlemen at the bar. His submissions to me have been exemplary. I am sure his original defence will prove more than adequate to acquaint the court with matters from your client's point of view without all the extra window-dressing you propose. And I am equally certain that a barrister of your reputation can take over another case in extremely short order. You mentioned seventy-two hours, madam, and I shall take you up on that. I have a cancellation later this week and an unexpected pressing public engagement next week. If Mr Standing is ready to go at short notice . . . Yes? Good. Then I will see you here in three days' time. Thursday morning. Ten o'clock.' He got up, bowed, and was gone before even Maggie, the quickest silver tongue at the bar, could think of anything to say.

They all sat, stunned, in Maggie's office.

'Can he do that?' asked Richard, his voice husky with shock and suppressed fury.

'He's done it,' answered Maggie. 'Brian, how many witnesses were you and Sir Harcourt talking about?'

'Three. Richard here, John Higgins who was the captain. We have a written submission from Ann Cable, the writer, who we thought probably couldn't guarantee to be here, and finally a young chap who was the third officer on *Napoli* when she went down. Fellow called Marco Farnese. Saw everything.'

'I've seen Ann Cable's submission. I'm surprised Standing has agreed it. He's sure to have some way of discrediting it in court. Where is Captain Higgins?'

'On his yacht in Peel on the Isle of Man.'

'Waiting for our call.'

'Precisely so.'

'And this other man, Farnese?'

'On the beach in Piombino, where he lives.'

'Also waiting.'

'He's out of work,' supplied Richard. 'We'll give him a holiday in London. Everything first class. He's looking forward to it.'

'So, Brian, did you expect to be doing anything before going to court which we couldn't in fact get done within the next seventy-two hours?'

'Well, no, I don't suppose so.'

'There you are then. We can be ready by Thursday morning. All he's asking us to do is to work a little harder.'

'To protect his public engagement,' nodded Brian glumly.

'And to save poor little CZP from going to the wall,' added Richard. 'And to facilitate these other lawsuits. I'm really beginning to feel as though I've been set up.'

Just as he said this, the clerk from the front office came in holding a fax. 'I thought you'd want to see this at once,' he said, and handed it to Maggie.

They all sat in silence while she read it, a frown gathering between her perfectly arched brows. At last she let the flimsy fall from between her long, dark, elegant fingers. They watched it float downwards like an autumn leaf and settle on the table.

'Bad news?' asked Richard.

'That's pat. Just what we were discussing. No need to wonder about further suits in New York.'

Richard raised his eyebrows, fearing the worst. And she handed it to him.

'I had a friend at the American bar sniff around. Didn't need to sniff far at all. Apparently Disposoco already have their feelers out. The law is really expensive on the far side of the pond, so they're flying a kite here, where it's cheap. Pretty smart. Word is that if you lose this case, they'll have every shyster in the Big Apple pouring lawsuits on your head in a matter of days. They've already got half a dozen ambulance chasers ready to shout "No play, no pay". They're getting ready to hang you out to dry, Richard, and they must really think they're on to a winner! I'd stiffen up the sinews if I were you. If we go down on Thursday, than it looks as though you're dead and buried.'

CHAPTER NINE

Day Six

Monday, 24 May 12:00

'Prepare to batten down. We are running into foul weather. We will come into thick fog first, then storm-force winds. Prepare to batten down.'

The captain's voice, distorted by the amplification, echoed over the tannoy to almost every corner on *Clotho* as she turned onto the heading which would take her to her stricken sister in the shortest possible time. To almost every corner. But not quite all.

Clotho's bow, like that of her sister, was of a slightly unusual design. The rest of her hull was based on the standard container design with its cruiser stern, all-aft bridgehouse and its long weather deck, distinguished only by the tall travelling gantry perfectly amidships. Instead of the raked and bulbous bow which would normally have completed the design, however, the sister ships both had Maier-form bows which cut back sharply below the water-line. Above and below the waterline, the bows had been massively strengthened to work in ice and they were broader than usual, too. At the base of the bow, where it curved back onto the keel, there was a manoeuvring propeller or fore screw, fitted aquadynamically into the hull so as not to detract from the vessel's overall performance. The bow was designed to smash through thin ice and to ride over thick ice. In the hull, above the slope of the bow, was the forward water ballast tank. This was unusually large because the designers of the hull had calculated that the weight of the water in it would crush all but the thickest ice once the bow had ridden up over it. *Clotho* was not really an icebreaker, however. She was not designed to clear long channels through thick ice. Her beam was not particularly wide and although there had been some changes to her ballast tank system, she did not have the side tanks which allow a real icebreaker to rock itself out of trouble. The bow was designed to smash in and out of ice-bound harbours. It was not really made to break heavy sea ice at all.

So big was the forward water ballast tank that it was only three-quarters full even now, when *Clotho* was running in ballast anyway. The tank was normally sealed, but there were inspection hatches, accessible from the deck, which led down into it, and, if there was a design fault at all in the big vessel, it was that these hatches could be opened without any warning lights flashing on the bridge. One of them was open now, though this fact would only have been apparent on close inspection. It was the hatch exactly at the forepeak, precisely between the pair of machines comprising the split windlass there, and very near the most forward point of the deck. The hatch led down to a long iron-runged ladder which plunged into the bowels of the ship, at first vertically, then at an angle following the rake of the slightly rounded cutwater. It was, in fact, an iron-sided tube reaching down the forward wall of the chain locker until it reached a tiny room just above the waterline. In the floor of the tiny, icy, iron-smelling room was a second hatch. This hatch opened directly into the forepeak's water ballast tank itself. Below it, the ladder continued to follow the slope of the bow down until it was covered by the restless, filthy surface of the ballast.

The hatch in that tiny room stood open now and on the studded metal of the floor there rested a small but powerful waterproof lamp. The lamp should have been stowed safely in the lockers under the whalebacked after section of the forward port lifeboat. Now it cast its steady light downwards onto the head and shoulders of the stowaway as she stood with her feet just clear of the restless water, carefully moulding Semtex against the forward plates.

She had been careful to remove the things she wanted from one lifeboat. This had required two midnight expeditions to the stern of the ship so far. If nothing happened within the next few hours, she would have to do something more obvious so that at least one officer would be certain there was someone unaccounted for aboard. She didn't actually want to give herself up: that would be too obvious. It might prompt a detailed search of the vessel, which she wanted to avoid if possible, though it was inconceivable that anyone would think of looking down here in the least accessible place aboard that she had been able to find. Once the Semtex was placed and the detonators primed, her simple plan required that she be found and taken to the captain before *Clotho* and *Atropos* met near Kap Farvel. She proposed to pose as some brainless, penniless student trying to hitch an illegal lift to the United States. She would have no trouble in angering everyone, especially the captain, so much so that, when the two ships passed one another, she would be transferred onto *Atropos* and sent ignominiously back to England. Once on *Atropos*, she would meet the man she had written that letter to last week and they would have no trouble in setting the second bomb using the Semtex he would already have smuggled aboard in Sept Isles. By the time the sister ships exploded in the nuclear waste shipping facilities on either side of the Atlantic next week, she and her lover would be long gone.

As she worked, she hummed the old French air called 'Frère Jacques'. She had just reached the stage where the timing mechanism was being backed up by a makeshift impact detonator made of safety flares – the only really telltale theft of all the ones she had made. But then the flares were so rarely required it would be a miracle if anyone noticed they were gone before she was gone herself. She was concentrating so fiercely that she noticed nothing of the ship's changing movement through the water nor the new sound the waves were making as they burst against the far side of the steel in front of her face. As she was not a sailor, nor an expert in the design of ships or the behaviour of metal, she also failed to notice that the solid curve of alloy was behaving in a way it should not have been behaving at all.

Robin stood at the front of the bridge, looking through the angled clearview at the fast approaching wall of fog, grey eyes narrowed fiercely as though she could see into it if she looked hard enough. Sam Larkman had relinquished the wheel to Errol and the massive shoulder of his boiler suit was the only thing between Robin and the terrifyingly abrupt change in sailing conditions.

'Steady,' she growled at him. 'Watch for a strong westerly drift as soon as we get in. Sing out if you feel it's pulling her off course.'

The engine room intercom buzzed. 'Coming to full ahead now, Captain,' said Andrew McTavish's quiet Scottish voice. Behind him the whine of the two gas turbines running in tandem could be heard – compact, specially adapted Rolls-Royce RB211 aeroengines, each delivering forty thousand pounds of thrust to the single, massive, variable pitch screw. Charging into the fog wall at 30 knots in any other vessel would have been close to suicide, but *Clotho*'s high-tech equipment promised clear seas up to five miles ahead and so versatile was the propulsion system that *Clotho* could come to full ahead or to a dead stop on less than a mile. And any slight risk was more than offset by the overriding necessity of getting to *Atropos* at the earliest possible moment.

There would be no help nearer in the Labrador Sea; the storm had sent almost all shipping scurrying for port and according to reports from station after station, the working of the currents up and down the coasts was closing everything in with drift ice. Except for the tip of Greenland. Kap Farvel itself, it seemed, was unseasonably clear. In the clear waters they were just leaving, there was a great deal more shipping, but they were the nearest vessel and, in any case, the best adapted to the conditions.

Robin's only thought of hesitation arose from the horrifying possibility of both Heritage Mariner ships being lost on their maiden voyage. That would be a disaster to put even *Titanic* in the shade. But, typically, the hesitation had lasted for mere microseconds and not even Niccolo, who had been watching her like a hawk since the distress call came in, had noticed anything at all.

'We're going in,' she said, as the forepeak disappeared. 'Log that, please, Mr Sullivan. Entered the fog wall at twelve hundred hours local time exactly.'

Sullivan, as watchkeeper, crossed obediently to the log

book. Because he was busy following her orders, Robin herself crossed to the console on Errol's left, hesitated for an instant, and sounded the siren as the opaqueness hit the clearview and *Clotho* was struck blind.

'Mr Niccolo,' she said as soon as the first peal of banshee wailing died, 'we have perhaps an hour of this weather before we come out into the storm. Would you please take out a team and check the weather deck. I don't want to have to worry about any of our fixtures or fittings. We'll probably be offering a tow. When you're happy we will be able to handle the weather, make sure the cable is free and easily available. Make sure the windlasses and the capstans are working. The storm is supposed to be moderating but it'll still be rough when we get to *Atropos* in ten or so hours' time and I don't want to wait until then to discover the deck auxiliaries aren't up to scratch. Mr Curtis, go with the first officer and watch him. You'll learn a lot. If you can stay aboard.'

'She's pulling west hard, Captain,' growled Errol.

'Mr Biggs, do we have an estimate on the current?'

Biggs, looking for all the world as though he was working at NASA control, called up the information on one of the screens in front of him. 'Strong westerly drift, Captain, moving at a mean of five knots. I say again, five knots. Still no ice heavy enough to show up on the radar. Clear for five miles ahead.'

Robin crossed to Errol's shoulder and looked at the digital compass. The heading clicked another degree to the west. The massive power of the current was forcing her round off course already. Robin turned, her mouth open, but Biggs was already checking their proposed course against the reading from the satnav. The satnav system gave a constant read-out broadcast from a series of satellites in low orbit overhead, placing *Clotho* to within a few yards of the surface of the earth. These readings could be married up with Robin's directions as to speed and heading, to ensure that the ship stayed on course in spite of the sudden change in the movement of the water beneath her racing hull.

Robin walked past the third officer to the door into the radio room. There she paused and looked back. 'Make sure everyone has caught up on their breakfast,' she ordered Sullivan. 'I don't want anyone going into this hungry.'

Sullivan grinned and nodded, then he crossed to the bridge telephone to pass the orders down. Not many captains would have thought of that, he mused happily.

'Tell *Atropos* we're on our way,' Robin ordered Bill Christian. 'Then get me Heritage House. I'd better tell one of my men what I'm up to.'

Young Jamie Curtis had never realised that the air could be quite so thick. His hand held out arm's length in front of his face came and went like a ghost. Niccolo had picked Sam Larkman and Joe Edwards to assist them, but Jamie could only guess at their whereabouts. Anyone out of reach was out of sight. But, as though to make up for the lack of vision, sound was unnaturally amplified. While testing the McGregor hatch on number one hold, furthest forward, nearest the forecastle, he had carried on a conversation with the invisible Niccolo, believing the first mate to be standing at his shoulder, only to discover that they had been many yards apart. It was strange to be out here where the breeze seemed solid. It only existed because *Clotho* was moving so quickly through the fog-bound dead calm. And whereas a real wind actually moving through a fog would thin it, this phantom wind only seemed to intensify it. It was as though the suspended condensation in the air was piled up ahead of *Clotho* as the ship ran through it, heaving and thickening, like waves.

When they had checked that nothing was likely to tear free or blow loose on the expanse of the main weather deck, they went back behind the bridgehouse to check the deck auxiliaries. There were two double capstans, one pair on each side of the square stern. The capstans were not solid, but designed so that the upright cable lifters could be rotated by big motors on the deck below. The machines had been the only ones to give any trouble so far in the voyage and Niccolo wanted to check them over first, especially as, all things being equal, they would be doing most of the work. True to form, the port-side winch fired and snarled. Nico went down on his knees beside it, as though worshipping the thing, and made a slow panto-mime of banging his head against it. 'Jamie,' he said quietly, but his voice carried to the anxious youngster hovering over him – it was less than six hours since he had saved the cadet's life, after all – 'Jamie, go and ask Chief McTavish if I can have an engineer up here. A competent engineer; no, a consultant among engineers, not one of his mad axemen. *Comprende?*'

'Yes, Nico.'

'*Bene*. You tell this engineer where to come. Then I want you to go and fire up the split windlass. One motor at a time. Take Sam and Joe here to help. It's been running like a Maserati so it shouldn't give any trouble. Just run them. Don't engage the cable lifters on them or you'll pull the anchors in through the sides. If I have to use them I'll disengage the anchor chain. Run the independent mooring drums and the warp ends, though. Can you do all that?'

'Yes, Nico.'

'*Bene*. Off you go, then.'

The cadet and the two GP seamen set off together. Leaving the two men in the A deck corridor with orders to await him at the port side bulkhead door, Jamie ran on down to the engine room. He was unwise enough to relay Nico's message verbatim to the chief and was very lucky indeed that the Scot had a lively sense of humour. An engineer was despatched to the poop, with a fire axe, to help the first officer. Jamie went back up to his rendezvous, then the three of them went out through the A deck door onto the weather deck and began to walk forward into the murk.

The forecastle head was a little wider than usual, but Jamie had been on so few ships so far that he didn't really notice. As he had been walking down the port side, he led the little deck crew up the port side steps onto the raised level of the forecastle head itself. The tall cowls of the forward ventilators came and went in the mist beside him like spectral hooded monks waiting to steal a soul or two. The fog horn bellowed out and its terrible, lonely sound completed the doomladen atmosphere.

A sudden chill puff of air slapped Jamie on the cheek hard enough to make him jump. He realised that the silence out here, scarcely disturbed by the rumble of the bow wave at her teeth, was strangely underpinned by a distant raving, as though in the far distance ahead a great battle was going on. Had he been close enough to see Sam and Joe more clearly, he would have remarked the long, foreboding stare that passed between them at the sound.

The split windlass consisted of two motors which worked independently to raise or lower each anchor. They were heavy, powerful machines, each in three sections. No doubt Nico's plan had been for each of the experienced seamen to run one machine while the cadet oversaw the activity, and learned from it. But Jamie had other ideas. He sent Sam and Joe to the starboard windlass and took over the port one himself. The motor started with no trouble. He checked the cable lifter without pulling the port anchor aboard. He ran the mooring drum successfully and touched the spinning valley of the end warp with one wet finger to be sure that it was rotating as required. Then, pleased with what he had achieved in the way of supported self-study, he closed it down and crossed to the port rail away from the sound of the port windlass engine, the better to listen to that distant, disturbing cacophony of sound.

Another unexpected gust of wind spat a little rain in his face and jerked the veils of fog to one side. As this happened, something made him turn just in time to see a figure running back down the deck, blundering in apparent confusion. 'Sam?' he called. The figure hesitated and began to turn. A feeling of unreality suddenly gripped him. No way was that a GP seaman in wet-weather gear. 'Joe?' The fog was still thick enough to be deceptive, but surely that figure was a girl. He took a step towards her. She turned towards him and her right arm moved, lifting something from her waist, pulling something out of her belt. There was the quietest, most sinister, hissing sound. Just for a second, he was riven with terror.

'Jamie?' bellowed Sam Larkman. 'What is it, lad?'

The fog closed down again and the figure was gone, with the slightest whisper of sound.

'Jamie,' called Joe Edwards' voice and immediately his big square body loomed up behind it.

'Joe, did you see a . . .'

'A what?'

'A . . . Nothing.' Already Jamie was wondering whether what he had seen had been a figment of his imagination. He certainly wasn't going to run the risk of looking silly in front of these men. 'Nothing,' he concluded lamely.

'Yup. That's what I seen, nothing.'

Thank God he hadn't asked, he thought. He changed the subject. 'Your windlass running all right?'

'Fine.'

'Fine,' agreed Sam, heaving into view beside his big friend. 'And just as well. Let's get in before that wind out there gets any closer.'

And Jamie realised that that was what the distant sound had been. The wind, far ahead. And it was getting closer all the time.

'We'll be in it in about ten minutes, I guess,' said Robin to Richard over the static-laden radio link. She put down her cup of coffee then picked it up again at once; the movement of the ship was getting lively. 'I've never come across weather quite like it so it's difficult to be sure. If the calculations Nico and I have made are correct, we'll be coming into a strong crosswind along our starboard side which will tuck in under our stern after an hour or two and push us on up towards *Atropos* quite quickly. I'll be cutting speed as soon as we get in until I have a better idea of the conditions, but with a tail wind I'm still expecting to be up with them within twelve hours. Captain Black says the wind has swung them round and they have the seas to their back. They haven't any steerageway, and it's not too comfortable, but they've slung a sea anchor over the stern and that's holding them steady. There's ice around – it was ice that smashed their screw – but they're not in immediate danger. And they don't seem to be icing up either, thank God. They can hang on till I get to them all right. I'll report back then, and before if there's anything I think you need to know.'

'Good luck,' he said distantly. 'Nothing more to say.'

'I've got a lot to do, then. Over and out.'

Of course both statements had been understatement. There was an enormous amount to say. But this was not the time. And she had an unimaginable amount to do, or to ensure was done, from the correct disposition of the glass in the bar and galley to the rebalancing of the ballast for foul-weather running and the placing of the moveable gantry nearer the bridgehouse or the forepeak, depending on how *Clotho* rode in a blow. But most of it would have been taken care of by the steady team of cooks and stewards, seamen, officers and engineers. The rest she would have to make up as she went along.

But it did occur to her most poignantly in the instant after Richard broke contact that she hadn't sent her love to him, the twins or to her father. And she hadn't asked how the court case was proceeding. Still, it was too late to worry about any of that now.

The mist wall was snatched away by the black fist of the storm. 'Here we go, gentlemen,' she observed, and closed both her hands round her coffee cup. *Clotho* dipped and rolled off the back of a tall sea into the unremitting grip of the storm.

CHAPTER TEN

Day Seven

Tuesday, 25 May   04:00

The darkness was so solid it seemed to press against her face and the silence was so absolute she could feel it in her ears. Mouth wide, to help her breathe more silently, she felt her way along the corridor wall. She moved so slowly and carefully she could feel her joints creaking. Her knees seemed to grate as she lifted them, one at a time. The friction in her hip joints seemed to make her whole pelvis throb.

At last she felt the edge of a doorway with her fingertips. With languid movements, she began to trace the crack between the frame and the door itself until she discovered the warm round jut of the door handle. With a gasp, she jerked her hand back as though the slick knob had given her an electric shock. Mouth dry, she fought to control her breathing until the thudding of her heart had slowed. Only then did she take a grip on the handle and begin to turn it. The door opened inwards a fraction as soon as the handle was turned. At once there was sound and a glimmer of light. She stood, listening, stretching every cell in the auditory section of her brain, as though by an exercise of will she could hear yet more. There was the slightest of rhythmic creaking and the occasional throaty gasp. The familiar sliding and hissing of a body exercising on the big rowing machine.

She had her back pressed to the solid panel of the door, with the handle at her left hip. She pivoted round this, leaning forward from the waist, feeling the way the long muscles pulled all down her back and up her thighs. She tensed her buttocks to stop the movement and held the door with the firm length of her leg. Her hair swung forward in a veil and she reluctantly released her hold on the hot, slick handle to pull it back behind her ear.

The rowing machine was on the far side of the gym in a shaft of dim light. What could be seen was more a matter of shadows differentiated by slightly lighter surfaces. There was no sense even of roundness, though the muscle tone of thigh, arm, shoulder and breast was accentuated by the lightest oiling of perspiration. It was hardly recognisable as a human body, simply shapes in almost languid motion. But this slowly mobile piece of abstract art made sense enough to her wide eyes, as the sounds had made sense to her straining ears.

He was curling forward into foetal rest, massive hands by the naked splay of his feet, low light gleaming across the sweep of his shoulders, over the corrugations of his ribs, and on the mountain peaks astride the valley of his spine. Under his hips, the black padded seat was motionless at the furthest end of the square metal track, but across that track, resting on the twisted cushion of his vest and training shorts, the woman's crossed ankles concealed any more from Ann's eager sight.

Then he rocked slowly upright, the sculpture of his

back suddenly rippling into motion, and began to slide backwards. And as he did so, so his partner's body was released from the trap between his thighs and chest. As his shoulders slid back and down, so her body slowly rose upright in turn, seeming to float above him, held erect by the strength of her hands, clutched over his, on the handles of the rowing machine. At the full stretch of the machine's design, these handles rested vertically while his arms angled down towards his shoulders, supine now, above the crossed ankles under his heart. And she sat utterly erect, the handles on either side of her short ribs, arms trembling with the effort, head held high above the little exercise towel draped round her neck. This served to clothe her torso, and the rest of her was cloaked in shadow. Light stealing under her arm revealed the bowed corrugations of her ribs just to the palest swelling at the rear of her breast. The ribs ran down to a tall, sharp arch, beyond which her stomach plunged, concave, to the impenetrability of the shadows where their bellies met. Arched delicately astride this secret place rose the elegant curves of her thigh, spreading to the angle of her knee and the falling, fading shadow line of her shin as it plunged back towards her ankles, crossed beneath his trembling chest.

Silent and lissom as a cat, Ann crossed towards the pair on the machine as the man began to rock upwards again, and their faces, which had been masked by darkness, moved back into the light. His eyes were closed in the deepest concentration, and he was frowning with fierce pleasure as he worked, but there was no mistaking Henri LeFever's chiseled profile. The woman's face rolled back into the brightness, blankly expressionless, as though in the deepest sleep and curtained by tendrils of sweat-darkened hair. But, again, there was no mistaking who it was.

Ann's breath was jerked out of her by the impact of realisation. Her whole body seemed to liquefy with shock. It was as though she was looking in a mirror. The woman was Ann herself.

She found herself lying on her tumbled bunk staring up into the darkness, surrounded by the throbbing of the ship's generator and the restless jerking movements of the hull as it tossed helplessly through the power of the storm. But these were lost beneath the thumping of her heart and the jarring gasp of her breathing.

I'm going to have to do something about these dreams, she thought. I don't want the gorgeous Henri LeFever to become too much of an obsession.

But the obsession revealed by the dream extended to more than the infinitely attractive scientist. She was still prowling around the ship whenever she got the chance. And, since the storm had taken such a hold upon all their lives, she had much greater chance for exploration. The crew had proved to be as great a disappointment under these conditions as they had been in fairer weather. They reacted to the loss of propulsive power with almost universal acrimony. The officers blamed the captain who blamed the officers. The deck officers all blamed the engineers who had only just bothered to turn up for duty when the disaster struck. The only person currently free from blame in the incident was Reynolds, and that was because he was dead. He hadn't actually been the only competent seaman aboard. Captain Black at least had had sense enough to put a makeshift sea anchor over the stern so that *Atropos* rode more easily in the slowly abating storm while they waited for her sister ship. But once that had been done, the backbiting and recriminations had redoubled. The crew, led as usual by O'Brien the sexist

New York thug of militantly Irish descent and his sidekick the slimy Symes, wearily vanished from the scene and the officers of both sorts, with nothing much to do except to maintain power, communication and some kind of lookout, sat around in dazed silence. For four hours before retiring to bed – to dream of LeFever – she had prowled around the bridgehouse as though she had been all alone on the ship.

She jerked her left arm up to look at the luminous display on her watch. Either sixteen hours – or twenty-eight – since the propeller went. Something must be happening by now. It would be just like these men to let her sleep through *Clotho*'s arrival. She sat up and switched on the light. Her clothes lay in an untidy heap amid the general mayhem of her cabin. Never a tidy person at the best of times, she saw no reason to make an effort now. Her untidiness sent Nico right up the wall and had been the cause of some truly memorable moments in their stormy relationship. She swung out of bed, her mouth curling into the gentle smile she always wore when thinking about Nico. Then she shrugged herself to her feet and began to climb into her clothes. They were still damp. Her stiff, bruised limbs did not appreciate the extra difficulty that the recalcitrant cloth added to the task of dressing on the pitching, jerking deck.

The first place she went to was the galley. In truth, she doubted that she would really have slept through anything so momentous as *Clotho*'s arrival, and even had there been something of the most pressing urgency to be done, she would have been incapable of doing it without getting some coffee inside her first. When she went to sleep, the galley had been dark. The chef had refused to serve hot food under the storm conditions. It was bright and bustling now – someone had changed his mind for him. He was working grimly beside the massive, tightly clamped urn of boiling water and he needed no second bidding to hand her a huge mug of steaming coffee. As he turned towards her she saw that he had a badly swollen eye. She made no remark, but noted it. Who had changed cookie's mind? It could have been Hogg, desperate for a refill after emptying himself so spectacularly and so often. It could have been any of the crew, though the simple, brutal directness had O'Brien written all over it. It could even have been creepy Captain Black himself. On *Atropos*, one never knew.

The next place after the galley had to be the bridge and she made the perilous ascent without spilling a drop. The bridge seemed surprisingly quiet. There was no one to throw her out of the wheelhouse itself when she went in to look around. Timmins was asleep in the watchkeeper's chair. The door behind him swung restlessly, revealing the hunched but silent form of the radio operator, also apparently asleep. Hogg was sitting slumped by the bank of bright instruments she had last seen him vomiting over. They might as well all have been dead. There was no one else around. There was no steersman as they had no steerageway. There was no one, in fact, between Ann and the angled panorama of the clearview.

Drawn by dull fascination – there was nothing to see, so there was nothing to quicken real interest – she crossed to this and, standing where the helmsman would have stood, looked out. At first the darkness before her seemed to be as impenetrable as the darkness of her dream. The digital chronometer on the wall above the window read 05:04. It would be a long time to dawn, especially as they had been running north since the propeller went, so the

darkness was hardly surprising. But as she looked, learning
to blank out the reflection from the dimly-lit bridge in the
window, she began to discover a little more. There were
lights along the deck before her. Red lights one side,
green lights the other. On *Napoli*, Nico had shown her the
running lights and the riding lights, and all the special
signals which ships were supposed to show. If she looked
carefully enough, she guessed, she should be able to make
out lights somewhere up there which said 'ship running
without power' or some such thing. But the thought about
the lights made her mind begin to dwell on Nico once
again, and memories of her cheerful, laughing Latin lover
drove even the infinitely tempting LeFever from her mind.
Concentrating on these, she brought her hot mug of coffee
to her lips and sipped.

Just as she did so, part of the cloud cover was snatched
away. There was a full moon, impossibly huge, incredibly
low, which seemed to be sitting on the horizon dead ahead.
Its brightness was so dazzling that she flinched away and
then squinted back. It was wonderful to look outside,
beyond the confines of the ship; she felt as though she
had been blind and could now see again. The huge effulgent silver orb called to her and before she realised what
she was doing, she was outside on the bridge wing, to
meet its cheerful beaming countenance face to face. The
instant she was out, she realised her mistake. It was incredibly cold out here. The first breath she took was like
liquid nitrogen in her lungs. Sub-zero temperatures stabbed
through her damp clothes with lethal speed. She found her
feet slipping from under her and her coffee went over the
rail to fall in a graceful arc towards the deck below. She
fell against the railing but had the presence of mind not
to touch it with her bare hands. Her elbow thumped onto

the ice-clad wood of the railing and stuck there so that she had to stand outside for a moment or two longer while she tore the cloth from the freezing wood by main force.

And in those moments, she looked around herself. The moon's bright beams struck across the ocean directly at the ship. The lines of light seemed almost to be coming parallel to the surface of the sea, as though the moon were sitting over the North Pole looking down at the vessel being thrust towards it by the wind. Everything between the restless vessel and the still curve of the planet was heaving, gleaming, white.

From horizon to horizon, port, starboard, dead ahead, everything was white. She looked down along the side of the ship. Beyond the deck, down among the waves, it was black. Rough waves and black water. Yet dead ahead, from one side of the world to the other, it was white.

She ran across to Yasser Timmins and began to shake the little man with all her strength. 'Wake up,' she was yelling. 'You too, Hogg.' Over Hogg's shoulder, the radar screen showed a pale wall from one side of the deep green bowl to the other. A warning light was flashing but the sound was turned off.

She swung back and Timmins was blinking at her like an irritable owl. 'Something dead ahead,' she said. 'I think it's an icefield.'

'Oh sweet Jesus Christ!' sang out Hogg even as she spoke. 'Go and tell the captain, Yasser. We're going into ice.'

'I'll tell him,' snapped Ann. 'You'd better stay up here. Where is he?'

'Cabin behind the chart room,' answered the little man, craning round to look over his right shoulder as though his agonised gaze would be the best guide across the wheelhouse.

She was off at once and had only taken a step or two before the alarm bell, ringing from the radar, informed her Hogg had turned it on again. To get this close to an icefield without anyone realising – heads were going to roll, she thought. Reynolds would never have allowed it to happen. She was through the chart room at a flat run and hammering on the door beyond. 'Come,' said Black's voice, instantly alert.

She pushed the door open and stood on the threshold. He was sitting, back straight, on a narrow bunk. He had clearly been sleeping partially dressed, but his trousers still seemed to be impeccably pressed and the shirt he was buttoning might just have been ironed. For once he did not attack her for being who she was, what she was or where she was. 'Icefield, dead ahead, Captain,' she said.

'A *field* of ice?'

'Horizon to horizon as far as the eye can see.'

'How far can you see, Miss Cable?'

'Halfway to the Pole. The moon's out.'

'I see. And how near do you estimate—'

His calm questioning was interrupted by the first shock of contact since the rogue floe had smashed their propeller fifteen hours earlier. The grinding hesitation, coupled by the slight but unmistakable canting of the deck, made the rest of his question superfluous. He rose, punctiliously sliding his tie under the starched points of his shirt collar, a frown beginning to gather on his lean, lined face. 'Miss Cable, I wonder if I could ask you to find the chief engineer.' His faded, weary eyes flicked up to the clock on the wall. 'He will be in his cabin at this time in the morning, I expect. Give him my compliments and explain the situation. He will have to doublecheck that everything in the engine room is secure.'

She turned to go, but for some reason he continued, tricked into a fleeting intimacy. 'I should phone him, of course. That's what a captain should do. But he has disconnected the bells in his cabin and his workroom so I can't disturb him, you see.'

The chief engineer's name was Lethbridge and Ann disturbed him all right. For some reason, Captain Black's defeated words made her angry with the chief engineer. She hit his door like a small avalanche, battering it with her fists. He opened to her, his face thunderstruck. Nobody had dared summon him like this since he had been an apprentice. 'Now just what the infernal—'

'Captain says you'd better look to your bits and pieces, Chief. It seems the wind's pushing us up into an icefield.' And even as she spoke, a second, more serious impact came. *Atropos* seemed to jump to port as the starboard quarter bounced off a bigger floe. It was a movement every bit as sudden and almost as violent as any enforced motion during the storm. All through the ship – unnaturally quiet because the engines were shut down – came the rumble of the impact.

And something more. From far below there came a sudden reverberation, so bass in sound it seemed to make the whole bridgehouse shudder, so powerful it seemed to have no beginning or end. Only when it had been repeated several times was there any pattern discernible in it, as though a huge bell was tolling slowly in the deepest bowels of the ship.

The chief engineer came fully into Ann's view, pulling up the zipper to close his overall across his lean belly. He set off at a run and she followed him without a further thought. Together they plunged down the companionways while the air around them filled time and again with the noise of the icefield thumping and grating along the hull and the great bell ringing ever louder beneath their feet. As they went, they seemed to collect a team of men about them. The engineering officers appeared from cabins like hibernating bears in spring and ran down at their sides, Lethbridge's sidekick Don Taylor first among them. LeFever appeared from nowhere and joined in as they went down past A deck into the engineering decks. He tucked in beside Ann. 'What's going on?' he yelled.

Ann seriously considered trying to frame a verbal answer but he would never hear it, so she shook her head and hoped that would suffice as they reached the corridor where nearly sixteen hours earlier they had first learned about the propeller. Here the noise was almost overpowering. And the reason for the sudden plethora of engineers was explained: it was coming from the engine room. They ran towards it as though the damage each overpowering chime was doing to their ears was a thing of no account. Ann followed, though she was getting very frightened now. Anything which summoned so much unquestioning dedication from men who bitched unendingly about arriving in their work area at 08:59 or leaving it at 17:01 had to be something she wanted to report. And because she was going in, Henri LeFever followed on.

Like her sister ship *Clotho*, *Atropos* was powered by two compact Rolls-Royce RB211 gas turbines. They were so compact that it was possible to carry a third aboard so any serious problem could be rectified by lifting the damaged unit out and putting a complete new motor in. The third turbine was carried suspended from the roof of the engine room. It was secured in a heavy sling which was

held up by four lines, two to the fore and two to the aft
of the room. The shock of impacting with the icefield had
caused three of these lines to snap so that several tons of
engine was swinging from side to side of the metal-sided
room. The bell-like cacophony was caused by the fact that
at the apogee of each swing the turbine was thundering
up against a wall.

They crowded into the engine control room and froze,
petrified with horror.

A series of marks along the far wall and lines of gleaming debris which made an hour-glass shape on the floor
showed that the engine was not content to follow only one
arc of motion. 'It's coming this *way*!' screamed Ann and
shocked them out of their stasis. So it was. They scattered.
The wisest, perhaps, headed back out of the door they had
just come in through. The chief, followed by LeFever, Ann
and the second engineer Don Taylor, went out of the right-
hand door and onto the steps there which led down into
the three-deck-deep hole which contained the engines and
all the ancillary equipment. The third engineer, the panicking boy who had told them of the propeller, went the
other way.

The engine did not, in fact, hit the engine control room
on that swing, but it collected the little metal balcony and
the left-hand door which opened onto it and the steps
which led down from it and slammed the whole thing
against the wall. The young engineer never knew what hit
him. It was, perhaps, the closest a man could come to
being swatted like a fly.

The last line, the one from which the engine was swinging, was secured to a power pulley on the far side of the
room. But it was a big room and they had to get down to
the next deck level before there was a lateral walkway.

They were halfway across this when the engine crashed into the corner of the engine control room in an incredible explosion of glass and metal shards. 'We've got to stop it before it swings again, Don,' screamed Lethbridge to his deputy. 'All the computer controls . . .'

But the second engineer was more concerned to gesture ahead. The series of marks along the further wall led inevitably towards a sheaf of massive pipes. The engine would hit them on this swing. Like wild things, the engineering officers ran and, caught up in the drama of it all, Ann would have followed. But as the two crewmen flung themselves wildly down the steps towards the power winch, Henri's hand closed like a vice on her shoulder.

'Too late!' he screamed. 'We get out.'

Any protest she might have made was stymied by the power of his grip and his action. He hoisted her like a child and ran back along the walkway with her. The engine swung past them, whispering as it hurled through the air, like the deadly blade in Poe's *The Pit and the Pendulum*.

Lethbridge hit the power winch and the emergency release. The weight of the engine was enormous and the force of its motion cataclysmic. The released cogs spun at tremendous speed. There was an automatic safety but it burned out in an instant and the engine would have thundered to, and probably through, the deck had not the second engineer collided with his chief. Lethbridge's overall, still only partly zipped and hanging loose, caught in the whirling cog and snagged it. The big man hurled himself backwards so that none of his body followed the cloth to shred through the rabid steel jaws, but the hesitation gave the engine the instant of time it needed to complete its final swing. It cut only the outermost of the sheaf of pipes but that was quite enough. A spray of superheated steam thundered into the engine room. It billowed in boiling clouds around the two engineers. The other two were lucky to avoid the full force of it, saved by Henri's action.

Not so lucky, however, was the ship's generator. In an instant the cool metal was running with condensed water. In another, with a blinding flash and a crackling roar, the machine died. And in the echo of its death, the battered wreck of the RB211 engine slithered to the deck.

As the wind-driven, helpless *Atropos*, struck dark and blind, deaf and dumb, wedged deeper into the flank of the moonlit icefield, Captain Black in desperation screamed at the setting moon, 'Where is that British bitch with *Clotho*?'

CHAPTER ELEVEN

Day Seven

Tuesday, 25 May   05:40

Clotho was moving east again, one hour's sailing south-west, coming in at full ahead. Robin, pale, exhausted but grimly determined not to give in to fatigue, was on the bridge. From her position, the moon had almost set and the palest fingernail of it lay above the corrugated coalface of the sea in the thinnest gallery of clear sky trapped claustrophobically beneath the mountainous weight of the clouds. Just as it did set, the undersides of the clouds were suddenly dusted with the palest mother-of-pearl and the whole sky seemed to light up for a moment before the blackness clamped back down.

'You seen that before?' Robin growled at Nico.

'No, Captain. I'm a Mediterranean man. I know what it means, though. Icefield ahead.'

Robin crossed to the collision alarm radar and fiddled with the setting. Just for a moment, she wanted the big picture, in spite of the fact that it would probably be pretty vague. The range clicked up from five miles to fifty. Far up above her head, the equipment in the big golfball of the radome readjusted itself and the image in the bowl silently changed. Twenty miles to the north, the deep green of the image paled in an almost straight line east to west. Above it, the paleness went northwards towards the Pole. The bright spark denoting the silent sister ship shone on the edge of that sinister, pallid sea. According to the calibration, it was a little west of dead ahead. They were still allowing for the current, though the force of it had moderated, as had the force of the wind.

But just to the south of *Clotho*, the machine showed another area of paleness. The pallor represented another area of thick ice, and this was what had held them up.

Robin snapped the machine back to the detailed five-mile setting before they bumped into anything too small to feature in the big picture but large enough to do them harm. Then she crossed to the watchkeeper's chair. It was Nico's privilege to use it because he was on watch now, but the Italian was happy enough to be gallant. He had been tucked safely in his bunk since she had dismissed him at eight last evening. He had enjoyed eight hours' blissful slumber while Johnny Sullivan and Rupert Biggs had held their watches. She had been on the bed in the captain's day cabin behind the chart room and her sleep there had been restless and disturbed.

It was the ice to the south of them that had been the trouble. Sullivan, knowing how exhausted she was and wishing desperately to let her sleep, had nevertheless been forced to report to her when it had materialised right across their path a mere ninety minutes after she had gone to bed. By 22:00 hours last night, they had been off course, running due west with the wind behind them, looking for a way round the obstacle – or through it. The five-mile setting on the radar showed them parts of it, but not enough to get a clear idea of its size or disposition. The big picture went fuzzy incredibly quickly because of the power of the storm. It was impossible to tell much about it. It was big. It was in their way. It was made of ice. That was all.

Rupert Biggs, the electronics wizard, had guided them round the end of it in the dead hours of his watch and had woken Robin again when the situation warranted a major change of course. Blearily, she had ordered Sam Larkman, who held the con until Errol arrived with Nico at 04:00, to swing back due east and come up to full ahead. The engines responded nimbly; they would have done so under the direction of the automatic systems, but the automatic systems were redundant because Andrew McTavish's engineers were awake and keeping watch as well.

Now they were running up to their objective at full speed, cutting through the stormy water at nearly thirty knots, throwing up a bow wave like a speedboat. Robin crossed towards the spray-spattered clearview, feeling very much in charge of the whole situation.

As she did so, Bill Christian pushed his pale face out of the radio shack, calling, 'Captain! She's gone dead. *Atropos* has gone dead.'

Robin swung round to look at Nico, as she did almost habitually in a crisis now. He called himself a Mediterranean man with that wry Neapolitan gift for understatement, as though the term defined the limit of his experience. But he had been around. He had learned a lot. He had more than earned his papers. He was a good officer. They were a very good team. Automatically they were bouncing ideas off one another in an instant.

'Power loss, probably, Captain. Generators down.'

'Probably, Nico. So we wait and see if she comes back up when the emergency systems click in.'

'But if her generators are down, how will that affect what we are going to do?'

'The answer to that will depend firstly on how many auxiliary systems the back-up is designed to run.'

'Light, navigation, communication.'

'Heat? Galley? Deck equipment?'

'The split windlass works independently.'

'I know. Thank God. But we need to be certain about food and heat too, in this weather.'

Bill Christian called through, '*Atropos* is back. On emergency power. Their main power is completely lost – their generator's down. More details as and when they can. Could we give Captain Black an ETA? He's not a happy man.'

'Less than one hour. I want to know at once if he gets full power back.'

'Aye aye, Captain.'

'Right. That'll give us something to do other than sitting around worrying while we go on in. I'll get the chief up here and if he can't tell us what the back-up power systems do and don't run, then I'll get the ship's specifications out and we can look it all up.'

'As you well know, Captain,' said Andrew McTavish in his gentle Lowland Scots burr, 'the power on these ships comes from two alternators run in tandem. If one's gone, the other will have shut down automatically so they'll be running on battery power and that will give them only the very basics. And no heat. If both alternators have gone, they're in trouble. If one alternator has gone, it'll be a case of fixing it, starting it and bringing it back into phase with the other one or they'll burn out the switchboard and a whole lot else besides. How fast they can do that depends on the damage and the chief engineer over there.'

'*Atropos* is back on the radio, Captain.'

'Thanks, Bill, I'll come myself. Excuse me, Andrew.'

'What do you think, Nico?'

'I don't know, Chief. I thought this was the unlucky ship. Looks like her sister is worse.'

'Oh come on, Number One, you're not serious about all that claptrap, are you?'

The Italian looked at the bluff Scot and wondered whether to be insulted. His Neapolitan pride was hurt and his hot blood would have been happy enough to declare a vendetta. But he knew that he was tired and that if he took umbrage then he would just be giving in to the *mala fortuna* of the whole situation.

'Right,' said Robin tensely, returning before either man could add another word. 'The situation is this. They've lost one alternator. It fused out because it was sprayed with superheated steam from a fractured pipe. Their chief and first engineer have both been boiled alive by the same steam, the third has been crushed to death and they'll need help to put things right.'

Andrew looked at Nico, his eyes wide and his dour Calvinist education trying vainly to come to terms with the Italian's dramatic concepts of fortune. They suddenly seemed to be absolutely accurate after all. 'I should think they will need help,' said Andrew feelingly. 'When we come alongside I'll have to go across myself. And I'll take Harry Piper my third engineer along with me. He's young but he's keen. It'll be good experience for him. That'll leave Lloyd Swan, my number two, to look after you until I get back.'

'Would you like to take Jamie Curtis as well?' asked Robin. 'The experience would be good for him too.'

'Aye. He's another one who's bright and keen. For a deck cadet. He'll do to carry any messages back and forth that I mightn't want to broadcast.'

Andrew's eyes met Nico's. The pair of them looked across at their captain and she met their gazes imperturbably. 'Are you suggesting that all might not be well aboard our sister ship?' she asked quietly.

'It's Nico,' answered Andrew. 'He's got me thinking that maybe she's bad luck.'

They saw her lights within the hour and slowed to a crawl while Robin talked to Captain Black first on the radio and then on the walkie-talkie. With the deck lights on and the searchlight atop the stubby communications mast just behind the forepeak blazing at full power, it was possible to judge how far the wind had pushed her into the mush ice and smaller floes along the edge of the icefield. The night was nearly over, and the storm likewise. Tall waves still rolled up from the south-east and it was these as much as anything that kept the edge of the ice broken up. When dawn eventually heaved itself up into view, Robin reckoned it would reveal the taming of the big seas down to ripples in a mile or so by the solid weight of the ice. But there was still some time to go until sunrise, and there was much to be done before it. Andrew McTavish, Harry Piper and Jamie Curtis were all dressed in bright orange survival gear and ready to go across. They would be using one of the lifeboats and, never one to waste effort, Robin was sending a cable across with them.

Jamie stood out in the gusty dark under the forward port side lifeboat. It was a raw morning still capable of

flinging unexpected squalls of rain and hail into the
unwary face, but the savagery had gone out of the wind
and things seemed to be improving. The young cadet was
excited. This seemed to him to be one of those adventures
which had peopled his dreams of the seafaring life. Even
when the wind forgot to gust and flap around him, the
noise was still incredible. The ice groaned and clashed
and rumbled as it heaved. It was solid enough to thunder
as one piece jarred down off a wave back onto the edge
of another. It was fragile enough to have bubbles, pockets
and chambers of air trapped within it, air which fountained
out in invisible geysers as the restless ice crust rose and
fell, roaring like the breath of monsters trapped below.
There was a smell to it – if one was unwise enough to
sniff and risk deep-freezing the adenoids. There was an
atmosphere to it, of wildness and mystery, of being at a
great frontier. There was a romance to it which even the
massive darkness beyond the lights could not cloak.

Joe Edwards' hand thumped down on Jamie's shoulder
and the big seaman gestured up to the lifeboat. Together
they released it and the gravity davits swung it down and
out. Then Joe held the tricing-in pendant, keeping the boat
close to the rail while Jamie released part of the cover
and scrambled in. So confident and nimble was he about
the little vessel now that it was strange for him to recall
that it was less than twenty-four hours ago that he had
fallen off the whalebacked bow. He turned just in time to
see the engineers scramble past Joe, then Nico appeared
and took the tricing-in line until Joe had climbed aboard
too.

As soon as they were settled, the first officer hit the
release and the lifeboat slithered down the falls, the speed
of its descent automatically controlled by the centrifugal

brakes. In the lee of *Clotho* the sea was still enough for the lifeboat to kiss the surface and bob as though sitting in a millpond while Joe busied himself about starting the compression ignition engine. Once it was running smoothly, they cut themselves off from their mother ship and began to move through the freezing water. At first their progress was easy, unimpeded by ice and undisturbed by swell. They ran down *Clotho*'s side and paused under the overhang of her stern as a great looped end of cable was lowered to them. This was not the towing cable itself; had that monster been lowered to them, it would have pushed them straight to the bottom of the sea.

With the cable safely secured, Joe turned the lifeboat's head towards *Atropos* and off they went. It continued easy sailing to begin with. The first strain on the little craft came from the drag of the cable she was pulling, but wisely foreseeing that the short voyage would not be all that easy in any case, Robin had sent a buoyant line with them which bobbed merrily in their wake, almost luminescently orange in the brightness of the lights. Next, they met the ice. A thin crust first, which whispered under the bow; then little pieces big enough to hiss and thump quietly. They had little more than twenty metres to traverse but soon the chief engineer had caught up the boat's oars and was using them handily, reaching over the bow to push baby ice floes out of the lifeboat's path. Jamie had thought they would be flat and round like frozen lily pads, but he found instead that the small ice floes were shaped like anvils. They had thin necks near the water with broad shoulders beneath the surface and bulbous heads above. At the edge of the pack it was like sailing through a sea of solid, slightly grubby little thunderclouds.

It was not until they reached the tall black side of the

stricken ship that the third obstacle was revealed. This far away from *Clotho*'s shelter, the waves rose high enough to have the lifeboat rising and falling considerably, waves which curved, not into breakers, but into hills and valleys which slammed up and down against *Atropos*'s flank. Even Joe's evident skill could not stop the little craft from being thrown against the forbidding steel cliff several times as they explored along the length of it, looking for a way to get aboard.

At last, near the bow, where the ice was getting threateningly thick and the waves dangerously high, they found the end of a Jacob's ladder dangling just above the sea, its upper reaches lost in sinister, silent darkness. Not that it would have been possible to hear anything but the loudest whistle down here among the cacophony of warring, roaring ice in any case. It would clearly be impossible for any one of them to carry the line aboard and so Andrew told Harry and Jamie to secure it to the bottom-most rung while Joe held the boat still and the chief himself fended off the ship on one side and the ice on the other. When it was tied, the three who were going aboard scrambled up, certain that it would be easy enough to pull up the ladder, and the line along with it, as soon as they were safely on deck. And so it proved, though they did not need to do the work themselves. *Atropos*'s first officer was there with a little team of men ready to get the line up to the windlass and the tow rope pulled aboard. In the meantime, Jamie and the engineers ran on down the deck. They had no need of a guide, of course: this ship was identical to their own ship.

At least, the layout and general disposition were the same. The atmosphere and the crew could hardly have been more different. They reported to the captain first and were graced with the curtest of welcomes. You would have thought they were bringing plague, not help, Jamie thought bitterly. Harry and Andrew were sent down to the engine room like plumbers going down to mend a broken lavatory. Jamie followed because the captain hadn't acknowledged his existence and the enormously fat officer by the radar had met his friendly smile with a cold stare. He was glad enough to plunge into the dark corridor after his friends.

It was uncanny to be aboard so silent a ship. Normally a ship was only ever this quiet when she was tied up in port, powered by land lines from the dockside, with only a harbour watch aboard. But this ship was miles from anywhere, full of people, stirring restlessly at the direction of deep waters and communing lumpily with ice. She felt dead and dangerous, like a ghost ship. Jamie hurried to catch up with his silent shipmates hurrying through the dim glimmer of the emergency lighting.

In the wreckage of the engine control room, Andrew stood looking down. By all accounts things were pretty grim and dangerous down there. It was all very well for him and Harry Piper to stumble through it in the dark, but . . . He looked at Jamie. The lad was eager and bright enough, but he wouldn't be much use to them down here. 'Laddie,' said the engineer softly, fatigue tricking the accent of his Greenock childhood out of him, 'go and find out how the chief and the second engineer are keeping, will you?' He saw Jamie's face fall, and smiled understandingly. 'You can come on down and see what's to do when you report back to me,' he promised.

The chief was in his cabin on C deck, just below the bridge. Jamie was like a spooked animal by the time he got there through the shadows and the unnatural silence, frightening himself further with the atmosphere which seemed to emanate from the unnaturally silent crew. He felt alien. Or, more accurately, like a boy lost in an alien, hostile, dangerous place. He tapped on the door and waited. He remembered Captain Mariner's words, repeated from what Captain Black had said to her and repeated to him on the way over by a shocked Andrew McTavish: 'Boiled alive.' How could someone be boiled and still be alive? He didn't really want to find out. But Jamie had been brought up to obey orders. He knocked on the door again, a little harder, and this time he heard someone move behind it and he steeled himself to meet a man who had been boiled alive. But when the door opened, a beautiful woman was standing there. Well, her face seemed lovely and also vaguely familiar. It was difficult to tell about the rest of her as she was bundled up in jeans and pullovers against the cold. 'Who are you?' she asked abruptly.

He was dazzled, dazed. He thought of the figure he had seen on *Atropos*'s forecastle in the fog. That had been a girl too. Should he report that sighting to someone? 'Jamie Curtis,' he answered. 'Officer cadet, *Atropos*.' He explained what he was doing here and she smiled wryly.

'So, you're a knight in shining armour. A trainee knight. Come in.'

Inside the chief engineer's day room, a tall man was sitting. He and the woman had obviously been deep in conversation when he tapped on the door. Normally, Jamie would have gone through the full ritual of introductions but his orders were clear and his time was short; he was eager to see what was to be seen and make his report to Andrew. He went on through and looked at the heavily bandaged figure lying in the bunk. Only eyes, puffy and closed in restless sleep, could clearly be seen. He returned to the day room. 'How is he?' he asked the woman.

'He's badly scalded and he's only asleep because he's drugged up to the eyeballs,' she answered. 'But I guess he'll pull through. First Officer Timmins is our acting medic but Henri here seems to know more about it. What do you say, Henri?'

The tall man looked up and even in the shadowy room his natural charm seemed to glimmer. It was as though he was smiling, but his face was serious. 'He's *hors de combat* at the moment but it's not bad enough to require hospital treatment. Not that he could have it out here anyway. He'll be back at work in a few days, I guess. Stiff and sore, but functioning. Same with Don Taylor, but the chief took the full blast of the steam so he's worse.'

Jamie nodded and exited. At the door out into the corridor she stopped him. 'How is Nico?' she asked quietly.

Echoing the strange drop in her tone he answered, 'Fine.' His mind was racing. How did this dazzling creature come to know his boss?

'Will he be coming aboard too?'

'I doubt it. Not unless you lose your deck officers as fast as you lose your engineers.'

'We've lost one already. Third Officer Reynolds. Just before the propeller went.'

He took that one in silently. Then he said, 'He won't come over unless the captain sends him. I don't think she'll do that unless there's a bad emergency.'

The woman's eyes glinted. 'They sound as though they have a very close relationship,' she said.

He was young. He was not a gossip, nor was he a lover of dirty talk. But he was callow and he wanted to say something which would have the same impact as the tall man called Henri could obviously command.

'Very close.' He gave an experimental leer. 'Mistress and mate, you might say.'

The nautical pun eluded her. The innuendo did not.

Jamie Curtis would never know exactly what he had done. He noticed only that his witticism had made an impact on her and he turned away happily and bustled down to the engine room to make his report.

Andrew next sent him down to the windlass to see the towing cable being winched aboard. Dawn was beginning to glimmer, the distant promise of the sun just starting to lighten the steely oppression of the clouds and spread across the face of the frozen north. Jamie looked around, stunned by the slow revelation of the white wilderness on their port bow, glancing up every now and then to look again at the wilderness stretching out and away towards the Pole. But the major part of his attention was held by the task of winching up *Clotho*'s towing cable. The smaller cable which they had brought was all but aboard now, and behind it, rising up from beneath the black surface of the water like the Loch Ness monster, came the main cable. It was thicker than two men wrestling chest to chest and, like the ocean, it was black. Belching great fountains and falls of water, it rose up towards the cleats in the forepeak, and as it did so the sheer weight of it started *Atropos*'s head swinging to starboard. Impulsively, Jamie ran across to make sure that Joe was all right in the boat beneath the swinging bow. But the canny old seaman had pulled the boat well back to avoid the motion which he had obviously expected and to keep clear of the tumbling water.

Once the towing cable was aboard and safely attached, Jamie had only to report one last time to Andrew McTavish and get any last message to take back to his

captain on *Clotho*. He found the chief together with the
two more junior engineers going over the alternator with
every evidence of satisfaction. 'I'll soon have this up and
running, then we'll put it in phase with the other one
and give *Atropos* her power back. Tell the captain three
hours at most.' Andrew slipped his arm round the cadet's
shoulders and bluffly pulled him a little apart. He dropped
his voice and added rapidly, 'But tell her I'll be staying
aboard longer than that. I want to go over the engine room
carefully. No engine sling I ever heard of broke three lines
at once. Unless it was helped.' Then the big Scot swung
the stunned cadet back into the hearing of the *Atropos*'s
second engineer and boomed, 'Don't forget to pay your
respects to the captain before you leave his ship, either,
young fellow-me-lad.' And his gaze met that of Harry
Piper with just the hint of a wink.

On the bridge it was possible to see the full extent of
the ice to the north of them now, but Jamie had little time
to appreciate the view. He took his leave of Captain Black
and received a grunt in reply. Then he was rushing down
to the head of the Jacob's ladder and on down into the
lifeboat. 'Just you, is it?' grunted Joe Edwards.

'Just me. Gosh, but that's a funny ship.'

Jamie was big with news, but he had the good sense
not to tell Joe too much as they bucketed and bounced
back to *Clotho*. It was obvious to the old hand that the
youngster was holding a great deal back, and precisely
what that was would become a ripe topic for speculation
in the crew's wardroom in the not too distant future.

His captain welcomed Jamie back aboard hardly more
warmly than the other had dismissed him, and he was
slightly hurt, even though she was clearly preoccupied
with the mechanics of getting the tow under way. She was

not in fact on the bridge itself, so Jamie reported in the first instance to Nico Niccolo. It was clear that the Italian wanted to ask the boy some questions of his own, but there were other priorities to be met. 'Captain's out on the bridge wing,' he said and Jamie went out to find her standing at the rear of the open space, looking down over the stern of her ship to where Johnny Sullivan and his team were keeping an eye on the tow rope. She was talking quietly into a walkie-talkie, in communication with Sullivan and Nico on the bridge as well as with Captain Black on *Atropos*. As he arrived, breathless and self-important beside her, she said, 'All right, Nico, dead slow ahead and take the strain.' Even as she spoke, Jamie felt the ship begin to move.

'Johnny, how is it down there?'

'Fine, Captain. Settled down and holding nicely.'

'Captain Black, we are at dead slow ahead and taking the strain.'

'I can see that. We're coming round.' There was a hiss of static, then the chilly, abrupt voice was back. 'My first officer tells me the tow is holding well.'

'Thank you, Captain. When we've pulled you free of the ice, I propose to proceed eastwards towards Greenland. I have received word that Frederiksdale is currently free of ice and I propose to shelter there until help arrives. I have been warned that we are likely to be in another storm by nightfall.'

It was clear to Jamie that he would have to make his report a little later and so he wandered away across the bridge wing to get a good look at what was going on. The wind was almost still now and the air was clear. The clouds were a lightening grey overhead with the most distant hint of blue away to the north where the moon had peeped through the overcast. Far to the west, on the other hand, the sky was black and threatening. The sea beneath *Clotho* was still running tall with the memory of yesterday's storm and the threat of today's. There was enough light now for the water to be brightening like the sky, but the waves were still strangely dark, as though clear green pigment had been poured over deep grey crystal. The waves rolled northwards, past the rocking hull of *Atropos* coming slowly round at the messy edge of the ice, tugging sulkily at the whipping, straining tow rope. Beyond her, the icefield proper began. As the waves passed under the ice, they lifted the floes until their sheer sides rose out of the water to reflect the sullen daylight in shades of blue and green.

After a few moments of watching the apparently random restlessness, Jamie began to see a pattern in it. The waves rolled north in majestic series without seeming to diminish in size. As they did so, they moved into lighter air, brighter conditions. Here it was dull but the millions of ice mirrors along the flanks of the floes seemed to multiply the light so that in the middle distance his narrowed eyes could see the occasional dazzling ultramarine gleam. And right at the far end of the horizon, at the extreme edge of his vision, blinding searchlight gleams of pure sapphire showed that the floes were stirring under clearer, brighter skies. The gleams brought tears streaming across his vision with their power and their beauty.

All around was the sound that their movement caused. The wash of the water disturbed in its progress by the floating blocks. The splash of their rising, the plunge of their falling. The hiss of the spray from their landing. The thud of the smaller pieces thrown together, the hush of the plates and lily pads big enough to slide over each

other. The crash of those small anvil-headed floes large
enough to hit against each other, the thumping and cracking of the medium-sized floes being ground down like
pebbles on a shore; and the distant, never ending roar of
the big floes, the thick ice, driven to war with itself by the
motion of the waves.

'Welcome back aboard, Jamie. Anything to report?'

'What?' He swung round, still dazzled, to find his captain standing just behind him.

'Anything to report?' she repeated.

'Oh. Sorry, Captain. I . . . Yes. The chief says he doesn't
think the damage was accidental . . .'

Jamie's report to Robin took five minutes. Her exhaus-
tive questions fifteen more. The whole process was completed in the warmth of the bridge while *Clotho* slowly
continued pulling *Atropos* clear of the ice. It was well into
Johnny Sullivan's watch now, but Nico had stayed on the
bridge. Obviously, he wanted to be available until the
second officer was called back up to the bridge from his
oversight of the tow, something which would happen when
both ships were in clear water and the tow was properly
under way. Also he wanted as much as the captain did to
hear Jamie's report and he had a few shrewd questions of
his own. But mostly he wanted news of Ann Cable. Jamie's
report made it clear that he had met her without having
any idea of who she was, or of the fact that she and Nico
Niccolo were lovers of long standing. But the news, when
it came, was not what he had expected to hear. She had
asked about him but sent no message to him. Jamie
seemed surprised that the first officer should think she
would. Especially as she was so obviously carrying on
some kind of relationship, said Jamie, with the incredibly
good-looking man called Henri.

So it was that something of *Atropos*'s dark atmosphere began to seep across into her sister.

The tow started in earnest and the two ships began to move at five knots due east towards the shelter of the southern tip of Greenland. As they passed through that wide channel of fairly clear water with thick ice on either side of them, the dark clouds of the next storm chased them like coursing hounds. In the crews' quarters, the men talked darkly of what might be going on aboard the crippled ship behind. And in the places where he performed his duties, Nico would pause to indulge in viciously jealous thoughts. In her day room, Robin tossed in restless sleep, wondering who had sabotaged the engine sling on *Atropos* and why.

And in her eyrie on the gantry halfway down the deck, *Clotho*'s saboteur reviewed the changing situation and began to redraw her plans, wondering whether to risk another chancy visit to the bomb in the water ballast tank. Down at the waterline, right at the most forward part of the ship where hard waves hit and increasingly massive chunks of ice rammed home increasingly frequently, the first signs of buckling began to show on metal fatally weakened three months earlier by the blast of the Belfast bomb.

CHAPTER TWELVE
Day Eight
Wednesday, 26 May   04:00

Nico signed on for his watch at 04:00 the next morning more exhausted than he had ever been. The day had not been particularly hard, but they seemed to have made barely any headway at all. Their progress eastward had proceeded at a snail's pace. It was fortunate that the westward current had moderated from its earlier fierceness or the two ships would have remained stationary, pushing eastwards at five knots through water flowing westwards at the same speed. Now for every five knots they went eastwards, at least they only fell back one. And drifted south one more, he noticed, glaring blearily at the figures in the impeccable record before him. In eighteen hours, the distance sailed had been less than one hundred miles. The distance actually covered was about seventy. There were another couple of hundred miles to go before they sighted the forbidding cliffs and fjords at the southern tip of Greenland. It was going to be a long, hard slog by the look of things. And the weather was closing in again.

Nico checked Rupert Biggs's neat notes with frowning

concentration. The glass was falling with increasing rapidity and it looked as though there was a sharp north-easter rushing down from Hudson Bay to overtake them. It would be at its worst around dawn at the end of his current watch if the weather reports were correct. It would make the daylight hours pretty foul and then it would clear. Even if it pushed them along at a better pace, it should still be over some time before Greenland presented itself as a lee shore. Unless there was a lot more bad luck in store.

And there probably was, he thought to himself morosely. Over a week ago, on the day she sailed, Richard Mariner had asked him if he thought *Clotho* was an unlucky ship. He had indeed thought so, but he had underestimated the damage such bad luck could do. And he had been ignorant of the fact that *Atropos* was worse luck still. From the sound of Jamie Curtis's report, *Atropos* had been slaughtering her complement with vicious regularity since she had set sail. And poisoning the relationships between those who had survived. It made him feel at risk even to be tied to her. But that feeling was nothing compared to the feeling that the rest of Jamie's news had stirred up in him. For all he hated and perhaps even feared *Atropos* and her bad luck, he would have given almost anything to be aboard her so that he could find out the truth about Ann and this Henri. The thought of them together putting the horns on him was more than he could bear. He was a modern man. He saw himself as being liberated. Not for him the quiet, half-educated girl from his home town living under the eye of his parents, made pregnant at each homecoming and existing in the abject expectation of those homecomings. No. He had found the mate of his dreams in this intelligent, articulate, modern woman. But now, at their first time of testing, what had he found? Infidelity. That Ann, with her face of an angel, had the soul of a whore.

No. This could not be true. It was impossible that this should be true. He seriously considered going down to Jamie's cabin and pulling him out of bed to go over the story yet again. And these thoughts filled his brain to such an extent that he did not notice the increasingly strange way that *Clotho* was behaving.

To be fair, even had he been wide awake and sharp as a tack, he would have been hard put to distinguish much amiss. The north-easterly was winding up behind their left shoulder and it was cutting across the generally south-westerly set of the sea so that *Clotho*'s progress through the steep-sided waves was lumpy and ungainly in any case. And the sea lane between the icefields was by no means as clear now as it had been earlier, so, among the sharp swoops which had their origin in the sea conditions came the occasional juddering impact with a solid piece of ice. Finally, among all this ungainly, uncharacteristic motion, was the fact of the tow. It was inevitable under the circum-stances that *Clotho* would run away every now and again only to be brought up sharp by the restraining leash tether-ing her to *Atropos*. This situation was now complicated by the fact that *Atropos* was upwind in a strengthening breeze and every now and then would be blown down towards *Clotho*, allowing her an unaccustomedly long run before jerking her back to heel.

The collision alarm radar showed the ice to the south of them very clearly but the edge of the icefield to the north was increasingly vague and ill-defined as the wind pushed the floes south across their path. There was nothing in front of them big enough to register, however, so there ought to be nothing out there big enough to do them any damage. Because *Atropos* was so close behind, they had turned off the sound alarm which would have been screaming all the time, but this meant that the watchkeeper had to be particularly careful to keep a visual check.

Nico looked up at the ship's chronometer above the helm and noted the radar read all clear. Next, he checked their position according to the satnav, marked the movement on the chart and logged that too. He checked their heading on the automatic steering equipment. Biggs's last modification of their course – too slight to be called a change – was holding good. If they were drifting south towards the ice there, then the ice, too, was drifting south at about the same speed.

Idly he wondered what it was, that strange, unexpected area of ice. But then he shrugged. He was a Mediterranean man. Why should he care? The ship plunged and jerked. He slammed forward and winded himself on the tiny rally wheel of the helm. *Jesu!* That one felt as if they had run into a brick wall!

He pulled himself back to the watchkeeper's chair and sat. It could not be said that he dozed, for had the warning light on the radar flashed, he would have seen it and reacted. But as soon as he sat, he became lost in those thoughts which had kept him restlessly awake during the last four hours when his body would have given almost anything to sleep. How could she betray him? And so soon. They had been apart for little more than a fortnight. What manner of man was this Henri who stole women so easily and with so little thought? He drew up a mental picture, based on what the boy had said. Tall, magnetic, powerfully handsome. Irresistible.

The first real sign of disaster would have communicated

itself to Nico's feet, had they been resting on the deck. Thence they would have sent warning messages flashing to his brain, had he not been so preoccupied. Even as things were, the tiny super-sensitive coils in his ears which attuned his sense of balance would have registered the first changes in the mean horizontal had they not been coping with the pitching and the rolling – and the fact that his head was thrown back against the headrest while he stared abstractedly at the shadows on the ceiling above him. And, just as there was no warning system to alert the bridge that the hatches to the water ballast tank in the forepeak were open, so there was no warning to alert the bridge that the ballast itself was flooding through the fractured and increasingly buckled bow. The only warning of that was the fact that the angle of the deck was sloping increasingly upwards and the activity of the ship was becoming increasingly frenetic as the ballast drained away.

As the front of the ship was slowly battered from a sleek wedge to a rough wall, the automatic machinery overseeing their progress interpreted their increasing loss of speed as being due to sea conditions and the engine revolutions clicked up accordingly. An engine room watch would have noticed, but none of the automatic warning systems did because the increase was so slight and so steady. So, to begin with, nobody aboard *Clotho* registered the fact that her forecastle head was being beaten flat as though it had been made of tin, not steel, as though each succeeding wave was a huge hammer flanked with carbon and each floe was a titanium ram.

The stowaway had come through the rough weather of the rescue dash relatively unscathed, although conditions had been pretty extreme. There was something about the way

Clotho was smashing into the steep waves now, however, that she was finding most distressing. All thoughts of going back down to check the timer in the Semtex were put aside as, with dogged determination and absolute practicality, she sought to make sure that her increasingly uncontrollable *mal de mer* did not soil her clothing or sleeping bag. The operating cab had been well made, and then well repaired after the bomb. It was utterly weatherproof even under these conditions and as long as she stayed wrapped up and dry, the slim saboteur was snug enough. But bouts of uncontrolled vomiting made it difficult to ensure the snug dryness and threatened to overcome entirely the makeshift toilet arrangements she had been forced to employ since *Clotho* had plunged into the stormy Labrador Sea. The ten-gallon plastic water drum she had stolen from the lifeboat and adapted was filling with disturbing speed and, had she been feeling stronger, she might have been tempted to drag it out onto the little balcony outside the cabin door and empty it down onto the deck where the rain and spray would scour it away in no time. The roll of toilet paper purloined from the same place was nearly used up too. If things went on like this, her paperback edition of *Les Travailleurs de la Mer* was going to come to an ignominious end indeed.

Because she was lying acrossways, with her head to starboard and her feet to port, she did not notice the increasing cant of the deck as the lightened bow strove to rise. Because it was still dark in any case, and because the ten-gallon drum was wedged between the end of the operator's bench and the wall above her head, she had no longer any view at all down the length of the deck. She did not realise that, beyond the stubby forward communications mast, immediately forward of the firmly founded

engines comprising the split windlass, the deck of the
forepeak was slowly buckling upwards, pointing towards
the stormy sky as the wreck of the bow beneath it was
being battered relentlessly back against the unyielding forward wall of *Clotho*'s number one hold.

Robin knew there was something wrong, and had her sleep
been less deep and exhausted, she would have reacted
more quickly. She was in the cabin down on C deck, not
in her day room on the bridge. Down here she had the
luxury of a double bed and the privacy to undress and
pamper her exhausted body with a shower which was just
this side of boiling, before slipping into silk pyjamas and
crawling between fresh starched sheets. All these things
she had done beginning at 23:00 hours last night, but the
six hours' sleep she had enjoyed in the meantime nowhere
near made up for the effort of the days before.

Her bed lay along the length of the ship, so that she
slept with her head towards the bow and her feet towards
the stern. Her body was perfectly attuned to the disposition
of her command in the water and it filled her dreams with
images of mountain slopes. Her ears were equally well
attuned to the steady throbbing of the engines, and as the
revolutions rose to force the damaged bow yet harder
against the almost solid sea, so their urgency also fed into
her subconscious until she had visions of Richard and the
twins standing distantly atop some precipitous, never-
ending alp while she hurled herself up the vertiginous
slope towards them at ever increasing speed but with ever
dwindling hope of reaching them.

She jerked awake into the instant knowledge that something was badly wrong. There was no bleary, half-awake
time when she wondered where she was or what was going

on. Her brain switched from the mountainous dreamscape
to the cabin's reality in a micron of time. She sat up
and reached unerringly for her bedside phone, her thumb
automatically folding over to press the bridge button. Nico
answered on the third ring, by which time she had switched
on the bedside light, checked her watch and swung herself
out of bed.

'Bridge here.'

'This is the captain. What's the matter?'

'What? I—'

'*Nico*! Can't you feel it?'

Now that he was on his feet, yes, he could certainly
feel it. '*Jesu, Capitan*! What—'

'I'm on my way. Get Johnny Sullivan up. Tell him to
roust out a work team. I want them up at the sharp end
reporting to me in bloody short order.'

She hung up before he could even acknowledge her
order. The silk pyjamas were expensive and well made but
the buttons rattled like hailstones against the wall as she
tore the jacket off and the seam in the seat of the trousers
yielded to her impatient hands. It had long been her habit
to leave clothing ready for quick dressing before she
turned in, no matter how exhausted she might be. She
pulled on the strengthened sports bra and hooked the cups
together down the front while she strode across the little
room. Then she caught up a thick quilted vest from the
end of the bed and pulled it over her head without pausing.
Tugging it down, she stepped into the circles of her trouser
legs and pulled up briefs, long johns and trousers all at
once. Pausing only to tuck each layer above into its equivalent below, she sat and pulled on thick socks, smoothing
the longjohns' elasticated ankle cuffs into them and pulling
down the turn-ups to her trousers before pulling on her

thick-soled foul-weather boots. Moving without pause again, she caught up and pulled on a heavy polo-neck sweater in oily natural wool. By the time her tousled head burst out of the tight neck, she was at her cabin door. She shoved it open and jogged out into the corridor, tugging the thick, warm, waterproof wool into place. The rest of her foul-weather gear was in her day room on the bridge. She made it to the bridge within four minutes of waking up.

'Andrew McTavish has Harry Piper on *Atropos* with him,' she rapped out, walking through the door. 'Get Lloyd Swan up and ask him to check the engine. The revs are higher than they should be and I want to know why, if he can tell me. If he needs any help, send Jamie down with him.'

Nico was ringing the third engineering officer before she had finished speaking and had spoilt the cadet's beauty sleep before she dumped herself into the creaking leather of the watchkeeper's chair. Nico stood at the helm, rocking up and down on the balls of his feet, feeling the tilt of the deck beneath them. He was silent, but he was inwardly cursing himself for his failure as a watchkeeper. Well, he thought, at least he had rigged the extra safety lines this afternoon; Sullivan and his team wouldn't have too rough a ride up to the bow, though he noticed the wind was freshening fast now. He should be going down there him-self, really. He wasn't a practising Catholic but he was Italian enough to appreciate the concept of penance.

Robin's walkie-talkie squawked and she spoke into it. Sullivan's voice answered. 'They're on the way out onto the weather deck,' she told Nico. 'Hit the lights.'

He strained to see all the way down to the forecastle, but the gantry was in the way and the clearview was

spray-spattered and salt-grimed and he couldn't make anything much out. Except when the spray exploded up from
the bow wave, there was something wrong with the shape
of it. He shivered and shrugged his shoulders, suddenly
nervous. Could this be real trouble? Abruptly he felt an
overwhelming desire to turn to his captain for reassurance.
But he did not. It was not sexism, it was a more deep-
seated pride than that. He would not have turned to a male
captain either. Not even to his father, had he known who
his father was.

The walkie-talkie squawked again and Robin said,
'Yes?'

Sullivan's voice came gabbling out too fast for Nico to
make out exactly what the second officer was saying. All
he could hear clearly was the howling sound of the wind
and the hollow thunder of water and the panic in Sullivan's voice.

'Calm down,' ordered Robin. 'Just tell me what you can
see.' She kept her voice gentle, and the fact that it was
obviously an effort for her to do so made Nico more
nervous still.

Robin looked at him. 'Nico, I think you're going to
have to take over while I go down there and see for
myself. Sullivan's not making too much sense but it sounds
as though there's something the matter with the bows.'

Eventually, when the shaken Sullivan had assumed his
watch and held the con, after Robin had had an exploratory
look in the last of the dark, Nico at last accompanied his
captain onto the deck. They both went down and stood
side by side between the crouching metal of the split
windlass in the first light of the grey, gusty dawn. The
green deck immediately in front of them was buckled,

then it rose steeply into a disturbing copy of Robin's dream alp, the peak of it pointing upwards. The little flagpole at the very front of the ship seemed to be immediately above their heads. The forecastle head railings were twisted and several uprights had torn out of their footings. The wind howled mournfully through these and buffeted against the flat metal in front of them as the waves thundered in below. Keeping her hand tight on the loop where her personal safety harness hooked over the deck safety lines, Robin crossed to the nearest solid railing and craned over as far as she could. 'I can't see much without going right over,' she shouted. 'I can't see what state it's in at the moment and I can't see whether or not it's getting worse.'

'That's the most important thing,' he answered, dazed by the amount of damage he could see. 'But how are we going to be able to tell? How can we be sure?'

'We're going to have to heave to and turn until the bow is more sheltered. I'll have to go over and take a close look, unless there's someone better qualified.'

'We could get Andrew McTavish to have a look from *Atropos*,' he suggested.

'Yes, we could, but I'll need to have a close look too.'

'You'll certainly have to go over the side to do that. There's no way in from here any longer.' He gestured at the useless inspection covers which, had they been open, would have been little more than makeshift portholes now. 'I'll go down into the number one hold and see what it's like down there.'

'Good.'

They had slowed *Clotho* right down until she was making little more than steerageway, which meant they were effectively being carried back along their course by the current. Invisible below the horizon, Greenland and their hope of safe haven were getting further and further away.

'Well, let's get started,' she said decisively. 'I think it's about time I had a word with Captain Black. Then I'd better call the office in London. Dear God, this is a mess.'

Not a mess, thought Nico. More like a curse.

CHAPTER THIRTEEN

Day Eight

Wednesday, 26 May   09:00

Andrew McTavish stood on the forepeak of *Atropos* and looked at *Clotho*'s bow with absolute horror on his usually open, cheerful face. The sight of his ship in this state drove everything else from his mind and all the nagging worries of the last few watches were swamped under the impact of this new nightmare.

It had taken him a little longer to fix the alternator than he had calculated, but bringing it up to power and phasing it in with its partner had gone smoothly enough. Then he had taken a fresh work crew and gone to work on the fractured pipe. Four hours of careful metal cutting and spot welding had fixed that and he could turn his attention to tidying up the engine room. This was what he had wanted to do right from the beginning, not because he was house proud or because he thought Chief Lethbridge ran a dirty workspace, but because the simple task would allow him to look around for clues.

As he had stated in his message to Robin, he was convinced that the accident could only have been caused by sabotage. It seemed impossible to him that three lines could all have failed like that. They must have been weakened on purpose. And the more he thought about it, the more it seemed an ingenious way of crippling a ship. The cradle containing the spare engine would only have been moved under normal circumstances if the spare engine was required. It would only be required if one of the other engines was damaged or faulty. So the effect of having the spare engine come crashing down onto the heads of engineers with a motor already out of service would be devastating – two dead engines and a fair chance that the third would be damaged in the incident, engineers dead and wounded, as now, and the whole ship crippled.

But he was not a trained investigator and although he had a lively imagination, he did not have the analytical mind of a detective. When he had reported to Captain Black last night that the engine room was spick-and-span and ready to work as smoothly as the alternators whenever it was required, he had been sent down to a tasteless dinner and a spare cabin without a word of thanks. He had spent a restless few hours in shallow sleep, convinced that he had missed some vital clue down there, for he had found no evidence of sabotage at all. A restless sleep from which he had been awoken ten minutes earlier with the news that there was yet more trouble.

Harry Piper came puffing up the deck clutching a walkie-talkie. 'Tightship says Captain Mariner wants you,' he said, handing the machine over.

'Who says?'

'Captain Black. It's what they call him.'

Andrew shook his head in displeasure. But Harry was too senior a man to be corrected over such matters as proper respect. And anyway, in the Scot's experience, captains generally got the respect they deserved.

He brought the walkie-talkie to his lips and pressed the SEND button. 'Captain Mariner, chief engineer here.'

'Andrew, what can you see?'

'Well, it's a hell of a mess, Captain. I'll start with what I can see of the deck, then work my way down towards the waterline.'

While Andrew began to describe what he could make out and his interpretation of how it might have happened, Harry Piper stood beside him at the rail, straining to see what was going on. *Clotho* had released the towing cable from the capstans at her rear and had fed out enough slack to allow the ships to come together almost bow to bow. It had been easy enough to do this because each ship was equipped with a full set of manoeuvring screws as well as a massive main propeller. The new relationship between the vessels gave anyone on *Atropos*'s forepeak a chance to look at the damage. The two engineers were the only men here now, but Piper reckoned there would be more sightseers soon.

He had a clear view of the damage which Andrew was describing, from the buckled underside of the folded back deck section to the twisted mess of corrugated metal beneath it looking like a multicoloured, almost concave cliff from the rust-streaked beak of the forepeak down to the choppy water. And each time a wave slammed up against it, water washed in through the metal, though no holes could be seen at this distance until it poured back out again into the next deep trough. When this happened, it was chilling to see the tears and rents in the buckled metal looking like multiple stab wounds gushing reddish, foaming liquid from the bilge and ballast tanks. Harry watched in sick fascination until he noticed something else

was going on. On this side of *Clotho*'s forepeak, as far up
the slope of metal as possible, two makeshift davits were
being pushed over the damaged rail. As Harry swung
round to look askance at Andrew, the chief pulled the
walkie-talkie away from his mouth. 'The captain's going
over for a closer look,' he said.

'She's mad.'

Andrew's countenance darkened into an old-fashioned
look and he broke the habit of a lifetime. 'You'll not say
anything disrespectful about my captain again, Harry Piper.
Not a word. Ever.'

Harry, who had truly meant no disrespect, had the grace
to look contrite.

Andrew's expression lightened. 'She wants us to continue observing things from here. So I'd like you to present
my compliments to Captain Black and ask him if I can
borrow a pair of binoculars, please.'

Nico was overseeing this himself. He knew he had said
he would check out number one hold, but with Sullivan
on watch, to do so would leave only Rupert Biggs to
ensure Robin's safety. And, what with one thing and
another, that was simply not good enough. Biggs was a
competent young officer under most circumstances, but he
was too breezy and over-confident for this job. Nico was
convinced that one slip, one mistake, one error of judgment, one oversight, no matter how small, would allow
Clotho to kill someone. And he very much did not want
that someone to be Robin. Sam Larkman and Joe Edwards
stood at the securely anchored feet of the metal frame.
Errol held the fall. Nico had triple-checked the block
and tackle and now, with rough familiarity which was
unconsciously near to being patronising, he was tugging

and testing the straps of Robin's harness – and giving her breasts quite a pummelling as he did so.

There was mildly affectionate amusement in her voice when she asked, 'Satisfied, Number One? May I proceed now, please?'

At last he nodded curtly and she turned to the railing. Because of the angle, it was difficult for her to climb and he gave her a hand up. 'Ready, all,' he called automatically as she teetered there for a moment. She thrust out her hands automatically, regaining her balance, and it was as well her walkie-talkie was attached to her wrist by a strap. Then she pulled in her hands to hold the rope like a climber about to abseil down a cliff and glanced down over her shoulder. 'Okay, Errol?' asked Nico. He was uncharacteristically hesitant, not really wanting her to go at all.

'Take the strain, gentlemen,' she ordered crisply and stepped back confidently over the side.

Her disappearance coincided with the jarring impact of the largest wave yet and a squall rushed down from the north-east just behind it. Nico hurled himself to the rail and looked down but she was standing solidly against the metal, engrossed in her task. Soaking, but safe.

The metal before her was slippery with spray but at least the ridges resulting from the damage made it easy for her to move across it. The buckled steel gave her so many hand- and footholds that her task proved easier than she had thought it would be. Easier but far more worrying. Even with the vision of the forepeak deck buckled right up in the air like that, she had still not imagined there could be so much damage down here. It was as though *Clotho* had been in a major collision. The metal of her bows had just collapsed back, cracking and splitting as it did so. How could strengthened steel behave like this? Thankful that she had thought to wear thick work gloves as well as the bright orange survival suit, she wedged her left hand in one of the cracks and swung herself round the corner onto the wall which had once been the cutwater. The walkie-talkie buzzed immediately and she reported in to Nico who had now lost sight of her.

She was effectively hanging halfway down a twenty-foot cliff which rose into the twisted wreckage of an overhang above her and fell in concave confusion to the gushing mess immediately above the waterline little more than five feet below her foul-weather boots. The bow had collapsed straight back, without buckling to one side or the other. That was something. She had suspected this was the case, however, or Nico would have reported trouble maintaining course as uneven damage would have pulled them one way or another quite sharply. They had clearly lost the forward water ballast tank and the ballast within it, hence the ship's head-high disposition in the water, but Robin reckoned that she could correct this by running the mid-deck gantry as far forward as it would go. That would settle *Clotho* back on an even keel before the weather deteriorated any further. But it would also put those parts of her hull immediately behind the damaged area under increased strain. And that could be disastrous. So far, in spite of this damage, the rest of *Clotho* had remained watertight, or she wouldn't still be afloat. Would it be wise to trust the forward wall of number one hold?

Robin put her walkie-talkie to her lips. 'Andrew, can you hear me?'

For the better part of an hour Robin scrambled about on

what was left of the bow section. She all but chopped the toes of her boots off on sharp edges, and the extra thick work gloves were seriously abraded long before she was finished. At last, using the harness more like a safety net than an actual support, she clung precariously to the sharp-edged hand- and footholds and actually climbed down the iron cliff face until she could feel the wash and tug of the wave tops at her heels. It was dirty, dangerous, freezing, depressing work. But at least she could make a full assessment of the detail of the damage while agreeing the big picture with Andrew on the walkie-talkie. The actual cutwater, the point where the two flanks of the bow met at the very front of the ship, seemed to have been welded. There was a crack running inconsistently but discernibly right down the centre of the wreckage. Here obviously the two massive bow plates had met and been attached to each other. But the welded seam was broken and, like the other fractures which had appeared, large and small, it now sucked in and spewed out water with each succeeding wave. And through the crack before her face Robin noticed something on the far side of the cracked weld. Something actually on the inside of the water ballast tank.

Around her waist she had a belt with work tools attached to it. She pulled a torch off this and flashed its bright beam through, but at first it showed her nothing new. A space, all too narrow, and then the solid brown wall of the number one hold. But there was something there, she was certain of it. She put the torch back and unhooked her crowbar. The crack was widest at the top and she wedged the roughly fashioned length of iron in there and jerked it down with all her force. So much force did she use, in fact, that she nearly pulled herself off the front of the ship and had to release the bar and grab another handhold to pull herself back from disaster. As she did so, something rattled against the metal on the inside of the plates before her face, then tumbled, clattering against the wreckage, to land with a tiny splash in the heaving water below. Robin did not see it and had no idea what it was. It sounded to her like something small and light, perhaps with metallic parts. Beyond that, there were no clues. She dismissed it from her mind and pulled the crowbar free.

Without looking at it she put it back against her belt, but the gloves were thick enough to make her fingers clumsy and she failed to attach it properly. As she looked down, another wave heaved the whole ship upwards and her precarious footing slipped again. The crowbar tumbled into the sea at once and not even Andrew McTavish, who was watching the incident as closely as possible through Captain Black's second best binoculars, caught the telltale flash of white from the long smear of Semtex which had got stuck to the end of it when Robin pushed it into the saboteur's makeshift bomb and knocked the clock-timer free of the primary detonator.

'The number one is dry. The forward water ballast tank is gone but the other tanks are secure. If we're careful she'll still get us home,' said Nico.

Robin nodded. 'And *Atropos*?' she asked.

There was a brief silence, underpinned by the blustery rain outside and the hiss of the open walkie-talkie channels. They were on the bridge with Johnny Sullivan in the early part of Biggs's watch and they were having a conference with the men on *Atropos*'s bridge.

'Will you still be able to tow us?' Captain Black's voice was shaking with strain. Even over the airwaves, the fear was audible.

Nico looked at Robin, his eyebrows high in mute query. He had spent the morning, since thankfully pulling her aboard, checking the damage from this side and as far as he was concerned, there was no chance at all that they would be able to tow *Atropos* home. In the Italian's eyes, Black was now the captain of the *Titanic*, and he could rearrange the deckchairs on his own.

Robin leaned forward towards the walkie-talkie. 'Andrew, are you there?'

'Yes, Captain.'

'How well will *Clotho*'s engines run in reverse?'

There was a brief silence as they took that one in. Clearly it was such an unexpected question that it caught them all unawares.

'In reverse?' asked Andrew faintly.

'Yes. How fast? How far? With what power?'

'*Jesu*!' Nico understood. She was going to turn *Clotho* round and run the tow rope to *Atropos* across the wreck of the forecastle head, and then she was going to *reverse* all the way to Greenland. That way the stern of the ship would face the brunt of the water and the weather. It was risky, of course, but infinitely safer than proceeding with *Clotho* facing the normal way round. It made sense. It could work.

He slammed his palm against his thigh and rose, too excited to stay still any longer. His understanding of her thinking brought a multitude of questions teeming into his head. Questions she was going to want answers to before very much longer. Was *Clotho*'s split windlass strong enough? If it wasn't, where else could the rope be attached? If it was, what would be the effect of the tow on the way the front of the ship sat in the water? It was sitting high at the moment and needed to be pulled down in any case. The effect of towing would be to lower it –

the simple weight of the rope, the drag, the effective weight at the far end. But would it lower the damaged bow so much that there would be danger of yet more damage? Impossible to tell. He would have to have a constant watch up there. And it *would* be dangerous. Should they move their people off, all except a skeleton crew? Or should they bring *Atropos*'s crew over here? Which vessel was in the greater danger? HMS *Devil* or HMS *Deep Sea*?

The saboteur watched the work on the bow from her secret eyrie with increasing desperation. It was hardly surprising that her situation, so far from what was planned and spiralling out of control, should have made her feel paranoid. But she was far further away from sanity than even she supposed. She had not been isolated for any great length of time – little more than a week so far – but the stress had been enormous, the danger and the deprivation so real. And she had hardly slept at all. Now they were moving about like ants down there, up to some scheme. All to thwart her and her plans, no doubt. She watched them secretly, a pale, dark-eyed face framed with yellow rat's tails of hair pressed against the glass. She watched them test the windlass and run ropes up to the ruined bow. She watched them send teams of men up the green slope with cutting equipment and hammers to cut a safe channel for something to lie in. She saw them carry the tow rope round and secure it into place and then she felt the engines throb. The angle of the deck changed as the rope tightened and her view of the world swung round until she was no longer looking out over wild water or wild ice, but across towards the gantry of the sister ship, with the tall bridge-house standing behind it as she knew *Clotho*'s stood behind her – as though she were in front of some huge mirror.

Utterly entranced, unaware of what she was doing, she came out of hiding then. *He* was over there somewhere. In the invisible heart of that tremendous, oddly beautiful sight, the great ship framed against the storm clouds and the black water, her partner in adventure waited. And even as she looked, she saw smaller boats begin to ply between the two vessels carrying people from one to the other. Suddenly she couldn't wait any longer. There was nothing to be gained from further hesitation and if she told someone she was aboard now, then she and he would be together all the sooner. She rose to her feet as though in a dream only to realise that she had been curled on the bench seat looking down and was now standing precariously on the seat itself.

The gantry lurched forward at that moment, controlled by the master system on the bridge, to fine-tune the balance of *Clotho*'s angle in the water, and the saboteur went over the back of the seat and smashed her head open on the floor of the cab behind. Had her sleeping bag not been there, she would have died at once.

When the tow began again towards the end of Rupert Biggs's midday watch, there was only a skeleton crew left aboard *Clotho*. This consisted of the captain, the first, second and third deck officers, the chief, the second engineer, and the cadet who had been an insistent volunteer. Last man off apart from these was the chef who had remained until the bitter end, preparing pile after pile of sandwiches, as well as soup and coffee which only needed microwaving to heat. Andrew McTavish and Harry Piper had come back across on one of the boats transferring everyone else the other way because, as Andrew had put it, 'No one other than me and my men will look after my propulsion system running backwards, by God.'

There was no need for any GP seamen as there was really no more deck work to be done and the helm would be best controlled by laying in a direct course for the southern tip of Greenland and running it in reverse on the automatic pilot. Equally, as everyone aboard proposed to camp in the wheelhouse and its immediate environs, there was no need for any of the stewards to stay to look after them. But it proved impossible to get Sam Larkman to desert his ship. And where Sam went, Joe and Errol followed. Robin was prepared to be indulgent. Three more first-rate men were a heartening buttress against the unexpected.

To begin with, the tow went very well. It was strange to be on the bridge looking backwards through the clear-view, seeing *Atropos* following doggedly out of the darkening afternoon, her lights coming into brighter focus as the day began to die. It was an odd sensation to be studying the reverse angles of the collision alarm radar to see what dangers lay behind their slowly reversing ship. Robin went outside and stood at the back of the bridge wing, wrapped warmly and dryly against the gathering north-easter, looking over the stern towards the invisible cliffs and fjords of what has been called the world's largest island coming towards them at five knots once more.

As night fell, the threatened storm arrived and the conditions of the tow deteriorated dangerously. In the engine room, Andrew and Harry kept a careful watch on the revolutions of the propeller as it rose and fell increasingly sharply through wildly varying water pressures and even began to threaten to tear itself out of the sea altogether.

The steepening waves put more and more strain on the rope and on the two windlasses securing it between the ships. One moment both hulls would be pointing down together into the same trough as *Clotho* climbed carefully down the back of one wave while *Atropos* was on the rushing face of the next. Then they would be thrown apart, separated by the crest of the same wave. Luckily the waves were not yet big enough to throw a destructive strain on the all too fragile arrangement, but the night was young and the worst of the weather was yet to come.

Ann Cable and Henri LeFever sat facing each other over a table in the officers' dining room. It was late and under normal circumstances *Atropos*'s chef would have closed up shop, black eye or no black eye. But the presence of *Clotho*'s complement, and her galley staff and stewards, had put all of *Atropos*'s men on their mettle and so there was food. Good food, too. Both Ann and Henri were vegetarians and so far this voyage they had subsisted in mutually supportive misery on salads which would hardly have been suited to the arctic conditions even had they been fresh. Tonight, however, they were in seventh heaven, despite the worsening weather conditions. The galley had produced a curry. Onion bahjees and vegetable samosas were crowded together on plates encrusted with jewels of chutney and pickle. Piles of naan and stuffed parathas sat fragrantly steaming beside a crazy tower of golden poppadoms surrounded by more condiments compounded of tomatoes, coconuts, chillies, cucumbers and yogurt.

A vegetable vindaloo was in prospect, to be served on pilau rice flavoured with coriander, cardamons, bay and cinnamon bark, and accompanied by a saag of spinach decorated with toasted almonds, mushroom and sweet pepper bahjees and a thick dahl of red lentils. Although they both avoided meat of all kinds, neither was particularly self-sacrificing in the matter of the grape or the grain, and they accompanied this feast, as was only right and proper, with glasses of Carlsberg's golden Elephant beer so cold that only its high alcohol content kept it from freezing.

Their conversation wandered, as it often did, over the concerns which were closest to their hearts: conservation and animal welfare. It had come as a pleasant surprise to her to discover that the scientist shared so many of her attitudes of mind. They had both donated much time and money to protect the world's dwindling populations of various endangered species. But, given that they were afloat in one of the great traditional hunting grounds, it was perhaps inevitable that their discussion should turn most urgently on the protection of whales. She explained how much of her income from *The Leper Ship* was being given to Greenpeace and how she was planning a book called *The Whaling Ship* as soon as she had finished writing up her current work, *The Sister Ships*: the unexpectedly exciting tale of this voyage so far.

Henri had never struck her as a boastful man but now he smiled and a fleeting look of superiority came and went across his face. He folded a delicate wing of paratha and dipped it in dali ratha. All through the main course, he told her of a long fight he had pursued across the southern ocean as a crewman on an anti-whaling vessel chasing a Russian factory ship and her fleet of lethal whalers. It was a tale guaranteed to appeal to her, full of hair's-breadth escapes and dangerous encounters. They had harried the Russian fleet, forcing themselves between the harpoons and the humpbacks. When they failed to spoil the aim or arrived too late to interfere, they filmed what was going on, and she remembered having seen the films that he'd shot. He rolled back his sleeve to show her the scar left by a harpoon which had come too close. 'But if you really want to see something impressive,' he joked, 'come to my cabin later and I'll show you what I lost to the frostbite.'

And so, in fact, she did. It was the atmosphere, the food, the story and the magnetism of the man, combined with the worm of jealousy sown in her trusting breast by Jamie Curtis's poisonous words about her Nico and his blonde-haired grey-eyed captain: *mistress and mate*. Henri had a bottle of bourbon in his cabin and he poured them both a glass. They sat on armchairs about a metre apart and watched each other speculatively. 'So, what's this about frostbite?' she asked, in a tense attempt at levity.

Henri gave a bark of laughter and slipped off his left boot and sock. The little toe was missing its top joint. 'Lost to the cause,' he said. 'I'm a Goddamned hero.'

It was the first time she had heard him swear. And it suddenly occurred to her that she did not really know this man all that well. But when she looked up at him, his face was so full of wry, self-deprecating amusement that her thoughts turned again to how attractive he was.

'I've never met anyone who would die to save the whales before,' she said.

'Die?' he laughed. 'Hell, I'd kill to save the whales.'

When he stood, the powerful fluidity of the movement seemed to make him seem even taller. Still with one shoe off, he took a step and stooped. Rock solid, even on the pitching deck, he stood above her, silently daring her to tell him to stop. When she remained silent, he suddenly swooped. As though she were a child, he lifted her, and the amusement remained in the laugh lines at the corners

of his eyes as he held her, feet dangling, her lips level
with his. The palms of his hands cradled her ribs, fingers
across her shoulder bones reaching towards her spine. His
thumbs rose towards her collar bones and the heels of his
hands closed gently into the softness of her breasts. She
could feel her heart beating importunately against the
steady pulses in his wrists. It was not only his grip which
made it so difficult for her to breathe. He smelt of Bourbon
and coriander and there was a little blue devil in the back
of his eyes which laughed and danced and told her this
would be fun.

But then there was something more within those merry
depths and the lines on his handsome face were no longer
a smile but a frown. As easily as he had swept her up, he
put her down. 'No,' he said. 'This isn't right.'

She said nothing. Truth to tell, she felt cheapened by
his assumption of moral authority. Who was he to tell her
what was right or not?

'Look,' he said quietly, revealing a hesitant side to himself she hadn't seen before. 'I don't know about you, but
I think this has got a lot to do with being far away from
the folk we really love and drinking a little too much beer.
I think it would be just dandy to go to bed with a woman
like you ... No, hell, to go to bed with *you*, Ann, but it
wouldn't be right for me. I'm in a relationship right now,
you see, and it's the best thing that ever happened to me.
Does that sound corny? Yes, I guess it does. But it's true.'

'She'd never know,' temporised Ann, thinking – distantly
– of Nico, but carried away with desire.

'I guess not, but *I'd* know. Don't get me wrong, though.
This isn't some kind of nineties man angst thing with me
– Gee, but it's hard to be sensitive if you've got balls, if
you see what I mean. No. It's just that I'm in love. Totally.

Completely. Utterly. Madly. And not with you. And no matter how you look at it, that has to carry some weight.'

She stood there, looking up into his reasonable, gentle, concerned, sensitive face and she thought what he had said was just about the sexiest thing she had ever heard. She really hoped Nico would have the strength to say something similar in the same circumstances. In the meantime, there was a little devil burning in her loins which said with irresistible force that any man this good deserved every sexual pleasure she could possibly afford him.

At first she thought the crashing coming from the cabin next door was a result of the storm. But it went on after the tossing waves of the squall had stopped. Long enough to bring a frown between those delicately curved eyebrows of his.

'That's the Wide Boy's cabin,' he said, more to himself than to her. 'There shouldn't be anyone in there.'

'Henri . . .' She sounded, in her own ears, as though she had just run a marathon.

Disregarding her entirely, he opened the door of his cabin. She had no choice but to follow when he went out.

Together they stole out into the corridor and along to the next door, which was standing wide as though it had been torn open with desperate force. The lights were on, so this was hardly some secret burglary. Nevertheless, they went in side by side as though expecting something nefarious to be going on. The cabin was an utter wreck. Hardly anything remained whole. The bed was strewn over the floor and the contents of Reynolds' wardrobe and clothing drawers lay on top of it. As they entered, the late third officer's bedside cabinet joined the mess, torn bodily off the wall. A washbag spilled out of it, only to be caught up at once by white, shaking hands.

'It's in here, it has to be,' said Captain Black, though it was by no means clear who he was talking to. The wash-bag burst open, shaving equipment falling hither and yon. 'He promised,' screamed the captain in scarcely sane frustration. 'He swore.'

He swung round to face them, the movement of his head spraying spittle from his thin white lips into Ann's astonished face. 'Enough for the whole voyage. *Enough to keep me going! HE SWORE*!'

And on the last word he flung himself at Henri like a wild man. The big scientist, more by instinct than design, drove his fist into his assailant's face. There was a sharp *crack* and the captain flew back into a heap on top of Reynolds' possessions. The force of the blow rolled him backwards to smack his right temple against the low side of the bunk. He rebounded forward and then lay there, still as death. With the welt across his forehead rapidly darkening and blood seeping from the sag of his jaw, he would not have made a pretty picture even had he been dressed as punctiliously as usual. But, in a crumpled shirt, half buttoned, with the sleeves rolled to expose pale, pocked arms, and crumpled uniform trousers which had all too obviously been slept in, the corpse-like captain looked almost as untidy as the dead drug dealer's things.

A voice from the doorway screamed, '*Captain*! What'll we do? Oh sweet Jesus, what'll we do?'

The erstwhile would-be lovers swung round to see the terrified, indecisive face of Yasser Timmins, first officer and acting master of the good ship *Atropos*, hovering in the doorway. 'What the fuck are we going to do now?' he asked again.

'You'll have to go across, Captain,' said Nico quietly.

'There's nothing else for it. Two full crews, but no competent deck officers left. You're the only person who can sort it out.'

'I think you're right,' said Robin. 'All of our people are aboard her. I can't risk anything going wrong.'

'Anything *else* going wrong,' amended Nico.

She gave a bark of laughter at his unregenerate superstition and it never entered her mind that only a fortnight ago she, too, had been expecting the worst in every situation she faced. Now that the danger was so massive and so immediate, she was back to her old self: cool and confident. 'No sense hanging about. The weather's getting worse. I won't be able to go soon.'

'It'll have to be the lifeboat.'

'I know. And I'll have to take the three musketeers, I'm afraid. There's no way I can do it on my own.'

'You're welcome to them. They'd only make me feel inadequate. I'll be all right with Sullivan, Biggs and Jamie, if he'll stay. And the engineers, of course.'

'Okay. Look on the bright side – there'll be twice as many sandwiches for you.'

'Be still, my beating heart.'

It took her scant minutes to prepare. She had no intention of wasting time by packing a bag. She would take what she was wearing and what would fit in her pockets. Sam, Joe and Errol took an equally unsentimental view of their possessions. The increasing savagery of the squall gusts focused their minds wonderfully. They took the forward starboard lifeboat, tethered on a long line. Once it was in the water and released from its falls, Rupert Biggs and Jamie Curtis walked down the deck, holding the line, until they could pay it out from the wreck of the forecastle by the creaking, straining windlass and let the bobbing boat ride back through the darkness towards *Atropos*.

While all this was going on, Nico was in contact with the crippled ship, alerting them that the lifeboat was on its way. Hogg and Henri LeFever prepared to get the lifeboat aboard as soon as it came alongside, and there were willing hands in plenty when *Clotho*'s crew heard who was aboard.

The exchange was made safely and Robin was on *Atropos*'s bridge long before the full fury of the north-westerly struck.

'There were some really strange noises down there, though,' persisted Jamie.

Nico nodded. 'Rupert, what do you think? Worth checking?'

Biggs shrugged. 'What could we do?'

'Warn the captain, of course.'

A squall raved against the bridge windows. Biggs crossed to his satellite weather equipment and pressed a button. A weather map printed itself out and rolled onto the desk. It was a diagram based on what the weather satellite immediately above them could see. He held the black and white paper up for Nico to see.

Nico took it from him. 'Another nasty little depression whipping through. If it wedges against that Greenland high pressure ridge like the last one, it'll just get worse and worse. But if it takes the southern track, it'll be here today, and gone tomorrow. In any case, if we're going to have a look at the bow and the cable, then now is the best time to do it.' He consulted the paper for a second or two more. 'Well, not so much the best as the least worst. It's going to get rougher very soon indeed. And while you're

down there,' he added innocently, 'you might as well check
in the number one hold.'

'This is all your fault, you little moron,' grumbled Biggs
all the way along the pitching, soaking deck.

'But there *is* a strange noise.'

'Strange noise. Look at you, been at sea for ten minutes
and you know it all already.'

'Look, Rupert, do you want me to go down into the
hold instead?'

'Don't be an idiot. And it's Lieutenant Biggs to you.
Or Number Three.'

'But if Niccolo is acting captain now, doesn't that make
you Number Two?'

'Yes, you're right. I suppose it does. Number
Two.'

'When I was a kid,' said Jamie, apparently apropos of
nothing, 'my parents had this kind of code so I could tell
them if I needed to use the bathroom. When we were in
public, you know? Number One was code for pee.' He
slowed and unhitched his safety clip, to put himself beyond
Biggs's reach. 'And Number Two was crap!' he yelled at
the top of his voice.

Biggs's reaction was muted. The wind was almost strong
enough to knock them both off their feet out here and the
blustery rain was making the deck slippery. Biggs was no
fool; this was not the time or place to give the young
cadet the thumping he deserved. 'Clip back on,' he barked,
and Jamie was wise enough to obey. Then the two of them
stood side by side in the stormy darkness and listened.
'Damned if you weren't right,' said Biggs at last. 'I'll be
buggered if that isn't a funny sound.' He put his walkie-

talkie to his lips. 'Can we have some light down here, please, Number One?'

Clotho swooped and staggered. Even this way round, the bow still took a powerful thumping from the sea. The lights came on and dazzled them. So bright were they that *Atropos* was lit by them, though they cast no illumination on the sky or sea. They checked the windlass and the buckled bow. They checked the forward radio mast which stood dangerously close to the damaged area. But there was nothing to be seen. 'Right,' said Biggs at last. 'I'll go down into the hold for a look-see. Give me a hand with the hatch, would you?'

They didn't open it all the way, just wide enough for Biggs to ascertain that Nico had switched on the hold lights and to scramble onto the first rungs of the ladder down the forward wall. Then, pausing only to clip his harness to the safety rail beside it, he was gone. Jamie could still hear that strange sound, a kind of extra wheezing creak, following every buffeting wave. It was coming from forward of the hatch cover. But when he got to the windlass, he found it was coming from further forward still. A wheezing groan with a low, vaguely familiar bass humming. But it wasn't a metallic sound at all, although there was nothing up there except metal.

Except for the tow rope. *Of course*. It was the tow rope. He swung round, ready to dash back to warn Biggs that there was something the matter with the tow rope.

But there was a girl standing close behind him. The same girl.

'Hello,' she said.

'What . . . Who are you?' he gasped, stunned by her presence, and by her proximity.

'I am a stowaway,' she said. 'Take me to your captain, please.'

'What?'

'I said, I am a stowaway—'

'Biggs! BIGGS!' He charged forward, bellowing at the top of his voice, shoving her roughly out of his way.

This was not at all the reaction she was expecting and it triggered a response in her which was born of the paranoia that had gripped her even before she concussed herself.

Jamie felt his left hand being taken in an almost gentle grip, and agony lanced up his arm. He froze, up on his toes, with his arm straight, elbow up, hand twisted to point at the sky. The wind paused and he heard the strange whispering sound her big camping knife made as its carbon steel blade hissed out of its plastic sheath. The position of his arm widely separated the ribs on the left side of his chest so that when she punched the eight-inch blade into his side, it cut through his lung and sliced his heart in half. The shock of it made his dead muscles convulse as though he was winded and his ribs closed down on the blade which had killed them.

She tugged at the handle twice, to no avail, and when she let him fall, he tumbled forward into the hold with the knife still wedged in his chest.

Biggs was halfway up the ladder on the very edge of panic when Jamie's body collected him and plunged the pair of them down into the five feet of restless water which should not have been there at all. Biggs was lucky. The way he fell, with Jamie somehow draped across his back, caused his head to hit the rungs with brutal force, so that he too was dead before he hit the water.

The girl stood at the top of the hatch, looking down at

the two dead men, stunned by what she had done. Instinctively, she looked around the deck, but even in the pitiless brightness, there was no one to see what she had done. Good, she thought. She still had a chance, then. Even so, there were tears on her ice-pale cheeks which did not have their origin in the terrible pain in her head.

But then the world went mad around her and she found she had no chance after all. She was never to understand the sequence of events, but it was simple enough, and all but inevitable in the circumstances. A big wave punched at last through the wall of number one hold and the weight of the water flooding in jerked *Clotho*'s head downwards with terrible force. That massive downward motion caused the tow rope to part. About fifteen feet out from *Clotho*'s forepeak there was a weakness in the rope which had caused the sound Jamie had heard, and here the line parted. Much of it whipped back to writhe uselessly like a dying serpent down into the sea by *Atropos*. The rest of it chopped backwards with all the force of a helicopter blade to cut across the murderess's slim hips. In an instant even shorter than the blink of an eye that had dispatched Jamie, she was broken and destroyed.

It smashed her spine and splintered her pelvis. It obliterated her womb and what that womb had carried. It ruptured her kidneys and her liver and the shock of it stopped her heart even before she landed in the dark sea a hundred yards away.

The last thing she was aware of was a sudden resurgence of the agony in her head and she never knew that what she felt was her left heel hitting the wound in the back of her skull as her broken body folded neatly in half.

CHAPTER FOURTEEN

Day Nine

Thursday, 27 May   00:00

'She's gone!' screamed Yasser Timmins. 'Oh, sweet Jesus.'

Robin stood, rigidly, willing her eyes to make out more details on *Clotho* as the sister ship whirled away. As chance would have it, she had been looking through Captain Black's best binoculars at *Clotho*'s suddenly illuminated forepeak when the tow line parted. Because of the tilt of the ruined forecastle forward of the windlass, she had been unable to make out whether there had been anyone on the deck, but she rather feared there might have been. Why else would the deck lights have been on?

During the last thirty seconds she had seen the flat front of her command suddenly collapse. Right at the foot of the metal cliff, a cave had appeared with startling suddenness, and she had seen a big sea foam in through it, obviously flooding number one hold. She had seen the whole bow snatched downward and the foredeck plunge under with terrifying rapidity. She had seen the thick black line of the tow itself burst apart and come writhing back towards her.

She was holding the binoculars with one hand and her walkie-talkie with the other. Almost without thinking she was speaking into it. 'Nico! Nico, can you hear me?'

But there was no reply. She wouldn't have heard much over Timmin's horrified exclamations in any case.

'Be quiet please, Mr Timmins,' she snapped, and there was silence on the bridge.

Clotho's deck, as far as the repositioned gantry, was now under the raging water.

And worse was happening. It was like a nightmare over which she had no control at all. As the white horses foamed around the feet of the gantry halfway back along *Clotho*'s deck, suddenly it became all too apparent that the gantry itself was giving in to the terrible forces which surrounded it. The squat, powerful square of the mobile crane tipped crazily backwards as its footings tore loose. Then a violent wrench of the waves turned *Clotho* so that she tossed the whole contraption overboard.

Timmins was quiet, but Robin heard someone on the bridge stifle a sob. It was Henri LeFever, with the spare glasses. He had borrowed them from Ann. She was crying silently. All at once Robin regretted the advanced technology within the binoculars which allowed them, all too clearly, to see the death of their sister.

'Nico,' she persisted. 'Come in, Nico.' But Nico probably had things to do at the moment which did not include taking telephone calls. The problem was that they were rapidly moving out of walkie-talkie range. Already the distance between the ships was widening as *Clotho* leaped forward almost bodily, free of her sister's weight, and *Atropos*, the way going off her rapidly, began to swing round beam on to the wind.

At last a squall came between them and the sinking

ship plunged into darkness. One moment she was there, bright and solid for all that the waves were breaking over the tracks which had guided the spread feet of the gantry and the foam was up and beating against the bridgehouse itself. There was one sad, hopeless, haunting gleam as the searchlight on the radio mast shone from underneath a wave, then everything went dark. Where there had been the pallor of her white-painted bridgehouse, now there was only a winding sheet of driving rain.

Robin turned away, lowering the binoculars and letting the walkie-talkie drop to arm's length by her thigh. There was nothing more to see and any contact now would have to be made by radio.

Or by a spiritual medium, she thought grimly.

But it was across to the door into the radio shack she went. 'Any contact?' she asked the radio officer.

Numbly he shook his head. 'Her frequency just went dead,' he said.

She turned round and leaned her shoulders against the door jamb. She took a deep breath, filling her lungs until her ribs hurt. Suddenly she felt very lost and lonely and not very sure of herself. She remembered Nico's faith in her when they were discussing whether she should come across to *Atropos*: 'You're the only one who can sort it out,' he had said. Well, perhaps. But she had never really thought that she would have to sort it out on her own with her most trusted officers swept away and in all probability dead. But when she looked across the bridge at Timmins and thought of the drug-addicted captain lost in his own private hell below, she knew that she had no option but to try. She let the deep breath out slowly and then crossed to the radar station.

It never once occurred to her that she could get on the

radio and ask Richard in London what he thought she
should do. Strangely, the radar station smelt of vomit. Or
was it the enormously overweight young man sitting beside
the bright displays who smelt? 'Have you got her echo?'
she asked.

A plump finger pointed to a bright spark on the green
disk. It was surprisingly far away.

'It's set at five miles?'

The crewcut head nodded, making the rolls of fat at the
back of his neck tremble. She stood behind him, looking
down, watching the spark get fainter and further away.

It was tempting just to stand there and let hopelessness
wash over her. But that is not what captains are supposed
to do. Better get things organised, she thought. Automatically her eyes went to the ship's chronometer just above
the clearview window. The time was just after midnight.

'Who holds the midnight watch?' she asked. She hadn't
been aboard long enough to find out the ship's routines.

'Reynolds,' answered Timmins, 'but he's dead.'

The storm wind thundered down from the north-west
and buffeted against *Atropos*'s port side like a tidal wave.
She heeled and swooped, corkscrewing. The clinometer on
the wheelhouse wall swung dangerously through the
degrees. Twenty, thirty, thirty-five . . .

Clotho would have rolled right over at sixty degrees.
But *Atropos* was fully laden. She might make sixty-five,
if her cargo didn't shift. Still, if the wind could roll her
to nearly forty, they'd better get a sea anchor out before
the big seas joined in and piled up against her windward
side to complete the roll.

Before she whirled into action, something made Robin
pause and think. They had a rudimentary sea anchor out
already and that was one of the reasons *Atropos* was

swinging round so quickly. The tow cable was dragging from her forecastle, for nearly a hundred yards out into the sea. With her all-aft design, the long-hulled ship would ride forecastle on to the wind anyway. The big bridgehouse would act as a sail and it would take the lead, towing the long weather deck behind it. And the tow rope dragging out from the forecastle would only make this arrangement more stable.

She shook her head and almost laughed. She was a team player, captain or not, and was used to discussing things. It was a conscious decision which she made early in her career as a captain. She saw herself as being impulsive to a fault and, not to put too fine a point on it, overbearing. It was natural for her to lead from the front and to charge into things without consulting anyone. This was a management style she deplored in others, for it gave juniors no room to grow by experience or discussion and it led to alienation between captain and crew. So, in all ships she commanded, there were full and detailed discussions before major decisions were taken. It was the way she had done things for many years now. Indeed, it seemed strange to her to be taking decisions at lightning speed without discussing them with anyone else on the bridge. This fact had undermined her self-confidence a little. The afterthought about riding backwards was the sort of comment she was used to getting from Nico or Andrew McTavish. It was heartening to know she could still work things out quickly for herself.

What needed to be done next was to get all of the tow rope over the side and hope *Atropos* swung round quickly. She would take a team of men and do that herself. She didn't like the look of Timmins, and his reactions to the two crises he had faced recently made her think that she would be safer to leave him where he would feel least stressed.

There was a chance of a big sea rolling *Atropos* over before the long hull swung right round, however, so there was one more task to be done before she went out onto the deck. 'Mr Timmins,' she said quietly. 'I'm going to call everyone to emergency stations, but I do not expect anything will go wrong. Then I'm going to take a team of men out onto the main deck. How much tow rope did you take aboard?'

He was silent for a moment and she thought she was going to have to repeat everything when he answered, 'About five hundred metres,' and she realised he had just been following everything she had said very slowly indeed.

'Very good. I'm going down to the windlass and I'm going to put it all over the bow to act as a sea anchor. Do you understand?'

'The captain ... Captain Black ... put the sea anchor over the stern when the propeller went.'

'I know, but this will be better.'

He fired up a little at that, clearly not liking the suggestion that she was better than Captain Black. But he said nothing.

'I want you to stay on watch until I get back. I don't want you to do anything. Mr Hogg will warn me if anything comes up on the radar and Sparks will alert me of any incoming radio traffic. Is that clear?'

'Yes, miss.'

'*Captain*.'

'Yes, Captain.'

'Good.' She crossed to the console and hit two buttons on it. These triggered the ship's alarm and opened the tannoy.

'Your attention, please,' boomed her voice as the last

echoes of the emergency alarm faded. 'This is the captain speaking. As a precaution only, I repeat, *a precaution only*, I would like you all to assemble at your emergency stations until I dismiss you. Our tow line with *Clotho* has parted and we are turning into the wind. Do not go outside, but put on your life jackets and be prepared to abandon ship if she begins to roll.'

She lifted her finger off the Open Channel button and snapped, 'Not you, Mr Timmins!' She waited until he had put his life jacket back under the chart table, then she said quietly, 'Ann, take Henri to his station, please.' The big scientific officer seemed more affected than anyone by the situation. Ann nodded, and crossed to the dazed man. Robin pressed the broadcast button again and added, 'Larkman, Edwards and Jones, meet me at the starboard exit onto the weather deck, dressed for work outside. That is all, thank you.'

She checked all the emergency stations quickly on her way down. She did not want panic aboard and she was concerned that her precaution would cause confusion and friction among the two crews aboard and unnecessary distress to the sick and wounded who would have to be moved. But there was surprisingly little to concern her. The movement to the stations was orderly for the most part. The badinage seemed goodnatured. Captain Black was still comatose, as were Chief Lethbridge and his second engineer, Don Taylor. But Ann Cable was pale with worry. She had seen at once the implication of the parted tow line and perhaps the toppled gantry. 'Is Nico all right?' she asked.

'I expect so. At least he's got an engine that works. You worry about us.' She smiled to give her grim words some lightness and turned away.

Ann stood at her emergency station, with Henri silently

at her side, and watched Robin bustle off to try to save
them all. The feverish action which had followed the parting of the line had kept the full impact of the loss of
Clotho distant in the reporter's mind. Even her question
to Robin about Nico had been delivered in only a partial
realisation of what they were discussing. But the idleness
now, waiting either to abandon ship or to be dismissed,
allowed the scene to play over and over in her memory
until the impact finally came in full. Henri was leaning
back against the white-painted metal of the wall like a
massive statue and she sagged into the angle made by his
side and the cold, ringing iron. The whole bridge-house
shook as the wind beat against it like a hammer on a gong.

Clotho had just vanished. Snuffed out like a candle in
the wind. How could a vessel so large, so substantial,
simply have disappeared like that? There had been something almost supernatural about it, as though she had been
taken by an alien force – or a demonic one. Nico would
have no doubts on that score: Mala Fortuna. Ill fortune
was his particular demon, always waiting just behind his
shoulder to snatch away anything important to him. She
had tried often enough to tease him out of his Neapolitan
superstition, but she knew she was fighting a losing battle.
And now it seemed Nico had been right all along. It
looked as though bad luck had snatched away everything
this time; *Clotho*, the crew, the man himself.

Nico. His face seemed to swim before her eyes, something about the apparition bringing the horrific suspicion
that he must have drowned already. She knew more
about that particular fate than most. Richard had described
in detail to her his own experience of being trapped aboard
Napoli as she plunged deep into the black depths of the
Western Ocean. She knew all too well what would be

happening to Nico if he was going down with *Clotho*. The last of the precious air would be rushing through rooms and corridors in strange submarine gales as the water boiled into the bridge-house. There would be a wild scramble to escape from the sinking coffin. But how could anyone push out through doorways against tons of green water flooding in? To get out of a certain death trap into the near certainty of death in the freezing water. Even if he got out, even if he avoided being sucked down, he would survive for mere moments unless there was a lifeboat nearby. And even if there was a lifeboat close at hand, how long could it hope to survive in the grip of a storm which had squashed a ship like *Clotho* as though it were a waterfly on a pond?

He was dead.

The certainty hit her like a vicious blow in the belly. Low in the belly, deep within her, just where he could ignite the most delicious fire with one of his tiny smiles, with the merest fleeting twinkle of his wise brown eyes. She sagged further against Henri's rock-like flank. The wind thundered against the exterior of the metal wall again, but she noticed nothing of it.

How could she have doubted Nico? How could she have given any credence to what the young cadet had said? How could she have thought for an instant that Robin would be unfaithful to Richard? But why would the boy have lied? Was there any proof one way or the other? Her mind, shying away from the contemplation of the near certainty of Nico's death began to side-track itself busily into working out whether there was any evidence at all of a relationship between her lover and her closest friend.

Almost an hour later, in spite of having been dismissed back to her quarters, in spite of the fact that Henri was

sitting opposite her, still statue-like beyond a pair of fra-
grantly-steaming coffee mugs, she was still trying to
remember precisely how Robin had reacted to the loss of
Clotho, when all the lights went out.

The sea anchor was out, the turn completed and the crew
dismissed back to bed within the hour and Robin returned
to the bridge, soaking and frozen but much more at ease.
Timmins was sitting in the watchkeeper's chair, little more
wide awake than Captain Black, who was catatonic in
Reynold's cabin below. Hogg was still sitting like a buddha
at the radar station. She went to the radio shack first to
talk to Harry Stone, but there was still no news from
Clotho – or from anywhere else, really. Certainly nothing
specifically for them, just general warnings about weather
and ice. And still no sign of any other shipping nearby
either. 'I haven't sent a Mayday,' said Harry. 'Should I
send one now?'

'Not yet. What's the use? Who is there to come in
after us?'

He gave a depressed laugh. 'No one. There hasn't been
anyone except us in the Labrador Sea for a week. And
we're only here because the captain's insane.' He caught
his breath, realising what he had said. 'Our *old* captain.'

'I wouldn't be too sure about your new captain either,'
she said, and crossed to Hogg.

'Anything showing, Mr Hogg?' she asked quietly.

The buddha head shook, the fat neck trembled. The
five-mile-radius radar screen was blank.

'Go to ten.'

The ten-mile radius was blank too and Robin shivered,
feeling as though freezing water was trickling down her
spine. The vital emerald spark of *Clotho* should have been

registering somewhere on the green circle in front of the silent pair. But nothing registered except an almost white line seven miles to the south, stretching from side to side of the screen.

'Give me the big picture.' Her voice was gravelly with strain.

The display went fuzzy and then re-formed. There was still no bright green contact. The pale line of ice to the south persisted. To the north of them, however, little more than ten miles away, the second area of paleness reminded them that they were still between one great area of ice and another. On the radar display, the two pallid areas looked disturbingly like a pair of jaws closing in on them.

This picture was the last thing Robin saw before the alternator failed again and all the lights went out.

Jesus Christ, this is all we need! she thought fiercely, but she said nothing and stood there without moving, breathing through her shock-widened mouth, trying to control her panic and waiting for the emergency power to come on as Captain Black had told her it had done the last time this had happened.

But this time the emergency power did not come on.

CHAPTER FIFTEEN

Day Nine

Thursday, 27 May   10:00

Magdalena DaSilva had not known fear since childhood, but her nervousness now bordered upon it. She looked down at the pile of papers on the lectern before her and ran through the summary of the pleadings in her mind. Brian Chambers and Harcourt Gibbons had prepared a full but simple defence to the charge that Richard Mariner as a representative of Heritage Mariner had wilfully caused the loss of the motor vessel *Napoli*, the property of CZP, valued at a certain sum of money, and Richard Mariner and Heritage Mariner stood liable to pay that sum.

But there was more going on here than this simple case. She had known that intuitively even before the fax from New York had revealed Disposoco's plan for further, massive suits against Richard in America. She felt like the hero of a childhood story who had slain a monster after a terrible battle only to discover that it was a baby monster and its mother was on the way, looking for revenge.

CZP's registered offices were in Cayman, Zurich and Palermo; the initials of the places were the company's name. Disposoco, so closely linked with the shipping company, had offices in Rome and Palermo. Palermo was in Sicily, and Sicily was, by reputation at least, the Mafia's headquarters. Could Richard have unwittingly crossed swords with organised crime?

Unbidden, a line or two from an old song came into her head: 'Foul infidel, know you have trod on the toe of Abdul the Bul-Bul Amir.'

Whose toes were they really treading on here in court thirteen of the Royal Courts of Justice, London?

The clerk of the court called her back to the present by asking the court to stand up, and the judge swept in, just as he had done last Monday. When he bowed to the assembled court, his grey face was reflected coldly in the silver paddle lying across his bench to signal that this was a case of maritime jurisdiction.

They sat, and there was silence. Then, with a discreet cough, Clive Standing rose to open the case for the plaintiff and Maggie tried to forget her worries as she began the next, and most crucial, stage of her job. It most resembled a duel, because of the elaborate ritual which surrounded each thrust and counter-thrust. Normally, she gained enormous satisfaction from the interplay of truth and partiality which was the backbone of adversarial law, but her earlier fears could not be so easily dismissed. If this was a duel, it was like the duel at the end of *Hamlet*: at least one of the swords was poisoned.

'My lord, the case before us is at once simple and complex,' Standing began. 'It is simple because, in the final analysis, it turns upon the actions of several terrified people, lost in the grip of panic, who felt that they were confronted by circumstances wherein it was better to destroy their ship, with all the criminal responsibility which that terrible act implies, than to try and take her and her cargo to her agreed port of destination. The defendant will explain that the nature and state of that cargo left them no other reasonable course. His case will suggest that in actual fact an act of almost divine providence made the ship go down because the hull burst open spontaneously before they had, in fact, carried out their criminal design.

'We will prove to Your Lordship's full satisfaction that the cargo was properly packed and carefully loaded – though under difficult circumstances, it is agreed. We will show that this cargo was carefully protected throughout the voyage and regularly checked by experts placed aboard for the purpose and found to be safe. We will finally prove that, in spite of these facts, at the prompting of Richard Mariner, aboard as a representative of Heritage Mariner, a company of which he is a director, and by whom, in fact, the then captain was employed, the ship was wilfully scuttled off the east coast of America. The defendant does not dispute that he was involved with the placing of explosive charges in the bow and at the stern of the vessel, nor that he placed these charges with the intention of sinking the ship. We will leave Your Lordship in no doubt whatsoever that it was the exploding of these charges that caused an otherwise perfectly seaworthy vessel to sink, incidentally with the loss of at least two lives, if such a thing can ever be incidental.

'Now, I said at the beginning that this submission is at once simple and complex. The simplicity, as I have already intimated, lies in the act of sabotage itself. The complexity lies in the background to the situation. The cargo, technically the possession of the Italian company Disposoco, was caught up out of the Libyan desert from under the

guns of the local people and of the PLO. It was loaded
aboard in the most extreme circumstances, and yet we
have submission that it was properly and carefully loaded,
even though the captain, Enrico Fittipaldi, was actually
lying dead at the time, slain by these selfsame guns. He
was later to be replaced by Captain John Higgins, an
employee of Heritage Mariner, through their subsidiary
company Crewfinders . . .'

Throughout the morning, the case unravelled. Unusually,
Standing did not put the plaintiff, Signor Verdi of CZP,
on the stand first. Instead he began with the lugubrious
Signor Nero of Disposoco. Taking the story in chronologi-
cal order, the tall, pale, dark-eyed Italian explained how
his company had purchased land in the Lebanese desert
where they hoped to dispose of the waste which was their
stock in trade, but how they had been forced to remove
the waste, under threat of death from the Palestinian Liberation Organisation who had agreed to help the local Lebanese people. He described the care with which the waste
had been moved and loaded on *Napoli*. He listed the
names of scientific experts employed by Disposoco to
oversee the process of removal, loading and transportation.

Maggie, her silky manner concealing her steely purpose,
got Nero to agree that the situation in the desert had arisen
because of fear about leakage from the waste, particularly
the nuclear waste. In so doing, she made him describe the
waste itself: drums of extremely caustic chemicals and
blocks of dense concrete protecting hearts of high-yield
nuclear by-products. Importantly, she made him repeat that
his main motivation to move the waste from the desert
had been a threat from the PLO that if no action was
taken, then Disposoco's directors would be assassinated,
one by one. Further, she elicited the unthinking agreement

that, when the ship was refused entry to the ports of Naples and Liverpool because of fears about her cargo, Disposoco had simply agreed with the suggestions of CZP as to the continued shipping and the final destination of the containers full of waste. But she could not shift him one inch on his statement that the cargo was properly loaded, fully monitored and at no time was there any real danger from it.

Next up for Standing was the plaintiff, Signor Verdi, who sang the praises of his company CZP and their small fleet. *Napoli* had not been young, he admitted, but she had been fully refitted at least once since her launch, had been treated to a new engine, and had been well maintained since she came into his company's hands. He also sang the praises of the captain and the chief engineer, both regrettably now dead. They had been long-term company men and he was certain that neither of them would ever have been a part of anything questionable.

It was with CZP that the original Crewfinders contract had been drawn when John Higgins had replaced Enrico Fittipaldi as captain. Crewfinders had been contacted by the first officer under the advice of a passenger who knew of the firm. Who and why was not important. CZP had been happy to accept the representative of such an apparently respectable company. And when, to their surprise, the cargo had not been accepted by the authorities in Naples, CZP had been happy to continue the association rather than start looking for a new captain. Verdi said he had been deeply shocked by the refusal of the Liverpool dock workers to unload his ship, but the combined circumstances of an offer to accept the cargo from a company in Canada and the preparedness of Richard Mariner, director of Crewfinders and its parent company, to help his captain take the *Napoli* there had put his mind at rest. Then he began to receive reports that his ship had been lost under questionable circumstances and that some of his people had died in the incident. When he had arrived in America himself to speak to the survivors, he discovered that these reports were less shocking than the truth – that the Heritage Mariner people aboard had become so terrified of the harmless cargo that they had actually scuttled a perfectly seaworthy ship rather than carry on to safe haven in Canada.

Verdi was a smooth, self-confident little man with a bristling moustache and a habit of bouncing up and down on his toes which concealed his icy intelligence, as Maggie's cat-like charm concealed hers. They sparred warily, but he would not be moved on any important particular. The most she could do was to establish that all he knew about the actual loss of *Napoli* on that fateful morning nearly two years ago was hearsay, gathered from the few crewmen involved who still wanted to work for him.

As she sat down, Standing rose to say, 'As the defendant has admitted he planted the explosives, and all I can do to further our cause is to await my cross-examination of him, that concludes matters for the plaintiff, my lord.'

The judge nodded. 'We will hear from the defendant's camp, and the defendant himself, I imagine, after luncheon.'

She didn't actually eat any lunch because she couldn't shake off the feeling that there was much worse to come. Hunger made her wits sharper, she had found. And she would need sharp wits this afternoon. She returned to her office and went over the pleadings and the summaries again. It all turned on who the judge believed about the actual loss. The fact that Standing allowed his case to be apparently so weak just at that crucial point made her suck her teeth and hiss in a most unladylike manner. On her side, Richard and Captain Higgins, as well as one of his officers, Marco Farnese who had been on board at the time, would appear as witnesses. Harcourt Gibbons and Brian Chambers had also secured an agreed statement, to be read in her absence, from Ann Cable. The late lamented barrister and the wily little solicitor had understood how easy it would be for the Italians to be presented as innocently injured parties, and the defendant Richard Mariner as a strongly manipulative business tycoon relying on the partiality of an employee, Captain Higgins, to cover up for his panic and criminal misjudgment. And there was no avoiding the hard fact that, as Standing had pointed out yet again, Richard admitted to planting explosives with every intention of scuttling the ship in the first place.

Maggie suspected she was going to be like a blind man in a minefield this afternoon if she wasn't very careful indeed.

If Richard had been too preoccupied to see much of the law courts on Monday, this afternoon he seemed to find every yellow brick, every grey slate of their ornate, Gothic frontage indelibly seared into his memory. He walked slowly up from the Strand, climbing the three shallow steps, their edges marked in white, and coming under the shade of the cathedral portal with its great pointed doorway before climbing the next four.

He had been in the area all day, starting out down in the City at Heritage House where he had been forced to camp last night by the hellish behaviour of the twins who were missing Robin every bit as much as he was himself. Because he was so close to the heart of things, he had been unable to sleep a wink, expecting each succeeding minute of the long, long night to bring some word of her; but there had been nothing. After Heritage House, he had gone to St Clement Dane's Church in the Strand, scant yards away from the law courts. Here he had sat restlessly beside his father-in-law throughout the long funeral service for Sir Harcourt Gibbons. The barrister had served in the Royal Air Force during the Second World War, starting out as a Wellington pilot and rising onto Bomber Harris's staff. It was apt that the statue of Harcourt's old commander should watch him being carried in and out. And ironic that a man who had dropped so much destruction from the sky should have died in such a way himself.

Like Maggie, but for far different reasons, Richard had eaten no lunch. He had phoned the office and discovered that there was still no news. He seriously considered dropping everything there and then to go off to the Labrador Sea to find out what was happening for himself. But of course he knew that he could do nothing until this case was settled, one way or another. Finally, trying with diminishing success to contain a black enormity of rage at his own helplessness, he strode into the law courts exactly at the appointed hour.

Inside, too, he noticed more than he had done before. The awesome space of the central hall was lessened just a little by the security wall and the sensor door through which he had to pass. For some reason, this afternoon the metal bolts supporting his knee joints set off the alarm. They had given no trouble on Monday. A lesser man might have been flustered, but Richard remained calm. On the outside, at least. As he walked slowly across the great hall

towards the mahogany and glass-fronted cases containing
the trial list, however, he hoped that it had not been a bad
omen. He and Robin needed so much luck at the moment,
and luck suddenly seemed in very short supply. Perhaps
you only ever got a limited amount of luck, he mused
grimly. Robin and he had used up so much of theirs that
they might well have no more to come. If there's any left,
he thought, let Robin have it. She needs it even more than
I do, wherever she is.

He got his wish.

The trial was in the same court and yes, he *was* superstitious about the number thirteen suddenly. The defence
began at two. He would be on the stand as soon as Maggie
had completed her opening remarks for the defence. He
had been in many a tight spot, not the least of which was
being trapped on the bridge of the ship in question as she
went down into the dark depths of the west Atlantic. This
was worse.

As he had noticed everything about the building outside,
so the courtroom itself seemed super-real. The wooden
door, ornately carved, through which he entered at last,
the slope of dark-padded seats, the wooden walls cased
along one side with shelves full of fat law books. The
thrust of horizontal brass poles with curtains gathered back
like furled banners on either side of the judge's bench.
The length of that pale wood bench, with three doorways
into the wall behind it. The overhang of wood like a half-
deck above it. The smell of dust and age and leather and
polish. It all swirled around him, much more real in its
impact than the quiet preliminaries in which he joined
with Maggie DaSilva and an unrecognised officer of the
court. Much more overwhelming than his dangerous predicament, until his own counsel asked him, 'Captain

Mariner, why did you sink the *Napoli*?'

Step by step from his first strong statement that he never
sank the ship, Maggie led him through his involvement
with the doomed voyage – the background to Captain
Fittipaldi's death as it had been explained to him, his
dealings with CZP and Disposoco, his decision to go
aboard at Liverpool, his desire to support his associate
and friend John Higgins who should have been on his
honeymoon, not trapped with his new bride in a dangerous
and deteriorating situation. And she brought him round
full circle to the sinking once again. The chemical waste
on the deck was leaking badly, especially after being
swamped by a severe storm. It was damaging the hull and
dissolving the protective coating round the nuclear waste
in the hold. Ann Cable and Professor Faure, Disposoco's
chief scientist, had read dangerous and worsening levels
of radiation. They believed the cargo was going critical.
Professor Faure and he had planted the explosives in the
forepeak. No, they had not detonated them. The chief
engineer had placed explosives in the stern of the ship.
No, he had not detonated them. Before any action along
those lines could be taken, the hull, weakened by the
corrosion of the chemical waste and by the ravages of
the storm already mentioned, had failed. The ship had
gone down at once. Those who had survived had been
lucky to do so.

  Maggie sat down. Standing rose. 'I have only two questions for Captain Mariner,' he said. 'Professor Faure saw
the danger to the cargo and consequently helped plant the
explosives in the bow. Why is he not here to testify to
the fact that the explosives he planted were never
detonated?'

'Professor Faure did not survive when the ship was lost.'

'I see. And the chief engineer planted the charges at the stern. Why is he not here to testify that they were never detonated?'

'The chief engineer did not survive when the ship was lost.'

'What an unfortunate coincidence, Captain Mariner.'

'Yes, sir.'

'Captain Mariner, I put it to you that this tissue of lies rests precisely upon the fact that these men cannot testify.'

'No, sir.'

'And that the whole unbelievable farrago about a sound ship suddenly going down as though it were made of sugar instead of steel has been concocted to cover up the fact that you blew the ship wide open and in all probability blew up the professor and the chief engineer when you did so.'

'*No, sir!*'

Richard sat, dazed, and watched John Higgins going over the same ground. He could hardly remember a word he had said, so great had been his concentration at the beginning and his outrage at the end. In his youth he had been a keen amateur actor and it was as though he was in the grip of post stage fright now. Then he had been able to recite complete plays – except for the lines spoken by characters he had portrayed. It was as though the fire of performance burned his dialogue out of his memory while he acted. Now he tried to recall his words in the witness box, looking for damaging admissions. But nothing would come.

Then, with a start, he realised he had missed most of John's evidence. Concentrating again, he followed his friend's description of the loss of his command.

At the end, Standing was on his feet again, rustling his papers vaguely, appearing almost absent-minded. 'Can you tell me why you stayed aboard this hell ship, this leper ship, Captain Higgins? The terms of your Crewfinders contract specify that you could have been air-lifted home at any time. The cargo was banned from Naples and Liverpool. You were not. You could have got off. Why stay?'

'My wife's sister was aboard. My wife and I did not want to leave her.'

'Most commendable. What was your sister-in-law doing aboard?'

'She was a passenger.'

'So why could she not simply have got off along with you?'

'She is a member of the Palestinian Liberation Organisation.'

'I see. And did the chief engineer plant the explosives at the stern alone?'

'No, Salah and she helped—'

'Salah? Who is Salah?'

'Her . . . friend . . . My sister-in-law's friend and associate.'

'Also a member of the PLO?'

'Yes.'

'I hope at least one of them survived? No other explosives expert except Captain Mariner seems to have done so.'

'My sister-in-law did, yes.'

'So this man Salah did not?'

'No. He was killed in the engine room. My sister-in-law was the only one who escaped from the engine room.'

'And returned to her surviving terrorist associates . . .'

'Yes.'

Maggie stood up. 'My lord, neither the captain nor my learned friend can be certain—'

'Quite, Ms DaSilva. I shall take that into account.'

'But you have heard nothing from her or the PLO since?' Standing continued.

'Only that they hold Disposoco to blame, not us.'

'Oh, that is most convenient . . .'

'I don't know about that.'

'Suffice it to say, then, that you and your boss and your sister-in-law were the only people who actually made it off the ship.'

'That's just the way it happened.'

'Quite, Captain. But we must observe how conveniently it all fell out, especially in regard to your enhanced professional status and your employer's good name. No, you need not say any more. I think we have heard enough, thank you.'

Ann Cable's agreed submission was read into evidence next. It was brief and to the point. She had come aboard at Naples as a representative of Greenpeace, to keep an eye on a dangerous looking cargo. She had stayed aboard at Liverpool in spite of the fact that CZP and Disposoco were less welcoming than they had been earlier. Her readings of the radiation levels in the holds had led her to contact Greenpeace and had given her increasing cause for concern as they crossed the Atlantic. After a severe storm, she had feared that the deterioration of the protective casings below would lead to meltdown, which would in turn lead to a terrible 'dirty' nuclear explosion as soon as the hot nuclear core melted through the hull and hit the cold ocean water.

In the silence after this deposition, Standing rose again,
holding a book. 'I would like to point out to Your Lordship
that the person who wrote that deposition has made a
considerable personal fortune out of the incident. The book
I hold here in my hand is called *The Leper Ship*. It has
topped the bestseller lists both in London and New York
for the better part of a year. Ms Cable wrote it soon after
returning with the survivors from the *Napoli* and it pur-
ports to be a true account of her experiences aboard. I
understand there is talk of film rights currently under
negotiation. Sums in excess of three million dollars have
been mentioned. Her fame as a writer, broadcaster and
conservationist, the personal fortune I mentioned, and, of
course, the film rights, all turn upon her contention that
the cargo in the *Napoli* was about to go to critical mass
and explode. And, as we have sadly become used to hearing in this case, the only expert witness who could confirm
or deny what she alleges – the only expert witness not in
the PLO – went down with the ship and is dead.'

Maggie was on her feet again at that. 'My final witness,
my lord, has no association with either Heritage Mariner
or any terrorist organisation. He was employed by CZP
but is no longer. He was an officer aboard *Napoli* and he
did not go down with the ship.'

In the two years since Richard had seen him, Marco Farnese had aged well. Aboard *Napoli* he had seemed almost
stupid, a big bumbling boy, overwhelmed by the responsibilities of being the junior deck officer and the butt of the
mutinous crew's frustration. His blond curls were close-
cropped now. His eyes had lost that bovine vacancy. He
wore a uniform of the Italian merchant marine with badges
and braid denoting a first lieutenant. And he looked every

inch the part. His English had improved, too.

'Yes, I remember the loss of the *Napoli* very clearly, though I was not involved in the placing of the explosives, you understand. I was officer in charge of the lifeboats.'

'Can you take us through what you remember from the time you began to lower the lifeboats, please.'

'Of course. There were two lifeboats. Everyone went aboard except Captain Higgins who remained on the bridge, Captain Mariner and Professor Faure who were in the bow, and the chief and the two terrorists who were in the engine room. They were planting the explosives, you understand. I remained on the deck, while the lifeboats were in the water just below me. It was not easy to stand on the deck, you understand, because of the slope. The bow was down very badly since the storm.

'Then suddenly Captain Mariner came out of the hatch to the chain locker and he yelled to me to get the boats clear because she was going down. He ran into the bridge. I turned to jump down into the lifeboat and I heard a strange sound from the bows. Is a deep rumbling sound. Captain Mariner told me later it was the anchor chain going through the hole in the bow. It must have been a big hole. She started to go down at once but we pulled clear very quick. As soon as the stern came out of the water, the propeller started to turn very fast. Too fast. There was an explosion in the engine room. The propeller fell off. She went down very fast after that, with more explosions in the engine room. And when she was deep, one big one – *BOOM* – blows the bridge right off!'

'Thank you, Lieutenant. Now, the explosions in the engine room. Do you think they were from the explosives being detonated?'

'No, I do not think this. I think they are from the engine

over-revving when the propeller spun too fast. I think they
are the motor burning out. I think they are the engine
blowing up.'

'Thank you, Lieutenant.' Maggie sat at last.

Standing rose. 'Just one or two questions, Lieutenant.
Now, you say there were at least three explosions in the
engine room?'

'I count the big one at the end, yes.'

'What makes you so certain that none of these was
caused by explosives going off?'

'The ship was going down. What for to blow it up then?'

'Do you understand the idea of a delayed fuse?'

'Yes. That way you can set off one explosion and then
a second one after a while.'

'Were you aware that Captain Mariner has said in his
written submission that they planned to use just such a
delayed fuse to set off the explosives?'

'No, but I don't understanding—'

'If you cannot be certain that the explosion in the engine
room was not the second half of the delayed fuse, how
can you be certain that the strange noise you heard at the
bow just before you cast off and rowed away was not
the first part of it, detonating the explosives deep under
the water?'

Comprehension flooded Farnese's face. 'So the sound
was not chain falling through the hull. It was the bomb
exploding first at the bow, and then at the stern on a timer,
a delay . . . *Now* I understand! Of course! That's how they
pulled it off!'

Maggie and Richard and Brian Chambers lurched back
in their seats as one. The trap was sprung. Whether Farnese had just been tricked by Standing's cunning or had
been bribed or threatened, they would probably never

know. But all the positive witnesses on whom Richard's defence rested had been undermined one by one, and this final friendly witness turned out to be damningly hostile after all. Maggie was on her feet in an instant, making him rethink and reconsider. But the damage was done. There was no way it could be repaired. The case had hung in the finest of balances, right up until the end. And now it was lost.

The judge found in full for the plaintiff, CZP, and the court was empty by teatime.

PART TWO

The Sisters

CHAPTER SIXTEEN

Day Nine

Thursday, 27 May   10:00

'Hard over,' snapped Robin, her voice rusty with exhaustion. She cleared her throat as she hesitated for an instant, calculating feverishly. Her eyes were slitted and streaming against the combination of cold, fatigue and sudden brightness. The overcast low above her reflected the dullest of mornings and the grey light was intensified to a seemingly impossible degree by the continent of ice which confronted her and upon whose frozen shore the wind was driving her. 'Starboard. Hard a' starboard.'

In the wheelhouse, Hogg, rendered useless as a navigator by the failure of his machines, automatically hit the green button beside the helm as the captain's order came over the walkie-talkie. But the button was electrically powered, and as useless as most of the other equipment on the bridge.

Sam Larkman, who held the helm in his calloused but delicate engineer's hands, shot the fat officer a withering look and swung the wheel hard over. The telemotor control indirectly joining the wheel to the rudder was independent of the other power systems aboard and so it answered his command and Robin's order.

Atropos did not have steerageway, or anything like it. She was riding backwards across the last few hundred metres of that stormy channel between the two great areas of ice which were the last thing Robin had seen before the power went, nearly ten hours earlier. The ship was being driven south-east by the remnants of the north-wester which had been raging for the last thirty-six hours. Because her high bridgehouse acted as a more effective sail than did hills and even cliffs of ice, she was moved by the wind more quickly than the massive ice barrier she was bearing down upon. Because her hull was sleek and aquadynamic, she was pushed across the current which was actually flowing north at this point and pulling the massive sunken portion of the ice barrier northwards with it. Thus the powerless vessel was closing with a seemingly infinitely wide and absolutely adamantine coastline of thick sea ice at perhaps six knots. She was moving back-wards towards a line of low green cliffs which rose sheer above the stormy water for about ten feet. They looked to be as solid as any made of rock, and the first part of her likely to make contact was her all too frangible rudder.

Robin had calculated that if she ordered the helm hard over, the rudder would, within twenty seconds, swing forty degrees to her left and pull the stern of the ship round with it so that the right-hand quarter of her stern would make contact first. The cliffs were sheer and there seemed to be no ice projecting beyond them above the surface or below. The ship's stern was ice strengthened, though not as thickly as the bow. Damage there would be minimal, with luck. And with the rudder out of the way, the propel-ler, already rendered useless by contact with the ice, should protect the hull from further damage.

But the damage would only remain within acceptable limits if she acted fast once contact was made. Teams of men would have to go down on the ice and arrange mooring ropes to hold the ship in place until the swell moderated and they could think about other alternatives. If the cliffs were as solid as they looked, then there would have to be some heavy-duty fenders placed between them and whatever sections of the hull came into contact with them. Robin knew well enough the solid force that water could exert when it was liquid. What it could do in its solid state was ten times more terrible.

All these thoughts raced through her tired head while she waited tensely for the stern of her ship to pull away to her left. She was standing on the port bridge wing – now the right-hand one, as they were sailing backwards – looking over the poop deck and the stern. She was bundled up against the cold until even her slim form seemed squat and shapeless. It was a very necessary precaution, for only the wind-chill factor differentiated the temperature outside the bridgehouse from that within it. They had joked in the galley that for a time it had been warmer inside the ship's refrigerators than outside them. Everything she owned which Damart made was currently padded round her, and she bitterly regretted the rest so casually left aboard *Clotho*. Her outline now, in fact, was very much the outline she had mentally given her body during the long months since the arrival of the twins. But she wasn't thinking about her outline now. Or her children, for that matter.

All her attention was on her command. All her thoughts and concerns were utterly involved with what she would do if the plan to swing the rudder away from rapidly nearing danger did not work. More distantly, what she would do if her current manoeuvre did work. More distantly still, what they would do once they were tied up safely; sleep first or restore the power? That decision really depended on how Chief Lethbridge and his officers were. So she needn't worry about it yet. A long way down the line, she wondered what she would do when they got the power back on and the radio working. How she was going to tell Richard that *Clotho* was lost and *Atropos* herself in a trap from which only a fortune in salvage payments was likely to extricate her. That Andrew, Nico and the rest, close family friends for years, some of them, were frozen, preserved until the end of time, in all probability, somewhere in the glacial depths of the Labrador Sea.

She had an image of them being pulled by the current, year upon year, up to the black depths of the Arctic Ocean where only the weight of the water and the ice above it could keep the brine from freezing. The image was so vivid and so terrible that she cried aloud and understood why Dante in the great poem she had read at school had made the lowest reaches of his *Inferno*, where Satan himself was held condemned, an infinite sea of ice.

The cry she gave jerked her awake and she cursed herself for being out here alone. How long had she been asleep on her feet? What if she had nodded off completely? She was tired enough, heaven knew; tired, exhausted and drained. She should have been lying down, to be summoned only in the direst emergency, conserving her energies to overcome the next inevitable crisis. But who else was there to keep watch here and give the orders? She was caught as surely as was her command. But, now that she was awake, she noticed that the shore of ice cliffs seemed to have jumped appreciably closer, and to have swung to a new angle.

Atropos was turning. It was working. Robin battered on the after rail with her numb fists in jubilation and all but dropped her walkie-talkie. 'Hogg! Pass the message that we will impact with the ice barrier on the port quarter in about five minutes' time. I want all the work teams already told off ready to go into action then.'

'Yes, Captain.'

Timmins had been able to arrange that at least. She hoped he'd made a halfway decent job of it and wished she could have overseen the selection of the most important teams from among the men she knew and trusted aboard *Clotho*. But that hadn't been possible and there was no point worrying about it now. Nothing should go too disastrously wrong – and she did need to know to what extent she could count on the thin, startled-looking creature everyone else aboard seemed to refer to as Yasser.

She took the opportunity of checking with another of her officers, one nearer at hand even than Hogg. The radio officer. 'Sparks, come in.'

'No luck, Captain.'

'What do you think?'

'This is the last of the lifeboat radios now and it's no better than the rest. What do you know about PCA?'

'Polar cap absorption. Interferes with radio transmission in high latitudes. Happens soon after solar flares. Can last days.'

'Got it in one.'

'That's what you think it is?'

'I guess so. Somewhere up above those never-ending storm clouds I think the sun just gave out the mother of all solar flares and I don't think these mickey-mouse transceivers will communicate over the length of the weather deck before next weekend.'

Things on deck got off to a promising start as men came boiling out of the bridgehouse at weather deck level to stream darkly along the poop beneath her. She suspected that many of them would have been up since first light, watching the enormity of the ice growing inexorably clearer as they swept down towards it, but there were still yells of shock – and, she guessed, disquiet – as some of them realised just how colossal and how close was the glacial barrier between them and the rest of the world. They did not come empty-handed. They brought with them an assortment of lines, ladders, fenders and the sort of equipment Timmins reckoned they would need to secure their vessel to a piece of ice which looked to be about the same size as a small country.

Robin felt the urge to be down there with them. To find out the sort of things she would need to know about them, officers and crewmen alike, that could be learned most quickly and accurately by being in action with them. But her place had to be here, for the time being at least. The captain had to remain on the bridge until the ship had stopped moving. Really, she should stay until *Atropos* was secure, but she wasn't sure she had the patience to wait that long. Right at the back of the excited crowd, she suddenly saw the slower, steady figure of Errol Jones and Joe Edwards. 'Be careful down there, Joe,' she yelled without thinking, and the pair of them turned to look up. Whether they heard her clearly or not, they welcomed the sound of her voice. Joe's massively gloved hand rose to salute her, and beneath a large cold-weather hat Errol's square face split into a broad grin which seemed to reach from one thick earflap to the other.

The fenders were over the side and clustering thickly around the point of impact a moment or two before the collision came. As there was no beach below the cliffs of ice, there was not much surf or backwash from the waves, though the ice itself was so massive that it reacted not at all to the arrival of the swell from the north-east. *Atropos* slid down off the back of one such wave and crashed into the top of an ice cliff as the next came up under her. Thus her arrival against the ice barrier was a sort of shoulder barge, as though the ship was playing American football. But this shoulder was well protected. The power of the impact shocked through the ship and even those who had been preparing for it were staggered. Robin was only kept erect by the fierceness of her grip on the railing in front of her, and the yell of shock which the impact jerked out of her was lost on the overwhelming sound of the collision.

As though the mass of men had been shattered by the convergence of ice and ship, they split up into their teams. One team moved watchfully down the port side, fenders at the ready as the hull swung round parallel to the ice cliffs and then tried to smash full length up against them, still at the mercy of the wind and the waves. At the stern, men were already swarming over the side and down quickly deployed Jacob's ladders. The descent to the solid surface of the ice barrier was little more than ten feet. One man, more excited than the rest, seeing how close the surface seemed to the level of the deck, climbed over the safety rail and jumped. He landed on a slope of solid ice and his footing went at once. He crashed out full length on his back and his head hit the glass-hard surface with the sound of a rifle shot. Everything stopped for an instant, then Timmins bellowed an order. A group of men clustered round the fallen acrobat and passed his unconscious body back aboard. Some of the excitement died down after that and the teams went more quietly to work.

Robin thumbed her walkie-talkie. 'Hogg. Go down to the bows and tell me when we're secure there, please.' Certain that the second officer would be puffing his way down the length of the ship at once, Robin walked out to the far end of the bridge wing. As *Atropos* swung in, so the wing came to overhang the ice and Robin had an increasingly excellent view as the ship came to rest. Down to her left she could see Timmins and his team making all secure aft. Away to her right she could see the dark bustle of work beginning at the bow. But it was the scene in front which claimed the greatest share of her attention.

The wind was still gusting from behind her. It bore on its back the last low storm clouds and it carried within it the last misty rain. But it was a brisk wind and, for all that it was cold, it was clear because it blew round and down directly from the Pole. The misty rain and the ice dust which it lifted from the surface of the ice served to obscure the distance. It was impossible for Robin, the better part of forty feet above it, to see the far edge of the barrier or even to guess how wide it might be at this point. Her horizon might have been ten miles' distant or it might have been twenty, but there was no sign of water.

All she could see was ice. It was grey because it caught the colour of the sky. But it intensified the dead hues so that they seemed to be hesitating on the point of bursting into light. It was as though the whole barrier as far as she could see was made of steel trembling on the verge of melting, the snowy surface just an ashen crust which at any moment would crack and flow apart to reveal the

white-hot heart within. The barrier seemed to be flat, a
white plain so featureless as to fool her eyes, like nothing-
ness, into focusing mere feet in front of her face. But
when she made an effort – or, later, when she brought her
binoculars into play – she soon saw that this was an effect
of the wind and the drifting crystals it whirled along in
its skirts. In fact, the barrier was made of folded ridges
which went from east to west, as far as her eyes could
see. They were all parallel to the coastal cliffs and there
was no way for her to estimate the true depth of them,
for although the tops of the ridges seemed to be below
her line of vision, there was no way at all for her to
calculate the depths of the valleys between. The frozen
waves could have risen for ten or twenty feet from valley
floor to ridge top if all the ice was as solid as the coastal
section seemed. Or they could have plunged from ridge
top fifty feet sheer to the water and then on down to
untold abyssal depths if the valley floors lay open to
the sea.

For maybe ten minutes she stood studying the barrier
through the binoculars but at the end of that period of
concentrated study she was really no wiser than she had
been at the end of the first dazzled glance. There was only
one way she was going to find out any more about it, she
reckoned grimly. And that was to get off the ship and go
and look properly.

Her walkie-talkie buzzed and she lowered the field
glasses before raising the importunate instrument to her
ear. 'Timmins here. Stern secure.'

'Thank you, Number One. You may recall your teams
and report to me in the chart room, if you please.'

Idly, for she was waiting for the twin of this call from
Hogg at the bow, Robin crossed to the starboard bridge

wing. Just as the port wing stood out over the ice they were secured – and trapped – against, so this one stood out over the tall waves which held them there. The wind was bitter here, but the view was clearer than the view across the ice. The last of the rain was gone now and the distant horizon was clearer. The cloud cover was thinning up there too and the gathering light was cutting in great silver blades down onto the corrugated surface of the sea. She pressed the icy rounds of the eyepieces back beneath her frowning brows and tried to plumb the distance of the Davis Strait. At the furthest edge of the magnification the glasses revealed to her a band where the sea went palest pale and a reflecting band above it where the air went velvet dark. For minute after minute she stood, willing her eyes to see more. Willing her body to ride the pitch of the deck beneath her feet so that the field glasses would stay solidly fixed on that horizon.

And just in the final instant before her concentration broke, even as Hogg buzzed up to tell her that the bow was now secure, her vigilance was rewarded. In the heart of that pale band which warned of more ice sweeping down with the wind towards them out of the Arctic Ocean itself came a gleam as though an invisible hand had ignited a giant flare. The distance and the ice haze reduced the gleam by a million per cent and it was there for less than a heartbeat but it still had the power to burn the back of her eyes. She lowered the glasses and raised the walkie-talkie.

There was something out there, something big. As long as the wind stayed in the north-west, it would continue to come down this way. The thought made her as cold inside as the weather was making her outside.

*   *   *

Timmins and Hogg weren't much, but they were the only deck officers she had. And, in that they were bona fide deck officers, with the papers to prove it, they deserved her respect and support. Inclusion in her deliberations was the least part of that respect. So the three of them met next in the chart room and Robin spread the charts out in front of them and began to point to the huge white spaces in whose empty heart they lay. 'We'll keep this brief, gentlemen,' she began. 'We've all got work to do and I want to detail the next few tasks we've got to face as soon as we've discussed our position and situation.'

She glanced up at them. They were both standing, stunned with fatigue, staring down at her like dummies. She would very happily have shaken the pair of them, banging their heads together until they woke up a bit.

'According to my copy of the British Admiralty's Arctic Pilot for these waters, the Greenland Current usually pushes a big ridge of solid sea ice round the end of Greenland at this time of year. It usually blocks the coast from Kap Farvel north and sticks out into the Labrador Sea for a couple of hundred miles. I'm sure both of you are as fully aware of this fact as I am. But what you may not know is this: for the last couple of days, Frederiksdal has been reporting that its harbour is clear of ice. Frederiksdal should be right in behind that ice barrier. If it isn't, then the barrier must have moved. Gentlemen, I think that the south-easterly storm in which your propeller was damaged broke that ice barrier free and drove it out into the Labrador Sea, and I believe we are currently moored to its northern coastline. This means we could have as much as a hundred miles of ice to each side of us. And anywhere between one and ten full miles of ice to the south of us. Any comments?'

'Ice to the south is very bad for us,' said Timmins slowly, 'because of the ice to the north.'

'That's right,' agreed Robin. 'How bad it is depends upon how far west we are and we can't really estimate that.'

'We were pushed right back towards the middle,' said Hogg. 'I know the tow got us back towards the east and the wind will have drifted us further, but the fact is we're a long way out.' He drew out the word 'long'.

'And you know what that means.' Timmins was almost animated. 'It means we're still on the edge of the Labrador Current. This time of the year it can come east right out over the Newfoundland Banks, especially with the wind behind it. If the Gulf Stream's running a little further north than usual or is pushing a little harder, then the Labrador can move at two, two and a half knots. And it can shove all sorts of shit south out of the Arctic Ocean through the Davis Strait. Oh, sorry, Captain. I—'

'What sort of shit, Number One?' She already suspected. She had been warned by that one blinding gleam of green light.

'Bergs like you've never seen. Ice islands. Half the size of British Columbia. Half as high as the Rockies.'

'Maybe once a century,' she said soothingly. She didn't want Timmins frightening himself. Or anyone else for that matter. 'But your point is well taken. We are, as the Americans say, between a rock and a hard place. We're effectively stuck on a north-facing shore with ice being pulled south against it. The size of the bits that the ice comes in is immaterial for the moment. It's the situation we need to worry about. We don't want to stay here any longer than we have to.'

'But how are we going to get out of it?' asked Hogg.

'Even if we fix the alternator or restore emergency power and radio for help, we're going to need an icebreaker to get us out of here and every icebreaker north of New York must be iced in solid until June. I mean, how much time do we have?'

The three of them looked at each other. Nobody had an answer.

'Your priorities are exactly right, Mr Hogg,' said Robin after a moment. 'We must get power back first, now that we seem to be so snugly berthed. Without power we are in very deep trouble indeed.'

'We could starve,' said Timmins, with a bitterly ironic glance at his fat second lieutenant.

Hogg threw him a fulminating look and opened his mouth.

'We could,' interrupted Robin brusquely. 'But we're far more likely to freeze first. And it is as sure as death and taxes that things will not look any brighter or get any better until we have warmth and hot food, quite apart from our instruments and our most powerful radios. Have either of you got any idea how the chief engineer is?'

He was in a deep sleep and neither Ann Cable nor Henri LeFever was keen that he should be disturbed. But Robin needed an engineer. So, inevitably, she turned her attention to Don Taylor, who had suffered less badly. Here, too, the makeshift nurses were hesitant, but Robin, for all her quiet concern and courteous attention, was as irresistible as a glacier. When she pulled the curtains of Taylor's cabin window open, the light flooded in to illuminate a figure more suited to the British Museum's exhibit of Egyptian mummies than to the bridgehouse of a modern ship. Her heart sank, for without his help and advice at the very least, she would be helpless. As befitted his seniority, his bed was almost double and she perched on the edge of it and called his name.

'Taylor. *Don!*'

'Robin, don't touch him,' hissed Ann from just inside the door.

The two women had been on friendly terms for nearly two years now. But when Robin glanced up, the American was taken aback. She had known Robin Mariner, wife and mother. Captain Mariner was quite another kettle of fish. The grey eyes, every bit as chilly as the ice barrier outside, froze any further words on the writer-cum-nurse's lips.

Frowning, Ann turned and went back into the engineering officer's little dayroom. Henri saw her expression at once.

'What?' he asked quietly.

'Nothing. I'm just being stupid.'

Ann had never really resolved the speculation about whether Robin and Nico had been having an affair. Every now and then she would find herself speculating, like a child picking at the scab on a healing wound. The sudden change in her friend stirred these thoughts again. Ann had supposed she knew Robin intimately. She was a writer, after all, adept at summing people up at a glance; and she had known Robin for quite long enough to be confident that she knew every side of her friend. And here was a new side. What else had Robin managed to keep concealed?

Ann looked up, pulling herself out of her momentary brown study. Henri's bright eyes were still looking quizzically at her. 'It's nothing,' she said again. 'I'm just too suspicious for my own good. Forget it.'

For a moment his gaze continued to rest on her, then he shrugged and turned away. But just for that instant, she wondered whether she had said the wrong thing to him.

For the shortest, fleeting micron of time she felt that her words had an impact on him far beyond their thoughtless intention.

As it happened, Robin was not driven to shaking the scalded man by his shoulder – which she'd had every intention of doing if she'd needed to. As she approached his bed Taylor's long brown eyes blinked open and focused blearily on her. It took him a moment to remember that this woman with her gleaming riot of salt-curled, windtousled hair was a senior officer, but once he got that clear in his mind, he began to fire on all cylinders. Or nearly all.

Her words crisp and to the point, she outlined their current predicament to him. The long eyes grew wider as she talked, but nowhere near as round as Ann's who overheard every doomladen phrase. When she had finished, Taylor lay silently for a moment, then he began to struggle under the blankets. His movements were so unco-ordinated that Robin at first thought he was having some kind of seizure. But after a moment or two it became obvious that he was trying to sit up. She touched him then, sliding her hand gently round his warm, thick-bandaged shoulders, to help him into a sitting position.

Once there, he paused for breath.

'Are you all right?' she asked him, sounding very English and slightly fatuous in her own ears.

'No, Captain, I am not all right. In fact the whole of my lily-white body hurts like a son of a bitch, and I surely pity the poor chief if he was harder boiled than me. But if you can get me on my feet, then I can get some clothes on. And if I can get some clothes on then I can get down in that engine room and fix that fucking alternator. And if I can fix the alternator, then maybe you can get us all the hell out of here.'

Put in those terms, Robin began to believe that maybe

they could do just that after all. But she was damned if she could see how they were going to pull it off.

CHAPTER SEVENTEEN

Day Nine

Thursday, 27 May   12:00

Timmins was even more exhausted than Robin, so she was forced to invest some of the energy her resurrection of Don Taylor had given her in order to get him up and running. There was nothing they could do to further their plans for survival and ultimate rescue until Taylor and the third engineer from *Clotho*, Lloyd Swan, restored the power. There was a lot she had to do as the new captain of this ship, however, no matter what the situation. She had to perform a captain's inspection at the earliest possible moment. A full inspection was out of the question right now, of course, but she did need to look over as much of the ship as possible. When the power came back on she didn't want to be wandering around looking at things she could perfectly well check on now. And it occurred to her quite forcefully that with Timmins on the edge of exhaustion, he might very well be less guarded than normal in answering several pertinent questions she had in mind about the officers and crew now serving under her command.

They left Hogg in the watchkeeper's chair, though he was too comatose really to be on watch. Harry Stone the cheerful radio operator said he was willing to remain on the bridge as well, though there was nothing he could do in his professional capacity until the power came up or the solar flares died down. 'There's no heat, no light and no food below,' he observed. 'It's worse than winter back home in Grand Falls, Newfoundland. Why should I want to go down there? No, I'll stay here and watch Hogg keeping watch.' Like Timmins, he seemed to use an ironic tone as a matter of course when talking of the second officer. But unlike Timmins he seemed competent and reliable.

They started at the top of the bridgehouse – right at the top, on the open deck at the foot of the main radio mast. Robin would have climbed even higher, but that would have been stupid because the temperature was beginning to tumble further as the cloud cover thinned. The iron rungs up the front of the mast itself were already coated with ice. She kept her mind on the equipment up here and the way it had been maintained, refusing to let her attention wander to the spectacular views northwards over the floe-flecked Davis Strait or southwards over the ice barrier. Everything up here seemed to be neat, clean and properly stowed. She could order none of it to be run or tested until she had power back, so she had to be content with looking.

'This all seems shipshape,' she said conversationally, making her tone warm and approving.

'Yeah, I guess.'

She walked back to the aft section and leaned against the railing, looking down to the lower deck with the funnel rising from the middle of it. That too was neat and tidy, everything well stowed and unobtrusive. 'Captain Black obviously likes to run a tight ship,' she observed.

'Now you look here, lady, that man was good to me. He's a good captain, he's just sick, is all, and I won't hear nothing against him.' His obvious anger brought out something like a southern drawl in his voice. She found the unexpected accent distracting. Like everything else about the man, it diminished him somehow.

She swung round to face him. His watery blue eyes were gleaming with genuine anger. The frizzy monk's haircut sticking out from under his warm hood above his ears seemed to be sparking with electric anger. 'I meant it, Mr Timmins,' she said. Her tone was quietly placating. Her eyes held his until they dropped. 'I wasn't being disrespectful.'

That took the wind out of his sails a bit. 'Just sick, is all,' he repeated. 'He'll be up and about in no time.' The way he said it made it sound almost like a threat.

And that gave Robin something else to think about. What would her position aboard be if Captain Black did get over his craving for whatever illegal substance the late Mr Reynolds had supplied him with? If he took over control of his command again, where would that leave her? Out on a limb with Ann, she suspected. Just another woman for the crew to fantasise over. It was not a pleasant thought. But then, this was not a pleasant ship.

She turned back and looked down. The ship rose and settled beneath her. The lines holding her stern against the ice flexed and eased. The movement made either the vessel or its anchorage groan as though there was something out there in deep pain. Something big and dangerous. Abruptly she moved off to the starboard companionway and went down onto the deck beside the funnel. Crossing it at a brisk walk, with Timmins like a sulky spaniel at her heels,

she paused to look down at the lifeboat from above. 'When
was the last lifeboat drill?' she asked.

'Well, I'd have to check in the log to be sure.'

'Roughly. Last Tuesday? Monday?'

He shrugged. She frowned.

'When did you last check all the lifeboat stores and
equipment?'

'Can't rightly say. The Wide Boy—'

'I beg your pardon?'

'Third Officer Reynolds. He did all this stuff.'

The penny began to drop then. The late third officer
had been the only really active deck officer aboard. And
of course he would have been extremely happy to look
after everyone else's responsibilities. God alone knew what
must be hidden among all this beautifully stowed gear.
And now that the weather was moderating and the ship
was temporarily safe, the crew had leisure to do a little
thinking and she suspected she would not be the only one
to wonder.

The next companionway was a ladder reaching down
behind the funnel to the small deck where the stores crane
was footed. This was quite a solid machine which pointed
its short boom out towards the stern, and was used for the
purpose its name implied. Like everything else, it was
well stowed and had handled the foul weather of the last
week surprisingly well.

The final companionway was a much more decorative
affair, coming down like a staircase onto the fair-sized
poop. There had been much debate with the shipbuilders,
she remembered, about whether to place a swimming pool
here for the use of the off-watch officers and crew. In
Heritage Mariner supertankers there was always a pool in
this spot, overlooked by the windows of the gym. But

the courses these ships were destined to follow reached exclusively across the northern seas, and the designers questioned the need for such a frippery. Richard and she had insisted, however, and in the end they had come to a grudging agreement. There was a little pool beneath the decking before her, empty and carefully covered until the heat of the summer months. So well designed and fitted was the ship that the deck seemed solid and seamless. What a superb hiding place for Reynolds' loot that would make, she thought. Perhaps she might even have the leisure to check it out herself in due course.

Without pausing as these thoughts sped through her mind, she strode across the deck to the capstan where Timmins had anchored the shore lines. She glanced at them from a distance as though her interest was on other things. She did not want to alienate him further by seeming to mistrust his work. Nor was there any need to check too closely. One glance from her experienced eye confirmed that he seemed to have done a good enough job. But having come this close to the edge of the deck, it was impossible to ignore the ice any longer.

It exerted its own atmosphere and the power of it crept up coldly and swept aboard with an almost physical force like a mist, a miasma or a ghost. It was something far beyond the everyday rough and tumble of the jostling between the fenders and the crystal cliffs. It was something quite apart from the grating rumble with which the ship and her floating dock rose and fell in relationship with each other. There was a mesmerism which could not be denied. Inexorably it called her to the railing and held her there, looking down.

In fact the ice was moving very little, but the ship was still rising and falling on the swell. Robin could see why the nameless sailor had been tempted simply to jump down onto the soft-seeming white slope. When *Atropos* was in a trough and the barrier was on the back of the wave, there was little more than five feet between the green deck and the ice. A counter-breeze suddenly swept back into her face and she really smelt the ice for the first time. It had not occurred to her that the ice would smell of anything but, just as the oceans have their own odours, so did this frozen segment of Atlantic water. Oddly, for this was sea ice and thick but not old, it had a timeless smell. The sort of smell she imagined would inform the still air of undisturbed tombs. But there was something rich there too, rich but rancid. A touch of whale's breath, of seal's bark. So slight as to be little more than her imagination. So powerful as to make her close her eyes and sniff at the freezing air again, for all she knew it was refrigerating her adenoids and probably giving frostbite to her nose tip. But it was gone.

Disappointed, she opened her eyes. And frowned with sudden worry. The ice was at its relative highest, hovering tantalisingly close. The fenders were bunched up high enough to be oozing water over her feet. The ropes from the capstan were at full stretch past her shoulder, angling down to a spike hammered into the snowy crystal to act as a makeshift bollard. And as the full strain came onto it, the spike moved. 'Number One,' she said, just as though she was talking to Nico Niccolo. 'This is funny, look at this.'

He crossed to stand at her right shoulder and followed her gaze downwards. 'That was well in,' he said defensively. 'Hammered hard home. I checked it myself.'

She nodded. 'I'm sure you did. But there's something . . . Let's go down for a closer look.'

No sooner had she spoken than she was off, climbing nimbly over the railing and swarming down the Jacob's ladder onto the green-white frozen surface. It was so still and solid it almost made her knees buckle. From the heaving deck of her command it had been so easy to imagine that the ship's movements were reciprocated by the barrier, but this was not the case. She had no real idea how big was the body of solid water she was standing on, but it was moved not one whit by its liquid cousin rolling by beneath it. Surprised, she staggered back and found herself skidding. Again, it had deceived her. The surface behind the vertical faces of the cliffs had seemed flat but it was not: it sloped down with increasing steepness into the first of the corrugated valleys and it was all Robin could do to stop herself sliding away.

As she turned, *Atropos* heaved up above her and the ten feet between her and the deck became fifteen, and she appreciated anew the size of her command. Forty feet above, on the way up to being fifty, was the overhang of the bridge wing. Sixty feet to the topmost railings. Nearly a hundred to the top of the main radio mast on the bridge-house. And the great curve of the funnel was only ten feet shorter, just behind. The roaring of the surf between the steel and the ice was incredible. She walked forward to where Timmins was standing, looking down at the spike. Sure enough, the ground in front of it, the snow-caked ice nearest to the ship, was a different colour and as the black column stirred, pulled forward by the pressure of the ship's movement, so water bubbled up and flowed away to freeze again. 'It's the pressure,' she said. 'Pressure causes ice to melt. We'll have to think of some way to anchor it more securely. After a while that stake will just pull itself out of the ground. It's okay for the moment,

though, so we've time to take a look at the other one as
well. Odds are that Hogg won't have done as good a job
as you did.'

Automatically Timmins turned to go back aboard.

'Don't bother,' she said. 'We can walk down the ice
from here.' She turned and was off without further
thought, her eyes busy on the treacherous but fascinating
surface in front of her boots. She had likened the powdery
coating over the crystal to snow, but in many ways it was
more like sand. When she kicked her toecap into it, it
behaved like any beach half remembered from her holidays. Except that there was no real depth to it. Not here
at any rate. She looked away to her left, down the deceptive slope into what looked like a shallow valley at the
foot of another, higher cliff face.

She suddenly envisaged this section of the barrier like
a wide staircase which had been tilted backwards so that
the absolute verticals and horizontals of the steps had been
softened into a rising series of escarpments and valleys,
each a little higher than the last. The angles in the feet of
the valleys had been cloaked in this drifting ice sand.
Then the whole aspect of the barrier seemed to change
and in a matter of a few feet she found herself looking
through the ice cliffs up a valley she hadn't realised was
there. She had been so busy thinking about the main
structures in the ice running east to west parallel to the
coastline that it came as quite a shock to see a feature
running north to south, separating the cliffs into blocks as
though the whole barrier had been bent upwards to crack
open at this point.

The sound of the surf thundered hollowly beneath her
and she suddenly realised that this was what had happened.
The seemingly solid ground on which she was standing

was probably a thin crust over a crevasse reaching straight down into the freezing sea. She glanced over her shoulder but Timmins was a good way behind still, watching his feet as though he expected them to vanish at any moment. Fascinated, and with no sense of danger whatsoever, she paused there for a second, waiting. Sure enough, another sea thundered in. This time the sound was louder. And she felt the ice stir. A sort of ripple fled past her insteps, strong enough to make the soles of her feet tingle even through the boots and all the socks she was wearing. And about ten feet down the slope, exactly in line with where she was standing, a geyser of spray and ice crystals shot up into the air as though a whale was breathing there. She skipped off this section at once and turned to warn Timmins of her fears.

The thoughtless action was enough to cause her boots to lose their purchase and she fell forwards onto her face. The ice was as hard as concrete. No sooner had she hit the treacherous surface than she was slithering down the slope into the first of the valleys. As much with frustration as because she believed it would help, she beat at the ground with her gloved hands and her fists jarred painfully along corrugations which were the miniature counterparts of the series of hills behind her. Thinking quickly, she pushed her chest and stomach into the air and ground her hands, knees and toe tips into the surface. At once she slowed and after a moment or two she was able to start crawling back up the slope.

At the crest of the shallow slope, Timmins stood watching her with a strange, unsettled, uncertain look on his face. He wasn't too scared to help her. It was something other than that. Still, she thought grimly, she didn't need his help now and she'd be damned if she would ask for it. Then she realised where he was standing. She looked up again and he saw the desperation on her face and utterly misunderstood it. A slow smile spread across his thin lips and the sight of it sickened her just enough to choke off the warning in her throat. He straddled his legs, put his hands on his hips and got ready to enjoy watching her suffer.

Then the black side of the ship which framed him stirred and began to rise. The trembling thunder started again beneath her. 'Timmins!' she yelled and the force of her warning sent her sliding again. Her warning was wasted because the wild sound of the surf drowned it out. *Atropos* continued to rise and rise. Somehow Robin managed to tear herself to her feet, just in time to see the stake Hogg put into the ice at her bows tear loose. The length of the ship rocked back and then slammed forwards into the ice cliffs, adding the massive inertia of twenty thousand tons to the force of the surf in the chamber just beneath the surface of the ice. The flat ram of the side shut tight against the mouth of the cavern, forcing untold amounts of water and air into it like gas into a balloon.

From the point where Robin had seen the geyser of ice crystals and spray, right back along a line to the side of the ship, the ice crust blew open. It came close enough to knock her off her feet again but she knew how to stop sliding now and she remained on her knees, looking up. The force of it went straight up into the air between Timmins's arrogantly spread legs and took him with it. He was blasted into the air, the one dark object in the heart of a dazzling cloud of purest white. He didn't go up very far but from Robin's point of view he seemed to hang in the air, arms and legs spread as he performed a lazy back-flip worthy of a circus acrobat. And perhaps he did actually hang there, supported by the fountain of air like a ping-pong ball sitting on a water jet.

But the situation couldn't last. The overwhelming power of the explosion began to falter. The spray-soaked body fell. But where there had been a solid crust beneath him brief moments ago there was now a broad crater at the heart of a long crevasse shafting down to a subterranean cavern made of emerald crystal. He hit the edge of the crater with his chest and, once again, his body seemed to hesitate in the grip of powers beyond control. He lay there, legs down the glacial slope and arms thrown out towards Robin as though beseeching her help. It was clear that he was in fact unconscious, and at first there did not seem to be any great rush for her to go to his aid. She was anyway more than a little shocked by the impact of what had happened, and her reactions were slowed to a dream-like pace by the sudden rush of adrenaline into her exhausted system.

In the heart of a hollow silence, she picked herself up, stumbled, and danced until her footing was firm. All the time she was watching Timmins lying face down on the ice and it was only when her feet were steady that her brain had leisure to consider the fact that naked skin on bare ice at temperatures like these would be frostbitten within seconds. But that thought was overwhelmed almost at once by the realisation that the apparently still body was not in fact stationary at all. It was slipping backwards with increasing rapidity into the throat of the crevasse.

Reality arrived with the sound of a slamming door. Speed came back to normal. There was sound and sensation. And bitter self-recrimination. Timmins was likely to die here and the fault was hers. All because she wanted to walk on ice instead of steel. Stupid, stupid,

stupid! She hurled herself forward with almost masochistic force in a long dive for his hand. She landed on her stomach with bone-shaking force and skidded forwards spectacularly but she was still too late to save him. She froze, spread like a starfish at the top of the green-glass slope, and watched him slither downwards. At the bottom of the crater was a hole wide enough to admit his body and to show her a cavern maybe twelve feet deep, in the jumbled gravel ice of whose floor the waves foamed restlessly but shallowly. She realised at once that only the tops of the biggest seas could get in there. The cave was long but not deep. Its floor stood above the waterline. It stretched fifty feet at least into the barrier, but it wasn't deep enough to flood properly. And as she realised this, among the restless, rolling boulders which tumbled like giant lustres from some gargantuan chandelier in the shallow foam she saw the dark jumble of Timmins's body and realised there was still a chance to save him, if someone was willing to go down there after him.

No sooner had the realisation hit her with dizzying force than a huge pair of boots slammed onto the ice beside her. She looked up to see who was surefooted enough to jump down from the deck without slipping and recognised the massive frame of Henri LeFever. Round his waist was tied a rope which had held him erect when he landed. Above him at the rail hung a group of worried faces: Ann Cable, Errol, Sam and Joe.

LeFever reached down for her but she yelled at him, 'No! Give me the rope. I'm going down there after Timmins.'

LeFever froze and his eyes narrowed, his mind was clearly racing, calculating the odds.

'You're too big,' she pointed out breathlessly. 'You would never fit through.'

But he had already seen that and was untying the rope. 'What you need to do, Captain, is calculate how much he's actually worth. He's worth a couple of bruises and maybe a bad head cold.' He leaned down and pulled her to her feet – she had already scrambled up to her knees. He supported her in a gentle but unshakeable grip as she tugged her gloves off with her teeth and held them in her mouth like a puppy while she secured the rope round her waist. 'He isn't worth a broken bone or anything worse.'

She thought he was being jocular but he wasn't. He was advising her with absolutely calm calculation.

'When you get down there you'll want to take risks. Don't. If you get too badly hurt to run the ship then we're all in very bad trouble indeed. The only way we can rely on Captain Black, obviously, is if we find his stash of coke or whatever it is Reynolds supplied him with. There's no way we can trust Timmins or Hogg if anything goes wrong down there. You're all we've got, Captain. He's maybe worth one hair of your head, as they say. But he's not worth a hell of a lot more.' His grip tightened. 'You remember that, now.'

Aboard *Atropos*, the others kept a long loop of rope coming down to him independently of the half-tethered ship's wave-driven motion, and he eased her down the slope with as much easy power as the cargo crane. Throwing dignity to the winds, she slid down the icy incline on her bottom as though she were a child too poor to afford a toboggan. When her feet dropped over the gleaming green edge she called, 'Stop!' so loudly that she gave herself a fright. She jerked to a halt and looked down. She had reason to be tense. She seemed to be sitting on a wedge of ancient glass, green and full of twisted planes, veins and bubbles. She could see through it only vaguely, enough to make out light and darkness, movement and vague shapes only at its thinnest edge underneath her knees. Under her hands, which were on either side of her hips, it was thick and dark, almost smoky. And, amazingly, it was dry. There was no sign of moisture on it.

Until, with unexpected ferocity, a combination of air and spray roared up past her at considerable pressure. Only LeFever's iron grip kept her safe but neither the ice nor she was dry by the time it had passed. 'Go,' she bellowed when she had regained her breath, and he eased her forward until her buttocks were just sitting on the edge.

Then she was in, and he lowered her swiftly so that her hips, torso and head followed each other rapidly into the hole. As her shoulders went in, she twisted round so that she was hanging upright in the chamber, ready to look around herself as soon as her head came below the level of the roof.

It was as though she was inside a little dome of ice. The thinness of the crystal on either side of the crack let the light in untinted, but all around her the crystal coloured it to different hues so that even at its deep-sea darkest, it seemed to give off brightness. It was breathtakingly beautiful but she soon discovered that the chill rapidly eating into her bones was matched by an equal chill working its way out. This tomb of ice was utterly, inhumanly, terrifyingly alien. Life forms of any kind had no business in here, for this was death solidified. Its chill, petrified beauty was the negation of anything warm with pulsing life. And she remembered that of all the witches, goblins and monsters in the fairy tales which had filled her childhood, the Snow Queen had scared her the most.

Air hissed past her as though the place had whispered a curse, and green water snarled beneath her dangling feet.

The clear green boulders trundled along the floor like giant uneven balls of glass, and in among them was Timmins. He was just beginning to come round and his eyes were wide with more than panic. He had no idea she was just above him for he could no more hear her shouts than she could hear his screams. Wildly, fighting free of the deadly swirl of water and ice boulders, he managed to stagger to his feet and when he looked up – and not with any hope of salvation – she found herself staring into the face of a man who was looking hopelessly at death.

He was so utterly surprised that she should have come into this terrible place after him that something like madness fled across his dead-white countenance. The backwash slithered back from the dark bowels of the cave and he danced in it insanely, fighting to keep his feet, and when he looked up at her again there was a strange conflict of borderline sanity and terrifying hope in his washed-out, bulbous eyes. She had never seen it but she knew it: this was the look of the drowning man who would drag his rescuer down. She looked up. Why wasn't LeFever lowering her more quickly? She saw that the rope was cutting deeply into the edge of the ice. But then something dark fell across the crystal roof and was forced down ruthlessly, lifting the rope out of the lethal rut.

As soon as the rope was free, she was lowered rapidly until she was standing opposite Timmins. While standing listening to Le Fever's advice, she had in fact been tying two hitches into the rope – one for her waist and one for Timmins's foot, but looking at him now, she knew he would never be able to do something as simple as putting his foot through a loop and holding on to her knees as they went up. So she untied the loop round her midriff and tied it round his. Two quick tugs and Timmins left

the ground. As his knees came level with her face, she
stepped onto the loop at the rope's end and hung on for
dear life.

When her head hit the ice roof, it shattered around her
and tumbled like stained glass. Her shoulders and hips
were scored by blunt but bruising claws as she was jerked
bodily up over the bulk of the fender which had stopped
the rope from snagging. The force of the motion flung her
head backwards and forwards several times, and then her
forehead hit the ice with stunning force. The last thing
she knew was that LeFever had tossed Timmins to one
side and was reaching down for her.

When she woke up she was warm but she hurt all over.
She moved and discovered she was tucked up in bed. She
felt silk beneath her fingers and realised she was wearing
a nightdress. A head and shoulders swam into view. Ann
Cable was sitting on the bedside, lamplight gleaming on
her hair. Robin's head rose fractionally off her pillow
and her ears savoured the sound of alternators throbbing
purposefully, supplying her ship with electricity; with light
and warmth and hot food. Everything else could wait.
Even Richard. Ann said something, but Robin didn't hear.
The lullaby of the alternators sent her back to sleep at
once.

CHAPTER EIGHTEEN

Day Nine

Thursday, 27 May   19:30

The top floor of Heritage House on Leadenhall Street in the City of London was split into two halves. In one half, the twenty-four-hour secretarial staff of Crewfinders kept tabs on every officer, man and woman who worked for that great agency, placing them on Heritage Mariner ships as a matter of routine and also maintaining their traditional function of being able to replace any crew member from the captain to the third assistant chef within twenty-four hours, on any ship, belonging to any company, anywhere in the world.

In the other half was the nerve centre of Heritage Mariner Shipping itself. One complete wall displayed a map of the world. The huge display was electronically illuminated and contained information on the disposition of every Heritage Mariner ship anywhere in the world. As the room was nearly twenty feet tall and this wall was the better part of fifty feet long, the map easily filled 450 square feet, and it contained a great deal of information.

Against another wall stood an antique bookcase

containing in serried blue ranks every volume of the
Admiralty Pilot with all the updates; and at least one copy
of every other publication that Sir William and Richard's
combined century or so of seagoing experience had found
to be useful, interesting or amusing. It was a very big
bookcase indeed, and a set of library ladders stood beside
it on castors in case anyone wanted to consult a book on
an upper shelf. Below it, thrusting out too far to balance
aesthetically, was a chart chest containing every modern
Admiralty Chart and a scarcely legal collection of increasingly elderly ones – they really should have been destroyed
each time a replacement was published – going back to
1800 and, for some seas, even earlier than that. In a
mahogany magazine rack which had graced one of the
chambers in the original Lloyds building was a set of
weekly and monthly publications all on the same theme,
from *Lloyds' List* to *Boating World*.

Opposite the bookcase and at right angles to the huge
map was a wall which seemed to have been recently
transferred down from a space shuttle. Here were screens
and displays, keyboards, dials, meters and gauges, prin-
ters and scanners. It was a massive IBM computer system
constantly in contact with its equivalents in New York, San
Francisco, Sydney, Hong Kong, Tokyo and, more recently,
Archangel and Murmansk. It could reach hundreds more
at the touch of a button via the telephone modem. There
were ten telephones, five of them constantly manned by
secretaries, but so many lines out that it had its own
international switchboard and a mini exchange in the cellar
below, beside all the company records. On the roof was a
transceiver and satellite monitoring system so sophisticated
that it had been installed by some of the same men who
had worked on the roof of Century House, the new head-

quarters of the British Secret Service.

The final wall was wood-panelled round a tall, ornate doorway flanked with mock Doric columns and a triangular lintel inspired by the Acropolis. To the right of this door, which opened into the passage from the Crewfinders office, the panelling was a fitting background for a series of paintings, all, in keeping with the room, on nautical themes.

On the left of the door was a picture window, placed there by a combination of 1940s architecture and a German thousand-pound bomb dropped during the Blitz. The window looked south across Fenchurch Street and East Cheap. On the right as you looked out lay the Monument and the span of London Bridge; ahead, Billingsgate and the Custom House; to the left lay the Tower of London and, beyond it, Tower Bridge. The backdrop to all these was the dark flow of the River Thames. The window was so designed that the central section could be raised to give access to a tiny balcony outside from where a keen-eyed observer could see everything from Shadwell and the distant tower of Canary Wharf in the east to the great dome of St Paul's in the west, and over the south bank halfway to the Old Kent Road. Churchill himself had once remarked that there was very little worth looking at in London which could not be observed most satisfactorily from Bill Heritage's balcony.

None of the men in that room on this particular spring evening was at all interested in the view, least of all Richard Mariner. Sir William had brought back from Harcourt Gibbons' funeral his old friend Sir Justin Bulwyr-Lytton. Or, more correctly, Sir Justin had, for reasons of his own, attached himself to Sir William and stayed with him relentlessly through the afternoon. Now Sir William and Sir Justin were seated opposite each other on the pair of leather chesterfields on each side of the low antique table, each man nursing a drink. But Richard could not settle. He was caught between two crises, still strung out on adrenaline from the court case, and he could not bring himself to sit down.

At least the conclusion of the case had finally liberated him to go to Robin's aid; but now that he could do so, there was nowhere for him to go. Clad in a dark pinstripe City suit, he strode up and down the room from the map wall to the communications consoles, brushing past the chesterfields and kicking up the corner of a priceless Persian carpet. The last reported positions of *Clotho* and *Atropos* were marked in the southern section of the Labrador Sea, one behind the other, as reported when last contact was made. But these positions were more than twenty-four hours out of date now because the last contact had been made yesterday, and he knew that there was something badly wrong. In these waters, in those conditions, with ships in that state, no news was bad news.

He was helpless without direct contact with one of the sister ships. The cloud cover was too heavy to be penetrated by the keenest-eyed satellite and while the pyrotechnics of yesterday's spectacular solar flare might well have sent astronomers into transports of ecstasy, it did nothing for men and women struggling to communicate over half the world. There was no news of the ships from any of the transmitters on the west coast of Greenland or the east coast of Labrador. The only news from Newfoundland was that even the fishing boats were avoiding the ice-clogged banks. The Labrador Sea from the Davis Strait in the north to Belle Isle in the south and across to Kap Farvel in the east was a no-go area for shipping and a black hole for communications.

The only thing that anyone seemed to be certain of was that part of the great barrier of ice which normally bearded the chin of southern Greenland had broken off and the better part of a thousand square miles of ice, most of it a hundred feet thick, was in the same place as his ships.

'I've got to get out there,' he said, not for the first time, fighting to keep his voice level.

'But where are you going to go, my boy?' asked Sir William. 'Be practical. Until we know where they are exactly, then you're better off here.'

'But—'

'But nothing. You're exhausted. You're under enormous stress. You're not thinking clearly. If you go, what will happen? You'll end up either in Federiksdal in Greenland because it's fairly ice-free at the moment or you'll have to go to New York or somewhere and wait there.'

'I'd go to Gander. It's closer.'

'Even in Newfoundland, you'd just be sitting around waiting for news. Wait here, Richard. Really, I—'

'He's making sense, old chap,' interposed Sir Justin quietly. The weight of their combined opinion gave Richard pause for thought. The two men had been school friends together between the world wars. They had been in the navy together fighting the Nazi and Japanese imperial fleets. Bill and Bull had been a maritime legend lasting from 1939 to 1945. Then Sir William had left the navy to set up his first shipping company and Justin Bulwyr-Lytton had joined the Diplomatic Corps. He had returned to his maritime interests after retirement, however, becoming adviser to the International Maritime Bureau, specialising in Middle Eastern terrorism in the eighties before Saddam Hussein turned the Gulf on its head. Now he advised the unofficial INTERPOL of the sea on terrorism in general. Few men had more contacts in the widest range of relevant organisations – official, clandestine and just plain illegal – than he did. And no one in the country knew more about terrorism than he did.

'You're right,' admitted Richard at last. 'I'd be silly to leave home base. I've got everything I need for quick action here. If I'm anywhere else in the world at all when word comes in I'll be lucky to be able to move. But if I'm here, then I can use my own facilities.' He glanced at the Greek-inspired door through to the adjacent office. 'Crewfinders will deliver me anywhere in the world faster than anyone else could hope to do. And that includes the middle of the Labrador Sea.'

Sir William patted his son-in-law on the shoulder in a way that only Richard's real father would ever have dared to do. 'That's better, Richard. You're talking sense now.' He paused, lost in thought for a moment, then he stirred himself as a new thought occurred to him. 'Well now,' he began, but one of the secretaries interrupted him quietly.

'Excuse me, Sir William. I have a call incoming for Sir Justin.'

Bulwyr-Lytton put down his black rum and pulled himself up out of the burgundy leather chesterfield. 'Let this rest until I find out what this call's all about,' he requested gently. 'Richard, why not break the habit of a lifetime? Have a drink, man, and settle down.'

That was asking too much, but Richard at least forced himself to perch on the leather arm of his father-in-law's sofa and flip impatiently through the latest Western Ocean weather reports to see if there was anything he might have missed.

Sir Justin talked on the phone for a moment, unconsciously pulling at the white point of his naval whisker beard. Then he put his hand over the mouthpiece and said,

'It's a friend of mine. He's faxing something over to me. What's the number here, Bill?'

Sir William told him, and the old naval commander passed it on to his mysterious 'friend'. Richard looked up, distracted from the weather reports, intrigued in spite of himself. What was old Bull up to? For the first time it struck him that Sir Justin was behaving rather strangely. Richard's eyes met the old commander's square on and it was as though Bulwyr-Lytton suddenly read his suspicious thoughts. 'It'll be here in a minute,' he said blandly. 'My friend says it's not just for my attention. He says you should take a copy as well. But it's for me to pass on to my people at the International Maritime Bureau, of course. It's apparently the sort of thing we might need to know about in our unceasing efforts to keep the seven seas safe from wrongdoers of all sorts. And something you need to see too. I don't know what it is, but he doesn't think you'll like it.'

'Bull, what on earth are you talking about?' asked Sir William, looking between the other two, suddenly aware that their gazes had locked and held. 'What is going on here?'

'It all blew up in New York this morning,' said Sir Justin. 'I heard about it at ten, just as I was on my way to Harcourt's farewell do. It came out in the first editions of some of the papers there. No one knows how it got circulated so widely. Looks as though there was quite an organisation involved. And that's very worrying. Very worrying indeed.'

'What is?' asked Richard, goaded to frustration by the old man's deliberate obscurity. But before Sir Justin could answer, the secretary brought in the fax and they could all see for themselves.

It was a handbill. Either it was cheaply produced or it had not copied well. But there was no mistaking what it showed. Most of it was taken up with a black and white photograph of jumbled wreckage. After a moment's study, it was possible to make out two faces among the splintered wood and twisted metal. They belonged to the late Secretary of State for Northern Ireland and to Richard. It had clearly been copied from a newspaper picture in one of the many reports worldwide about the explosion in the Harland and Wolff shipyard. Underneath the picture in large, bold letters it said: 'SOME WOULD DIE TO SAVE THE WORLD. WE WILL KILL.' And under the slogan it was signed 'La Guerre Verte'.

The three men pored over it with disgust and horror, and not a little confusion. At the bottom of the faxed sheet, Sir Justin's 'friend' had scrawled simply, 'Who is the message for?'

'What is this all about, Bull?' Sir William asked again. 'No more beating about the bush now. Lay it on the line, please.'

'The group calling themselves La Guerre Verte are ecological terrorists. Like any other terrorist group, they believe in killing and maiming in order to enforce their beliefs.'

'The Green War,' said Richard, his voice trembling as he looked down at the blurred image of his own rage and agony beside his friend's dead face. 'What does it mean?'

'You've heard of Greenpeace? The organisation dedicated to trying to preserve the earth and endangered species on it?'

'Well yes, of course. Ann Cable belongs to it, quite apart from anything else.'

Sir Justin nodded. 'Well, La Guerre Verte believes in

the same basic things, so I understand. The difference is that they will kill in order to preserve the planet. Kill and maim and destroy. Whatever it takes.'

Richard was looking down at the poster, at the picture of the wreckage in the Belfast shipyard. 'So this wasn't the IRA after the Secretary of State,' he said slowly. 'It was these Green War people.'

'This makes it look that way.'

'And if it was Green War, they had no reason to kill Sir Jeffrey at all. He was a noted green campaigner and a powerful voice for the environment.'

'But so are you, Richard,' spat Sir William.

'Yes, but I'm also the man making money by transporting nuclear waste across the North Atlantic. And the boats we were launching when the bomb went off are the boats designed to do it.'

'Certainly looks as though my friend might have a point,' said Sir Justin.

'That's insane,' growled Sir William.

Richard was up on his feet again, looking at the massive map. 'Say he's right and the bomb was a message for us. We didn't listen to it, did we? The ships have been launched and fitted. They're in service, for heaven's sake! And these Green War people must know that.' He strode back to the table and snatched up the fax. 'This proves that they have access to explosives and the willingness and expertise to use them.' His hand trembled slightly, like his voice, as he put the flimsy sheet back down on the coffee table. 'If they tried once and failed, what's to stop them trying again?' He looked at his father-in-law and then across at their oldest friend. And he asked the question clamouring on the tips of all their tongues: 'How do we know they *haven't* tried again?'

All three of them looked up at the map with new horror as they realised what the twenty-four hours of silence might in fact mean. The storms were dangerous enough in those waters, but the ships had been designed to ride them. The ice was worrying but, again, they had been designed to meet it. But who would ever have conceived that *Atropos* and *Clotho* might have had to overcome terrorist bombs as well?

They were still looking at the map when the same secretary suddenly spoke up. She didn't say it to anyone in particular, but announced excitedly, 'I have an incoming.'

The tone of her voice made the three men swing round. The secretaries here were every bit as deeply involved in the wellbeing of these ships as their owners and operators were. Emotionally if not financially.

Richard strode across to her. 'Put it on the amplifier, please, Rachel. I'll take it.'

Rachel's long fingers pushed a switch and suddenly the big room was full of the hiss of static.

'. . . *Heritage Mariner London* . . .' it said through the whispering ether and fading away again.

'What's the wavelength?' asked Richard.

Rachel's dark eyes flicked up to a display in front of her. 'Company standard. But it's coming in from the Labrador Sea. I'm certain of that. If I get a fix on them for long enough I'll tell you exactly who it is and where they are.' She broke off for a second, then said, 'Strength building again.' On the screen in front of her, the vertical bars denoting reception strength climbed as the computer registered reception below hearing level and tried to filter the message out of the solar static so it could boost it up for them.

'. . . *Mariner London, are you receiving me?*'

'Yes! This is Richard Mariner. You are faint but we can hear you! What ship is this, over?'

Silence again, except for that faint, sinister whispering.

'They're not broadcasting,' said Rachel, her eyes on the green bars in front of her. 'I'd say they received you. Wait for it. Here it comes!'

'. . . *hear you, Heritage Mariner. I have the captain . . .*'

'You are very faint, over.'

'*I say again, this is* Clotho *and I have the captain for you, over.*'

'Thank God!' shouted Richard and he yelled jubilantly into the transmitter, 'Robin, this is Richard. We have you intermittent strength ten.'

'*Richard. I hear you. I'm sorry, Robin isn't aboard. This is Nico. I'm afraid I have some very bad news . . .*'

CHAPTER NINETEEN
Day Nine
Thursday, 27 May   20:00

Richard turned on his heel and walked through to the Crewfinders office. In many ways the room was a smaller version of the office he had just left. There were only two secretaries. He crossed to the senior one, who in fact had a major stake in the company these days and a seat on the board. She had been the secretary with whom he had started the business, more than fifteen years ago, in the old offices in St Mary Axe which had been destroyed by the IRA bomb at the Baltic Exchange. 'Audrey,' he said crisply, 'I need to be on our ship *Clotho*. She's presently in the Labrador Sea. Here's her exact position.' It was written on a piece of paper which he placed on the desk in front of her. She picked it up and her practised glance went at once to the point on the world map about 150 miles off Kap Farvel, slightly to the south and west.

'How soon?' Her voice was quiet, calm and deep.

'Now. Immediately. *Atropos* is gone and there are several dead. Jamie Curtis and Rupert Biggs at least.

They're damaged and in a bad situation. There may even be terrorists involved.'

'My God! Those poor people. I'll contact the Portsmouth police to break it to Jamie's mum and dad. At least Rupert Biggs didn't have any relatives, but . . .' She pulled herself together. She could cry later. She had to get Richard out there now. 'You go and get your travelling bag together. We have your passport and papers in the safe here. Pick them up from the doorman on the way out.'

He hesitated for a second longer. He knew she saw Crewfinders as her own family. She had just lost two sons.

'Hurry,' she said. 'I'll have a cab outside the front door in five minutes.'

Suddenly aware that he had not used the services of his own company in this way for nearly a decade, he said, 'Where shall I tell the driver to take me?'

She glanced up at him, her green eyes shaded by her long lashes, as calm and deep as her voice. And as full of tears. 'You don't tell him anything, remember? We take care of all that. We take care of everything.'

On the floor below, beside their own office, he and Robin kept a tiny bedroom with toilet facilities and changing rooms en suite. Here he put together a case of the basic necessities. He wasn't really paying attention to what he was doing, however, because his mind was totally preoccupied with the news Nico had given him, trying to see the hand of Sir Justin's mysterious eco-terrorists. It was worse than almost anything he could have imagined. But at least one ship was still afloat, so the extra element which the poster from La Guerre Verte had added to the situation did not seem to have come to full force yet. But two dead so far. Dear God in heaven! He couldn't think what he needed. He grabbed his washbag, chucked in some shaving equipment and dumped it automatically in his briefcase. Should he bother with flannels? Soap? Towel? The thought of taking any clothes was too complicated even to consider.

With an attaché case ill-packed with little more than his shaving kit, he rushed downstairs. Sir William and Sir Justin were waiting for him in the lobby, as was the driver of the black cab at the door. The farewells were brief and understated. 'Is there any way you can get the twins back up to Cold Fell and look after them there?' he asked. Fortunately, it hadn't even begun to dawn on him that little William and Mary might be targets for terror. He just wanted them out of town.

'Of course we will, lad. Janet will take them up at once. They love Cold Fell. They'll probably think they're on an early summer holiday.'

Richard gave a cough of laughter at the bracing words. It seemed unlikely that even his children, whom he indulgently supposed to be outstandingly intelligent, would actually understand about holidays yet.

'When Helen gets back from Moscow at the weekend, we'll go up and see them settled in, I promise. But you and Robin will probably be back yourselves by that time.' Helen Dufour was the chief executive in the Heritage Mariner office. Sir William was retired now and the Mariners came and went. They needed someone whose presence could be relied upon unless, as now, negotiations were called for which needed a special negotiator. Sir William missed the French executive particularly; they were in the throes of an affair.

'I doubt we will be back,' said Richard. 'So give my love to Helen and kiss the twins good night from both of us . . .'

The security man came forward with Richard's travel documents. Richard took them automatically and rushed out through the door with the cabbie in tow. 'You relax, guv,' said the driver as he slammed the door behind his fare and climbed into the front. 'We're off to the heliport beside City Airport. Ten minutes in this traffic.'

Richard leaned back into the seat, eyes closed and mind busy. But really there was little enough for him to think about; nothing positive anyway. He had worries aplenty and speculations without number. But he was not a man who worried unless he had something specific to worry about, or who planned without basis. He had a habit of checking ahead for bridges to cross, but he never tried to cross them before he came to them.

Damn! He hadn't packed his hairbrush. Had he remembered his aftershave? He used to be so organised! Not tonight, apparently. He took a deep breath, stopped worrying about what he had or had not remembered to pack, and cleared his mind.

So, he was in the velvet grip of his own organisation and, although he had not the faintest idea of where he was going in the short term, he was absolutely confident that he would be aboard *Clotho* as quickly as humanly possible. When he got there, he would be able to work with Nico Niccolo to decide the next step. If the weather continued to moderate and *Clotho* stayed afloat and out of trouble, then he would go and search for *Atropos*. In every other circumstance he would have to head for safety and leave Robin to fend for herself. She was an extraordinary woman and a captain of real genius. If circumstances conspired to overwhelm her, then her situation would have been far beyond anything he himself could have remedied in any case. Especially if the only steed he had upon which to ride to her defence was a ship with no bow section left. Some knight in shining armour, he thought wryly; not so much El Cid as Don Quixote.

The heliport building was a blaze of light in the gathering gloom of the spring evening. The cab pulled up outside it and the two men hurried in. Richard was at first surprised to find the cabbie so solicitous, but it soon became obvious that this was all part of the system. Richard himself was disorientated. His mind was full of the everyday concerns from which he had been torn away. He could hardly believe that he was about to travel a quarter of the way round the world with fewer preparations than were normally required to go shopping in the local supermarket with Robin and the twins. He was quite incapable of making sensible decisions about travelling at the moment. Much of Crewfinders' success had been based on the fact that Audrey and he had realised this when they set up the system in the first place.

Another stranger swam into view and the cabbie handed Richard over to him. 'Good evening, sir,' he said. 'I'm your helicopter pilot. We're off to Gatwick. Follow me, please.'

Well, that was something, Richard thought, feeling a bit more in charge at once.

Together they hurried out of the building by another door and across a concrete apron towards a flock of helicopters. All but one were at rest. They crossed at a half-run towards the one which was winding up. 'Sorry to rush you, sir,' yelled the pilot. 'But you're on the nine o'clock flight to Reykjavik. Time's a bit tight.'

The helicopter heaved itself straight up into the air and Richard leaned forward. He loved helicopters, though it was Robin who had the licence to fly one. As the slim fuselage tilted, swinging them across the river, he craned like a child to see familiar landmarks. Then the sleek craft tilted forward as the pilot dropped her nose and began to race south towards the lights of the Oval, Brixton and

Streatham. The pilot was too busy clearing their flight path and contacting Gatwick to indulge in conversation, so Richard had leisure to sit back and return to his thoughts.

He would take command from Nico. The big Neapolitan did not have his master's papers yet. Not that there was any need to have very advanced qualifications in order to sit and wait for your ship to be rescued. His mind sheered away from the financial implications of the salvage claim on the sister ships if they both had to be towed home. Thank heaven they had been so punctilious about insurance, crippling though the premiums had been. But if the tow could be resumed, if *Clotho*, no matter which way round she was facing, could bring *Atropos* home herself, or at least to a safe haven, then that worry at least was sorted out.

Toothbrush! He had forgotten to pack his toothbrush. Good God Almighty!

Gatwick pounced upwards, an angular blaze of white and gold light against the satin blackness of the Sussex hills. Once again, the sense of purpose and urgency gripped Richard. He forgot about toothbrushes and pushed all the other worries to the back of his mind. He sat up and held his seatbelt, ready to jump down as soon as the wheels touched the ground. Again, the pilot accompanied him, carrying the ill-packed briefcase, guiding him into the maze of buildings and safely, swiftly, through the disorientating labyrinth of multi-level corridors.

His ticket was being held for him at the departure gate and the helicopter pilot took him straight there. The ticket was not the only thing waiting there. One of the Crewfinders secretaries lived in Cowfold, a village near the airport. She kept a small cabin-sized emergency suitcase packed and ready in her spare room. While he had been winging his way southwards, she had been driving north with the case. As he rushed through to the waiting aeroplane she pressed it into his hand so that when at last he sat back in the big, comfortable airline seat, his worries about forgotten necessities were at least quietened.

He had assumed that the grasp of the commercial airline would be impersonal when compared with the very personal service of Crewfinders, but this was not the case. The stewardess took him under her wing and made sure he had a clear view of where they were going and when they were due to arrive. This, too, returned his sense of control over the proceedings and he decided to use the next two hours to check on the contents of the suitcase and then do some serious planning as the plane beneath him hurled down the length of the runway and climbed into the air.

'Captain Mariner, wake up, please. We are beginning our descent into Reykjavik now.'

Dazedly he opened his eyes and found himself looking into bright blue eyes fringed with dark blonde lashes and framed with ash blonde hair. For one confusing moment, he thought he had made it to heaven after all. It didn't occur to him that this was less because the hostess looked like a Nordic angel than because he had been dreaming of death.

'What time is it?' he asked automatically. His watch said 23:20 but it was set to London time.

'Iceland is on London time, Captain Mariner. We're due to land at half past eleven. I have some documents for you to sign here. You will disembark first. I will be taking you straight across to your next plane.'

His eyebrows rose, and she smiled. 'A message from your office was routed through direct to the flight deck. I think the pilot will be going to dinner with your Audrey the next time he's in London.'

Reykjavik was extremely cold and for the first time he realised just how unsuitable his pinstriped suit was for travelling this close to the Arctic. The airport lights were bright as the hostess walked him across the windswept apron, her heels tick-tocking purposefully on the concrete in front of him, her shadow pointing darkly southwards as though suggesting he should go back home at once. At least the night was dry, though the wind felt as if it was sweeping directly from the Pole and it was strong enough to hurl his bags against his knees with jarring force. He was not looking forward to being on board a pitching ship in rough seas. He hoped fervently he had a good supply of painkillers in his washbag just in case. Heritage Mariner were unusual in that they kept doctors aboard their super-tankers but they relied upon senior officers and paramedic calls on their smaller ships.

The executive jet was small and fast-looking, and the engines were whining urgently as the hostess hurried him up the steps into the cabin. In the doorway he turned and looked back at her as she stood on the concrete beside the man who was waiting to roll the steps away. The cabin was warm and quiet behind him but he lingered until she looked up. Then they exchanged waves and wide grins as though they had been friends for years.

There was no one in the long cabin so he dumped his cases on a seat and went on up to the flight deck. The two pilots were busy, one balancing the engines and the other talking to the tower. 'Welcome aboard, Captain Mariner. Sit down and make yourself comfortable, please. I'll be back to talk to you once we're in the air. We hope to be in Julianehab in two hours' time.'

They touched down in Greenland's major city two hours later, but because they had crossed two time zones, it was still just coming up to midnight. The airport would not normally have been open this late, unlike the port, which was open twenty-four hours. Richard's Danish was severely limited, but the officials who saw him through the little airport and put him in a taxi down to the harbour spoke enough English for him to know what was going on. The formalities were basic, though the Danes had a reputation for punctiliousness, because he was only passing through.

As it was so dark, he was no more able to make out the countryside from the back seat of the old Volvo taxi than he had been from the window of the executive jet. He could feel gentle undulations, and gained the impression that the road was leading down a slight incline, but there was little to see beyond the headlight beams until they breasted a low rise and the little town clustered around the bright port was spread out below them. Beyond the citrine jewels of the street lights and the clustered whiteness of the dock lights, there was an enormous blackness. Close to the shore, it revealed itself in pale lines of foam. Further out, lines of brightness ran across heaving restlessness. Perhaps only his imagination saw the faintest reflective gleams on the big seas further out. He wound down the window and sniffed the icy sea wind until the taxi driver asked him to close it again. Even in Danish, there was no mistaking the message. When Richard had obeyed, the driver turned up the heater with a vicious twist of his wrist.

He had recovered his temper enough to help Richard across to the little heliport lying on a promontory to the east of the brightly lit port. Here a battered old Sikorsky was winding up. The pilot must have been warned that his passenger was on the way by the people at the airport, Richard guessed. He climbed aboard and strapped himself in as the taxi driver dumped his travelling cases in beside him. Then he slammed the door and the helicopter swooped up into the sky.

At first, Richard was content to sit and think. He had slept on the Lear jet as well so he was four hours' rest better off than he had been at eight. His head was quite clear and he was in a position to start making some plans. He noticed that, like his brain, the sky was becoming clear as well. The buffeting from the wind did not lessen, but he suddenly realised that he was looking down at the broad white track of a full moon lying across the waves. If he looked up, he could see the familiar formations of the northern stars. 'It's clearing up,' he bellowed to the pilot.

The pilot pulled the right earpiece off his ear and let it rest on his cheek. 'What d'you say?' He had an American accent. But that could mean anything.

'The weather. It's clearing.'

'Yeah. We're in for a spell of winter high pressure.'

'This'll be the last of the north-westerly storm, then.' The helicopter bucketed and bounced through turbulent air.

'That's about it. Great big high-pressure system on the icecap's fallen over westwards. There'll be no weather systems through here for days. This'll be the last. When it's gone, the rest'll all run south through the States. Screw up springtime in Vermont.'

'What sort of temperatures are you expecting?'

'Daytime middling high, nighttime low.'

'How low?'

'Out on the icefields, maybe minus twenty. This air is cold as well as heavy.'

'So it'll start freezing up again.'

'Maybe. More likely further north. This ship of yours we're going out to, this *Clotho*, she should be okay. She's south of the cape, south of the ice barrier. She can run on down through the calm if there's a problem. Time it right, fit in your passage between depressions, and you can run her back to England in the warm between the storms.'

'Yes. But I wasn't thinking of *Clotho*. What'll it be like further north? North of this ice barrier, say?'

'Not so nice. Storm before this was a south-easter. Blew a lot of ice back up into the Davis Strait. This one will have fetched it out again. Freezing temperatures will keep the floes big and nasty. And I heard tell of an ice island out there somewhere too, but that's more likely just a big berg. Still and all, I wouldn't like to be up in the Labrador Sea till it all gets sorted out and comes back down south to melt.'

They found *Clotho* an hour later, though the pilot had increasing trouble keeping in contact with Bill Christian on the radio. 'Combination of anticyclonic conditions, solar flares and the good old Borealis,' he said cheerfully. 'Ain't life great up here in the frozen north?'

She was lying still, in a blaze of light that they could see from miles away. The pilot didn't bother circling. He charged straight on in and set down immediately in front of the bridge. Nico's radio message had forewarned Richard about the missing gantry and the shadows born of broken lights effectively hid the rest of the damage up forward. He pushed the door open and slung his bags out. Then he automatically checked his wristwatch. As he did so, the pilot bellowed over the roar of the rotors,

'Remember we crossed another time zone, Captain. It's just coming up to midnight here.'

'Thanks,' yelled Richard and hit the release on his seatbelt.

He stepped down onto the throbbing metal of the main deck, thinking, 'I only left London at eight. That's pretty good, even for Crewfinders.' Then he caught up his cases and, doubled under the screaming rotor blades, he took his first steps aboard his new command.

Audrey had stayed on duty even after she had ensured Richard would get through quickly. She had phoned the police while he was in the taxi on his way to the heliport and she knew that if she went home she would simply sit and brood about the utter ruin of Mr and Mrs Curtis's lives. Just the thought of them made her cry again, though she had never even spoken to them. Richard had, she knew. He had been down there and talked to them. And it was only the current emergency which had stopped him from going back down to break the news himself. As she had observed, Crewfinders took care of everything.

At 4 a.m. she rose and stretched. There was a pot of particularly excellent coffee on the simmer in the Heritage Mariner office next door and although they worked for different firms on paper, the corporate spirit made them all a team together. This was particularly true of the twenty-four hour secretariat. Many of them became fast friends during the long night hours when they had to be ready to handle emergencies of all kinds but had nothing to do for most of the time except sit and keep boredom at bay. War conditions, Audrey called it.

'Any traffic?' she asked as she crossed beside the chesterfield.

'Nothing much,' said Jane, nearest of the two night guardians of the company radio waves. 'Come in for a coffee?'

'I'd kill for one. It smells wonderful. Is it still the Blue Mountain Captain Hammond brought?'

'It is. Liquid ecstasy.'

'Hot, strong and goes on for ever?'

'Very witty. Sharon, do you want one?'

'In a minute, thanks, Jane. I think I've got an incoming . . .'

Audrey poured Jane a cup and carried it across to her, not really paying any attention to the one-sided conversation Sharon was having.

'You are very faint . . . Say again, please . . . No. I'm afraid not . . . You are fading. Please say again . . . *Damn!* Lost it.'

The others looked over at that, for Sharon only raised her voice in the direst of emergencies and neither of them had ever heard her swear.

'Who was it?' asked Jane.

'I'm not certain. It was very faint . . .'

'It's that solar flare.'

'. . . but I think it was Captain Mariner.'

Audrey's eyes flicked up to the bright spot marking *Clotho*'s position on the big map. 'He's there already?' she said, surprised. 'That was quick.'

But Sharon swung round, frowning. 'No!' she said. 'The other one. Not him. *Her!*'

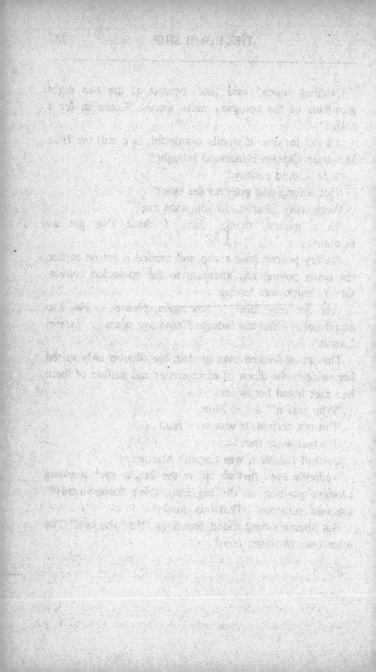

CHAPTER TWENTY

Day Ten

Friday, 28 May   00:00

'*Jesu*, Richard, you look dead beat.'

'It's been a long day, Nico. Twenty-eight hours long, quite apart from anything else. You don't look too bright yourself.'

'You think I look bad, you wait until you see *Clotho* in the morning.'

'I can look round now.'

'You can look. You won't see nothing. All the lights down at the bow, they're—'

'Fucked?' It was an old joke. The swearword was the Neapolitan's catch-all for anything that wasn't working properly, from a door handle that wouldn't turn to a tanker that wouldn't float. Nico gave a weary smile, hardly more than the crinkling of his eyes.

'So,' said Richard, still in the grip of the momentum that had carried him here, so far so fast. 'Let's get everyone up here for a council of war.'

'That won't take long,' said Nico flatly. 'But if I was you I'd make it a quick one. The others are as tired as you look and I feel. If you got the energy, I would ask you to take the next watch and we see what to do in the morning. But you are the captain now so we do whatever you want.'

The current complement of the good ship *Clotho* stood at six, including her new master. It was almost with awe that Richard surveyed them a few minutes later. Two deck officers, Nico and big bluff Johnny Sullivan; two engineers, Andrew McTavish and Harry Piper; Bill Christian the radio officer. Together these five had saved the ship and pulled her through the last of the north-wester. The tow had parted twenty-four hours ago exactly; their day had been every bit as rough as Richard's.

'I'm going to send you all to bed in a moment,' he said. 'The first watch is mine and it will run for six hours. But before I dismiss you, I must get some things clear in my mind. Bill. You first. No word from *Atropos* at all?'

'Nothing, Richard. But things have been pretty bad on the airwaves.'

'The solar flares. I know.'

'I'll leave her on open frequency and turned right up before I go.'

'Right. Andrew, you next. If I was thinking of going north to look for *Atropos*, maybe to take her in tow again, could you give me the power?'

'Aye, I could. She's running very sweetly, Richard, and we've plenty of bunkerage.'

'Nico. What about the bows? Could I take her north?'

'You'll see for yourself in the morning. And you can read my rough report if you feel like it tonight. But yes. She's afloat and she'll stay afloat. If the good weather arrives.'

'Johnny. Will it? What do the machines say?'

'That was Rupert Biggs's area really, but the system's

running pretty well and, yes, the weather's set to stay fair for the better part of a week. Warm sunny days, cold clear nights. No wind to speak of. Typical winter anticyclone. The sea will be flat calm to go with it, I should say.'

'All the local stations confirm that,' added Bill Christian. 'Air pressure going through the roof.'

'All right, then—'

'Even so,' interrupted Nico quietly, 'you got to think of your insurance. If your insurers ever find out you deliberately took a damaged vessel into a sea full of ice on anything except an immediate answer to a distress call, your policy will be—'

'Fucked,' said Richard. 'Yes, Nico, I know.'

They were going nowhere. There was no point in even trying for steerageway until they could get some idea of where *Atropos* was, so that they would know what course to set. The engines were idle and only the alternators were running. According to the positions punctiliously marked on the chart and confirmed by the satnav read-outs, they were hardly even drifting. Maybe five miles in the last twelve hours. From the look of things, not much further in the next twenty-four, now that the wind had dropped. They seemed to be sitting in a pool of still water at the convergence of the currents. They could certainly stay here quite safely through the night watches. Far north of the usual sea lanes, and lit up like a Christmas tree to boot, they were hardly a threat to shipping. In any case, the collision alarm radar was functioning every bit as well as the satnav; anyone foolish enough to be running this far north who also happened to be blind would set off the alarms and get a pretty sharp warning from Richard – if he could reply on the radio; he couldn't raise Heritage House.

Well, even if voice transmission wasn't reliable, he could always send in Morse code. The simple pulses would cut through the solar interference much more efficiently.

He boiled a kettle, made some coffee so strong that it seemed to hang upon his teeth, and sat down, as Nico had suggested, to read the report.

It had been the loss of the gantry that saved her. The hole in her bow which had let water into number one hold with such disastrous results had not been big. Nor had it been low on the front. When the weight of the gantry was removed, the deck had lifted. The hole had been jerked a good ten feet into the air and the water had stopped coming in at once. Even without power, the ship had remained steady, swinging sluggishly across the wind to settle with her bridgehouse acting as a sail and taking the lead. By that time, the long hull had spun round once through 360 degrees and the weather had abated considerably. Power had been restored as the dawn had come up and Nico had run due south. His radar showed him the end of the ice barrier at the twenty-mile limit to the west of him, and he had observed nearly ten miles of it. Then it had finished, cutting away northwards in a clean, almost rule-straight line. By the time he had cut his power and allowed her to drift to her present position, he was clear of the ice and safe enough.

All morning Bill Christian had broadcast in clear and code, on company frequencies and on open channels, with very little success. Morse signals drifted in and out of the static, but they were never strong enough to make sense, let alone contact. Things improved midday and peaked at four when he raised several local radio stations, one or two ships running to the south of them now that the storms were clear, and a Scandinavian Airlines 747 flying over the Pole. And, of course, Heritage Mariner. But with the onset of evening, communications had closed down again almost as though the god of the airwaves wanted to enforce the old adage 'If you can't see it, you can't speak to it'.

Once Richard had read the report, he put the log away and hauled himself to his feet. As much to keep awake as for any other reason, he began to check everything on the bridge. It was an old habit. One of his tricks of command. He tidied up the chart desk, sharpened all the pencils and set them in neat rows like soldiers on parade. He opened the Arctic Pilot and left it on page thirty-three where the heading said ICE. He crossed to the collision alarm radar and checked the detail of the five-mile setting. Then he turned the alarm down and checked the ten- and twenty-mile settings. Only when he set it at maximum could he see the ice barrier. A square corner of it palely disfigured the otherwise flawless deep green circle exactly at the eleven o'clock position. He reset it to five miles and turned the alarm back up. He checked the satnav and momentarily regretted that he did not have a sextant because the stars were huge and brilliantly clear and he would have enjoyed taking a sighting. But then he remembered how cold it was out on the bridge wings – and he was still dressed for a board meeting in London. He got a printout of the latest weather position from a satellite in low orbit over-head and would have given anything to ask it to scan the sea to the north of him for *Atropos*.

He forced himself to go through Nico's report of the separation and the loss of the two men on the forecastle head and realised he had been doing much of the fiddling and tidying around the bridge as an unconscious stratagem to avoid doing just this. The report was bald and direct. Its conclusions were inescapable. The men had been on

the forecastle head when the tow had parted. They did not
return. As soon as possible under the circumstances, Nico
himself had gone out to look for them. They were no
longer there. They were lost overboard. There was nothing
to be done.

Richard sat for a moment, wondering how he would
feel if he heard that the twins were dead. If he heard that
Robin was gone. It was too painful for him to contemplate
for any length of time.

At last he went through to the radio room and sat
looking at the bright red and green displays, listening to
the hiss of the open channels.There was a range of radios
here and he knew enough about them to know which he
could touch and which to leave alone. He took a pair of
earphones and slipped them over his head, then idly he
began to search the ether. As he concentrated on what
he could hear, so his eyes went slightly out of focus, but
they never left the warning light which would alert him
of a signal incoming on any of the other radios, nor the
display beneath it which would record the band, frequency
and strength.

And so the night passed while he fruitlessly searched
the short waves for any sound of even faintly human
origin. At about three o'clock it occurred to him that the
sound the empty waves were making was exactly the
same sound as bacon and eggs in a frying pan and he
realised he had eaten nothing since breakfast exactly twenty-four hours ago at 7 a.m., London time. It hadn't been
bacon and eggs, either.

He took off the earphones and got up. In the chart
room, in the corner beside the kettle and the instant coffee,
there had been a stack of cling-wrapped sandwiches. He
strolled through to investigate. The first one he opened
was shrimp in salad and mayonnaise. It must have been

there for the better part of two days and was starting to smell a bit sorry for itself. The same was true of the tinned salmon and cucumber. The thick, sliced, tinned ham was better, but the tomatoes had soaked through to leave sticky circles on the outside of the bread. But then he hit paydirt: beef and mustard. Three pairs of triangles. Perfect. He strolled back out onto the bridge, trying to find out where the edge of the cling wrap was.

He was concentrating on the near-impossible task so absolutely that he did not notice the warning light flashing from the radio room and it was not until he tore the wrapping free that he looked up. As soon as he did so, he dropped the unprotected sandwich and ran forward. The still wrapped pair went onto the watchkeeper's chair as he went past and he was wiping butter and Coleman's English on his lapels as he went in, in case he got the chance to transmit. It was the short wave. He turned the volume up until the hiss was like a big wave breaking, and right at the back of it, far, far away, he heard a whispering pulse: . . . *dot dot dot* . . .

He was in the seat at once, twisting the volume up until it was like sitting under Niagara Falls: . . . *dot dash dash* . . .

He caught up the handset in direct communication with the radio officer's cabin. He didn't even have to dial; just picking it up rang Sparks's bell.

He found he was whispering, 'Come on, come on, come on.' But whether he was talking to Bill Christian or to the signal, he never knew.

. . . *dash dash dot dot* . . .

'Yes?' So loud, it made him jump almost out of his skin.

'Bill, I've got something. Morse. Sounds as though it's coming in from Mars.'

'On my way.'

Richard put the handset back. His lips were moving with the Morse pulses, saying letters. His hand was scrabbling for a pencil, ready to write the letters down as soon as he understood them.

... *dot dot dot* ...

'S.'

... *dot dash* ...

'A.'

... *hissss* ...

'Missed it! Come on, come *on*!'

... *dot dash* ...

'A again.'

... *dash* ...

'T. It's T. God ...'

... *dot dot dot* ...

'S. It's an S.'

When Bill Christian came dashing onto the bridge, he heard his captain in animated conversation with the radio, yelling jubilantly over the thunder of static. When he swung round the door to look down into the radio shack itself, he saw Richard aglow with almost uncontrollable excitement.

On the pad in front of him were the capital letters written in his clear, bold hand:

A T S A T S A T S.

'ATS,' said Richard, beginning to calm down a little. 'It's *Atropos*'s call sign. We've got her, Bill, we've got her.'

They woke Andrew McTavish long enough for him to get them under way and put the engines on automatic, then Richard turned the wreck of *Clotho*'s bows towards the ice barrier and they began to feel their way northwards, following that scarcely audible Morse code call sign, with

Bill Christian sharpening up the reception and broadcasting *Clotho*'s Morse call sign CLO in return.

Once they were safely under way, Richard split his time between the helm and the chart table. To begin with, they simply followed the bearing where the reception was strongest, but this, even if it was giving them an accurate direction, only gave them the line *Atropos* was lying on, somewhere between *Clotho* and the North Pole. Once Richard was confident which direction the signal was coming from, he started to swing more and more widely off course to east and west, checking the new bearings which Bill gave him, trying to make that all-important triangle on the chart at whose point *Atropos* would be lying. It was slow, painstaking work which nevertheless required fierce concentration on the part of both men. The night fled by and it was not until the signal began to fade with the first hint of light that Richard realised he had given Nico considerably more of a lie-in than he had intended.

He sent Bill Christian down to bed, then went round the bridge one last time himself. He ended up staring disconsolately down at the bearing lines chinagraphed on the clear sheet over his chart. Where there ought to have been a dark-sided, clear triangle, there was something which looked more like a hedgehog. He narrowed his eyes, trying to make the darkest part of the figure coalesce into something positive, with no great success. Still, he had a ballpark. He would find the diamond later. And the striking plate, in due course.

Trying to coin an equivalent English analogy using cricket pitches instead of baseball parks, he walked over to the helm, pressed the communications button beside it and summoned Nico onto watch. When the Italian arrived, much refreshed, Richard explained how he and Bill Christian had spent the night. While he did this, he punched a course into the automatic pilot which would take them straight towards the point where most of the lines on the chart seemed to come closest to crossing each other.

Then he went to bed. 'Wake me in four hours,' was his final order. 'I want to look at the bows before we get anywhere near the ice barrier.'

Nico nodded, watched Richard stagger into the captain's day room behind the chart room, walked over to the watch-keeper's chair and proved how wide awake he was by removing two beef sandwiches from the seat before he sat in it.

'Captain Mariner went right over and climbed around on it,' said Nico, four and a half hours later.

'She would,' said Richard. 'But you won't get me over there, Nico, so don't draw up any plans to resume your command just yet. Still, that's a hell of a mess. What about the hole into number one?'

'It should have sunk us. We were lucky. But . . .'

'But?'

'The two who were down here at the time. They were not so lucky.'

Richard nodded. He had known Jamie and had met his parents; he had not known Biggs personally but he felt their loss equally keenly. They had both been Heritage Mariner men. More than that, they had been Crewfinders men.

Clotho was ploughing determinedly along the course Richard had set. Johnny Sullivan was on watch, Bill Christian was trying to raise Heritage House and Andrew was working on the pumping system with Harry Piper.

They were sailing deeper and deeper into the area of high pressure. The conditions were idyllic. High, clear skies of picture-postcard blue, and long, quiet seas one shade of green off the same colour. No wind to speak of, and a high, bright, early afternoon sun. The two men on the battered deck should have been wearing shorts and T-shirts, not the cold-weather gear they still required if they were going to be outside for any length of time.

Any thoughts of summer wear, however, were cancelled by the view dead ahead. The barrier was just below the horizon, but it made its presence known with breathtaking power. There was the faintest haze of fog above the corrugated raft of ice. It was hardly thick enough to be called cloud, but the suspension of water droplets and ice crystals extended quite a long way up the sky. Sunlight blazing off the dead-white surface below lit the fog like neon so that only *Clotho* could bear to look directly towards where they were headed. There the blue of the sky faded as though it was increasingly frosted over itself. At its lower edge, pale blue became blazing white and that whiteness seemed to contain the brightness of a chain of nuclear explosions burning all along the very top of the world.

'Have you checked the hole at all?'

'No. Like I say, Captain Mariner went over. But I won't.'

'Neither will I, but we need to have a look. I think we might be able to make a full assessment from inside the hold itself.'

'You don't think it's enough that we know the water has stopped coming in, that we have balanced the weight with the pumps so that the hull sits well in the water and we know we can sail safely forward? Why do you want to look at the hole?'

'How near the surface is it? Will it start to let in water

if the conditions get to force five on the Beaufort scale?
Force six? Will we be safe in a force-nine gale? Force-
ten storm?'

'What storm, Captain? Is dead calm—'

'How is the ice-strengthening at the waterline? Does the
hole come through it? Over it? How far over it? Yes, it is
a dead calm, but we're heading into ice. What thickness
of ice can we go through? Six inches? Will she ride over
six feet?'

'The hole into number one hold won't tell you much
about that, Captain.'

'But it will tell me something. And, when we get nearer
the ice, I might well find ways to look more closely
from the outside. Looking from the inside now will save
time then. And it might tell us something we could find
useful in the meantime. Was this hatch closed when the
hold broke open?'

'No. I came down and closed it later. Hard job, too, in
the dark with the safety lines all tangled here and where
the gantry went overboard. Tow line writhing around on
the deck like some great big snake. I don't like your
Western Ocean. I prefer the quieter seas. I am a Mediterranean man.'

'Yes, I know. Well, you've got some nice Mediterranean
weather today.'

'Don't get that much ice off Napoli, *Capitano*.'

Section by section they rolled back the McGregor hatch
and daylight flooded in to reveal a dark, dirty-looking little
sea of water restlessly heaving down in the number one
hold. Striking in across the wave tops and throwing them
into stark relief was a searchlight beam of brightness from
the hole in the forward wall of the hold.

'That's enough,' said Richard after three sections were

back. 'I only want to go down the forward wall and look at the hole itself.'

'Ladder don't look too safe no more,' observed Nico. 'You'd better wear a lifeline if you don't want to go swimming.'

'Good idea. It's a bit cold for a dip.'

A few moments later, Richard had clinched the line round his waist and Nico had tight hold of it. Then Richard carefully climbed over the raised edge of the hatch and put his feet on the first rungs of the ladder. It had been attached to the forward wall of the hold but the inrush of water through the hole had ripped a good deal of it free. After the first few steps, he found himself apparently climbing down a ladder made of rubber, which bounced and wavered with each new step and movement, no matter how slow and careful.

But Richard wasn't really concerned with this. There was no real danger, simply the outside chance of an unwelcome swim. Only if by some unimaginable accident was he thrown through the hole in the wall before him down into the Labrador Sea was there any actual chance of him coming to harm. By the look of things, the hole was quite big enough for him to fit through. It was near the top of the wall, centred perhaps two-thirds up from the inundated floor. It seemed to be very roughly circular with a radius of perhaps three feet. The edge was an obscene bloom of twisted metal petals not only from the hold wall but from the ruined bow immediately beyond it. In a strange way, the damage seemed to be acting almost like a monstrous rivet, joining the two layers of metal together.

Another few careful steps down brought him to a position from which he could see almost vertically down the cutwater of his ship to the creamy mess of her bow wave.

It was very difficult to judge distances in these circumstances, but it seemed to Richard that he had about eight, maybe ten feet of solid bow there between the hole and the wave tops. There was even a section, maybe a metre, of seemingly undamaged bow immediately above the tumbling foam. He would have to consult Andrew McTavish about that. 'Nico,' he called up, 'did Robin say anything about an undamaged section just at the waterline?'

'No, Captain. But I think she is riding much higher in the water since she lost the gantry.'

'That would make sense. Okay, I'll just go down a step or two more, then I'll be up again.'

Here, in fact, the ladder was almost horizontal, bent far back by the force of the water which had burst through the wall. Its base was another ten feet down in the water, bent back in towards its original attachment points. But it was no longer actually riveted to the wall, and really it should have been jumping up and down much more actively under Richard's weight. He had no way of knowing it as he moved across the twisted rungs like a monkey on a trampoline, but he was being held safely in place by the inertia of two dead bodies whose safety lines had bound them to the metal. But the more he moved, the more these bindings were loosened, so that, just as he decided that there was nothing more to see and began to climb back up, the body of Jamie Curtis followed him in ghastly pantomime up the rungs from under the water, the handle of the assassin's knife chiming faintly against the hollow rungs as he moved.

'What was that?' Richard called up to Nico.

'What? I heard nothing.'

'I don't know, a kind of ringing . . .'

As he spoke, Nico's walkie-talkie buzzed urgently. The

Italian turned as soon as Richard's head came out of the
hold. '*Pronto*?'

As Richard pulled himself onto the deck, Johnny Sullivan's voice boomed out excitedly, 'Tell the captain I think
we've got *Atropos*.'

They left the hatch as it was and ran up the deck
without a further thought. In the wheelhouse, Sullivan was
standing with a big flimsy printout. 'I think this is it,' he
said as they charged breathlessly in. 'The conditions are
so perfect that the satellites are sending down brilliant
weather pictures.'

He spread the printout on the chart table and Richard
could see what his lieutenant meant. He was looking at
an enhanced weather picture of the Labrador Sea. Not a
whole picture but a highly enlarged section perhaps ten
miles by ten on the earth's surface.

'Where did you get this?'

'We're back in contact with Heritage House. Not just
the radio. The machines too. They enlarged it. They faxed
it over.'

Richard nodded and leaned forward.

The picture, in stark monochrome, showed a long tongue
of white ice. To the south of it was black water. To the
north of it, black water, which gave way almost immediately to a stippling of white which thickened relentlessly
until the top of the picture was dead white again. To
the east, the ribbon of black water was wider before the
stippling warned of gathering ice floes. To the west, it was
narrower, and right in the north-western corner there was
something else. What this extra section could be was not
clear, but it was big and it seemed to be pushing the floes
down in front of it – which meant that it was moving.

And that was worrying, for, nestled against the straight

edge of the ice barrier immediately in its path was a tiny speck of brightness too vivid to be a floe. Too vivid, in fact, to be anything but *Atropos*.

CHAPTER TWENTY-ONE
Day Ten
Friday, 28 May   00:00

Robin hauled herself up out of a seemingly bottomless black pit of exhaustion to find someone was shaking her. That was the first thing her reluctantly wakening body realised: that she was being shaken very forcefully by the shoulder. Then other sensations came – the fact that the shoulder was bruised and tender, the fact that she was in a warm and comfortable bed. The fact that the bed was on a ship.

Her eyes opened and a face slowly pulled itself into focus, broad forehead frowning with concern, wide blue eyes which crinkled at the edges into laugh lines stretching back to the ears. High cheekbones, with long valleys joining them to a square chin with just the hint of a dimple under the gold-dust stubble. The firmly sculpted mouth, its top lip framed by a moustache, was talking to her, revealing perfectly even teeth. 'Stone says he thinks he's getting through to your home base, Captain,' said Henri LeFever. 'Hogg wasn't sure whether to wake you but I figured you'd want to know.'

'You figured right. What time is it?'

'Just gone midnight.'

'Time I was up anyway.' She swung herself out from under the blankets without thinking and was relieved to find Ann had put her in a long silk nightgown. She rose and crossed to the pile of neatly folded clothes on the chair beside the doorway into her main cabin. 'I'll be on the bridge in five minutes,' she said and turned to face him. Something about his eyes made her look down and she realised that the light coming from behind her made the gossamer confection she was wearing almost transparent. 'Five minutes, Mr LeFever,' she snapped.

'Aye aye, Captain,' he answered and went past her looking studiously at the floor.

She dressed quickly, not quite certain whether she was angry with the scientific officer or not. It was strange that, after thinking that she might join Ann as ship's sex object if Captain Black recovered, she should find herself being so observed by the one man aboard she had not thought of as a rabid sexist. Perhaps she had been over-impressed by LeFever after all. Or perhaps she had been so busy being a captain that in a way she had forgotten that she was a woman. She had not forgotten her femininity, she had simply moved it down the list of priorities a rung or two. It was not a question of how she saw herself, it was a question of how she wished others to see her. When she walked into a ballroom, she wished to be seen primarily as a woman. When she walked into a board meeting, she wished to be seen primarily as an executive. On a powerless ship, out of communication with home base, tied up against an ice barrier in the Labrador Sea, she wanted to be seen simply and solely as the captain. Not the short captain or the tall captain or the well-groomed captain or the scruffy captain or the white captain or the black captain or the weak captain. The strong captain; yes, certainly the strong captain. But not the woman captain; not the pretty captain; not – heaven forfend – the sexy captain. Just the captain. As in 'Yes, Captain! No, Captain! Three bags full, Captain!'

This was something she had achieved in the Heritage Mariner fleet, to such an extent that she never gave it a second thought because no one else seemed to either. But LeFever's look showed her that she might still have some work to do here. The thought was very unwelcome; she had so much other difficult work to do. She missed her officers from *Clotho*. Had she not had so many of her crew aboard, she might have felt isolated.

Still lost in these thoughts, which had much of their basis in the fact that she was so tired and for once in her life had not sprung fully awake at the first touch, she walked out of her cabin onto the corridor and found herself face to face with Captain Black. Later she realised that this was hardly surprising – Ann Cable had put her in the captain's cabin and the drug addict had woken in Reynolds's accommodation and was trying to return to familiar surroundings. But it gave her a shock at the time.

She had the advantage. She was properly dressed in overalls which were marked with a captain's badges of rank. He was in pyjamas which had seen better days and an ill-tied silk dressing gown several sizes too small for him. He wore no slippers, he needed a shave and his hair was a grey mare's nest.

'Who are you?' he demanded in tones of trembling outrage. 'What's some damn woman doing in my quarters?' He drew himself up, gathering his clothing around him like King Lear putting on his dignity in his rags and madness.

'Captain Black, are you well?' she asked gently. 'How do you feel, sir?'

Her gentle approach nonplussed him. Made him actually think about it. 'Well, I . . .' He began to shake, as though he were in the grip of the arctic wind which had been blowing outside. He looked down, and then up at her again. In the instant he looked away, he had aged ten years and his eyes had overflowed. Tears streaming and nose beginning to run, he said, 'As a matter of fact, I am not quite myself, I . . .'

And he went down at her feet in a dead faint as though cold-cocked from behind. She considered leaving him there but she could not do it. Back she went into the cabin and called up to the bridge. Hogg answered. 'Mr Hogg. Captain Black is lying out cold outside the door to the captain's sleeping quarters. Have someone collect him and put him safely to bed, please.'

On her way back past him, going on up to the bridge at last, she paused to check his pulse and breathing. So it was nearly ten past midnight when she actually reached the wheelhouse. With a nod to Hogg sitting comatose in the watchkeeper's chair, she swung through to the radio shack, crowding in beside Ann and Henri. 'Well?'

Harry Stone looked up at her. 'I've got Heritage House about strength five at least,' he said, and handed her the microphone.

'Heritage House? This is Captain Robin Mariner aboard *Atropos*. Can you hear me, over?'

The airwaves hissed and whispered. Then, abruptly, there was a fierce crackling sound as though the radio equipment had caught fire somehow. '. . . very faint . . .' said a woman's voice.

'This is Captain Robin Mariner aboard *Atropos*. Can you hear me, over?'

'Say again, please.'

'This is Captain Robin Mariner. Is my husband there?'

'No. I'm afraid not.'

'Please get a message to him or to Sir William. All well at present . . .'

'You are fading . . .'

'Have you any news of *Clotho*?'

'Say again . . .'

'*Clotho*?'

'. . . *Damn!* . . .' And she was gone.

'Well,' said Robin to Harry, 'at least they know we're alive. And still nothing from your headquarters in Sept Isles?'

'They don't have the kind of equipment your guys at Heritage Mariner have. They may be closer, but that don't mean a hell of a lot in these conditions.'

'You didn't ask for help,' said Ann. She sounded shocked, almost accusatory. LeFever nodded as though he agreed with her.

'No need. Making contact should be enough. They have the progress reports I phoned in while we had contact. They know everything that happened up to the second part of the tow. Now they know which ship I'm on, which is one thing that's new; and they know I've lost contact with *Clotho*, which is the other thing that's new. They'll call up Canada on the phone or fax the information across. Or I guess the Heritage computer will update the Sept Isles computer automatically. In any case, the message will get through in next to no time.'

'Harry has set the short wave to broadcast our identification signal. It's more powerful than the voice radio because it works on Morse code. In theory, just from that transmission, and maybe from others that weren't quite strong enough for voice contact, either of our bases should be able to locate us, or our general area. If the weather clears and the clouds go, then there's a fair chance someone will be able to enhance a satellite picture enough to get an idea of our general condition. Then they'll know what to do. In the meantime, our priority is to try and get the ship working again one hundred per cent.'

'How?'

'Well, Mr LeFever, we've got a spare propeller and unless we're offered a tow within the next two or three days, I see no reason why we shouldn't set about putting it in place and sailing ourselves out of this mess.'

'But how—'

'Yes, well, I haven't quite worked that one out yet, Ann.'

The plump, crumpled figure of Hogg loomed in the doorway.

'Captain.'

'Yes, Mr Hogg?'

'You did say you'd left Captain Black outside the captain's quarters?'

Robin took a deep breath. The tone of the question made it perfectly obvious what was coming next. 'He'd gone by the time your men got there?'

'Yes, Captain.'

'Well, in that case, I'm sorry, Mr Hogg, but you just drew the short straw. Take your men and search this ship from stem to stern. If you find him, lock him up. If you don't, then report to me. Either way, I want to see you here again one more time before you go to bed.'

He looked, literally, mutinous. She could hardly blame
him. It was the end of a viciously long period of unbroken
watchkeeping for him. Even though it was a glorified
harbour watch, he had nevertheless been in charge of the
bridge since she and Timmins had gone on her first inspection. He was clearly all in. But who else was there to turn
to? Timmins was out for the count, and apart from Harry
Stone, Hogg was the only other deck officer aboard. 'I'm
sorry, Mr Hogg,' she said gently. 'If there was anyone else
to turn to, I'd let you get some well-earned rest. But there's
no one. And he must be found. As he is, he's a danger to
himself and anyone he meets. He could even do the ship
some damage, you know.'

'I'll come with you, Hogg,' said Stone. 'If Tightship
goes outside, he'll freeze to death in a couple of minutes.
You got to try at least. Come on, the guy's your uncle,
for God's sake.'

'I'll come too,' offered LeFever. 'I can catch up on my
beauty sleep while the rest of you are juggling with propellers the same size as house fronts.'

Hogg shrugged petulantly and the three of them went.
Stone turned in the doorway. 'I've left it all on open
channels,' he said. 'Anything incoming, any contact at all,
and she'll light up like a fireworks display. I'll keep a
walkie-talkie with me so you can call me back here at
once.'

When they were gone, Ann and Robin walked back
through into the wheelhouse. Robin crossed to the log
book and signed on. 'I'm on watch,' she said to Ann.
'Why don't you go to bed?'

'I hate being on my own on this ship quite enough
without going into a cabin alone knowing there's a woman-
hating coke head on the loose.'

'I hadn't thought of that.'

'Robin, you amaze me sometimes.'

'Why?'

Ann smiled at her and shrugged. 'Never mind.'

A little after one, Hogg came in to say that they could find no trace of Captain Black. At that, Ann decided to stay the night on the bridge. 'Tell me what you plan to do if no help arrives,' she said, and Robin described the plans she was beginning to firm up in her mind. Then she had to describe to her relentlessly inquisitive friend the communications system they had in place on the ships.

It was an extension of the system they had set up to monitor the Heritage Mariner tanker fleet and it was basically divided into manual and automatic, ship-based and shore-based. The ships had radio transceivers with standard wide-range facilities to communicate with other ships, port facilities, home base and anyone else who happened to be listening on the operational frequency. They also had automatic identification signal facilities which transmitted the ship's call sign in Morse, like the standard guidance buoys near harbour mouths and shipping lanes. These were supposed to register on radios tuned to the right wavelengths even over great distances, and were designed to give head office an idea of the whereabouts of their ships. In the current conditions, however, all radio traffic in high latitudes was being disrupted, so there was no guarantee that the call signs were being registered any more than the standard transmissions.

There were other systems aboard – the satellite systems. The satnav system was designed to place the ship to within feet on the earth's surface. It did this by broadcasting a signal to a low-orbit satellite which compared the source of the signal with a map of the world and gave back the correct co-ordinates. Heritage Mariner were pioneering a system by which the satellite would broadcast the required information not only to the ship but to the big dishes atop Heritage House. That way, every time one of their ships checked position, the big map would be automatically updated. But the system wasn't in place yet. For the time being they had to be content with the third system, which was land-based but also involved satellites. In this system, the low-orbit weather and old spy satellites whose functions had now been extended to civilian use could survey specific areas of the earth's surface in great detail so that thermal images could be read through cloud cover – something as big as a supertanker would register through quite heavy cloud cover. Or, if they got clear skies, it was quite possible to enhance photographs of the ground, and the ocean, until actual vessels and their immediate surroundings could be seen. Then these pictures could be despatched to ships to be married in with weather maps and navigational charts, to give a very accurate impression of the ship's position. By definition, as these went through head office before they reached the ship, they were used to update the information in the office's computers.

But it was the on-board equipment that most captains preferred to rely on. Robin laughed and reminded Ann that John Higgins, with whom the American reporter had sailed on the ill-fated *Napoli*, still preferred to use his sextant rather than his satnav and he was by no means alone.

But mentioning John and *Napoli* brought gloom back into the picture. Both women were too well aware that the court case would have been heard in the law courts within the last thirty-six hours, and they both regretted poignantly the fact that it was impossible to pick up even the

BBC World Service on the radio. Ann gave a bitter grunt
of amusement.

'What?'

'Haven't you noticed? No, I guess you haven't been
aboard long enough. Mentioning satellites made me think.'

'*What*?'

'We don't even have a TV aboard. Tightship's rules. No
mollycoddling the crew. I mean we may not be able to
pick up any radio stations, but we'd certainly be able
to pick up a TV station or two, even up here.'

'Never mind. We'll think of something.'

'I can't think of anything except bed at the moment.'

'Use mine in the room behind the chart room. I promise
to warn you if I see Captain Black.'

On her own at last, Robin sat back in the watchkeeper's
chair and allowed herself to wonder. How the case had
turned out. How Richard and the children were. Where
Richard was if he wasn't in Heritage House, waiting for
news of her, and what he was up to. How her father was,
and how he was taking yet more bad news – God, she
hoped *Clotho* was still afloat somewhere and the brave
officers and friends aboard were all all right. But most of
all, she wondered how in heaven's name they were going
to get *Atropos* out of the mess she was in. It was all very
well to talk glibly about putting on a new propeller but it
would be an incredibly difficult and dangerous under-
taking. She had only mentioned it for the sake of morale.
She would only think of actually trying it in the direst of
emergencies, if there was no other help being promised
and nothing else to be done. But this *was* a bad position.
The ice barrier they were tied to made any attempt to reach
them from the south almost impossible. The conditions of
the last week made it certain that every port to the north

of them – and they were few and far between – was iced up solid. The only help she could envisage was for an icebreaker to come round one end of the barrier or the other and work along the top of it until contact was made.

She stirred herself on that thought and went to record the state of sky and sea for the log. The temperature was plunging and through the solidly fogged windows she could see so little of the moonlit night that a visit onto the starboard bridge wing would have to be undertaken. It seemed such a bore to get all dressed up, but she did so. She was conscientious, and the observation needed to be made.

Steeling herself, she slipped outside and crossed the bridge wing to look out towards the Davis Strait. It was so cold out here that she stayed only an instant. But she saw a full, low moon shining on a vivid expanse of gathering white coming down at her over the horizon, swamping the black water like a great wave breaking infinitely slowly. Then she was back in the wheelhouse and she realised she had been holding her breath, the air had been so cold.

What she had seen allowed her not only to fill in the log but to return to her speculation. Any icebreaker coming up to pull them to safety was going to have to come in from the east. In a very short time indeed, the west was going to be closed off by that slowly-nearing icefield. And that ruled out almost all hope of help from the American seaboard. Even if Belle Isle was still free, a rescue vessel coming out of Labrador any later than tonight would have to sail all the way to Kap Farvel before turning round and coming on back for *Atropos*. Robin didn't want to imagine how long that would take – or how much it would cost. Perhaps trying to replace the propeller wouldn't be such a bad idea after all.

She was going through the logistics of it when she fell asleep. And her sleep was so deep that she did not even stir when the radio room lit up – not quite as brightly as a fireworks display, and nowhere near as noisily. While she slumbered on, in the quiet little room behind her the signal strength indicator lit up. Numbers flashed onto the liquid crystal display. The radio began to whisper, almost inaudibly beneath a waterfall of static interference.

... *dash dot dash dot dot dash dot dot dash dash dash* ...

... C L O C L O C L O ...

The only thing that Bob Black ever thought about, really, was heroin. Where to get it, how much to pay for it, how to cut it, how to prepare it, how to inject it. After he had injected, he could get on with his duties for a while but even as he did so, at the back of his mind he would be thinking about it. In the first rush of freedom he would think how he was strong enough to give it up – how he was strong enough to do anything, in fact. But as soon as the rush wore off he would begin to think about the next fix, long before he began to feel the need for it, before the craving set in. Long before the benefit of the present fix ran out, he would be thinking about the next one. How was he going to afford it? Where would he find a supplier? How much would the fix cost? How would he cut it? How could he inject it?

This situation had not been going on for long. No one, not even a man as single-minded and cunning – and just plain lucky – as Bob Black could captain a ship for long without his habit becoming known ashore. Before the death of his wife and son in an automobile accident little more than a year earlier, he had only been an alcoholic.

One of those cunning alcoholics who are impossible to detect. He had switched almost without thinking from Bourbon to vodka when he started keeping it on the bridge. He worked out a routine which was not noticeably different from a normal shipboard captain's routine, but one which fitted in a nip here and a snort there. He was a naturally taciturn man so nobody noticed when the black dog hangover was on him and it was only if he went too far at the other extreme and became almost expansive that anyone raised an eyebrow. He nurtured his reputation for distant authoritarianism and aloof rudeness. He surrounded himself with men who would have noticed little even had he been more obvious in his addiction: Timmins, who was a kind of puppet; Hogg, who was his nephew.

Later, when Mamie and young Luke were buried and the clear liquid had been replaced by the white powder in his veins, he added Reynolds to his team, accepting him with open arms for the very reasons that everyone else had rejected him. 'Typical of old Bob Black,' they had said, 'wanting to lick the Wide Boy into shape.' But the boot of course had been on the other foot and it had been the young dog teaching the old dog new tricks. The simple techniques Black had used to hide one addiction served equally well to hide the other, although he had come close to giving himself away. This voyage, for instance, Reynolds had warned him of a price increase immediately before sailing and it had only been by selling the ship's televisions and video machines that Black had been able to make up the difference. But again, the Tightship reputation had proved excellent camouflage. 'Doesn't want to spoil the crew, typical . . .' But he had known as he had done it that this was the last straw. Someone somewhere ashore, even in the corporate shambles left after Dan

Williams' death in Belfast, was going to notice that the
televisions and videos which had come off *Atropos* during
the extra hours she was delayed in port had simply gone
missing.

The Wide Boy had been as cunning as his captain. He
held the cards but he never played them too obviously.
He took orders, and insults, like the rest. He did what
he was told and never abused his position. Why should he?
He was more than seaman enough to handle his duties
and he was greedy, not lazy. He knew, too, as well as
Black did, that this was a berth which would not last for
ever. There would be other postings on other ships before
he retired to his mansion in Las Vegas or wherever. It was
one thing for people to gossip; it was another for them to
point the finger and give examples, dates and times. Reynolds wanted anyone pointing at him to be saying, 'Now
there's a fine seaman and an excellent young officer.' The
Wide Boy was just starting out. He needed to toe the line
a little. He had never given Black enough for more than
one fix at a time. He had other customers and other things
aboard and he didn't want to risk Black getting holier than
thou. And being young and full of life – and on a roll –
it had never occurred to the young, cunning, efficient and
increasingly rich third officer that he would die in a storm
at sea.

It had never occurred to Black that his ill-tempered
order to check the cargo would cost him his supplier and
his supply. How in hell's name could a man sent into the
holds contrive to get himself washed overboard, even in a
storm like that? He had had no conception that the loss
of his supply would have this kind of effect on him. He
had remained a man of fierce dignity even in the grip of
his addictions, but then he had never had to face a morning

in the cold knowledge of cold turkey. His pride, his character, any thought of any self-worth were all gone beneath
the rabid craving. He was hardly capable of any thought
at all, in fact, except *Where is it? Where is it? Where is it?*

He had eluded Hogg's desultory search with ease and
had gone through the bridgehouse. His destruction of
Reynolds' room and its aftermath had taught his craving
to be cunning. He wasn't wrecking as he went this time,
he was hiding even the evidence that he had looked. The
only parts of the ship's accommodation which had been
barred to him since midnight had been those places where
people congregated. And those he had searched when the
multitudes of the two crews currently aboard were fast
asleep – when everyone was asleep, in fact, and only his
need kept him awake.

Now he turned away from the noise and brightness in
the radio shack and tiptoed past the sleeping figure in the
watchkeeper's chair out of the wheelhouse, his bare feet
making no sound on the linoleum, and nothing to mark
his ghostly passing except the whisper of silk dressing
gown against the mahogany doorframe leading out into
the corridor.

If it wasn't on the bridge – and a glimmering of intelligence confirmed that it could never have been hidden there
– then it must be outside. Unknowingly, he began to trace
the course of Robin's inspection with Timmins, out onto
the rear decks below the navigation bridge, by the funnel
and down. Such was the all-consuming power of the need
which was driving him, he noticed nothing at all of the
splendour of the night through which he was stealing. He
did not notice the setting moon magnified to spectacular
size and brightness by the supernatural clarity of the quiet
polar air. He did not notice the stars hanging like fairy

lights just above his head. Reality had retreated so far
from his view that he took it as a matter of no remark
that he could see as well as if it were day, except that
colour was all frosted into bluey monochrome. He did not
notice the size of the night, spread out all around him
from horizon to horizon, or the way incredible distance
was seemingly brought near, his vision magically extended
by the clarity of the air. The ice burned in shades of
sapphire from electric neon to Stygian syenite. The barrier
swept away like a range of lapis mountains to the south,
their peaks seeming to contain cold fire like the volcanoes
of the planet Pluto. The ice crept down from the north, a
field of restless ultramarine and indigo riven with webs of
water as black as interstellar space. He saw none of it,
but he heard the distant ice floes boom in the silence and
the throb of the alternators grumble like a thunderstorm
all around him. The stillness of the air was like the first
intimation of a scream, and the minute he breathed it in,
he began to die.

Everything he touched blistered his naked skin but the
nerve endings were numb with frostbite so he never
noticed. Like a terminal leper he moved over the decks and
down the companionways, destroying himself but never
knowing. By the time he took the ladder down behind
the funnel, he was leaving tracks of frozen blood upon the
metal, for all the skin on palms and insteps had been
stripped off layer by layer. He fell and tumbled down the
wide stairway beside the wide gymnasium windows
because he was shaking too much to stand. But he had
been shaking ever since withdrawal set in, so he didn't
really notice this either. Lying there, face down upon the
patterned wood of the boarded deck, unaware that his
cheeks were white with frost, he looked along the ridges

thrown into such spectacular relief by the moonlight, and he noticed that a catch was standing up. A little circular catch like a ring set into the deck. It should have been lying flat but it was standing up and gleaming.

It was the catch that removed part of the cover from the empty pool. Hope surged through the prone body, such a fierce, hot surge of hope that it pulled the captain onto his knees no matter how much of his face was left behind. And he crawled over to the catch and lifted it, hissing with the power of his desire. He had trouble jerking his finger from the little metal ring but his desire would not be denied. He could not feel the fingers which prised the trap door up. He could not feel the steps into the shallow end beneath his buttocks and back as he slid down them, taking extra care to replace the deck section immediately above his head.

It is here, it is here, he exulted and he didn't want to share it with anyone. The darkness would have stopped him as not even the cold had done, but at the bottom of the steps there was a flashlight so big that he felt it underneath his spine as he lay in the dark almost beyond rational thought. He grasped this thing and knew it by its shape. His thumb found the switch on its own and light flooded out. Whimpering with excitement, he scrambled down the slope of the pool towards the pile of packages lying before him at the deep end. Gibbering with joy he threw himself upon them, too far gone in his delirium to think it strange that Reynolds should keep heroin which he always sold in tiny plastic bags or twists of foil in great square oiled paper parcels like kilograms of sugar.

His fingers would not open the first parcel he caught up and so he bit into it as hard as he could. The cold had made the contents almost completely solid and he broke his teeth. He tore the package away from his face, leaving the outline of his mouth frozen to it round the stumps of his teeth buried in it. He had made little enough of an impression, but enough to see that the contents were not heroin at all, but a white, doughy substance, like putty.

His scream of wild frustration was infinitely loud within his head, but from his lips came no more than the mewling of a drowning kitten. He hurled the package from him but it was frozen to his fingers and the action simply jerked him over so that he was lying on the stuff. He cried with uncontrollable frustration and his tears froze his eyelids shut. His rage still would not be contained and he raved there helplessly, wildly berserk, though in fact his epic paroxysms amounted to little more than a spastic twitch and an act of incontinence. But the wetness in his lap allowed the cold to enter his vital organs more rapidly than anything else would have done – except, perhaps, the knife of the girl who had hidden on *Clotho*. The partner of the terrorist whose Semtex this was. And once the cold was in, then life was utterly over. The man died long before the batteries in the flashlight.

CHAPTER TWENTY-TWO

Day Ten

Friday, 28 May   08:00

It was the sun that woke Robin and it was she who woke
the rest of the ship. It felt strange that she should have to
do so. She was used to ships which ran like Swiss watches
independently of the captain – and, indeed, of the officers
keeping their watches on the bridge. This was necessarily
so. It was all too often the case in her experience that the
officers, bound up in the requirements of their command,
relied upon the ship to run without their interference.

The ship's day should have begun with the rising of the
chef and his acolytes to prepare breakfast. At the same
time, the chief steward and his men should be up and
about, getting the common areas ready for the arrival of
the crew to eat, drink and get ready for work. The work
generally started between eight and nine, so breakfast
needed to be over by seven forty-five. Normally around
forty people needed feeding and that could take half an
hour at least. Traditionally, the breakfasts served at sea
would be as large as the individual crew members desired.
Anything from coffee and croissants newly made to

porridge, kippers, kedgeree; a full English fried breakfast of eggs, bacon, kidneys, pork chops, sausages, tomatoes, fried bread, or an American variation with hash-browns, grits, waffles and biscuits; toast, marmalade and tea. And this took no account of Chinese or Indian crewmen, or of the dietary requirements of vegetarians, Jews, Hindus and Muslims – all of which were of the first importance. Bearing this in mind, it was not unusual for the chef and his men to be up well before six.

Up on the bridge, in the watchkeeper's chair in the wheelhouse, it should have been impossible for Robin to know that the ship was still asleep. The alternators were grumbling steadily and their insistent throbbing should have been enough to cover quite a lot of bustle down below. But as Robin blinked awake, dazzled by the bludgeoning glare of the sun on an ice-bound world, she knew at once that she was the only one awake. It was as though, by assuming the captaincy of *Atropos*, she had grown nerves through the very fabric of her command.

She pulled herself erect and stretched. What to do? she thought. What to do? Her actions now would best be dictated by the requirements of her overall plan. It was worth rousing the crew – the crews – if she had something for them to do. Sitting here helplessly in what was clearly a dangerous and deteriorating situation with nothing to do except watch the ice thicken would be terribly bad for morale. But on the other hand, pointless action, especially if dictated by an unknown commander, could lead to trouble equally quickly. She had to bear in mind, too, that there were limits to the work needed inside the hull – and dangers to working outside the hull in these conditions. Even the decks could become no-go areas in extremely low temperatures.

'Damned if you do and damned if you don't,' she said to herself as she crossed to the helm and looked out. There was nothing to see; the clearview had frosted over. All that confronted her eyes was an intricate, beautiful pattern of ice crystals making the glass utterly opaque. The sight lifted her spirits a little, subconsciously reminding her of Christmases at Cold Fell when she was a child, before the central heating had gone in. Now, as then, she suddenly felt an overwhelming urge to run outside and look at the magic whiteness of the snow-covered world. She only just had the good sense to pull her cold-weather gear on first.

The door out onto the bridge wing opened stiffly and she half expected to find a pile of snow drifted outside. She breathed out gently through the scarf she had wound round her nose. A cloud of frosted breath rose to blind her and she felt the wool dampen and stiffen at once. Breathing in was like drowning in liquid nitrogen. Settling her sunglasses on her nose, she stepped outside and only the dark lenses stopped her from being blinded. It was not just that the world was white, so was her ship.

During the night, *Atropos* had snuggled up even more tightly against the ice barrier which now stretched away south, seemingly as solid as the Himalayas. This action had been caused by the first pressure of thin ice being pushed southwards by the ice floes and the icefield behind them grinding down out of the Davis Strait. *Atropos* was not icebound yet – there was no noise from her hull and therefore no real pressure on it yet – but she certainly looked to be so. The lethally low temperatures of the night had frozen white crusts over every lead, polynya and break between the floes to the north and had even put a rind over the quiet water between the floes and the ship. It

looked as though *Atropos* had somehow become beached
on the ice shelf, for there was no water visible at all,
anywhere around. The ship itself, too, was ice-covered. As
though the frozen water was some virulent contagion, it
had grown over every surface before her. The steps, the
banisters of the companionways and safety railings were
white and covered with thick spicules of ice. The equipment on the bridge wing, even the brass, was thick and
amorphous, as though coated with frozen foam. She took
several entranced steps forward and looked down. The
deck was a gleaming expanse of hoar frost, raised hatches
casting sharp-edged shadows on the white. The gantry
halfway down the deck, white-painted anyway, was effulgent now. The forecastle head and all the deck auxiliaries
upon it seemed to be drifted with glacial sand. Not snow,
it was too fine and granular for snow; the effect of it was
more like powdered glass. A hundred million tiny facets
seemed to catch the light at once, forcing her to look up
and away.

Beyond the confines of the ship, the whole morning
seemed to be braced and ready for action, tensed not only
against the massive cold but in preparation for something
more. The very horizons seemed to be trembling with
clarity, like black lines strung taut beneath the blue bowl
of the sky then sounded like the strings of harps. Except
right in the north-west, she realised. There the horizon
seemed to be obscured by thick black smoke, which took
the shine off the morning, somehow. She stood and looked
at it, staring intently. But she could think of no reason
why anything should be on fire there. Nor could she deter-
mine, squint as she might, how far or how near it was.

Back in the stifling wheelhouse, she referred at once to
Hogg's machines. The collision alarm radar showed

nothing major except the ice barrier on its five-mile setting, but there was something on the ten-mile register and
when she set it to twenty, the alarm sounded, but the
picture showed nothing she could understand. The satnav
confirmed last recorded position so, no matter what the
ice to the north was doing, the barrier and the ship secured
to it were not going anywhere at the moment.

It was coming up for half past eight now. Enough of
this shilly-shallying, she thought. Time to get them up.
She crossed to the console and pushed the broadcast button
beside the microphone there. The ship's tannoy chimes
sounded.

'Your attention. Your attention, please. This is Captain
Mariner speaking. I would like First Officer Timmins,
Lieutenant Hogg and Radio Officer Stone to report to the
bridge at their earliest convenience, please. I would like
the rest of the officers and crew to report to the ship's
gymnasium at oh nine hundred hours sharp. Galley staff,
serve coffee and tea there at that time, please. Breakfast
will be prepared after I have addressed the ship's complement. I say again . . .'

Ann came out of the captain's day room before Robin
had finished the repetition of her order. 'What are you
going to say when you get us all in the gym?' asked
the journalist.

'What I told you last night. Dressed up a little, maybe.
You can have the full text later to make sure you quote
me right.' The two of them laughed companionably. 'Sleep
all right?'

'Like the dead. No sign of Captain Black?'

'No.' Robin's answer was shorter than she meant it to
be because she was feeling a little guilty about dozing off
like that. She wouldn't have known whether Black had

been there or not, she thought. Like the black smoke on the horizon, it took the gleam off her bright plan of action.

LeFever arrived, obviously looking for Ann. 'You weren't in your cabin,' he said, his tone somewhere between mild accusation and insouciant explanation. Robin noticed that he didn't say exactly when he had checked in her cabin. But to be fair, even were he as much of a star in that department as he looked, he wouldn't have been up to many sexual antics when they had finally got to bed this morning. And, although Ann wasn't saying much, Robin suspected she was happy to keep the Canadian at a distance for the time being because she was really worried about Nico Niccolo. The Italian's main chance of beating his unknown rival at the moment was the possibility that he was dead. He might find himself ousted from Ann's affections if he turned out to be safe and well.

It was more difficult to fathom LeFever, however. He was so attractive and seemed to be so attracted to Ann. They made a good couple and they seemed to share so many interests – their vegetarianism, their ecological conscience, their burning desire to make the world a better place to live in for all species, not just for man. For all his worth and undoubted charm, Nico Niccolo really shouldn't have held a candle to Henri LeFever. And yet . . .

She pushed her thoughts about these two to one side as her senior deck officers entered with the radio officer in tow. 'I'm going down to address the others at nine o'clock,' she began at once. 'I'm really just going to lay our position on the line as I see it, and I'm sure it's as obvious to you as it is to me. Mr Timmins, I want you to hold the watch until I return. We won't be holding regular watches from here on in. We'll be making do the best way we can until we get out of here or until I say different. You're on watch from now until I relieve you later.

'Mr Hogg, I want you to find out what is scaring the collision alarm radar. It goes off whenever I set it over a ten-mile radius but I can't make anything out. I want you to contact any passing satellite that will talk to us and get some idea of what we can expect in terms of wind, weather, ocean currents and ice during the next few days. Most of all I want to know what is producing all that black smoke up to the north-west of us.

'Mr Stone, I want you to go back through the airwaves with a fine-tooth comb. Ideally, I want to talk to a nearby vessel, a not too distant port or weather station or, at a pinch, Heritage Mariner in London; but I'll settle for anything you can get me.'

'I got a New York cabbie on his way out to Kennedy the night this lot started,' said Stone cheerfully. 'But he couldn't hear me too well.'

'Anyone. It's time we knew what's going on around here. And not just around here. I'm going down to talk to the crew. LeFever, make yourself useful. I'll be wanting to refer to those two charts there. Take them down and stick them up on the wall so that everyone can see them. You're in charge of getting them back up here when I've finished talking. Then we'll have to discuss the best way for you to check the disposition of the cargo. I know this ship is strengthened, and that it would be incredibly bad luck if there was anything wrong with her hull like there was with *Clotho*'s, but I'm just not comfortable with the idea of all that ice squeezing our nuclear cargo too tightly. Right. I'm off now. Jump to it, Mr LeFever. And I want to hear from you three gentlemen the instant anything that looks or sounds important happens, please. Is that all clear? Good. Come along then, Ann; just grab that walkie-talkie there and let's go.'

Ann had never seen Robin in action with all stops out

before. She followed the determined dynamo off the bridge with the slightly dazed LeFever in tow. The three of them crossed to the lift and crushed in the car together, the big Canadian being particularly careful of the armful of rolled charts he was carrying.

'There are the better part of sixty men aboard this ship,' continued Robin as they plunged downwards. 'If we can get them organised and all pulling their weight, then there's nothing we can't achieve. Especially as the alternatives are pretty unpleasant. If we leave them with too much time to sit and worry, we'll have panic and trouble. Even when the weather's clear and calm like this, it's obvious that the ice around us is building up. Unless we get out of this position, we may find the hull gets badly damaged and we have to camp on the ice until we're picked up. If this weather continues, it will go from being difficult to get a rescue ship in here to being downright impossible. Then what are we going to do? Rely on air-dropped supplies and wait for the next storm to break up the ice and start praying for help again? No. If we can't rely on anyone getting in to help us, then we will simply have to get out under our own steam.'

'Well, gentlemen, here we are,' she began again, fifteen minutes later, standing in front of the charts LeFever had pinned to the wall and looking down at the expectant sea of faces in front of her. 'I am aware that when I say "Here we are", many of you do not know exactly where "here" is. Well, we're at this point on the chart *here*. Halfway between Hope and Desolation.' She pointed to the spot on the chart, and did so surprisingly accurately, considering she was using a steaming mug of coffee. She pretended not to hear the rustle of sound that went through the room at her dramatic pronouncement. 'Hopedale in Newfoundland is here on the Labrador coast,' she moved her mug, 'and Kap Desolation is here in Greenland. I can give you the co-ordinates though they probably won't make much sense to most of you. We're fifty-two degrees and six minutes west and a whisker over fifty-nine degrees north. The most important aspect of the situation for you to bear in mind is that we are well beyond helicopter range from either Greenland or Canada. The only way we can be contacted by air is if we make a landing strip somewhere near the ship. And, as we are beyond the limit of most small aircraft's range, it would have to be quite a big airstrip.

'You all know that we are secured against a barrier of ice. At this time I have no way of telling with any accuracy how thick it is, or how broad or long. We are on its north shore, so to speak. It is to the south of us, between us and the obvious courses for rescue. Judging from its general character and the very close look I got at parts of it yesterday, it is far too thick for us to break through, at this point at least. By the same token, it is too thick for any other ship to break through. So anyone coming to our rescue and hoping to pull us out will have to sail round one end of the barrier or the other, and that could be a long business.

'To the north of us there is still quite a wide stretch of open water before the floes and the ice field, but the water is crusted over with thin ice and cannot be seen at the moment. We do have the freedom to move through it if we can get under way, however, so you need have no worries on that score. But the ice field is moving southwards. There are currents beneath it pulling it down towards us and so that freedom of movement may well be limited by time. As is the hope of getting a tug or another icebreaker in to pull us free.

'So, how are we going to get out of here? We can't rely on helicopters coming close. We could leave the ship, try to find a big flat piece of ice and hope they send a couple of thirty-seater aircraft out to the right spot before we all freeze to death. We can stay with the ship and wait for a rescue ship to come in after us and pull us out – and hope they get here before we get really hungry or a storm comes up or the ice crushes us. We have enough food aboard to feed thirty people for six more days, before you ask. And, unless you know where the late Mr Reynolds kept his supply, we have no alcohol at all.

'Well, gentlemen, I would like to propose an alternative that I haven't mentioned so far. I would like to propose that we get up off our backsides and fix our own wagon. We still have the docking screws so we can manoeuvre, and even sail forward or backwards at a knot or two. It should not be beyond the realms of our wit or ingenuity to find a piece of ice that gives us at least the start of a slipway, reverse this tub up a little and see about sorting the propeller out. Remember, if it wasn't for that particular damage, *Atropos* is exactly the sort of ship that would be coming in here to help us out. She's ice-strengthened and powerful. If we can get the propeller repaired so that the turbines can start turning it again or, failing that, replace it with the spare propeller, she will sail us out of here with no trouble at all.'

It was at that point that the walkie-talkie buzzed urgently. Ann handed it up to her automatically and Robin thumbed the receive button.

'Yes?'

'Hogg, Captain. The communications console just lit

up. The whole shooting match. We're back in business again, even got a fax.'

'I'm on my—'

'Captain?'

'Yes?'

'This is Stone. I've got a queue of people on the radio for you.'

'Patch the first one through to me here. I'll talk to them while I'm on my way up.' She caught Ann's eye and jerked her head.

Ann was up and in action at once, only to collide with Robin who had stopped in her tracks as though she had been stunned.

'*Richard*! Darling, where are you?'

Ann was close enough to hear the reply relayed by the black handset. 'Fifty-two degrees, six minutes west; fifty-nine degrees north.'

'Halfway between Hope and Desolation,' whispered Robin, awed. As she spoke, she swung round and the two women's gazes locked while the walkie-talkie relayed Richard's voice.

'What? Oh yes, I see what you mean. Hopedale and Kap Desolation. That's right. Exactly. I'm on *Clotho* with Nico and the rest. We're less than ten miles south of you.'

CHAPTER TWENTY-THREE

Day Ten

Friday, 28 May   12:00

Sir William Heritage sat in the operations room of Heritage House with Helen Dufour on his right and Magdalena DaSilva on his left. The world map towered imposingly up the wall behind them. Beyond the dashing, dazzling Maggie, the bookcases stood, solid, reliable, traditional. Beyond coutured, business-chic Helen, the wall of screens and displays glowed, high-tech, efficient, impressive. In front of them, beyond the solid table hastily borrowed from the boardroom downstairs, in place of the chesterfields and the antique coffee table, stood the local representatives of the world's press.

'If I may begin by reading a statement,' Sir William said firmly. 'Then we can answer individual questions later.'

Silence fell, except for the quiet conversations of the people in charge of the communications boards beyond Helen. An occasional flash exploded as photographers tried to catch the ambiance of this carefully selected location. Tape machines whirred as though whispering to themselves. Pencils poised, dagger-sharp. Sir William cleared his throat and began.

'The two nuclear waste transporters *Atropos* and *Clotho* are at present in the Labrador Sea, exactly at the points you see marked on the map behind us. *Atropos* is fully laden with nuclear waste from the north American subcontinent on its way for reprocessing at the Sellafield nuclear reprocessing plant in Cumbria. She is currently moored to an ice barrier and is perfectly safe. There is no damage to her hull and no question of any damage to her cargo. She has on board not only a scientific officer specially trained in the observation and maintenance of such cargoes, but a member of the Greenpeace organisation with free access to all areas of the ship. And, of course, both ships have a full range of specially designed safety equipment as well as handpicked officers and crew. *Atropos* has been very slightly damaged and currently cannot make her way home unaided. She is under the command of my daughter Captain Robin Mariner who, as I am sure you are all aware, is one of Heritage Mariner's most senior and respected captains. *Clotho* is within ten miles of her and we confidently expect that a tow will be offered within the next few hours and certainly before the end of the day. *Clotho* is unladen and, although also damaged herself, is well able to offer assistance. She was in fact towing *Atropos* perfectly adequately until the line parted thirty-six hours ago in a storm. *Clotho* is currently under the command of Captain Richard Mariner, whose reputation will be well known to all of you.

'We do not at this time envisage any particular problems, especially as the weather in the Labrador Sea is calm and clear with every prospect of remaining so for the next few days. We have not, therefore, requested any help from ships or agencies outside Heritage Mariner itself, and do not envisage doing so unless there is a major change in the circumstances. Heritage Mariner would like to go on record as stating categorically that we believe the situation to be of little seriousness. We believe it will be satisfactorily resolved within twenty-four hours and we see no reason at all for concern.'

Sir William laid the paper on the gleaming mahogany before him and sat up straight. His hands, clasped on the paper, shook very slightly but at his age it could have been incipient Parkinsonism. His shoulders were square, his blue gaze clear and level. He looked every inch the commercial elder statesman that he was, with his perfectly barbered, carefully parted silver hair and his militarily clipped white moustache. No one would have suspected that he felt he was lying through his teeth.

The questions began as quickly as he had feared and soon took the line he had most dreaded.

'Andrew Pierce, *Shipping*. How badly damaged are the ships?'

'One has a bent propeller, the other has some weakness to her bows. But the hulls of both ships have been strengthened for icy conditions.'

'And how thick is the ice they are involved with at the moment?'

'I understand it is first-year sea ice. As such it is probably less than six feet thick.'

'Is that likely to do the ships any damage?'

'Highly unlikely, and of course we carry full insurance.'

'Who insures the world against the cargo?' demanded a new voice.

'Mr Stonor, would you please observe the proprieties. The cargo is sealed in containers which are guaranteed to withstand any extreme.'

'Utterly unbreakable.' Stonor's voice was a sneer of disbelief.

'Even stronger than the ones British Nuclear Fuel crashed a locomotive train into in that famous advertisement . . .'

'Andrew Pierce again. To what extent is it true that these ships have been designed and indeed financed with the expectation of transporting this nuclear waste in and out of the near arctic ports of Russia?'

'That is our hope, certainly, Mr Pierce. In fact Miss Dufour here has just returned from Moscow where—'

'Ms Dufour, have you completed an agreement with the Russians?'

'As you know, Mr Pierce, since the disintegration of the old Soviet empire, it has become impossible to make one agreement with all the republics involved, but the people in Moscow—'

'But these ships were financed on the expectation of the Russian deal . . .'

'*Mr Stonor.*'

'. . . so any slowing down of the process will add to Heritage Mariner's financial problems?'

'No, Mr Stonor, that is not true,' Helen Dufour told him. 'They were not so financed. And the agreement of one or two republics would in theory be sufficient. Effectively we are only talking about the ports of Murmansk and Archangel, though there is some possibility of the authorities opening St Petersburg to this traffic eventually. And, of course, Heritage Mariner's finances are absolutely sound.'

'Sam Duncan, *International Press*. Sir William, we hear from our Canadian associates that your partners in this enterprise, Sept Isles Shipping who actually own *Atropos*, are also on the verge of financial collapse.'

'Since the death of Dan Williams in the terrorist outrage at our launching ceremony three months ago, the company has been undergoing some restructuring but they are financially sound.'

'And word is that Heritage Mariner has every spare penny tied up in these two ships.'

'Heritage Mariner is a broad-based company with substantial interests in oil shipping and leisure boating . . .'

'Both shrinking markets, going from bad to worse.'

'. . . of established and longstanding reputation.'

'John Stonor, of the *Sketch*.' The piercing voice was heavy with ironic innocence.

'*Yes*, Mr Stonor.'

'Isn't it true that the insurance on these two ships, all of which your company is bearing—'

'As agreed with our Canadian associates.'

'All of which you are bearing is beginning to cripple you financially . . .'

'No, Mr Stonor, that is absolutely—'

'. . . to such an extent that if these ships go down, then Heritage Mariner goes down with them?'

'I have answered that already. Yes, Miss—'

'And, furthermore, that is the real reason you have sent *Clotho* after *Atropos* in spite of the fact that she is badly damaged and conditions in the Labrador Sea are so dangerous. Even the salvage cost of bringing in help from outside will put Heritage Mariner at risk. Isn't that so?'

'No. These allegations are absolutely untrue. You are speculating wildly. As you were with the question of the cargo.'

'How many people have been killed so far?' Stonor chucked the question in out of nowhere and it was so unexpected that Sir William flinched in spite of himself.

'Miss Silver—'

'Rachel Silverberg, *Economic Review*. Isn't it the case that the judgment outstanding against Captain Richard Mariner over the loss of the *Napoli* leaves your company wide open to further litigation, especially in America? Litigation which could destroy the financial base of your company?'

'That judgment is under appeal here and we know nothing about further—'

'If I may field this one, Sir William.' Maggie rose to the fray.

'Certainly, Miss DaSilva.'

'There is no question that our appeal here will fail, Ms Silverberg. And I am in contact with several of the New York law firms who were considering moving on the strength of yesterday's judgment but they are all as yet undecided.'

'And the United States government is considering making an order against Heritage Mariner, forcing them to retrieve *Napoli*'s cargo and dispose of it properly!' that sneering voice accused.

'Mr Stonor, that has nothing to do with the strength of our appeal—'

'It's got everything to do with the American litigation, though. Half the lawyers in New York are just waiting until the State Department makes up its mind. I have an American lawyer who will stand up and say—'

'*When* he stands up, we will answer his allegations. Not before.'

'Okay, then tell me how many are dead so far on *Clotho* and *Atropos*. Ten, Sir William? Twenty?'

Sir William's jaw squared and his lips thinned as he remained in solid silence, staring the reporter down.

Maggie sat, and the silence persisted for a heartbeat longer.

'Steven Palmer, *World News*. Could you comment on the terrorist involvement in the recent history of your company?'

'We do much of our work in the Gulf, Mr Palmer. We have dealt with people who also work in the Middle East. We build our ships in Northern Ireland. Terrorism is a fact of life these days, I'm afraid.'

'But your contacts with international terrorism go even further than that, do they not, Sir William?'

'No.'

'Isn't it true that the sister of one of your senior officers is a member of the PLO? Haven't you actually had an unofficial contact with them for some time now?'

Only after he had thundered another outraged negative did Sir William notice Maggie's covert signal begging him to be careful. But he was too enraged to stop now.

'If that was the case, Mr Palmer, do you suppose we would have allowed terrorists to murder and maim at the launching ceremony for *Clotho* and *Atropos*? Especially as it was our friends and associates who bore the brunt. My own son-in-law was nearly killed.'

'Now you mention that incident, Sir William, do you think it was wise of you to let your ships sail without a full naval escort? May I remind you that when the Japanese sent just one ship like yours to Europe last year, they sent a fully armed coastguard vessel with her to protect her from terrorists.'

'The Japanese were picking up weapons grade plutonium, Mr Stonor. And even they had nothing to fear from the PLO.'

'Ah, but of course it wasn't the PLO who bombed your ships in Belfast, Sir William.'

'PLO, IRA, what difference does it make? They were

trying to kill the Secretary of State and only used our ceremony by coincidence.'

'It was neither of them, Sir William. And it wasn't a coincidence.' Stonor's voice had lost something of its sneer and he deigned to stand up for the first time as he spoke. 'What do you know about the LGV, La Guerre Verte?'

Sir William's memory was jerked back to the poster Justin Bulwyr-Lytton had shown him yesterday. Trust old Bull to be right on the nail, he thought wearily.

'I heard of them for the first time less than twenty-four hours ago, I don't see—'

'They are terrorists whose concerns are ecological rather than political. They kill to save the world from people who pollute it, like oil transporters, like traffickers in nuclear waste.'

'This sounds like fantasy to me, Mr Stonor. I have never heard such arrant nonsense in my—'

'And can you tell me if you've ever seen this woman before?' Stonor held up an A3-sized poster of a young, long-haired woman.

'No, I have never seen her.' He looked from side to side. Both women shrugged. 'We have never seen her.'

'Her name is Joan Hennessy. She is an American citizen, wanted for murder in the United States and Canada. She is apparently quite a lady. Ex-US Army; highly trained explosives expert. Favours a kind of Bowie knife for close combat, I'm told. She and her husband are among the leading lights of La Guerre Verte.'

'Mr Stonor, I have never met or knowingly had contact with anyone called Hennessy.'

'I see,' said John Stonor. He began to fold the poster carefully and precisely, aware that every eye in the room and almost all of the cameras were observing his studied performance. When he spoke again, all of the hectoring sneer had left his voice and his tone was one of genuine, concerned enquiry.

'Would it surprise you to know then, Sir William, that this morning my paper received a fully authenticated communication from this woman? In it she stated that it was she who bombed the launching of your ships and it was the ships which were the target. And the statement concluded that members of her organisation have placed more bombs aboard *Clotho* and *Atropos*, and that they will stop at nothing to destroy them both. Would that surprise you, Sir William?'

CHAPTER TWENTY-FOUR

Day Ten

Friday, 28 May   17:00

Clotho was still capable of twenty-five knots and her turbines could take her up to full speed within a mile. Sitting high in the water, with the undamaged base of her bow cleaving the near calm at the southern edge of the ice, she raced eastwards, all of her high-tech equipment at the fullest possible alert for a way north through the ice barrier. While she sped towards distant Greenland, Richard and the others sat in the wheelhouse and held a council of war. Sir William's shocking news had come near to destroying an afternoon of careful, detailed planning between Richard and Robin. The detailed notes he had made from their initial radio phone conversation lay beside the further information which had arrived by fax a little later. The words '*explosives expert*' and '*Bowie knife*' had been underlined. Joan Hennessy's photograph glared at the ceiling, but because she had faced the police camera that had taken the original square on, her eyes followed anyone who moved around the room.

'I'll stay on watch,' Richard was saying. 'Johnny, I'll

need you at the radar, and Bill, you'd better stay at the radio now that it's working properly again.'

'If you're going to keep her at these revs, I'd like to stay in the engine room,' added Andrew.

'That leaves Harry and you, Nico. What do you think?'

'We can't run the risk that there is anyone aboard. We must look carefully. And if Sir William's information is accurate, we need to do it soon.'

'And not alone,' said Harry Piper feelingly, running a freckled hand through the curly shock of his carrot-red hair. 'I don't want to blunder into any terrorist stowaways. If they brought explosives aboard, they could well have brought guns too.'

'I think there might well have been someone aboard,' added Nico thoughtfully. 'I'm certain someone was tampering with the stores in the lifeboats. I remember, when we went over after poor Jamie . . .' His voice trailed off. There was nothing more to say. He had noticed something but what with one thing and another he had done nothing and told no one. Until now.

'Take the walkie-talkies and keep in touch,' said Richard. 'Sorry I can't offer you anything more in the way of protection.'

The two men went out of the wheelhouse and the last thing Richard heard from them was Harry saying, 'Let's look in the galley first.'

'You think they're going to start by making a sandwich?' asked Johnny Sullivan almost wistfully.

'No. I think they're going to borrow some of the chef's biggest knives and cleavers. Just in case.'

On *Atropos*, Robin was having a very similar conversation; but whereas Richard had nothing but senior officers, Robin had nothing much except crew at her command. As *Atropos* was still tied up and unlikely to be going anywhere before Richard had finished his exploration of the ice barrier and confirmed whether or not he could get in to help them, Robin had no real need to be on the bridge. She didn't really trust Timmins to do a thorough job yet, so she left him on watch. Hogg would have liked to remain at his nice warm radar post but there was no real need for radar scanning at the moment, especially as he proved to be no more capable than Robin had been of explaining what it was in the north-western distance which set off the collision alarm at just less than the ten-mile setting. Stone could remain at the radio because now that contact with the world had been restored, it seemed that everyone with access to a radio wanted to talk to them. The radio officer had a list of people Robin wanted to talk to, and he had discretion enough to be trusted with the rest of the calls. *Atropos*'s engineering officers were still technically convalescent, and Lloyd Swan was keeping an eye on the alternators, just in case. Robin was still fizzing with the excitement and extra energy which had filled her since Richard had got through.

'We'll split into two teams, then,' she decided. 'Mr Hogg, you take the *Atropos* complement, except for galley and dining saloon staff, and search the port side of the ship. Search everywhere except the cargo areas. Mr Le-Fever, I'd be pleased if you would go with them at first. I'll take the *Clotho* complement and search the starboard. Ann, you can go with either team. Crew will dismiss to dinner at eighteen hundred.' She paused for a moment as Ann gave a curt nod, then rushed on without noticing her American friend's reticence. 'Officers will report back to me here at that time, though we will stay in contact by walkie-talkie in the meantime. Mr LeFever, we will check the cargo holds after dinner.

'Mr Hogg, I would be grateful if you could assure your men that this is not a race or a contest of any kind. I really do not want to start any rivalries between the crews, but if we wait to draw up balanced lists and areas of responsibility, we will lose the light, and this job will be quite hard enough even when we can see what we're doing. And Mr Hogg,' she added as that worthy was just on his way off the bridge, 'remember that this will be an unrivalled opportunity to discover the whereabouts of Captain Black. If you find him, I want to know at once.'

'Yes, Captain.'

'Off you go, then. And I'll come too. Mr Timmins, you have her.'

Walter Hogg was in a near-panic. He had been sure for some time that the Wide Boy had kept at least part of his stash somewhere under the spare propeller at the forward end of the deck between the hatch to number one hold and the forecastle head. Quite by chance, he had seen him acting suspiciously one night while on the prowl for a cure for night starvation and he had followed him down the deck as far as he dared – far enough to see the rough location of the nefarious activity but nothing more. While Reynolds had been alive, he hadn't dared to look more closely. Since his death, there had been no real opportunity to check. This morning he had nearly had a heart attack when the new captain had announced that she was thinking of replacing the damaged propeller with the spare one. The sudden resumption of communications, however, had given him a respite and he had planned to have a look during the midnight watch tonight. And now the captain had ordered a stem to stern, truck to keel search.

He realised how stupid he had been not to take a chance earlier. If he wasn't quick about it, there was every likelihood that the limey woman would find Reynolds's merchandise. That would be a total disaster. He didn't like her, but he was not stupid enough to underestimate her. He was certain that anything she found she would simply destroy and no one would get any profit or pleasure from whatever it was at all. But what could he do? His team was made up of people he didn't know or trust – starting with LeFever. Hogg couldn't see any way of getting away from them to have a look on his own.

He split the team up into smaller and smaller groups. He was not an able officer. He was young and untried, considering his seniority aboard, but he knew the ship well enough to be able to delegate a lot of specific areas to increasing numbers of groups. He sent most of his team to look through the engineering areas, the galleys and the accommodation on the bridge. Half of those he had brought outside with him he put under LeFever's command to search down the decks behind the bridgehouse. Hogg himself worked his way down the main deck and he still had half a dozen men in tow.

The bright sunlight had melted the thick frost which had cloaked the vessel this morning and the decks were slick and slippery. The low sun kept the nearby ice ablaze and split the deck into absolute patches of burning brightness and freezing shade. Hogg was aware that the captain had dispatched none of her men into the engineering sections yet. She was using the daylight to examine the decks first. The only chance he had of getting down to the spare propeller before she did lay in the fact that she had not split up her team to anything like the same extent as he had and the search she was making seemed to be much slower and more painstaking. 'You three, swing that lifeboat out,' he ordered, 'and go through it with a fine-tooth comb.' Three men shrugged and went to work. He set off down the rest of the deck with the last of his team. As he came out past the front of the bridgehouse and onto the weather deck, salvation presented itself. He hurried forward excitedly, hardly even bothering to check anything at his feet.

'I want you three up there in that gantry,' he grated as his men came under it. 'Go over it inch by inch.' The three crew members nodded resignedly and began to climb the steps up the right leg, one after the other. Hogg hurried forward alone at last. His heart was thumping and his mind was racing. Actually finding the hiding place and recovering anything that was there would only be half the battle. He would have to find another hiding place guaranteed to remain undisturbed. One much more convenient and easier of access. Would it be sufficient to announce that he had looked under the propeller and found nothing? If the captain would believe that, then he could come back later and move whatever he found at his leisure. If last night had been anything to go by, he could drive a forklift truck up and down the deck and no one would stir. Everyone seemed to have been flat out, even the captain on watch. There was no other possible explanation for the hour at which the ship had come to life this morning.

The huge three-bladed propeller lay as flat as possible, its variable pitch blades in their minimum setting. Great hoops of steel pinned it to the deck and were secured by massive bolts to stop the propeller from moving in even the roughest weather. The first thing the captain would have to get done if she did go ahead with her plan to use it in the morning was to have those bolts cut off, Hogg calculated. He would probably find himself down here with the oxyacetylene crew first thing tomorrow, he thought grimly. The propeller had been swathed in tarpaulin which had been folded and secured neatly into place. It was like a Christmas parcel, he reflected, reaching it at last. Like a Christmas parcel in more ways than one. His hands were actually trembling as he began to undo the nearest lines.

He had to fight the urge to keep glancing over his shoulder as he worked. Keep cool, he thought to himself. Act like you're just obeying orders. The knots were surprisingly easy to undo. It was only a matter of minutes before he had the first rope loosened and stood ready to throw the tarpaulin back. He risked a glance around the deck. He was absolutely alone. The nearest people to him were the three men in the gantry halfway back along the deck. He threw the tarpaulin back just far enough to make an entrance. As though entering a tent in some childhood camp, he stepped inside.

It was the smell he noticed first, even before he registered the gloom. He turned his head as though moving his nostrils through the dank, foetid air would make the odour clearer. Automatically, his short hairs prickling on the back of his fat neck, he stepped back. The flap of tarpaulin swung open wider. Wide enough to let in light from the setting sun.

At first Hogg didn't realise that the figure crouching there was dead. He stepped forward, about to speak. But the movement allowed light to fall across the face and the frosted pallor of the skin was revealed. Hogg reached forward, stunned. The folds of the dressing gown were set like stone. The whole figure was like some kind of statue.

Shaking his head, Hogg stepped back again and, horribly, the corpse seemed to follow him, toppling forward to tumble at his feet, hitting the deck with the sound a balk of timber might make. Only then, when it rolled over, did Hogg see that the skin over half the face had gone, displaying muscle like a sheep's side hanging skinned in a butcher's shop. And no sooner had he registered this fact than he registered another, even more disturbing. The hands, reaching out strangely, as though bringing something up close to the late captain's face, ended at the tops of the palms. Whoever had hidden him here and tied up the canopy so neatly afterwards had cut off all of Uncle Bobby's fingers first.

By the time Nico and Harry Piper reached *Clotho*'s spare propeller, the sun had almost gone, but they were able to throw back the tarpaulin and check that there was no sign of any stowaway beneath it.

'That only leaves the holds, really,' observed Harry.

'Number one's full of water,' Nico reminded him.

'Worth a look, though.'

'Okay, but we'd better be careful. With the ship running full ahead, it'll probably be a bit restless down there. When the captain went down last, I had to secure him pretty handily with a line.'

'Better do the same for me, then,' said Harry.

By the time they had the line secured, it was twilight, the long, lingering luminous twilight of clear evenings in high latitudes. The hatch slid back and Harry climbed down onto the curving ladder every bit as carefully as Richard had done earlier. The twilight lit up the clear, almost colourless sky above, but it served only to emphasise the Stygian gloom in the hold itself. The ladder beneath Harry was unexpectedly firm, and he was able to move about quite well, but he found it very difficult to see anything much at all.

'I can't see,' he called up to Nico. At that moment the buzzer on Nico's walkie-talkie began to sound. He felt the rope round his waist adjust as Nico moved to answer. Then it was just a distant, one-sided conversation which did not make much sense to the young engineer.

'She said what? . . . Found him where? . . . Hogg did? I'm not surprised!'

While he listened distantly, Harry's eyes began to clear a little. He realised that the surface of the water just beneath him was behaving a little strangely. It didn't look quite right either. He put his right hand down towards it but found that he could no more reach it than see it properly. He moved down a rung or two, listening still.

'Yes, that's right. Someone must have . . . And done the fingers too, but why? . . . Frozen to death, yes . . . Until there's an autopsy, yes . . . Then *why*?'

Harry was well down on the ladder now. He reached down again and was surprised to find that the strange grey water in the hold would not let his fingers through its surface. He pulled his hand back, made a fist and punched down.

'*Ouch*!' It was ice, solid enough to bruise his knuckles.

'Even so,' Nico was saying above, 'there's something not right . . . Damn right . . . Yes, okay. Back we go.' The Italian leaned over the raised edge of the hatch. 'We're going back,' he shouted down.

'It's ice, Nico,' Harry called back. 'The water in here's freezing solid.'

'*Jesu*! We don't want that! Wait a minute . . .'

The first mate's shadow vanished and Harry wondered

what he was up to. Then abruptly the most unexpected thing happened. The hold lights went on. It had never occurred to Harry that they would still be working, but they were. Brightness flooded the great square chamber and it threw into stark detail the glacial sheet of ice which lay across the surface, pushing up against the hold walls and securing the ladder firmly in its crystal grip. And revealing, immediately beneath its surface, looking up at Harry as though watching him through a window, the body of Jamie Curtis, suspended in the water spread against the underside with his eyes and mouth wide open, as though screaming some terrible warning.

Robin looked down at the corpse of Captain Black, her face frowning with concentration. She was not examining the dead man, simply trying to work out the implications of the discovery and the strange mutilation. In the warmth of the bridgehouse, the body was beginning to thaw, tiny droplets of water condensing on the marble skin, a fold or two of patterned silk beginning to darken out of petrified rigidity. It was only a matter of time before he began to leak. There was no question about it, he would have to be wrapped carefully and reverently, then placed in cold storage until they could get him to a port. And to a coroner's court. Still, as she had said to Richard, he looked to her exactly like a man who had frozen to death. But perhaps he had been dead before he had frozen; she did not have the expertise to tell. And she had no way of knowing whether the skin missing from feet, palms and cheek – not to mention the fingers and thumbs – had gone before or after death. But there was no doubt in her mind that he had died – met his death – somewhere other than under the tarpaulin by the spare propeller. So he must have died early last night in one place aboard, then been discovered and moved much later last night. But where had he died? Outside, if he had frozen. Why had he been moved? Because he had found something or had died near something. Why had his fingers and thumbs been removed? Because he had touched something or had tight hold of something. She didn't want to consider the possibility of torture, and ruled it out anyway because of the noise which would have been involved in removing a conscious person's fingers. They had all, including her and with only two obvious exceptions, been asleep. But the screaming of a man having his fingers removed would have woken someone up, surely. And she could see no sign of bruising where the wrists might have been restrained. Most likely the fingers had been removed after death. So, who had done it? If he had been killed, then it seemed likely he had been killed and moved by the same person. And that left two areas of contention. Black must have been looking for Reynolds's drugs. Maybe he found them and one of Reynolds's associates found him. Or maybe the captain had found something else entirely. Like a bomb, for instance.

Her blood ran cold at the thought, especially as it was suddenly much more real to her now. More real even than it had been from her father's warning or even from the faxed poster and picture. Discussing both with her crews had got her nowhere, just as the search had been getting them nowhere until Captain Black had turned up. La Guerre Verte seemed so fantastic, somehow. But Captain Black's hands were all too real.

She crossed Reynolds's room – they had brought the Captain back here because it had been the last place he had been when alive – and picked up the phone. She dialled the bridge and Timmins answered. 'I want two men to take the captain's body to cold storage,' she said. 'You know the crew. You know who would be best for the job. Then, when you've sorted that out, I want you to get a list ready for me. I want to see everyone aboard in my cabin starting at nineteen hundred. I don't care about the order, but I want to interview everyone aboard tonight.'

When she had finished, she dialled Ann Cable's cabin. 'Ann, can you write shorthand?'

'It's a while since I took my Pitman's course, but sure, I guess.'

'Great. In that case, I've got a job for you.'

Richard drove the iron bar down as hard as he could but still it skidded off the ice and he grunted with frustration as he came near to dropping it. 'It's no good,' he called up to Nico. 'I'll have to strike straight down. The ice seems to be so thick that it shouldn't matter.'

Nico said nothing. This was not the time to start trying to explain just how much bad luck was involved in damaging the dead, even if you did do it by accident while you were trying to chip them free of ice. He strengthened his grip on Richard's lifeline and prayed silently that Johnny Sullivan did not hit anything too solid with the bow of the ship which he was currently in charge of as she ran full ahead into the thickening darkness. This was going to be delicate enough without any brushes with ice at twenty-five knots.

Richard had a firm grip on the iron bar now and, pointing it straight down at Jamie's midriff, he struck again. This time the ice cracked. He lowered his aim and struck again. Cracks radiated out from the two successful blows,

distorting the already disturbing expression on the young
man's face. Richard was on the verge of screaming with
frustration. The news that their boy had been lost at sea
would be hard enough for Mr and Mrs Curtis to bear.
Their modest terraced house would never really see sunlight again, he knew. But to have their sorrow compounded
by the inevitable coroner's hearing would be more than
they could bear, he suspected. Brutally, he drove the bar
down again just at the point of the cadet's armpit, and it
smashed through the ice and plunged into the water until
it vanished into the swirl of Jamie's wet-weather gear.

The tip of it struck something. Richard was a fisherman
and had been so since earliest childhood. He had never
ceased to be fascinated by what subtleties of information
could be transmitted up a trembling line and along a rod,
even to gloved fingers – as happened at that moment.
Whatever the tip of the crowbar struck, it was not part of
the boy. It should not have been there. The sensation of it,
ringing up the metal pole as vivid as a salmon's bite, sent
the whole of Richard's long body cold as ice. Then the
cracks in the ice spread far enough to release the end of
the ladder. The metal dipped and danced. The ice sprang
to life, its level surface destroyed by the heaving liquid it
had restrained. The silence in the hold was shattered at
the same time by the clashing wash of the hold's contents
and by the creaking heave of the dancing ladder. And
it suddenly became obvious that Jamie was not alone
down there.

Richard took a firm grip on the slippery rung with his
left hand, hooked the crowbar on with his right and called
up to Nico, 'Young Rupert Biggs is down here too by the
look of things. Throw me down a line with a loop and
I'll try to slip it over Jamie's head and shoulders.'

The line came down, but slipping it over Jamie was easier said than done. And even when he was secured, it was impossible to lift him more than halfway out of the hold because his safety lines were tangled. Richard climbed up past the dangling, cascading body and ran across to the nearest tool box for a knife. Then it was only a matter of minutes before the cadet was out on the deck and Richard was fishing for the third officer.

They were back at their original position just across the ice barrier from *Atropos* by the time both bodies were up out of the hold, and so Andrew McTavish and Harry Piper came down to help carry them back to the bridgehouse. They took them straight to the ship's cold store and laid them out side by side on the butcher's table there among the hanging carcasses. There were tears in Richard's eyes as he arranged them respectfully, with their arms crossed, before covering them and leaving them. As he folded Jamie's arms he remembered the strange sensation he had felt along the length of the crowbar and he searched among the jumble of soaking wet-weather gear, safety harness and black line wrapped round the boy's chest. And there, under his right arm, the handle of a knife protruded.

Richard looked at it for a minute, then he walked out of the cold store and gently closed the door. Moments later he was on the bridge, trying not to look too closely at the exhausted faces there. 'Bill,' he said to the radio officer, 'get me Heritage Mariner in London. I must speak to Sir William. Most urgent. When I've talked to him, I'll want to talk to my wife.' He looked grimly around the room. 'Then I'm afraid we're in for a busy night, gentlemen. We must go through this ship again in microscopic detail. Jamie Curtis was murdered with a Bowie knife.

That woman from the poster has definitely been aboard this ship and even if she's no longer here, you can bet your life she's left a bomb behind.'

CHAPTER TWENTY-FIVE

Day Eleven

Saturday, 29 May   08:00

The sense of freedom was overpowering. Robin had not realised how oppressive the atmosphere on *Atropos* was becoming. The exhilaration of being off the ship was so intense that it more than overcame the fatigue of a late and sleepless night. And the morning was utterly glorious. Clear and quite calm, for all that a little wind kept gusting insistently into her face and threatening to refrigerate her nose. The sea itself was as playfully restless as the air – not enough movement to disturb the purposeful thrust of the lifeboat as it explored westwards along the northern edge of the ice barrier, but more than enough to break up the thin ice which had formed overnight. With the low ice cliffs to the port and thin ice rubbing against the starboard quarter and breaking into wide white circles like enchanted lily pads, the lifeboat seemed to be sailing through fairyland. It was travelling with a serious purpose, however.

Richard's exploration eastwards yesterday evening had showed conclusively that there was no real chance of rescue from that direction. No real hope of rescue at all, unless they could find a break in the ice barrier to the west. But Robin's westward exploration, following in the footsteps of some of her Viking heroes, was more than a search for rescue. She had every intention of carrying out the plan she had first mentioned to Ann Cable all those fraught hours ago. She was looking for any formation in the ice which might be used as a slipway. Ideally she wanted a shelving beach which slid down to the waterline but remained well supported beneath the surface with a depth of ice strong enough to take some of *Atropos*'s weight. Fully laden, too. She was prepared to move the cargo around, but she did not want to unload the ship and then load it up again. That process, independently of the time taken to repair the propeller, would use up more than a day. Fixing the propeller, if it could be done, or replacing it, if that could be done, was bound to take at least forty-eight hours. And something told her that three full days was more time than she actually had to play with.

The atmosphere of gloom which the brilliance of the morning had begun to dispel returned. She could not shake off the feeling that there was something out there. Something even more threatening than the problems which she already knew about. Was it the thing – the force, the entity – that kept the collision alarm ringing so mysteriously while registering on none of the other instruments? Could there possibly be something out there solid and threatening enough to alarm the automatic system, yet hardly visible to the weather satellites and too insubstantial to show up as a contact on the radar bowl itself? Or was it just some formless feeling of doom engendered by the situation she found herself in? She was in command of a ship which was incapable of going anywhere faster than dockside manoeuvring speed. A ship overcrowded with two crews and trapped beyond immediate help. A ship with one dead man lost and another dead man aboard, whose condition made it clear, in spite of the lack of anything tangible from her interviews last night, that there was something sinister and illegal going on. A ship laden with potentially dangerous cargo which had a hidden fortune in drugs somewhere in the work or accommodation areas and which was also under threat of destruction by terrorists who may well have placed a bomb aboard.

Part of her earlier sense of relief arose simply from the fact that she was no longer close to such a disturbingly explosive situation. But she knew well enough that she would have to face it and sort it out. She was no shirker and the thought of running away had not occurred to her. If the terrorist threat was real and they were all destined to go the way of poor old Dan Williams, then so be it. She would be working her hardest to find a way out for everybody right up to the moment of detonation. But she had no vision of ultimate failure. She was nobody's martyr. Right at the foundation of her character, she was utterly confident of her ability to get *Atropos* and all aboard her safely back to port.

Distant gunshots brought her back to reality with a start. Her hand tightened on the tiller and the boat veered to grind quietly along the crystalline verticals, showering the others with feathery ice crystals.

'That sounded like gunfire,' said Ann.

'Difficult to tell out here, miss,' said Sam Larkman. 'Could have been ice cracking. I bet there's quite a sea-full of floes up north of here. Out beyond that fog barrier.' He nodded towards the north-western horizon, his movements, as always, bird-like and precise.

'Didn't know you was a man of the frozen north, Sam,'

said Joe Edwards, ribbing his companion with gentle friendship.

'Yeah, he's a proper what d'you call it – Nanook,' supplied Errol, cheerfully joining in the joke, though the big Afro-Caribbean was feeling the cold more than the rest of them and had been quietly reserved so far.

'I don't know,' supplied LeFever. 'I've been north, in Canada. Up around Hudson Bay. I guess I've heard most of the sounds ice can make.'

'So?' asked Sam who, unlike the rest of the crew, seemed to hold the big North American in scant regard.

'So that still sounded like a—'

A flock of seabirds exploded into the sky low above them in full flight, screaming and beating panicked wings. Robin jumped again and once more the forward quarter of the boat ground along the electric-green glow of the vertical ice wall. The sound it made was lost in the thunder of wings and the madness of the calling. There must have been several hundred, a mixture of species, sizes and sounds. But not of colours: they were all black and white. From the elegant length of the arctic terns to the comical puffin-like plumpness of the little auks, the screaming of the skuas to the keening of the kittiwakes, it was utterly overpowering. All the more so because these were the first living things they had seen in over a week. As suddenly as they had come, they were gone, leaving the crew of the lifeboat bewildered and disorientated.

'Where did they come from?' asked Ann, her voice sounding far away in ears still ringing.

'From the ice barrier?' suggested Errol.

'No,' said Sam decisively. 'They came from the north, not the south.'

'Then how did they get so close?' asked Errol, his round

eyes darting everywhere, as though their return might be
something to be feared.

'Out of the mist,' said Robin. 'Haven't you noticed how
it's been creeping down on us?'

'That's not so strange,' said Joe, in his slow, considered
way. He screwed up his wise, lined face as though he was
squinting – a sign that he was thinking. 'These sort of
conditions, up here. All it takes is a warm current in the
air or the water.'

'Or something very cold,' added LeFever. 'But you're
right, Joe. A mist is not so unusual in calm weather
up here and that sound must have been ice cracking,
not gunfire.'

'We'd better get on then,' said Robin. 'Our compass
may not be too accurate up this near the Pole. I can
navigate along the ice barrier if I have to, but I don't
really want to get caught up in too thick a fog. And
besides . . .' She let it trail off. None of the others seemed
to notice the last bit of her speech so she just let it lie.
This mist was very solid, very dark. It was more than some
warm wind or some cold current. It was the outskirts, she
suspected, of the black smoke which had been bearing
down on them out of the north-west. Unlike LeFever, she
had never been in the far north, but she had read and
studied the writings of men who had. And, although she
couldn't pin it down, she knew that black smoke meant
something up here in polar and near-polar latitudes. Oddly
enough, she was more worried about that than about
sounds which resembled gunfire and flocks of birds which
appeared and disappeared like magic.

The morning progressed without further incident. The
mist remained between them and the northern horizon on
the right hand. Robin kept a weather eye upon it but it

seemed to be coming no closer, though it was hard to tell just how far away in fact it was. The eye was tempted into the heart of it and what seemed to be a surface, a beginning to the mist wall, more often than not turned out with further thought just to be that part where it thickened, deep behind the first ghostly fingers of it.

Most of her concentration, however, was focused on her left. The cliffs of the ice barrier were becoming lower and lower the further west they went. After three-quarters of an hour, they came to a slight southward curve of ice shore. They rounded a low headland and seemed to have reached a wide, shelving bay. The ice on their left fell back as though it had been scooped out. The cliffs fell back also, though they were little higher than dunes at this point.

The water in the little bay was strange and oily, oddly coloured. In front of them, at the heart of the curve, it was black as though the blue through which they had been pushing was a shallow which had suddenly sunk to abyssal depth. So absolute was the change of colour that it was unsettling. Uncharacteristically, Robin was almost nervous of allowing the lifeboat to cross that inky water, as though she feared it would be sucked down. Or pulled down by something monstrous hiding in the blackness. But it was really only a trick of the light, the pitch at the heart of the lagoon existing only in contrast to the colour around it. For here the ice shelved out below the surface and the brightness of the late morning light struck down to catch the increasingly submerged crystal and dance upon its dazzling facets in a rainbow made exclusively of blue and green. No white light here, all the reds and oranges and yellows gone to warmer climes of earlier or later hours. Here were only the greens, blues, indigoes and violets.

The white thrust of the ice slid down like any beach until the washed silk of it was marked by the first wave of lightest aquamarine. Then stage by stage and shade by shade it sank, flanked by malachite and beryl, shadowed with lapis and turquoise, until the last pale fangs of it reached out, emerald, over depths of sapphire and cobalt and, immediately, jet black.

'This looks like the place,' said Ann.

'Well worth checking out,' agreed LeFever, and Robin nodded.

It seemed impossible, but the lifeboat's wake across that midnight pool was white and foaming. It spread out in a measured vee across the tranquil water until it disturbed the shaded gradations in the beaches to east and west.

The slope before them seemed so gentle that Robin risked running the lifeboat's bow directly up onto it, and such was the momentum of the little craft that it slid well up the slope. Joe and LeFever were able to leap out easily onto dry ice and pull the boat up still further. All of them climbed out without getting their feet wet, and it was easy enough to drop the little anchor into a dry rivulet and leave the craft securely held.

After her experience with Timmins and the ice cave, Robin was particularly wary of the ice. She looked first at the 'ground' beneath her feet, trying to make sure it was safe and solid. It certainly looked so; it resembled nothing more than the sort of icy slope she would spend hours perfecting as a child. Snow impacted and polished until it was white almost-ice, perfect for sliding and tobogganing at breakneck speeds. She almost expected the black rock of Cold Fell's grounds to be just beneath the surface. Lost in these thoughts, she walked forward, unaware that the others had gone on ahead, much less wary than was

she. After the sound of the birds, the relative quiet had
returned. The wind was not strong enough to make much
sound, though it was beginning to intensify now. The sea
was too quiet even to make the floes clash or the waves
roll, and, for all that it resembled a beach, the bay had no
actual floor or bed to make the waves tumble into surf at
the waterline. The quiet was utterly primeval in its intensity. Just the timeless whisper of wind over curved ice and
the sibilance of wavelets not quite breaking as they slid
up and down the frozen shore.

The others had stopped walking once they reached the
low crest of the ice dune, and they stood along the crest-
line, as black as the water in the heart of the lagoon,
silhouetted against the rolling plain beyond. From water
to ridge crest, the slope rose about ten feet in twenty
yards, then, like white foam frozen in ripples at a cliff
foot, it dipped the same amount in the same distance
perhaps five times, then rose again, and rose and rose. It
was not a particularly high cliff, no more than fifty feet,
but it was sheer and solid and looked as impenetrable as
the Beardmore Glacier, a world away to the south.

'What d'you think, Captain?' asked Sam, quietly. And
it was fortunate that he had not raised his voice, for the
dead-white surfaces a hundred yards away picked up his
voice and echoed it, each repetition building on the sound
until it reached an almost deafening pitch.

The six of them looked at each other in surprise at first,
and then in horror. The bay had looked quite promising
to Robin. As long as the ice was solid, it seemed about
right and the slope of the beach fine. Ideally she would
have preferred something longer with steeper sides, perhaps even with a cliff nearer to one side to make anchorage of the beached vessel easier, but it would have done

at a pinch. This strange echo, however, made it totally unsuitable.

At last the echoes died. 'Do you think that would happen with every noise?' whispered Ann, glancing nervously at the cliff. She turned her face towards the ice on the word 'every' and the frozen facets picked it up.

'Every... Every... EVERY... *EVERY*...' said the ice, booming the whisper out until the sound pounded at them like fists.

Robin gestured and they turned to walk back down to the boat. Once they were off the ridge, going back down the slope, she dared to try an answer. 'It would have been okay. But we're going to be pretty noisy, what with heaving and hauling and winching, not to mention hefting propellers about and cutting and hammering and welding. I'd hate to hear what that echo made of a couple of big hammers trying to straighten out a sheet of buckled copper.'

'Or of a gunshot,' added LeFever, clearly still worried about the sound.

'It was the ice,' insisted Sam. 'Who would be firing guns up here? Where would anyone *be* to fire any guns?'

'And what would they be firing at?' demanded Joe, only to have this question answered immediately and unexpectedly.

Three polar bears abruptly heaved themselves out of the water immediately beside the lifeboat and came pounding up the slope of the ice towards them. The bears were so close and the sight of them was so unexpected that perhaps shock added to the general perception, but they seemed to be massively huge. Their bodies, covered in slick ivory fur made as smooth as otter pelts by the moisture running off them, seemed incredibly muscular and powerful. Their heads were wide between the laid-back ears behind the black pools of the eyes, then they narrowed to long, almost snake-like faces with black-lipped mouths bristling with long, forward-reaching teeth.

The group of humans exploded out of the way as the trio of deadly predators sped up the ice towards them. Robin lost her footing and tumbled onto her side, rolling over and over across the camber of the slope. On one roll, as her back bounced on the unforgiving ice, she was aware of a neck hollow, haunch and flank, of a surprisingly long leg and a huge foot padded with glistening fur and armed with huge black claws. She gasped with shock and was suffocated with the seaweed stench of rotting fish. Then the ice swung up to slap her in the face and the apparition was gone. The fear of being savaged was abruptly replaced by a horror of skidding off the edge of the ice shelf and plunging down into the black water, and she spread her arms and legs wide, grimly determined to stop herself rolling at least. This proved an effective way to stop sliding too and soon she was picking herself up and dusting off the ice crystals as though she had been rolling in sand. The bears were gone and her companions were picking themselves up carefully and painfully, as though they had aged fifty years in a few seconds.

'Everyone all right?' she called softly. 'Ann?'

'Okay, Robin. All in one piece and shaking like a leaf.'

'Henri?'

'Fine. We were lucky.'

'Yes indeed,' said Sam cheerfully. 'Lucky that was a retreat and not a charge.'

'Damn right,' agreed Errol. 'I thought I was going to end up like some fish supper.'

'Where d'you think they came from?' asked Joe, looking back up the slope towards the crest over which the panicked bears had vanished. All the others followed his gaze. Except for Robin, who was facing the opposite way and looking out to sea. And, in a voice trembling with awed revelation, she whispered an answer to his question: 'There!'

During the time they had been ashore, a subtle change had overcome the view to the north-west. In itself, it was no great change. The mist had thinned, the pale sky above had resolved itself a little more firmly. The wind had attained sufficient strength to pull away a cloud or two. And everything had changed. What had been a vague wall of insubstantial vapour joining the sky to the sea some indeterminable distance away had now attained form. Seemingly shifting shadows within it had attained substance. Bright beams of sunlight became surfaces. Cloud tops became mountain slopes. Insubstantiality had become reality and the incredible had happened.

They stood, stricken by understanding, like observers unexpectedly finding themselves at the birth of a new continent, the discovery of a lost world.

The fog was still there. A dirty-looking grey band of it stood on the surface of the sea perhaps five miles distant, hardly more. It rose for maybe a hundred feet into the air before it thinned and became transparent. Above it, rising out of it in silent majesty, was a cliff of ice. No mere ripple, like the echoing toy behind them, but an alpine cliff, the shoulder of a mountain. Above the cliff, a slope began, reaching up towards a ridge which cut across the blue sky like a razor. So sharp and absolute was the edge of that ridge that the white of it was black at the very top where it sliced the blue at the sky's zenith. The slope swept up towards a peak jutting like a Himalayan rhinoceros horn, the first of a line of peaks reaching back into the table-topped body of the thing. Robin's head began to ache as she fought to comprehend what she was seeing. Her eyes were striving without success to focus on the further reaches of that flat mountain top where it reached back and back and back beyond the power of her sight.

She had never imagined anything so big. Never imagined that anything could ever be so big. She staggered as though the mere sight of it had a physical impact, then dragged her dazzled gaze away to see that the others were staggering as well. The ice barrier had moved. The lifeboat stirred and began to slither down towards the sea. That was what broke the iceberg's spell upon them: the need to catch the boat. It was their one hope of survival in the suddenly hostile environment, and they fought to control it and clamber aboard. Only a fight for survival like that was motive enough to look away from the mesmerising scale of the thing before them. It was as though Everest itself had been launched into the sea, and its fascination was greater than if the Gorgon had sprung to the aid of the Sirens.

Henri LeFever and Sam Larkman held the line and scrambled aboard last. Robin went on just before them and staggered down the length of the lifeboat to start the motor. As soon as the two men were aboard, she was under way, skirting round the edge of the bay and out into the sea proper, just as the little hollow of water suddenly filled with ripples. Automatically, she looked ahead for the incoming waves which had caused the ripples but there were none. Her head lifted, questing for a wind strong enough to move the fake fur of her hood, but there was none. A sound like distant thunder came, however, so quiet as to be almost imagination and she began to understand.

The wavelets came not because of any stirring in the air or water. They were born of the ice. The movement of the immovable ice barrier, so solid that not even a full storm had lifted it. So solid that she could imagine only one thing in all the world which might cause it to shake like that. The iceberg.

'Where are you going?' asked Ann, her voice cutting with unexpected urgency through Robin's thoughts.

'To take a look.'

'What? Surely we should be going back to the ship, not—'

'Nonsense. The day is young. We can be over beside it inside an hour. Maybe do some exploring. I've never seen anything like it, have you?'

'God! No!'

'Any of the rest of you?'

They all shook their heads by way of reply and one by one their faces turned and their gazes followed the shining eyes of their captain, directed towards the massive iceberg which now seemed to be bearing down upon them with disturbing speed.

After about half an hour they entered the fog belt caused by the extra chill the iceberg's meltwater gave even to these icy waters. It was a dank, disturbing mist. Thick enough, seemingly, to interfere with their breathing. Certainly solid enough to deaden sound and cloud sight with what looked like grey rags hanging in the air. The surface of the water around them seemed to glow dully as it exuded a never-ending miasma. They felt as though it should be boiling fiercely somewhere nearby but there were no bubbles and no intimation of heat at all. If the air in the sunshine had been cold, here there was a subterranean chill which seemed to go beyond anything which belonged in nature. There was more than a smell to it, there was a taste, as though the foetid breath from the throat of the polar bears had been rendered into oil and suspended in droplets among the grey fronds of the mist. This sargasso of the air lasted for twenty minutes but it seemed a much longer time. The gloom of it bore them down. They were like explorers trapped in the heart of a dank mountain, wandering aimlessly through uncharted tunnels, lost and without hope.

Coming out into the clear was indescribable in contrast. The fog ended in a wall where the air of the iceberg's own microclimate was too cold to contain moisture. Here the day was dazzlingly clear and the sun struck down, its rays bright as falling stars but wholly devoid of heat. The iceberg rose in unutterable splendour, magnified by the total clarity of the air. The variety of hues which had coloured the plunging shelf of ice was echoed and extended here. Every shade of emerald and sapphire was contained in the crystal galleries behind the white surfaces of the ice. Here a shadow revealed a depth of Prussian blue which ought to have contained distant galaxies; there a cavern carved in bottle green might have contained a cathedral. Their necks ached from holding their heads far back as they tried to see the peaks of the thing. Their eyes watered from trying to focus on the depths and distances of it and their heads throbbed, fighting to comprehend its enormity.

They had been silent for nearly an hour when Robin swung the lifeboat off on the port tack and began to follow the line of the berg from a distance. This side of it was where the cliffs plunged hundreds upon hundreds of feet sheer into the sea and vanished equal numbers of fathoms straight down. There seemed nothing to say which would

not be as trivial as they were themselves, like insects –
like microbes – beside it. The puttering of the lifeboat's
diesel muttered against those crystal flanks, but there were
no echoes in answer. Instead there was a silence as deep
as space itself; it appeared to soak up sound like a black
hole gulping in light. It seemed as if the iceberg could
control time as completely as it controlled everything else
around it. Certainly no one aboard the lifeboat had any
idea how long Robin ran them along the cliff sides before
the form of the glacial mountain range began to change.
Abruptly, the sheer faces began to swing out and where
there had been cliffs, now there were slopes. And where
the ice had disappeared straight down into the black water,
now it reached out milkily towards them.

Robin was taking no account of bearing or direction,
she was simply following the coastline, like the first Viking
exploring the vastness of Newfoundland from his tiny
longship. Her narrowed eyes following the curves of the
ice were guide enough for her, and for the other five as
well. Automatically, she pulled back a little from the thrust
of the submerged ice, but she knew she need not have
worried, it was fathoms below her keel and presented no
real danger. The action swung them out onto a wider reach
and gave them a view round a headland which the sloping
shoulder made. Here, the ice stepped down like a staircase
before settling on a cliff of sixty feet which fell to a
sloping tongue of ice before rising again on the other side.
It was as though the tongue of ice were a frozen river
reaching out from between icy river banks. The whole
glacial valley was a couple of hundred feet wide.

The curve away to the left was reversed and Robin
sailed round on a starboard reach, heading straight for that
frozen river which stretched out into the liquid element

between them. The valley banks stepped back symmetrically on either hand, and swung round in galleries dead ahead. The nearer they came, the more they could see and the more artificial did the whole thing seem to become until at one point it was as though they were looking at a balcony in a giant's theatre. The frozen river flowed out, sliding into the water like a stiletto into green silk. The smooth surface sloped back up above the tide line to become the narrow floor between the stepped levels of ice which surrounded it completely on three sides.

Robin held her line and the lifeboat sailed up the tongue of ice exactly as it had sailed onto the slipway on the ice barrier. Except that here she could easily see the anchorage points and the work areas.

Terrified that there would be another destructive echo, she raised her voice and called, as though speaking to people far away, 'You know what this is, don't you?'

There was no echo. The others allowed her words to hang in the silence for a heartbeat as they, too, waited for the ice to answer. But when it did not, Sam called back to her, his voice as loud as hers had been and every bit as alive with excitement, 'Yes, Captain, it's the best-designed dry dock I've ever clapped eyes on.'

CHAPTER TWENTY-SIX

Day Eleven

Saturday, 29 May 08:00

Richard leaned far out over the front of *Clotho*'s ruined bow and looked down to watch her strengthened cutwater ride up onto the ice. As the grinding shudder of the first contact began, he found he was holding his breath and praying that this section of his command was stronger than the ruin immediately above it. He was desperately worried about Robin and felt that the situation was rapidly spiralling out of control. He trusted her to do everything humanly possible, but could see no way for her to escape her current predicament, in spite of her confidence in her plans for self-help.

He was worried about his own position too. There was no doubt in his mind that the Green War woman had been aboard. She had murdered two of his men and then in all likelihood had been swept overboard herself. He could see no other explanation that fitted the facts he had to hand. Or rather, the lack of them. For there was no trace of her, nor of her hiding place or her bomb. During the last ten hours they had fruitlessly searched the ship again, from

her stern to as near her stem as they could manage. And
there lay the rub. One area was beyond their power to
search. And he was standing on it now.

They had exchanged reports with *Atropos* and had been
torn between sickened surprise and great relief to hear
that Robin was in exactly the same situation: there had
been a body found but no bomb. At last they had grabbed
a few hours' sleep.

This morning they had come west along the southern
edge of the ice barrier. After five miles or so the ice had
swung northwards into a wide bay on their starboard side.
On the lookout for a way through, Richard had gone in
to explore. In the middle of the bay, near the shore, he
had reversed his almost idling propeller and come to a
stop. It was the most promising location so far and at first
glance seemed to offer the best chance of breaking at least
some way through. The ice had sloped down seamlessly
into the water, like a gently shelving beach. Above the
tide line, a series of ice dunes reached back to a more
precipitous central ridge. Richard was totally immune to
the beauty of the scene. All he wanted to do was to find
out whether the ice would yield him a way through. A
hurried conference with Nico and Andrew had set the first
part of his experiment up.

Clotho eased forward under the irresistible impulse of
that one great screw and Richard felt the whole bow
section begin to lift as his ship rode up over the ice. Then
there was a grating crack, a sharp, loud percussion like a
gunshot followed by an immediate roaring. The bow
beneath him slammed down and he staggered, all but
pitched overboard by *Clotho*'s motion. Surprised by the
unexpected power of the ship's continued movement, he
slipped on the icy deck and sat down with a decided bump.

Through the deck plates and his bruised hindquarters, he felt the forward impulse ease as Nico slammed her into reverse – or, more correctly as this was not a Range Rover they were driving, altered the pitch of the propeller blades and called for full astern. In a moment or two the ship was motionless again.

When he regained his former post, Richard found himself looking down at a semi-circle of ice floes all rocking in agitated motion and clashing together with a deafening combination of sharp cracks and dull thuds. Following the line of the shore, but reaching inland for perhaps twenty metres, the ice seemed to have shattered like glass. Excitement welled in him. This was better, he thought, allowing himself a wolfish grin. Now they were getting somewhere.

He counted as nothing the enormous amount he had achieved during the last few days. It all came down to the fact that Robin was on *Atropos* and the ice barrier was between them.

Richard put his walkie-talkie to his lips. 'It's working, Nico,' he said. 'We'll try again, please, but you'll have to hit it harder this time.'

'You'd better hold on tighter, then,' said Nico's voice over the machine. 'And pray she didn't put the bomb up there.'

Mind-reader, thought Richard, but he said nothing out loud.

Clotho eased back under Nico's guidance, as though the first officer had been working on icebreakers all his life. Richard paid careful attention to his advice; having eased back a couple of lengths, they moved forward at what felt like full revs and the impact as *Clotho*'s sharp bow slammed into the ridge of ice shook the vessel from stem to stern. The bow seemed to jump up over the ice and then come crashing down with added weight and momentum. The noise was deafening, and a cloud of freezing spray leaped upwards to be blown towards Greenland on the gusting wind. When it was clear, and the ship's pitching has eased enough for Richard to look down, he saw that they had made a good deal more progress – but had paid the inevitable price. Beyond the new section of noisy floes, the edge of the solid ice rose from the water in quite a cliff. The southern shore of the barrier was the better part of five feet high now. It shone with a baleful green fire which made it look very much like bottle-glass.

Richard looked at it thoughtfully, refusing to let his elation at getting to grips with his frozen adversary wane. Everything he achieved at the moment simply seemed to reveal a new problem. Very well. Every new problem would be overcome. He would get to Robin no matter what it cost. From this vantage point he could see quite clearly that the little cliff was in fact made by a low ice dune which had shattered at its crest. Behind the solid-looking vertical of the shore itself, the dune sloped down to thinner ice. If they could break through here, then there was every chance that they could do the same with the next dune-like ridge, and the next, until they had opened a channel right through to that central ridge which was so much higher than the rest. As he thought about it, he looked up at it. It resembled a rounded, snow-covered hill from this side, though it could be anything from a gentle slope to a precipitous escarpment on the far side, he supposed. It stood maybe twenty feet high. High enough to form a horizon against the pale, misty sky beyond. Would more be visible from the bridge? What lay beyond might turn out to be important if he could break a way up to the first slope of it. He put his walkie-talkie to his lips to ask Nico what he could see.

The flock of birds came straight over the ridge very low and with quite enough speed to make Richard jump. They seemed to pounce forward through the air towards him, a pandemonium of screaming beaks and battering wings. The size of the ship's bridge seemed to upset them, for they wheeled away in one tight body immediately above his head and sped westwards, their panic echoing on the air behind them.

The walkie-talkie sprang to life at once. 'Richard, are you all right?'

'Fine,' he answered. 'It was only a flock of birds, Nico.'

'I know but . . .'

'Yes. I know what you mean. We haven't seen a living thing since I came aboard. They were a bit disconcerting.'

'The last living thing I saw was a tiger shark trying to eat Jamie Curtis.'

'It's been a rough ride.'

'You can say that again. And it's not over yet.'

'Okay, Nico, let's go again. We have a five-foot cliff above the water so I guess it may extend the same amount under the water. But it falls away quite steeply beyond and I reckon if we can break through, we might be in business. Hit it with all you've got.'

'Okay. Remember to hang on.'

This time the ice turned them without breaking. Although the ship's bows were not only strengthened, but specially angled to ride up over obstructions, a five-foot wall went too far beyond the design specifications. *Clotho* slewed round to port and Richard was hurled against the safety ropes and almost lost his grip in spite of the fact that he was following Nico's sensible advice. He hung on with all his strength, one hand on the line and the other round a stanchion. His angle, disconcertingly wide of the ship's side, allowed him to see something that he had not included in his calculations so far. A great spray of water gushed out of number one hold through the hole in its forward wall. He was rolled back fully onto the deck by the counter-motion, and was able to hear the wild watery disturbance from within the ship just beneath him as he lay there, dazed and cursing himself for not being more careful. And as he lay there, looking at the impossibly beautiful blue sky immediately above his head, he suddenly had the strangest impression that he could hear voices echoing. It was too vague and far away for him to be sure of the words – or even of the reality of the impression. Voices rang in his ears, echoing on the wind, building to a kind of climax then fading into silence.

He lay for a moment more, listening to the wind and the hissing of the water below the deck. *You're cracking up, old son*, he thought, then he picked himself up. The shock of the fall, and the unnerving experience of hearing voices, had deadened that elusive elation slightly, but when he looked at the point of impact, he saw that the crystalline face of the ice had crumbled. Grimly he dusted himself off and slid his walkie-talkie down to his hand from the position at his shoulder it had somehow achieved while he was rolling about on the deck. He walked across to the nearest box of deck safety equipment and pulled out a harness. He slipped it on, buckled it tight and slid the catches over the safety lines nearest his favourite observation post. 'Right, Nico. Let's just try that again, please.'

And so the morning passed. Within three hours they had broken through four low ice dunes and gouged a straight channel the better part of half a mile in towards the lower slopes of the central ridge. Here their progress slowed dramatically. Once the ice wall at the water's edge was too high for the bows to ride up over, they were reduced to battering it aside, foot by foot. Slowly, inexorably, as the target ice thickened, the upper edge of it rose towards the damaged section of the bow and Richard at last was forced to call a halt.

'It's nearly time for the noon contacts in any case,' he said to Nico over the walkie-talkie. 'I want to know what's going on aboard *Atropos*, and I'd better report in to head office.' He pulled off his harness and left it hanging on the safety lines. At first he walked wearily, for the extravagant motion of the bows had taxed his knee joints sorely, but as he saw what they had actually achieved, as his vision rose from the ice immediately beside the ship and began to take in also the black channel they had created stretching back through the cracked and bobbing jumble of little floes to the emerald of the open sea, so a spring entered his step and he almost ran up onto the bridge.

Nico was poring over the chart table when Richard came into the wheelhouse. 'Talking of contacts,' said the first officer. 'This has just come in. I'm trying to sort it out. Look.'

It was another enhanced satellite picture of their section of the Labrador Sea. Even with the calm weather and the near-perfect conditions, not to mention the advanced computer enhancement techniques which had been used on it, the picture was not all that clear. 'Probably the solar flares again,' said Nico glumly as they stood, trying to make out the detail. Most of the picture was uniform white. From the top of the square, stretching down over what must have represented the better part of a hundred

miles, the white was featureless. Only in the bottom third
of the frame and in the western reach was there any
difference. Here the absolute white gave way to absolute
black. In the west it was as though something massive had
simply been dropped, shattering the glassy surface around
it, but the black spider's web of cracks seemed to fade as,
for some reason, the picture lost definition in that area.
The area of vagueness spread south, in fact, until the
shattered cracks around it joined the thicker line of black
which Richard had come to recognise as the clear water
along the north of the ice barrier. And, now that he could
recognise the ice barrier, he began to see more detail
within it. Certainly the picture gave some idea of the
overall shape of the solid adversary lying between him
and Robin, but when detail was required, it proved frustrat-
ingly vague.

More black at the foot of the picture showed the open
water from which *Clotho* had just made her inroad. In
fact, thought Richard, as his eyes began to water with the
strain of looking so closely at something so ill-defined, it
was just possible to make out the whole stiletto shape of
the ice barrier for about three-quarters of its length. Its
edges were perfectly clear in the east, but as the picture
came west, so things began to get vague, especially on
the northern shore. That hole where the black cut into the
white from the south must be the bay they were currently
sitting in. There was no channel marked, for the picture
must have been taken earlier. Yes. That bright dot east of
their present position must be *Clotho* and that one due
north of it *Atropos*. They were in their original positions
as they would have been soon after dawn early this morning. Since then *Clotho* had come five miles west. This
must be the bay.

What lay opposite it on the north shore? He strained to see, but that vagueness made it impossible to be certain. If anything, the pale unfocused area lying spread across the black made it look as though the ice extended north suddenly from this very point right to the western edge of the photograph. But that couldn't be true, surely.

Without conscious thought, he lifted the faxed photograph and walked to the clearview. Had he been reasoning clearly and consciously, his thoughts would have gone along predictable lines: here we are exactly to the south of this vague area. There is an ice ridge perhaps ten metres high half a mile in front of us, but from the bridge I should be able to see over it quite clearly. Even if I cannot estimate how wide the ice barrier actually is at this point, I should still be able to look directly into the vague area from the photograph and maybe get some idea as to what is actually out there. He was not thinking that clearly. He was simply a man walking across a ship's bridge with a fax of a picture in his hand, hoping to get something straight in his mind. He actually laid the picture on the console under the clearview and straightened it carefully, deep in his brown study, before he looked up.

When he did look up, he was looking beyond the crest of the central ridge of the ice barrier before him for the first time since perhaps ten o'clock. And what he saw had as much effect upon him as it had upon Robin when she had seen it earlier.

She had been looking at it from very much closer and a great deal lower down, but such was the impact that Richard, too, had his breath stolen and his sense of proportion and reality ravished. It was as though a man who had grown used to looking only at the tenements at the end of his street should suddenly have discovered that a mountain stood beyond them. His eyes ached as they refocused themselves, stretching his vision far beyond that suddenly paltry ridge to the silent majesty of the iceberg beyond. He looked down at the fax, but he hardly saw it. He made the gesture not as a man who wishes to check something but more like someone who squeezes their eyes closed when confronted with something incredible. When he looked up, everything was exactly the same; in fact the distant, lustrous cliffs seemed to have grown clearer and more real in the interim.

'Nico,' he said, quietly. 'Would you come here and look at this?'

Something in his tone alerted Nico who, frowning, joined him at the clearview. Alerted or not, the down-to-earth Italian looked out into the bright blue noon without actually comprehending what his captain was talking about. The mist made the base of it so vague, especially as the ridge of the ice barrier proved to be such a strong sky line against it. And above the grey backdrop, so far into the sky, who would have supposed the dazzling whiteness to have been anything but clouds? So his eyes, like those of the satellite looking for weather systems far above their heads, were fooled. 'What?' he said.

'You don't see it?'

'*Che . . . ?*' He did feel that something was amiss, enough to slip back into his native tongue as he concentrated, but still he could not see, until . . . '*Dio mio!*' he breathed. 'My God!'

Just at that moment, Bill Christian stuck his head out of the radio shack. '*Atropos* reporting, Captain,' he said.

Richard dragged his eyes away from the upper slopes of the distant iceberg and answered, 'Take it for me, would you, Bill, unless there's anything important.'

Bill vanished and Richard remained where he was for a few moments more, until Nico said, 'I didn't see it. I was looking at it and I didn't see it. It's too big. Too big to understand immediately.'

When his lieutenant put it like that, Richard suddenly realised that the people on *Atropos* might have their comprehension fooled in the same way. 'Bloody hell,' he said, and strode across to the radio room. 'Let me have that mike a moment,' he asked, just loud enough to overcome the buzzing in Bill Christian's headphones. 'And put it on broadcast,' he added as the radio officer looked up at him.

The microphone felt warm in his hand and he realised how cold he had become. It was shock, probably, he thought. '. . . reported on arrival at the first bay,' Harry Stone was saying as Bill flipped the switch. 'Wide and shallow, perhaps with a good beach for pulling her up. Then she—'

'*They're tearing the place up down there!*' an urgent voice broke in.

Richard frowned. 'Stone, what—'

'*They're out of control!*' screamed the voice from *Atropos*, magnified by the radio link.

'Stone! What's going on?' demanded Richard. '*Stone! Answer me!*'

But the radio was dead.

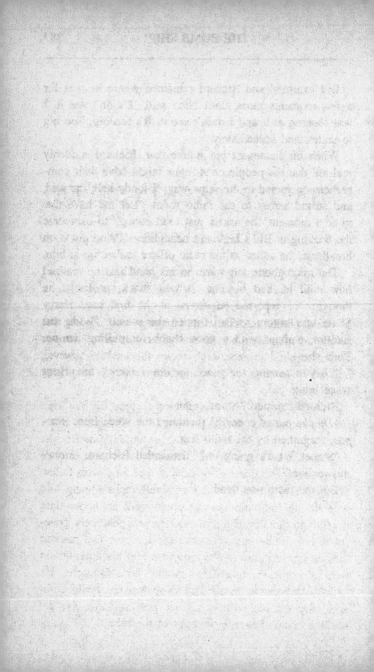

CHAPTER TWENTY-SEVEN

Day Eleven

Saturday, 29 May   12:00

It could hardly be said that Timmins was holding the watch any more than he was really in command of *Atropos* during Robin's absence. He was on the bridge, however, and on the verge of commanding action when Hogg found him.

Timmins had no real duties currently, and did not have the imagination or the inclination to think ahead. Since Black's sudden collapse, he had been rudderless. He was willing to take orders from Captain Mariner, but only in the same spirit that an orphaned duckling will follow anything that moves. He did not really relish being told what to do by some limey woman with an upper-class accent and the airs of a princess. He was genuinely grateful to her for having come into the ice cave and rescued him, but he was not a generous soul and his thoughts on that subject were tinged by meaner considerations. He hadn't liked anyone to see him so scared. He would probably have got out without all her grandstanding. He did not like being shown up in front of the men.

Black had run a hard ship as well as a tight one and Timmins was well aware that Captain Mariner had got away with so much in spite of her sex because she had her own crew aboard with her and had somehow earned their loyalty. At the first hint of disgruntlement from *Atropos*'s men, the word had gone out from *Clotho*'s that they would protect their captain, no matter what the cost. But there was no one looking out for Timmins, so being hauled aboard by a woman had damaged him in his men's eyes more than he cared to admit. He currently ranked only a little higher than Hogg and he knew it. The only officer left aboard who held any of the men's respect was Harry Stone. Then again, no; that wasn't quite true. LeFever never had any trouble and the engineers, too, asserted their authority when they needed to. But LeFever was away with the captain, the engineers were still convalescent, and when Hogg ran onto the bridge, Timmins only had Stone to turn to.

He had been hanging around the radio room half hoping that Captain Mariner would include some kind of order for him when she next radioed in. He was not a man who particularly relished being idle and, in truth, Captain Black had never allowed him a moment's rest and he felt the weight of his inactivity now when things were so obviously bad and there was clearly so much to be done. But it was the wrong Captain Mariner on the radio when he arrived and so he just sat and listened to Stone's report to *Clotho*, while anticipating some lunch. Since *Clotho*'s chef had come aboard, the food had improved one hundred per cent, for he had awoken the spirit of competition in *Atropos*'s own temperamental galley staff.

And, to be fair to her, Captain Mariner had found the time to do some checking and improving down there as well. Just like a woman: get the kitchen sorted out. And now he thought of it, the laundry service had improved too . . .

The captain herself broke in on these thoughts by making a connection on the radio. She came through to Stone first, but the tenor of her voice was clearly identifiable even coming out through his earphones. He switched over to broadcast and her words filled the room. 'Mr Timmins, I want you to retrieve the shore lines and start the manoeuvring system. It will only move you at a knot or two as though you were in harbour, but it will be better than nothing. Make what speed you can along the ice barrier following the course I took in the lifeboat this morning. I shall be coming back to meet you, but I want all speed made, please. Mr Stone, report to *Clotho* for me. Tell them I came west this morning looking for a natural slipway in the ice . . .' Stone flipped the broadcast button to off and listened to his orders in private.

When he signed off from his captain and called over to *Clotho*, Timmins was still sitting there. Captain Mariner had given him the one order he didn't want to hear: he wanted nothing whatsoever to do with the ice. The ice frightened him. It had tried to kill him only yesterday and had very nearly succeeded. He didn't want anything to do with getting lines back off the ice. He would delegate the job to Hogg and go wake up the chief engineer. Yes, that was it. He would send Hogg onto the ice and go down to the engine room with the chief to check on the best way to engage the little manoeuvring propellers. He certainly didn't want to make any mistakes about which propellers he wanted . . .

Hogg's face drove all thoughts from Timmins's mind, for it had trouble written all over it. 'Timmins,' gasped

the fat officer. 'You got to back me on this. It's O'Brien.
There's others too, but O'Brien's the ringleader.'

'What is it?'

'They're tearing the place up down there. They're looking for Reynolds's stash. I told them to stop it and go get
some lunch but they told me to fuck off. They're out
of control!'

Timmins swung round to look at Stone. The radio
officer's eyebrows had risen and he was looking out of the
radio shack at the two officers in stunned surprise. Hogg's
words had gone straight across the airwaves to *Clotho* as
a corollary to the half-completed report from *Atropos*, but
he didn't seem to have realised this. Still looking at them,
his mind clearly engaged in what they were saying rather
than what he was doing, he switched the radio off. He
was not in the habit of breaking contact in this abrupt
way, but this looked like a crisis to him and the two
officers in the wheelhouse clearly hadn't much of a clue
what to do.

'Log them. Dock them a day's pay,' suggested the first
officer uncertainly.

'You're kidding, Timmins. This is serious. They don't
give a rat's ass about a day's pay. In the first place they're
looking for thousands of dollars' worth of assorted drugs.
In the second place they don't think anyone's going home
to collect any pay in any case.'

'Well, what do you want me to do?'

'I don't know, but I tell you this. It's a direct refusal to
obey an order. That's mutiny, for fuck's sake, Timmins.
You got to do something.'

'You're winding me up, Hogg. Mutiny, for Christ's sake!
You can't call it mutiny.'

'I don't care if you call it musical farting, Timmins. I

told them to stop. They told me to fuck off. I told them I was referring the matter up to you. Now you've got to sort it out before they destroy all the accommodation areas.'

'Well, I—'

'And you got to back me up. How the hell we going to run this ship with no one paying any attention to the only two deck officers left?'

'He's got a point there, Yasser,' observed Stone quietly. He had removed his headphones and hung them on the hook beside the dark radio.

'So what do you think I ought to do?'

'I think you have to go down there and stop them. They'll be working on the assumption that with the captain gone and the chief still in bed, they'll have the run of the ship. You've got to stop them. If it was me, I'd go carrying something hidden but heavy and I'd lay O'Brien out at the first sign of trouble, then I'd lock him away as close to the cargo as possible and let the Irish bastard rot.'

'Sounds about right to me,' supplied Hogg.

'And who's going to discuss it with the Seaman's Union in due course? And the lawyers with the criminal assault charges when we get home?'

'Justifiable force, Timmins,' said Hogg helpfully. 'And like O'Brien said, no one here is ever going home.'

'You don't believe that, do you, Hogg? The captain'll get us out.'

'Sure she will, Yasser. But if she gets back to find we've allowed O'Brien and the rest of them to tear her ship apart, she'll likely dump us over the side before she goes.'

Hogg's words did little to reassure the hesitant man. He turned to Stone again. 'Stone, what do you—'

'It's no use contacting the captain,' he said. 'She might

be able to advise us, but you'll still have to sort it out. She won't be back for hours if her last report was anything to go by. We simply can't have a mob of men running amok round the accommodation area smashing up anything they want.'

Stone stood up, stooped and pulled a tool box out from under the radio bench. He hefted it up and placed it in front of his equipment. Then he opened it and selected three tools from inside it. To Timmins he gave a wrench, to Hogg a hammer, and for himself he pulled out a heavy-duty screwdriver. 'Let's do it,' said Stone. He slid his enforcer up his right sleeve and exited. The others copied and followed him more hesitantly.

Sean O'Brien and his men had followed their late captain's lead and begun in Reynolds's quarters. The destruction wrought in these rooms went far beyond what was required to discover whether anything was hidden there, and then they had simply continued along the corridor, looting and pillaging – except that they had left LeFever's quarters alone. By the time the three officers arrived, the men had destroyed most of the rooms on the corridor. There weren't many of them but they made a noisy and ugly little mob; Timmins, Hogg and Stone had three or four adversaries each to choose from. Or, more to the point, the crewmen were in a position to do very much whatever they wished to the officers. Had Timmins been in charge, they would most likely have done just that. But Harry Stone took over. Arriving outside the room currently being searched, the three officers spread out across the corridor in order to prevent the men from proceeding.

The first looter who came out stopped and waited silently and speculatively. The second arrived beside him, saw the situation and turned to call out, 'O'Brien!'

O'Brien was big. He was fat rather than well built, but he looked powerful and had a mean reputation extended by his thick-skulled, close-shaven bullet head and his battered, fighter's face. He came out the instant his name was called and walked towards the officers, opening and closing his massive fists. While he did this, the others followed and formed up silently behind him. Timmins stepped forward, squaring up to the big crewman. 'Every man here will be logged. You are all docked one day's pay for insubordination and the cost of any and all repairs arising from your actions will be fully deducted from your wages as well. Now go about your business.'

It was not a bad speech. Had Captain Black spoken those words, the men would have obeyed the final command at once. But Timmins had not the knack of leadership and the threats had as little effect as Hogg had feared they would. O'Brien paid no attention to him at all. He looked past the first officer at Stone. 'What're you doing here, Mr Stone? You'd better take a walk, sir.' His tone lingered on the final word, pushing it just to the edge of insubordination but still leaving Stone enough room to get away if he wished.

'You'd better do what the first officer says, men,' he said quietly. 'This will turn out badly for you in the end if you don't.' His eyes met O'Brien's and locked. 'Any stupidity now will just get added to the reckoning later on.' His words carried weight. Some of the crewmen at the back began to waver.

'You aren't going anywhere. You'll have to reckon with the captain when she gets back. She isn't going to let anything slip or pass and you know it,' added Hogg, hoping to press the point. But the words did not have the effect he had hoped for.

O'Brien threw back his head and laughed. 'You can't

hide behind old Yasser's gold braid so you'll hide behind the captain's skirts, is that it, Mr Hogg?'

Timmins raised his right arm and hit the laughing man over the head with his metal wrench. He made a bad job of his attack, however, and the metal jumped out of his hand to vanish over his shoulder so that the powerful *crack* which rang down the corridor from the impact was immediately followed by the thud of the weapon falling to the floor. Timmins stepped back, shaking his hand in agony. O'Brien stood, frozen with wrath as blood spurted out of his split scalp and poured down his cheek. Stone stepped in front of the first officer.

As though Stone's movement had broken a spell, everyone was in motion at once. O'Brien hurled forward towards Timmins. He went straight for the senior officer as though he had no idea that Stone was between them. His shoulder took the radio officer in the chest and spun him against the wall. Stone was a fit man and an active one in spite of the fact that his calling required him to sit around so much. He was not prepared for the impact of O'Brien's charge, however, and this was compounded when he smacked his forehead against a joist between two wall panels. Badly dazed, he sat down just in the path of O'Brien's confederates who were all eager to join the fray. A knee took him in the right ear and, as he fell back a foot took him in the temple.

Hogg was thinking with feverish speed. It was far too late to run away and the only alternative he could see was to join in as best he could. As O'Brien went past him, he hit him over the back of the head with the hammer. As he had not set out to murder anyone, the fat officer had reversed his weapon and was holding the heavy metal head in his sweaty fist. The hard wood handle was eighteen inches long and as effective as a British bobby's truncheon. It connected with all the accuracy and force which had been missing from Timmin's blow and O'Brien went down before he ever reached his target. Hogg swung back and, more by luck than judgment, he spread the next man's nose across his face. The man spun away, spraying blood everywhere. Hogg shrugged himself off the wall and stood astride the corridor. The next man in line was the one who had called O'Brien. He was a few feet back. Just far enough for him to have to think before he attacked Hogg. He hesitated.

The nine who were left behind him hesitated too. Unexpectedly, Timmins did the right thing. He stooped, then rose to the occasion with Stone's nasty-looking screwdriver reversed in his right hand. Above his clenched fist, the six-inch shaft of steel widened into a foot-long, ridged wood handle and it looked like an extremely effective cosh. In his left hand he held the wrench which had sprung back over his shoulder after that first, weak blow. It was covered with blood and it looked very businesslike now. 'Who's next?' Timmins grated. 'Those of you looking to get wounded too, remember this: I'm the only medic aboard now LeFever's gone cruising with the captain.'

'And anyone hoping to get away unscathed,' added Hogg, breathlessly, 'might like to think where they'll be locked up when the captain gets back. Down by the cargo.' His eyes raked over their faces, daring them to move. 'And I've got the name of every man here. Think about it.' The man with the broken nose sat whimpering, his groans the only sound in the corridor for an instant.

'Break it up and go to lunch, the lot of you,' ordered Timmins. And for once he sounded so much like a real first officer that they obeyed.

It was only when the men were gone that the victors noticed the state of Harry Stone.

CHAPTER TWENTY-EIGHT

Day Eleven

Saturday, 29 May   13:00

'Look, Captain, this isn't really my line of country, you know,' called down Bill Christian nervously.

Richard swung round and looked back up the Jacob's ladder to where the Cumbrian radio officer stood on *Clotho*'s deck. 'I thought you were with the polar team in eighty-nine,' he said. 'That was one of your qualifications for this post.'

'I was, but . . .' The radio operator suddenly looked almost boyish, torn between his desire to please Richard and his fear that his captain was doing something unwise. Desperate.

'If this is a stupid thing to do, I'm relying on you to tell me, Bill. If it's not, I'm relying on you to help me. I really do have to get across there. I need to know what's going on.'

'We could wait. They're bound to get back in contact soon . . .' Bill tailed off, knowing how weak this sounded. He could imagine how it would strike this man who stood to lose not only a ship but a beloved wife.

'Less than five miles, if that satellite photograph is accurate,' persisted Richard. 'I know we're not well equipped, but you're experienced and we'll be careful. The weather's clear and the ice seems sound.' He stamped down on it hard. 'There are ridges in the way, building up to that central chain of hills, but it's not as if we're aiming to climb the Matterhorn or anything. And we'll turn back at once on your say-so, no questions asked. You have my word. But I must give it a shot. Don't you see that?'

'Okay, Captain. As long as you realise I'm not an ice man. I'm a radio operator.'

While *Clotho* had reversed along her channel back to the open sea and then turned east once more, Richard had searched everywhere aboard for the items of equipment he might need to help him walk across the ice. This had seemed his best course of action if *Atropos* did not get back in touch. She had not done so, and now he was off across the ice barrier to find out what was wrong.

He had no intention of being on the ice for more than a few hours, no matter which way things went, so there was no need for anything other than warm clothing, basic survival equipment in case of accidents and a walkie-talkie to summon help in the face of a serious emergency. But the equipment which would have made the journey safer, easier and quicker was not to be found. There were no skis, nor anything that could readily be adapted into skis. He added ropes and harness to tennis racquets from the ship's sports equipment, but then left them because they seemed too weak and stupid. Stout walking boots would do if the ice was firm, and if it wasn't then he would just have to come back. Even though he had no skis, Richard found two lengths of metal which would double as ski poles and help him to remain upright on the slippery surface. It was when he had got enough equipment together for one person that Bill Christian had advised him just how unwise it would be for him to risk it alone. Richard was not as fit as he might be; he was certainly not experienced. Even one of the legendary polar explorers might hesitate before setting out alone on such an apparently simple journey as this.

In no time, Richard had produced a second set of equipment and now, with *Clotho* resting against the southern section of the ice nearest to *Atropos*'s last recorded position, he was eager to go.

All too well aware that Richard's confidence might for once be badly misplaced, Bill Christian climbed over the side and joined him on the ice. Despite his misgivings, he simply could not let Richard go alone.

Over their cold-weather gear each of them wore a safety harness and to the harnesses was tied a rope linking the two of them together. Each wore a backpack with extra gloves, boots, hats and dark glasses in it. They each carried two thermos flasks, one filled with soup and the other with sweet tea. They had grabbed a light lunch of scalding soup and freshly made sandwiches immediately before kitting up, so they carried no solid food except for some emergency rations of chocolate. Richard had wanted to bring Mars Bars as they contained the highest concentration of energy, but Bill had pointed out how impossible they were to bite into when they were all but frozen. Chocolate would have to do; at least it could be shattered like toffee and the shards sucked carefully. They had eaten enough soup to warm them but not enough to fill them. Neither man relished trying to relieve himself if they were caught short on the ice.

They each carried a compass and a walkie-talkie in case
they got separated, a knife in case they needed to cut
themselves free of their harness quickly, and a heavier
implement in case they needed to cut steps or handholds
in steep ice. Richard had an axe; Bill had the chef's biggest
meat cleaver. Each one carried two emergency flares purloined from the lifeboats, in pockets convenient to their
hands, though even careful Bill could hardly imagine any
situation in which they would be required. The walkie-
talkies would communicate with *Clotho* for the first mile
or so, and with *Atropos* if they got close enough to her.
Richard also had a pair of binoculars slung over his
shoulder. Apart from their poles, that was all they carried.
They were only going for a short walk on a sunny day,
after all.

Bill set off at a brisk pace with Richard slightly behind
him. There was no doubt as to which of them was the
leader, but the simple fact was that Bill knew more about
this sort of thing than Richard did, so he wisely put
himself in a position to get the best view of what the
more experienced man was doing. Immediately, Bill fell
into a sort of shuffling gait, back slightly hunched, leaning
on his makeshift poles. This way, apart from the occasional
glance upwards to confirm direction, he could watch the
ice at his feet – he was more interested in that than in
views or far distances. A moment's consideration convinced Richard that this was eminently sensible. The ice
seemed solid, but there was no telling when a crack might
appear unexpectedly. A dry crevasse would be as dangerous as a water-filled lead. A broken ankle might prove as
fatal as a plunge into below-freezing water. Indeed, a
simple clumsy fall might do as much damage as anything
else. Pushing the feet along the slippery surface rather
than lifting and planting them kept the walker stable and

cut down the chances of slipping over.

The unnatural method of locomotion seemed to be quite easy to begin with, but Richard soon found that it was taxing the muscles at the front of his thighs and, although his ankles preferred this strange movement, his knees did not. His shoulders began to ache next, as his arms were out in front of his chest for most of the time, and his ski poles were surprisingly heavy. He soon found that he was beginning to pant a little. The instant he did so, he found he had a choice: he could either breathe heavily through his nose, whereupon a lancing shock went from his adenoids up behind his eyes; or he could breathe through his mouth and transfer the discomfort to his teeth and chest. As soon as he began to perspire, his dark glasses threatened to fall off his nose and within a few yards his head was aching with the unaccustomed strain of keeping them in place. Surprisingly quickly, his world shrunk to the ice in front of his shuffling feet, and the discomfort, which soon attained the level of genuine pain.

The ice against *Clotho*'s port flank was five feet thick to the waterline. It began to slope upwards immediately, onto the back of the first corrugation running from east to west, right to left in front of them. From the ship, looking at the overall pattern rather than the detail, Richard had registered only the corrugations, building up and up onto that central ridge, as though a piece of corrugated iron had been folded into a rough 'A' shape in preparation for a simple roof. But this folded piece of corrugation was not level from one end to the other. It dipped and twisted along its length. Nor was it plain. There were outcrops in all sorts of unexpected places, telling of cracks which met and forces great enough to push ice up in individual blocks or jumbled, rubbishy piles.

The slope was not too steep at first and the crest of the

first little ridge, hardly higher than a sand dune, was soon
attained. Here they paused, for several good reasons. It
was an excellent place to regain their breath a little and
refocus their attention on terrain that would soon start
sloping away from them. Also, in spite of the apparent
ease of the gradient and shortness of the distance travelled
so far, this downward slope would take them out of sight
of *Clotho*. For the first time on the ice, they looked down
into shadow and here, oddly, the depth of the ice chose
to show itself. It did so only in places, for it was covered
here and there by drifts of ice grains like sand, obscured
elsewhere by solid blocks and piles of rubbish like gigantic
snowmen which had rotted and been weathered almost
away.

While Bill checked in with Johnny Sullivan who was
manning the radio in their absence, Richard had leisure to
look down at the bottom of the valley. Here the ground
looked as though it contained the sky within its depths,
but behind a surface which had been coated with thick
white swirls and piles of sugar frosting. The blue shone
through the white as though there was another sun somewhere down there, burning beneath the sea. As soon as
full light hit the slope of the next ridge ahead, the solid,
snowy whiteness returned and there was intimation of
sapphire only in the shadows of increasing numbers of
excrescences around and through which they were clearly
going to have to wander. The next ridge was like a maze
and, Richard suddenly realised, the one beyond that was
worse. And how many more to the central ridge? Then
how many more beyond that?

He understood with poignant clarity Bill Christian's
reluctance to come.

'Still no contact with *Atropos*,' said Bill, even as

Richard thought of him. 'Anything you want me to pass on to *Clotho*?'

'No. Let's get on.'

'Okay. That's it, Johnny. Over and out.'

They had to slither down the slope, and when they reached the bottom, they paused again, looking up and calculating how easy, or otherwise, it would be to climb it on the way back. 'I don't fancy carving a stairway all the way up there,' said Richard feelingly.

'You shouldn't have to. It looks just about do-able,' said Bill confidently. 'Still, no sense worrying. Let's go.'

As Richard had suspected, their way up the next slope was more complicated. They were forced to follow an almost drunken path weaving in and out of the surprisingly massive obstructions in their way. From *Clotho* these had appeared too insignificant to be worth considering. On the ground, the smallest of them was more than six feet high and ten wide. It would clearly be a waste of effort and time to try and climb them, even had it been possible to do so. Round and about they went, therefore, like children lost in a petrified forest, often with nothing to guide them but the upward slope at their feet.

At the second crest they paused again, looking back. In the clear, icy air, *Clotho* nestled at the edge of the ice, beam on, etched against the dark blue sky, massive and seemingly only yards away. This time Richard spoke into his walkie-talkie while Bill considered the next stage of their journey. Again, Johnny had nothing to report and Richard was now becoming really worried. He could think of no routine reason for *Atropos* to be out of contact for this length of time. After a few moments, they turned their back on *Clotho* and went on.

This time the escarpment was less steep and they were

able, with care, to walk down it. The shadow at the bottom of the valley seemed to be deeper, however, the crystal-blue sections more numerous, and the atmosphere of the place more sinister. Richard found that his legs were aching, not just because of the peculiar method of walking, but because he did not trust the valley bottom to hold him up. Each of his legs, from hip to ankle, was rock solid with the expectation that when he put his weight on his foot, it would simply break through the glacial surface and plunge down into a crevasse or into the ocean itself. It was like walking on a great sheet of glass, never knowing when it was going to crack.

Wryly, he considered his current situation and compared it to his experiences over the recent past. It had all been like this, he thought. Since the bomb in Belfast he had been walking on glass, knowing it was going to break beneath him, that it was only a question of time. Knowing of no way to avoid disaster other than to keep doing what he was doing. Ready for the first warning crack, certain it was coming soon, to rob him of reputation, standing, friends; ship, company, fortune; wife. Only the twins seemed safe, with their grandfather to rely on immediately, and the insurance after that. The rest of them were trapped and Richard felt himself to be most at risk, unable to see any way out at all. He had never been a man to look on the dark side. He had always been lucky and taken his luck for granted. No longer, it seemed. Here he was walking on thin ice and knowing how thin the ice had always been beneath his feet. It almost frightened him, in retrospect, to think of the risks he had taken, of the chances he had permitted those close to him to take. It certainly frightened him to think of the future; of the next second, the next hour, the next day, and the unlimited disaster it would surely bring.

So engrossed was he in his combination of pain, fatigue and depression that he didn't see the polar bear until it was almost upon him. When he did see the creature, it was so unexpected and so close that he shouted aloud with surprise. Bill slewed round at the sound. The bear, which had been running silently towards them along the valley floor, stopped in a flurry of ice crystals and sat back on its haunches. The three of them looked at each other, then the men, being quicker thinking and most at risk, began to look around for a safe haven. The nearest feature of any kind was a tall jumble of small ice blocks. With their eyes on the bear, they began to fall back towards this. It was the best thing to do under the circumstances, for at the very least they would be able to face the bear from above there and rob it of its obvious advantages of height and the reach of its long black claws. But their slow retreat served to tempt the animal into renewed movement.

The massive creature rolled forward off its rump and flopped onto all fours. Then it began to follow them step for step. This was not an attack; even its initial approach had been more of an enquiry than a threat. But it was an inquisitive creature, and the master of its realm on the ice. The man smell no doubt made it wary, but something more compelling drove it on. 'This could get bloody dangerous,' warned Bill hoarsely. 'If he gets interested, we'll have to scare him off good and proper. Or kill him.'

'Always assuming he doesn't kill us first,' said Richard. 'Look at the length of those claws!'

'Big teeth, too. Young male, I'd say.'

'At least he doesn't look as though he's starving.'

'Won't make much difference. He'll kill us anyway if he takes it into his head. We're probably on his territory or something.'

'That doesn't seem too likely, unless he's drifted here

from Greenland with the rest of this lot. And if he has, he'd look hungrier than this. We've seen no wildlife except those birds.'

As they talked, they began to work their way up the pile of ice blocks. They did this unhandily, their backs to the ice, watching the beast as it wandered forward, still on all fours, disconcertingly like some huge child playing a game of pretending not to be interested in them. It prowled around them, one eye fixed on them, never nearer than ten yards, never further than twenty.

'What've we got to fight him with?' mused Richard, more to himself than to Bill.

'The axe. The cleaver.'

As Bill said the words, Richard could see all too clearly how impossible it would be. Trying to stay firm on the treacherous ice pile, thumping away at the bear's head with the paltry weapons while it tore at their unprotected legs with teeth and claws. No. They had to get rid of this unwelcome, inquisitive creature long before it came to blows at close quarters. But then the time for thought was suddenly past. Bill's foot slipped and the square Cumbrian slithered past Richard's left shoulder, down towards the bear which suddenly looked very interested after all. Richard just had time to grab his companion's harness with his left hand. The downward slide stopped with a jerk that nearly dislocated Richard's shoulder. Luckily he was on firm footing and stayed put. He was incapable of further action for an instant, however, until his friend had regained his footing. As the two men struggled, facing outwards with their backs against the sloping jumble of slippery blocks, perhaps six feet above the surface of the ice itself, the bear began its charge.

'Your flares,' yelled Richard, his own hand still tangled

in Bill's harness. The radio operator needed no second bidding. As the bear rushed towards them, ten yards down and ten to go, gathering itself to climb up the ice after them, he scrabbled in his pocket for the long cylinder.

Richard tore his hand free, leaving his glove caught in the straps, just as Bill tugged the short lanyard on his first flare. With a vicious hiss the tube exploded into life and a green light sped towards the bear. It grazed past the creature's left shoulder close enough to singe the fur, but it did not have the desired effect. The charge slowed, but only so that the bear could draw itself up to full height. On its hind legs, with its arms spread wide, tipped with lethal black claws, each as long as a dagger, it began to walk towards them, roaring. Richard's feet were two metres above the ice but the bear's head was level with his groin. Its mouth gaped and it sucked in icy air to bellow again its intention to attack.

Richard just had time to take careful aim. 'Aim for its mouth but don't fire until I say,' he grated to Bill in whose trembling hands he could see a second flare. Then he fired his own. The spitting ball of bright green light whooshed like a misdirected skyrocket down onto the ice immediately in front of the bear's ankles and exploded there with vicious force. The great white pelt was suddenly pocked with burning black spots from ankle to waist, all across the great sag of its lower belly.

Bill's hand jerked convulsively.

'Wait!' rapped Richard, for the bear had stopped. Grotesquely, like a human, it looked down at its sullied belly and as it did so it dropped to all fours. It gave a grunting cry and turned. Its head, near the ice now, came close to the flare which was still hissing and spitting in a fizzing pool of water. And that was enough. With a noise disconcertingly like a bleat, it turned and ran away on down the valley.

'You were right,' said Richard. 'It must have been a male. Didn't like putting the family jewels in danger. You all right?'

'Fine,' said Bill. 'And that's one I owe you.'

'Forget it,' said Richard bracingly. 'You wouldn't have been here but for me. Let's go.'

'In a minute,' temporised Bill. 'I think I need a good big lump of chocolate after that. Put something other than adrenaline back into my blood.'

There were only two more ridges before the central hill. They and it were gentle enough. Bill and Richard pulled themselves across them quite quickly, although both of them began to suffer reaction to the stress of their adventure, and weariness added to the weight of everything else bearing down on them. But at last it was done and they dragged themselves up to the crest of that central ridge.

Richard had imagined that the two halves of the ice barrier would be roughly the same, but this was not the case. True, the folds fell away from this point, but the ridges were much higher, their sides more precipitous. The terrain they had just crossed was as nothing compared to the rough wildness before them. Just as the ridges were more considerable, so the blocks and jumbled rubbish piles were more colossal. The plain itself was wider too. They had crossed five ridges to reach this spot. The same number lay beyond. But even reaching the first of these was out of the question, for the hillside which sloped gently back behind them fell away in a cliff face a yard further on.

Richard stood immobile on the crest. Bill joined him

and looked down. The precipitous slope stretched away as far as their tired eyes could see on either hand. If they went down, they would never be able to get back up. 'We can't go on,' Bill said at last. 'You said I could call it, and I am. We have to go back, Captain.'

Richard said nothing for a moment. He pulled the binoculars off his shoulder and raised them slowly to his eyes. They made a slight sound, like ice striking ice, as they hit his sunglasses. From side to side he scanned the distance. Beyond the wilderness of crushed and tumbled ice it was possible to see the black line of the sea. But that was all.

There was a moment more of silence, then Richard said, 'Yes. We have to go back. She's gone.' He lowered his binoculars and repeated, his voice as desolate as the scene at his feet, 'She's gone.'

CHAPTER TWENTY-NINE

Day Eleven

Saturday, 29 May   15:00

From Robin's point of view, the best part of a bad situation was that Timmins had managed to get the shore lines in and the manoeuvring system working well enough to meet her halfway. The obvious damage to crew morale, the accommodation areas and the radio officer was not so acceptable. She fumed and spat like an irritated tiger, berating everyone involved, making no allowance at all for the fact that the first and second officers felt that they had dealt with a crisis quickly and effectively. As far as she was concerned, she had simply found herself forced into stopping and dealing with a petty lapse of discipline. This was an utter and dangerous waste of precious time when she needed every second of daylight to assure the safe disposition of her command and to prepare for what must be a busy night of detailed planning and an agonisingly hard day's work tomorrow.

O'Brien, Symes of the flattened nose, the rest of the search and destroy party, Timmins and Hogg all stood in various attitudes of sullen resentment in the captain's day

room on C deck while she introduced them to the rough
side of her tongue. Like Richard, like almost any captain,
Robin had a quarterdeck voice which would have carried
to the truck of the *Cutty Sark*. It carried now out into the
corridor and across to the stairwell where various assorted
members of both crews pretended to be about important
duties while they actually stood and listened.

'. . . Finally, I will not only dock your pay, I will with-
hold it until the damage has been repaired and paid for
out of it. If you are back at sea then, I will have what
little is left sent directly to your wives or bank managers.
It will be a pleasant surprise to them, I'm sure, and a
nasty shock to various brothelkeepers and publicans. One
more incident like this, *one* more, and I shall have you all
on permanent deck work, watch on watch, until we get
home and I'll sort it out with the union later. Is that clear?'

The sullen silence persisted until she thundered, 'IS
THAT CLEAR?'

'Yes, Captain.'

'Right. I'll be making an announcement about duties
later. Your names will feature prominently. Now, get out,
the lot of you! Not you two!' With an effort of will
she moderated her tone. 'Mr Hogg, Mr Timmins, remain
behind, please.'

As soon as the crewmen were gone, Robin began to
explain to the two officers what she had found and how
she proposed to make full use of it. 'I'm relying on you
two to get us there while I draw up the first set of plans
and detail the first working parties,' she concluded. 'You've
done well to get this far. Finding the iceberg and the
slipway should be easy enough for you. You'll need a
decent helmsman soon, though. I'll send Sam Larkman
up. You'll need to man the radio too, Mr Hogg. And,

talking of that, I'd better start by looking in on the sick and wounded. I want Harry Stone up and about as soon as possible, and I can't get much further with any of my plans unless I can get the chief up out of bed now so that he and his officers can help.'

Hogg was a little dazed at being berated one minute and confided in the next, but he was quicker on his feet than he used to be: 'You want me to contact *Clotho* and the two offices?'

'Yes. London and Sept Isles both need to know what we're up to, but I'm most concerned about *Clotho*. Her captain will have been worried that we've been out of touch. I hope he hasn't started to do anything risky.'

'Like what?'

'Like coming across the ice on foot, Mr Hogg. Mr Timmins, you're certain Stone hadn't told Captain Mariner we were going to move *Atropos* before he broke contact?'

'Fairly certain, Captain.'

She paused for an instant, sucking her teeth in thought. 'Well, there's no help for it,' she concluded. 'Let's get to work.'

Henri LeFever had been acting as chief medical officer and she found him in Lethbridge's day room, just outside the cabin door, sitting morosely reading a medical textbook from the ship's library. 'I'll want you to change hats again soon,' she said. 'I want to hoist *Atropos* out of the water up that slipway we found on the iceberg. It's difficult to be accurate, but I suppose it must be angled at seven or eight degrees. You'll need to advise me how the cargo will react to that if I leave it where it is or if I move some of it down towards the bow and pile it high in number one hold to lighten the stern.' Her voice was a little hoarse. She was still trying to control the anger which a brief visit to the cabin of her battered radio operator had caused.

LeFever looked at her, narrow-eyed, as though concerned that her obvious anger might be directed at him. When he spoke, his tone was almost defensive. 'Cargo's been fine through pitching of far steeper angles than that, Captain. It'll sit still for a sixty-degree roll to the side, and I guess it'd take an eight-degree angle to the front. I'll have to do some math if you're going to start moving it about, though. How much time do I have?'

'Lots. We'll be moving into position before dark tonight, but I won't be starting heavy work until the morning. If I start at all. How is he?'

'Should have been in hospital, I guess. It was worse than it looked. On the mend now.'

'I have to talk to him. It's too much for Don Taylor and Lloyd Swan.'

'Go ahead . . .'

She had gone.

The room was in darkness, but Lethbridge's voice greeted her as soon as she walked in. 'In position for what? Which slipway? What's too much for Don?'

She snapped on the light, sat herself in his bedside chair and began to explain her plans. As she did so, her restless grey eyes wandered over the chief engineer. She had hardly had any real contact with him. Certainly, if the deck officers were anything to go by, his absence from the engine room could have been caused by anything, including a certain amount of malingering, especially as she had brought young Lloyd Swan with her to take over the routine work. But LeFever had said he was genuinely hurt, and she trusted LeFever even if she couldn't quite fathom him. And Don Taylor had a lot of time for him, and she had a lot of time for Don. The bandages were nearly all gone now, revealing a strange mask made still and shiny by a combination of dead skin and ointment. His eyes were slitted and, although pale, looked like the result of a couple of hefty punches. The cheeks were unnaturally plump and the mouth pushed out into a kiss. The nose down the middle was straight and thin as a razor. Below the bloated jowls, the neck was lean and scraggy. It was an odd, unsettling face and she soon came to the conclusion that the chief was a thin man whose aspect was usually angular. The apparent rolls of plumpness were actually swellings from the scalding he had received three and a half days earlier. The whole effect was made a good deal worse, of course, by the fact that he hadn't shaved since Monday morning. It looked as though LeFever's diagnosis had been accurate enough.

As she described what she wanted to do and explained how she proposed to go about it, Lethbridge pulled himself up in the bed and began to join in the conversation. His questions were germane. Positive. Creative. The slitted eyes began to gleam with enthusiasm and it was with a burgeoning sense of relief that she began to recognise someone, like herself, who not only rose to challenges but enjoyed doing so. The only thing which gave her pause was the fact that when he began to gesture with increasing fervour, it became obvious that the boxing-glove bandages round his hands were still very necessary.

'Don's up, you say.'

'For a couple of days now.'

'Thank God he's not as bad as me. Where is he . . .?' Lethbridge paused, listening to the renewed vibration as *Atropos* got under way, powered laboriously by her manoeuvring propellers. 'No, don't tell me. I bet I know where he is. Wait a minute.'

Carried away by his sudden enthusiasm, the chief surged out of bed and began to search for some clothes. 'Give me a hand, will you, Captain?' he demanded unselfconsciously as soon as he found a promising pile of neatly folded clothing. 'Hold those trousers there so I can climb into them.'

In five minutes, with his pyjamas as underwear, the chief engineer was dressed in trousers and pullover. His white overalls covered the ensemble. As long as he had no intention of going outside, it was quite adequate. Had LeFever taken the opportunity of spying through the door at any stage, he would have been treated to the unusual sight of a captain dressing her chief engineer; had he done so now, he would have seen her tying his shoelaces. And he would have heard them talking. Talking nineteen to the dozen, like old friends who had been separated for years.

Lethbridge was right. Don Taylor was in the engine room with Lloyd Swan. The two young engineering officers were deep in conversation, speculating as to what their captain had in mind. As soon as she arrived, she explained to them what she had described to Lethbridge and then she left the three of them in close enclave, talking over the practicalities and working out how two senior officers with no hands might best direct the efforts of someone with less experience but more functioning fingers. The first thing they sent him to do was to find Henri LeFever and Ann Cable; it was time, the engineers reckoned, to see just how many more of these bandages could be dispensed with.

Buoyed up with that burgeoning feeling of hope, Robin ran up to the bridge and joined Timmins in the wheelhouse. No sooner had she done so, than Hogg stuck his head out of the radio room. 'I have *Clotho* for you, Captain,' he said.

Her heart leaped but she did not rush over. One glance around the bridge was enough to tell her that everything was going adequately. A slit-eyed look out into the opalescent glare of the afternoon assured her that they were just entering the fog bank which clothed the iceberg. She crossed to the radio room and caught up the microphone. 'Richard?'

'No, Captain Mariner, it's Nico. Lieutenant Hogg says you have moved *Atropos*.'

'Yes.' The elation was gone, punctured by Nico's statement as easily as a child's balloon. 'The radio officer was injured and we could not warn you.'

'So the captain and Bill Christian did not reach you.'

It was exactly as she had feared. 'They came across the ice.' She made it a statement, not a question.

'That is correct.'

'How long have they been out of contact?'

'Only an hour.'

An hour! Anything could have happened. She looked round the bridge but there was no help there. There was no help anywhere, she realised. Not for her. Not for Richard. 'He'll be back in contact soon,' she said, more for her own benefit than Nico's.

'I'll let you know,' he said. 'Can I have your current position? He'll want to know at once I should think.'

'I'll hand you back to Mr Hogg. He'll give you the details.'

She had no time to indulge herself in worry over Richard. Her first task was to stand at Sam Larkman's shoulder and will him safely through the fog. As soon as the fog began to clear and the glistening slopes of the iceberg shone through the thinning billows, she began to give more precise directions. In the lifeboat it had seemed to take them a considerable time to round the cliff face and discover the slipway with its surrounding stepped galleries. Even under the power of just her manoeuvring propellers, *Atropos* seemed to close with the glittering monster more quickly. It seemed little more than moments before Robin was directing the helmsman to steer hard over so that the ship could swing round in a slow half-circle, reverse her course and approach the slipway stern first.

It was going to be a long manoeuvre. As soon as it was under way, Robin handed over to Timmins once again, went into her day room behind the chart room and began to prepare for the next part of her plan. Overall, the scheme was relatively simple. When they were in position close to the iceberg she was going to put lines ashore from the stern on the port and starboard quarters. They would be long lines secured to the lower slopes of ice, designed to hold *Atropos* safe and still in the correct position vis-à-vis the slipway. As soon as the hull was secure, she would dismiss the crew to dinner and hold a council of war with her officers. She had no desire to do anything complex tonight. In the morning, at first light, she proposed to run two more lines ashore. They would run backwards from the port and starboard bows this time and be anchored on the upper slopes. Then, carefully, in agreed sequence and perfect harmony, all lines would be tightened. The stern lines would wind round the capstans and the bow lines would be gathered by the split windlass. So, inch by inch, *Atropos* would be guided backwards up the frozen slipway until as much of the hull as seemed necessary and safe was pulled out of the water, and the propeller could be inspected.

Precisely what would happen then could only be guessed at, but as far as Robin could see, it would follow one of two courses. Either they would fix the propeller where it stood, or they would simply take it off and replace it.

Simply. It was only twenty feet high, almost the size of a house front. It only weighed God knew how many tons. It was only welded onto a main drive shaft the size of a giant redwood's tree trunk which in turn contained a complex of variable pitch mechanisms which would need to be disconnected and then reconnected before the job was complete.

Hogg stuck his head round the door and caught her unusually grim gaze. 'Niccolo again,' he informed her. 'Your husband's just been in contact. He's fine.'

'Excellent. Get on to Heritage Mariner, would you? Tell them I want them to fax something out. In sections, if need be.'

'Yes, Captain.'

She followed him out through the chart room, then walked over to the clearview and looked out at the fog for a moment. It danced and wavered hypnotically, hiding the ice barrier just as effectively as it had hidden the iceberg. She let her thoughts drift for a moment as she brought her relief under control. Oddly, knowing that Richard was safe brought her much closer to tears than the news that he might be in trouble.

In a surprisingly short time, Hogg called through, 'Captain, I have Sir William on the line. He says what do you want?'

'I'll take it,' she said at once, crossing to the radio. 'Daddy, why are you still in the office?'

'Why do you think, darling?'

'Okay. Silly question. How are the twins?'

'Fine. Safe and sound up at Cold Fell. They'll stay there until you get back. Now, what is it you want?'

'I want the engineering drawings and architect's plans of the ship. Everything, in as much detail as possible. Especially the propeller.'

'I have them here. They'll be on their way in a moment. You think you'll have to go ahead then?'

'I'll know for certain tomorrow, but it seems more sensible to plan for the worst that can happen.'

'Replacing the propeller will be bad,' he said sharply. 'But I wouldn't call it the worst that could happen.'

'You're right, Dad.'

'Now, Richard has described your situation to me as he understands it, but I find it hard to visualise. Is there actually an iceberg in your vicinity?'

She began to explain that not only was the iceberg – which Richard must have seen only from a great distance – utterly real, but she was actually planning to use it.

After a while he broke in and said, 'You realise that it must have been moving south all along?'

The question stopped the flow of information and speculation. 'Well, yes,' she said. 'Of course it has. How else could it have come down upon us while we were waiting against the ice barrier?'

'Have you any idea of its speed?'

'No. I've been thinking, but even with the faxes you've sent out to us it's impossible to be at all accurate. And in any case . . .'

'Yes?'

'The barrier will slow it. Maybe even stop it.'

'I'd say that would depend on the relative masses and

the power of the currents involved.'

She tried not to let her sigh of irritation carry to the microphone and away across the airwaves. Of course it would. She knew that.

'It's impossible to see all of the iceberg because of the mist,' she said, 'but I think part of it has already come into contact with the barrier. I'm sure I felt it shake some time ago. The berg is the only thing I can think of that would make something as massive as the barrier shake. We'll find out more soon, I'm sure.'

'The point is, you see, that if you're caught between them, and it sounds as though you certainly are—'

'Of course. It's an acceptable risk. We'll just have to keep a weather eye out.'

'My elementary physics suggests, you see,' he insisted gently, 'that if the berg keeps moving but the barrier stops its progress to the south, then it might very well start swinging round to the side. To the eastern side, for instance, where you are positioned; then *Atropos* could end up like a nut in a pair of nutcrackers. It would simply crush the life out of you.'

'Even our manoeuvring propellers can still move us faster than an iceberg, Daddy. There really is nothing at all for you to worry about.'

'Still . . .'

'Still what, Daddy? Stop beating about the bush. What do you have in mind?'

'All right. I know you've a lot on your plate and all of it is more important than putting an old man's mind at rest, but what I have been thinking ever since Richard told me about the iceberg was this. If we haven't been able to pick it up on the satellites because of the fog surrounding it, then how can we track it accurately? I suspect that even

Atropos's visual trace will be invisible once you're tied up alongside that much high ice. If it's as massive as Richard said, it will be bound to have quite a cloaking effect, especially when added to the mist. And that amount of ice could even break up your radio transmissions again. We simply cannot see you here. Are you anywhere near an overhang? It's so frustrating, darling, not to be able to track *Atropos* at all.

'What we could track, however, is one of the rescue beacons from a lifeboat. I've been thinking, you see, that if you could send someone up onto the berg itself, preferably onto a high point on the ice, then we could pick up the signal and track the iceberg's movement very precisely indeed. Inch by inch, near as dammit.'

'Well, as you say, I have my work cut out for me . . .'

'But, don't you see, it'll let us give you a completely accurate description of the iceberg's movements and that could be absolutely critical if it is turning towards you for any reason.'

'Well, if the barrier stops it going southwards, then the odds must be fifty-fifty it might turn our way . . .'

'And if it does so, then we'll be able to warn you long before there's anything to worry about. Certainly long before you would actually be able to see anything clearly on the ground.'

'Okay. You've convinced me. I'll add it to the list.' She might have said more, but Timmins stuck his head round the door to inform her that Sam Larkman had swung *Atropos* onto the required bearing and now wanted permission to go to reverse. 'I'll come through, Mr Timmins,' she said decisively. 'That's it, Dad. Love to the twins. Over and out.'

* * *

The plans had arrived through the fax while Robin was talking to her father. She spread them on the chart table and then divided the next half-hour between them and the bridge wing where she guided Sam as he reversed *Atropos* painstakingly up towards the slipway. As soon as she was satisfied with the line of the great ship's reverse approach, she sent Timmins and Hogg down to gather teams of men in readiness for getting the long lines ashore and secured onto the ice. No sooner had she done so than LeFever and Ann brought a much recovered Harry Stone back up. While the radio officer went through to check over his beloved equipment and make sure that Hogg had looked after it properly, Robin looked speculatively at the other two.

'You know your way around on ice, don't you, Henri?' she asked. 'You were sure-footed enough helping me on the ice barrier when we went after Mr Timmins and I heard you say you had been far north in Canada when we thought we heard a shot this morning.'

'Yeah, I guess.'

'Do you think you could find your way to the upper slopes of the iceberg and put a transmitting beacon there? We really need to keep track of how the iceberg is moving and a beacon would be the most reliable way of doing so.'

'It's pretty steep this side. I'm no mountaineer, Captain.'

'I know. What I have in mind is this. You go ashore with the boats taking the lines and the anchor points, then you explore a bit back behind the slipway. If you can find a path up onto the upper slopes, all well and good; if you can't, come back down. If it looks dangerous, I don't want you to go. Remember what you said to me on the way down into that ice cave. This isn't worth the hair on your head.'

'What did you say, you smooth-talking devil?' asked Ann archly. But before the big man could answer, Timmins bustled back into the wheelhouse, heavily wrapped in cold-weather clothing and full of new-found importance. Henri met Ann's eye and gave a minuscule shake of his head.

'We're ready to go, Captain,' Timmins said, noticing none of this. 'My team and Walter Hogg's. I'm taking Don Taylor and a team led by your man Errol Jones. Walt's taking the chief and Joe Edwards is leading his team.' He rubbed his gloved hands tog ther, clearly eager to be off, and Robin felt an unaccustomed pulse of affection for the little man. He really seemed to be trying as hard as he could. He was beginning to grow into the role Robin had mapped out for him in her command structure. She couldn't begin to imagine how he or Hogg – was his given name really Walter? – had earned their papers, but the pair of them might make adequate officers one day if they kept this improvement up.

Henri went off to change into his cold-weather gear and Ann went off with him. Timmins and Robin went down to the stern and, while the teams stood ready by the lifeboats, the senior deck officers were joined by the engineering officers to discuss the finer points of what was due to happen next. They stood between the capstans, each one a pair of independently operated steel mushroom shapes designed to wind cable in or out in a controlled manner. They were integral to the first part of Robin's plan. The officers gathered at the after rail, the better to see what lay before and around them.

Inevitably, as they discussed the plans Robin had drawn up, she felt her eyes straying over the breathtaking view again and again. The bulk of the berg rose on their right, its crystal crest hanging above them like a great wave breaking over their heads, etched against the darkening afternoon sky. Beyond and above that deceptively absolute edge lay the upper slopes that LeFever would try and gain in order to place the signalling device, but the slopes and the peaks above them were hidden by the angle caused by *Atropos*'s nearness to the berg. This proximity and the waning afternoon brought a chill to the air beyond anything that even Robin had been expecting. The edge of high ice swung round in front of them and, as it did so, the slopes beyond it were at last revealed. The levels below it stepped down to the slipway itself before swinging further to form what looked like a mountainous isthmus on their left.

When the boats went ashore – and they would need to do so very soon indeed – they would take with them the spare anchor and a heavy anchorage spike. They would pull behind them the heaviest rope they were capable of carrying. When the anchor points were secure, the rope would be fed through a tackle secured to each and brought back aboard by the returning lifeboats. One small safety crew would remain ashore to stand by each anchorage point. Then Robin would use the capstans one at a time to pull heavy cable out from the ship's stern, through the tackle and back aboard as though she were threading a needle. It would be enough for tonight to have the cable doubled through each, the ends secured to the pairs of capstans. In the morning, they would wind the cables tighter until *Atropos* was nudging up the slipway and then they would send the other lines ashore from the split windlass forward. When the forward lines could take the strain, the cables from the stern would be singled and resecured so that one of each pair of capstans could be released. They would need to use the freed capstans later for other, more important work.

No sooner had the plan been reviewed than LeFever pounded up, well wrapped and ready to go. Robin took him to one side. 'You'll go ashore in one of the lifeboats,' she said. 'Take the emergency beacon from the boat you go in. And, now I think of it, take another one as well, just in case. I know the light's beginning to go, but the evenings are long in these latitudes and you should have plenty of time to decide if you can get it placed, place it if you can, and get back before I've finished. Then you can come back with the safety teams from the anchorage points. Okay?'

'Sure.'

'The beacons are simple. It's perfectly obvious how to turn them on and off. Put one of them where it can broadcast effectively and try to shield it from the worst of the cold if you can – low temperatures play havoc with batteries. Keep your spare one switched on all the time so we can find you in an emergency.'

'Sure thing,' he said.

She paused, wondering if she should discuss his mission in any more detail, then she decided she had wasted enough time. The first order of business was to get the anchorage points ashore and secure.

'Everybody happy?' she asked, energy cresting in her vibrant body at the thought of positive action and the beginning of the solution to their problems.

The answers she received were dubious, but at least in the affirmative.

'Right,' she said. 'Let's get this show on the road.'

Robin hardly noticed the slowly fading light as the end of the afternoon passed into early evening and gathering twilight while her teams went ashore and the plan began to work. She did not even leave the deck, content to send for layer after layer of warmer clothing as the temperature dropped steadily. She moved from capstan to capstan, Lloyd Swan in constant attendance for those moments when one pair of hands was not enough. It was fortunate that he was there, too, for in the end they had to run the capstans both at once, Robin pulling the cable through the tackle atop the spike hammered home by Timmins's team while the engineering officer copied her every action, pulling the cable through the tackle on the anchor Hogg's men had taken ashore and hooked securely into the ice. They needed to work so quickly and in concert because of the cold – the one thing Robin had not taken sufficient account of. Had they taken any longer, then the sodden cable would have frozen stiff before it was correctly in place and all their work would have been for nothing.

As things turned out, however, the ends of the rope came back aboard, bearded with icicles but still supple enough to coil round the capstan posts oozing oily water, and the job was successfully completed just as the lingering twilight gave way almost imperceptibly to the brightening promise of moonrise. Robin and Lloyd snapped the machinery off and the doubled cables sagged into their perfect curves, down to the still, black water, then up onto the distant, glowing ice. *Atropos* settled back a little, pulled by the weight of the ice-encrusted hawsers. The lifeboat purred back towards the shore to pick up the safety teams.

Robin was waiting to welcome them back aboard. She stood between the davits looking northwards over the little bay to the crystalline, gleaming cliff and the moon-bleached deep blue sky beyond it. Spellbound by the beauty of the scene though she was, she still had the presence of mind to breathe shallowly as though the air was tainted, trying to keep the deadly cold out of her nostrils, mouth and lungs. She had not gone down to a well-earned dinner with the rest of the crew, nor up to the wheelhouse and the watchkeeper's chair. Lloyd and Harry Stone were bridge watch enough for the moment. She wanted to congratulate her four most senior officers on a good job well done and take them down to the meal herself. What they had achieved that afternoon deserved a little pomp; a little show of congratulatory respect. She remembered that warmth towards Timmins this afternoon and she knew it was a mark of good leadership to act upon it. A gesture which, she suspected, the two deck officers at least would find something of a novelty.

But as she counted them back aboard, shaking gloved hands and clapping bulky coated shoulders, her good intentions froze and died within her. For there were too few. Two too few.

'Where are the others?' she asked, and the safety teams looked at each other as though they didn't know what she was talking about.

'What others?' asked Yasser Timmins slowly. 'Everyone else came back.'

'No,' she insisted. 'I counted you all out and I've counted you back. Two are still out there somewhere. Dear God, they're still out there somewhere!'

They all swung round to look up at the beautiful, unutterably dangerous cliff; all, like Robin, thinking of the deadly slopes it concealed. There could be anything up there. Crevasses falling into caves floored by oceans entombed. Unfathomable drifts of ice grains. Deserts, valleys, mountains made of ice old enough to be holding dinosaurs, frozen like flies in amber, fresh enough to eat.

More dangers and more ways of dying than could fill all their nightmares in this short, moonlit early summer's night.

And against them, Ann Cable and Henri LeFever had nothing but what they were wearing, what they were carrying and what the chill gods of the high ice might supply.

CHAPTER THIRTY

Day Twelve

Sunday, 30 May   08:00

Robin flicked the broadcast switch up to the off position and sat back, her grey eyes overflowing with tears. The echo of her last prayer lingered on the still air within the accommodation areas; the prayer in which she had brought to divine attention their desperate concern for Ann Cable and Henri LeFever. She closed the service book and placed it carefully in the drawer of her work desk. The drawer slid shut silently and her hand rose and fell, brushing thoughtlessly down her face, sweeping the tears off her cheeks. Just for a moment, exhausted and preoccupied, she felt lost and desperately lonely, though she was glad enough to be alone. It wouldn't do for anyone aboard to see their commanding officer in tears.

She was in the day room which formed part of the captain's accommodation on C deck, using it for the first time since she had interviewed the crew in her fruitless search for the disturbing person she knew was somewhere aboard: the saboteur who had cut off the dead captain's fingers. She was glad that she had made the decision to do so. Normally, she would have held the simple act of worship in the gym at 11 a.m. with the entire ship's complement assembled in front of her. Had she broken into tears in front of the whole crew, she would never have been able to repair the damage and they all would have lost their leader just when they needed one most. She had moved the service forward to before breakfast because she knew very well she wouldn't be able to stop work at eleven. They would have their work cut out if they were going to get the ship out of the water and the propeller seen to – particularly if they were going to have to take it off.

She didn't really like working through Sunday but there was no alternative. Her plans for last night had been interrupted by the need to look for the missing pair. She had hoped to find time after dinner to go through all the alternatives for today's work with everybody likely to be involved. Instead she had been ashore most of the short night, organising search parties in the moonlight and setting up a permanent presence ashore in case the missing couple turned up in the starlit dusk after the moon had set. The searchers had come back with nothing more than reports of lost trails and walls of sheer ice which no one could hope to climb. And yet it soon became obvious that Henri and Ann had found a way up, because from somewhere on top of the unclimbable wall the emergency beacons began to broadcast. But it was a way that no one else could find or follow, which meant the two of them really were beyond help.

On the ice, waiting for the carefully selected, fully-briefed search parties to report back, she had felt again that bone-deep feeling of foreboding. The iceberg seemed to be so still, so solid and sure. Yet it was in motion. Her father had been wise to want to know what forms that motion might take, for all that his simple plan had turned out so tragically. Evidences of the motion were suddenly all around her in a way they had never been aboard *Atropos*. The ice beneath her feet never seemed quite still. It seemed to tremble, almost to throb, as though the foundations of the iceberg went deep enough to be grinding gently along the bottom of the ocean far below. In stillnesses given preternatural force by the frigid weight of the air there always seemed to be the echo of thunder, as though the conversation just completed had covered a deafening peal. The gleaming, moonlit beach of crystal seemed so small, so cosy, that it further emphasised the unimaginable size of the phenomenon they were marooned upon, its mystery and its implacable danger. The Alps afloat. It was an image which had struck her when she had first seen the iceberg. It struck her now with renewed force. Especially as the Alps were also a place of ice and snow and storms and death. Of blizzards and of avalanches. The avalanches preyed on her mind particularly, for she knew how common they were at this time of the year, on slopes which were safely anchored in the heart of the earth, not tossing around on the bosom of the deep.

Once back aboard, she had held a brief but detailed enquiry, more to see if there was anything she might have overlooked in the rescue attempt than to make this a matter of record. No one could remember LeFever saying 'Goodbye'. No one could remember him actually leaving at all. Not one man there was certain whether Ann had left with him or had gone after him later. This fact alone gave Robin pause for thought. What had there been about that strange frozen beach which made the men stop paying attention to the person who had been their fantasy for weeks? Robin had not ventured far in the search herself, but another strange thing emerged from those who had. There had been no wind to speak of; certainly none worth remarking. Yet all those who had followed the tracks left by the missing couple over the first ridge agreed that they had faded almost immediately, as though a blizzard had blown across them. And all too soon, soft snow gave way to hard ice and any hope of following footsteps had gone.

She had slept little, haunted by unremembered dreams, and was still tired. Hence the tears, she thought grimly. There was really no point in getting emotional until she found if there was any reason for it. She stood up. No sense in brooding here. It was time for a bit of leadership. LeFever had been a popular crew member and Ann seemed to have fallen somewhere between a pet and a pin-up for most of the men. Their disappearance had cast gloom over everyone, especially the searchers who, involved in the failed rescue attempt, now felt a sense of responsibility. Robin knew she was by no means alone in having slept so little.

The atmosphere of gloom could only be damaging. The first order of business now was to try and dispel it, or at least moderate it somehow. Thank goodness some deep-seated foresight had led her to request that the chefs outdo themselves with breakfast today. At the time she had seen the order as a positive way of ensuring a good start to a hard day's work, but now it seemed the best way of lightening things up a little. No man she knew could stay depressed for long in the face of a full, hot breakfast, lovingly prepared and served. She didn't feel like eating, but she felt she had better get down and join the rest of them. Work was due to start in half an hour or so and she knew she would certainly be better for some of the food.

Soup and sandwiches on the job at twelve would hardly keep her going until dinner time unless she got off to a good start now and lined her stomach well.

The rest of the morning passed in a haze of activity. Robin was everywhere, overseeing everything. The crew of *Atropos*, leavened by men from *Clotho*, soon began to see her presence in any spot where important work was being done for the gesture of faith and support it really was. They were so used to having officers present in their work places only in order to insult and denigrate their efforts that the captain's enthusiastic presence and concerned advice was something completely new to them. Something increasingly welcome as the day wore on and the work got harder and more dangerous.

At first, the capstans at the rear of the ship pulled her back inch by inch, her careful progress dictated not only by the need to ensure that no further damage was done when her keel met the ice of the slipway, but by the fact that the cables were frozen solid and there was a real risk of snapping them. While this careful work was going on, two teams went ashore with enough equipment to set up makeshift cranes on the upper terraces on either side of the ship. Once the cranes were in position, the ship's anchors were carried in the lifeboats across to the icy beaches at the cliff feet. Then the anchors were winched up and bedded firmly, level with the decks on either side of the empty davits where the boats had hung. The anchor cables were still attached to the split windlasses on the fore deck, and, as soon as the anchors were firm, Robin oversaw the slow winding-in of the slack. *Atropos* continued to reverse towards the slipway, four ropes now holding her firm while guiding her in. So gentle was her movement that not even her super-sensitive captain felt the first impact of rudder foot and slipway surface nearly twenty metres below.

By the time steaming cups of thick vegetable soup came round, *Atropos* was at a decided angle and Robin – who found she had not quite foreseen the confusion even an eight-degree slope would bring to the icy decks – called a brief halt after all so that the stewards could have a fighting chance of getting the life-saving liquid to the men at the windlasses. All the bustle seemed to die for a moment, ashore as well as aboard, and a deep quiet overhung the little bay. The sky was high and postcard blue. The slopes were glittering white and the cliffs a frosted duck-egg. The air was utterly still and the inky water equally so. It was so still that there seemed to be a whisper in the air, as of a huge barrage of artillery firing at the furthest reach of hearing. The walkie-talkie in her oilskin pocket buzzed. Reluctantly – for she knew it would be cold before she could pick it up again – she put her soup down.

'Captain here.'

'Sparks, Captain. Incoming from Heritage House.'

She went back towards the bridgehouse at once, slightly surprised. She had agreed with Richard this morning before the service that he would be the communications centre. He was on the far side of the ice barrier now, back at the head of the lead he had opened, trying to bash his way on through to her, but his work was much easier than hers and he felt – and she agreed – that it would be far better for him to keep in contact with London and Sept Isles rather than have her interrupted and slowed down. What could her father want now? She was almost irritated. It had broken her concentration and had cost her a nice hot cup of soup.

Her irritation died as she walked onto the bridge and saw what her father had sent her. Hogg was laying them out on the chart table as she entered: a series of faxed blow-ups of the satellite pictures of their immediate area. They were dated and timed, one every two hours from eight o'clock local time yesterday evening. There were nine of them, all seemingly identical, an apparent waste of a great deal of money, for they did not come cheap. The picture of this end of the ice barrier was increasingly clear. It was possible to see the breadth of it – only a couple of miles now – and the black track of Richard's lead stabbing in from the south, with *Clotho* at its end apparently wedged against a high central ridge of ice. The northern edge was not so clear. In picture after picture, the telltale vagueness which was the fog shroud of the iceberg spread along it. In the earliest photograph it was possible to see part of the wide bay she had found, but that too was eaten up by that strange, amorphous paleness. Of *Atropos* herself there was no sign at all. So her father had been right. The cliff above them, with its slight over-hang, hid them completely from the satellites.

There was a clear sign of the iceberg however. It was the reason he had purchased, enhanced and faxed the pic-tures. On the first picture there were two points of light but, most disturbingly, on each one after that there was only one. It was the lifeboat's emergency transmitter. Robin looked at that point of light. There was no light there in actual fact, of course; this was just the visual representation of the radio signal. Robin picked the pic-tures up and studied them silently, one after the other, then handed them back to Hogg who was busily plotting the sequence of light points on the master chart. When he had finished, they put the pile of pictures to one side and looked down, still in silence. There was no doubt about it. The sequence of carefully plotted points made a line across the chart. A line which clearly represented a steady movement eastwards along a course just beginning to arc southwards.

The radio transmitter was doing a job which just might prove to have been worth the sacrifice of two lives. It was warning that the iceberg on whose south-eastern flank they were beached was moving along the north coast of the ice barrier, turning slowly, like the front of a steamroller, and in the fullness of time it would crush the life out of *Atropos* and anyone aboard her if she was still unable to move out of the way.

Hogg turned back to the first picture of the sequence. 'You know, they might just have turned the spare beacon off to preserve power,' he said quietly, but with surprising tenderness. 'It's what I'd do.'

'What I want you to do next, please, Mr Hogg,' she answered briskly, a telltale pricking in her eyes warning against sentimentality, 'is to contact both London and *Clotho*. They will be able to give bearings on our radio transmissions precise enough for you to sketch in our location in relation to the beacon there. Then I want you to use all the pictures Heritage House has sent us to draw as accurate a coastline as you can for the northern edge of the ice barrier. I want an estimation of when the movement of the iceberg will push us up against it. Ballpark figures will do to begin with. We'll refine them as we go.'

'Yes, Captain,' said the second officer. 'But I don't think we'll have all that much time to refine them. It looks to me as though the berg's beginning to turn quite quickly.'

'I agree. But let's keep it to ourselves for the moment. Certainly until we have some idea of whether we are likely to have enough time to repair the ship or not.'

'Do we know how long that will take?'

'No. I'm about to start up the winches again. We'll have the screw out of the water and the whole situation clearer by teatime.'

On her way back out of the wheelhouse, she bumped into one of the stewards who was carrying a tray full of sandwiches. 'Have these gone out to the men on the deck and ashore?'

'Yes, Captain. This is the last lot.'

'Good.'

She grabbed a handful and pushed one into her mouth. Then, still chewing, she pressed the walkie-talkie to her ear and thumbed the transmit button. 'This is the captain,' she said, not very clearly, through a mouthful of bread and tinned salmon. 'Lunch break is over. Start your winches, please.'

Atropos was in position just before three. Robin was all too well aware of the dangers the water would pose and so she had as much of the ship's length pulled ashore as possible. When the winches stopped turning, three hundred feet of her length were sitting on the ice. First, Robin wanted no risk at all of her workmen sliding down the slipway into the lethal tide. Secondly, she needed to be sure that the working areas on the ice and on the hull itself were dry. She needed a work surface which it was possible to walk on and, if necessary, to erect scaffolding upon. She needed heat down by the propeller to keep the metal dry. She needed power and welding gear and none of it could get wet. *Atropos*'s stores had been ransacked against this moment and as soon as the great ship came to rest, teams of men were at work. The opaque white surface of the ice slope was covered with some of the

clean safety sand designed to fight fires and other emergencies aboard. Canvas, any heavy-duty cloth, even some
curtain material was spread over the roughened surface.
Safety netting was placed over that and it was all pegged
down tightly. The hull was running with water which was
rapidly freezing in the cold air. The moment the netting
was safe to walk on, the first swabbing team began to
sponge the metal dry, while around them scaffolding went
up, allowing the second swabbing team to work above
their heads and the third team above theirs.

Robin came down at once with Timmins and her engineering officers by her side. All through the afternoon they
had been following the progress of the propeller as it came
up out of the water and slid back along the ice. Even
from the distance of the beaches at the feet of the cliffs,
it had been possible to get some idea of the damage and
how difficult it would be to fix it. But with the nets down
and the scaffold up, now was the time for a closer look.

The huge propeller was sitting with two blades pointing
down and the third pointing up. The lower port blade was
the most severely damaged, though all three bore graphic
evidence of hard contact with tough ice. Silently, the little
group of people looked at the screw and then at the shaft
behind it. Robin was the first to speak. 'You pulled off a
miracle here, Chief. How on earth did you manage to
disconnect the power in time to save the shaft? It should
be corkscrewed by rights but it looks straight as a die
to me.'

'I was lucky,' said Lethbridge. 'The light damage was
done under power and I managed to get the gearing off
as soon as I felt what was happening. That bad bit happened soon after, but the power was off by then. She slid
back down the wave and smashed straight into the floe. I

felt it happen and I heard it hit. Nothing I could do by then.'

'There's no way we can fix it, though, is there?' observed Don Taylor quietly. 'The whole lot's got to come off, hasn't it?'

They all nodded at once, silenced again by the way his simple questions had brought the reality of their huge task home to them.

They were standing fifteen feet high and their eyes were level with the point of the massive boss. Like the point of a giant military shell, it projected out towards them more than eight feet in diameter and over six feet deep. It was screwed onto the end of the main shaft and welded home. They had to cut the welding and unscrew it without damaging it. When they had unscrewed it, they had to lower it safely to the ground and stow it carefully, ready to be screwed back into place later and welded firmly home before they could sail. When they had done all that, then the first really difficult bit could begin.

'Time for a cup of tea, I think,' said Robin.

With her steaming mug in her hand and her mind purposely clear of any thought about the problem, she prowled round the winches, checking that all the lines were tight. As she had planned, she had secured the stern cables to the outer posts of the pairs of capstans only. They stretched back tautly now, angled outwards only slightly as though *Atropos* were an inquisitive insect with a long pair of feelers exploring the shore. The forward cables were almost at ninety degrees to the angle of the hull and seemed to be reaching upwards onto the terraces. She looked up, thinking about the careful instruction she had given for the securing of the anchors in the ice – she didn't want any repetition of the fiasco when the pressure against the spikes hammered into the ice barrier had caused them to melt the ice. She was standing alone on the deck behind the propeller they would have to cut free and move soon, below the gantry they would use to transport its massive weight, between the windlasses which would have to hold all this restless movement safely in check. And because, for the first time today, she was standing absolutely still, looking up, she felt a wind upon her cheek she would not otherwise have noticed.

It was a gentle wind. A kiss rather than a puff, hardly enough to stir the fur at the edge of her hood. It was cold as the kiss of death; it had come from the iceberg. It was damp, if anything so cold could be said to be damp. It was enough to make her look higher, frowning, wondering how many such warning movements of the air had passed unnoticed so far today. And what she saw when she looked at the crest of the cliff made her catch her breath in a mixture of shock and delight. What she saw was unutterably beautiful. What it meant was probably deeply sinister. The sky was no longer innocently blue. Scudding across it at a seemingly incredible rate were tendrils of vapour. They were too thin and insubstantial to be called cloud, and too busy to be mere mist. The vapour formed lively mares' tails like the warnings of an approaching storm, but the mares' tails were moving too fast to be products of the ionosphere miles above. It was as though a storm was coming in through the lower few hundred feet of the sky; and yet it was impossible to be sure the strange phenomenon was that low. Only the speed of its movement made it seem so close.

Closer still, and absolutely fixed in terms of height, a great banner of white, crystal-filled mist was streaming off the cliff top and away south immediately above her head. It was as though the frozen wave of ice was breaking at last. So real was the effect that she stepped back involuntarily, as though expecting the whole ice wall to come tumbling down upon her head. The movement against the sky was made to look even more frantic by the fact that the sun was well past its zenith and seemed to be casting its light from behind the streaming clouds.

As she stood transfixed, her breath caught in her throat, the strangest effect of all reached out towards her. As though the banner of mist streaming out from the cliff top were some sort of screen, a shadow was projected across it. The tea mug dropped from her nerveless fingers to shatter on the deck and the drops of tea within it rattled down around her feet like brown hail, frozen in the air. Her knees threatened to give out on her and only the greatest effort of will held her erect. Stretching out above her, cast across the flat plane of vapour in the sky, the shadow stumbled out towards her as though it would hurl itself down over the edge and into her waiting arms. It was clear and unmistakable, hooded, jacketed, and gloved. She could even see the bulges where its trousers were tucked into its boots. It was real in every detail, but distorted by the light. It hung like doom above her. Its hands reached out blindly, imploringly, seeming to reach towards her. There was a high keening sound which seemed to attain unbearable intensity and she thought it must be the sound of the wind in the ice cliff. Or it might have been a sound she was making herself. She blinked, slowly, feeling her tears freezing on her cheeks and tore her eyelids open again before they were frozen shut.

And the shadow was gone.

* * *

'Look,' said Lethbridge, 'if it was a real shadow then it has to have belonged to Miss Cable or to Henri. But it sounds as though it could have been a trick of the light.' He was shouting the words over the sound of the workers beginning to break through the welding at the back of the propeller boss.

'I agree. But what would they still be doing up there? It's nearly a day later . . .' Then she answered her own question. 'It looked so *lost* . . .'

'Well, I guess Harry Stone and his team will find anything up there. Unless the weather makes it too risky to go far enough to see anything. Hell, Captain, it certainly brings it home how sheltered we are down here. Anything at all could be happening on the far side of the hill. At least they've got the walkie-talkie with them and orders not to go beyond its range.'

Robin nodded. She bitterly regretted not doing the same with Henri LeFever. If she had realised that Ann would be going with him she would certainly have done so.

She shivered, but not from the cold. The strange feeling of disquiet that the experience had roused within her would not leave her. It was as though all the unsettling little things she had noticed about the massive iceberg had joined forces with her increasing worry for her missing friends to form that ghostly shadow. For the first time, really, she missed Richard. They were so seamless a team as to be almost one person. When they were together, their thought processes worked so closely in union that they verged upon the psychic. Together they would have worked out what was troubling her and the best way to put it to rest. Alone, she could only talk it through with one or two of her command and even then not fully. It niggled

away at the back of her mind like an itch she couldn't
scratch.

The team had finished their assault on the welding and
a length of cable came down from the deck above them,
uncoiling with all the lazy grace of a massive python. The
men caught it and began to wrap it round the hot metal
of the boss. Immediately above Robin's head, a lighter line
wound down and when it tapped her hood she jumped.
Lethbridge saw this, and wisely said nothing. 'Right,'
she said decisively. 'Time to get on. I hope this
works.'

'I'll keep the hammers and the oxyacetylene equipment
down here just in case,' offered Lethbridge.

'Yes. If there's any problem, then we'll heat up the boss
and give it a gentle tap or two. But we can't risk distorting
it. We'll be well up the creek if we can't get it back
on again.'

'And without our paddle with a vengeance,' he agreed.
'I'll be gentle, I promise.'

'I've heard that one before,' she said and began to climb
back up to the poop deck.

Her plan was simplicity itself in essence. The length of
cable which Timmins had lowered to the engineers was
secured round the starboard inner capstan post. As Robin
arrived beside him, Hogg pulled the end back up on the
line which had made her jump and secured it round the
port inner capstan. The cable now went from one post
twice round the propeller boss and back up to the other.
In theory, all they needed to do was tighten the cable to
the correct tension then feed it out from one capstan while
pulling it in to the other and the friction of the rope wound
round the propeller boss would cause it to unscrew. If they

failed on the first attempt, Lethbridge's men would heat
things up until the boss expanded and came loose, like
the cap of a jar held under a hot tap in the kitchen.

'Right,' she called back to the two officers behind her.
'Let's go.'

Half an hour later, the cheers of Lethbridge and his
men as the boss cleared its final screw thread were so
loud that they almost drowned the insistent sound of the
walkie-talkie. Robin's face was still split into a wide, vic-
torious grin as she slid the icy earpiece under her hood
and thumbed the buttons.

'Captain here.'

'. . . Harry Stone . . .' The signal was weak. They were
clearly at the furthest limit of their range.

'Come back, Harry. You've gone too far already. I say
again, give up and come home.'

'. . . bring . . . with us . . . too weak to walk but I think
we can . . .'

'Say again, Harry. I can't make you out.'

'. . . white-out here. It's a miracle we found him. I think
we can get him back all right, though. I say again, it's a
total white-out here, but we marked our trail and I think
we can get Henri back . . .'

'I hear you! I understand you have found Henri LeFever
and are bringing him back with you. What about Ann
Cable? I say again, what about Ann Cable?'

'She's gone, Captain. I'm sorry, but she's gone.'

CHAPTER THIRTY-ONE

Day Twelve

Sunday, 30 May   18:00

Ann Cable was lost, but not quite gone. She was staggering through the ice blizzard, her right arm crooked before her forehead, trying to protect her face from the wind. She could see very little now, for the vicious spicules of ice which seemed to be driving like needles into her cheeks were scoring the glass lenses of her goggles like diamond dust and settling in miniature drifts across them. She was staggering forwards, her skis long gone, into a tunnel of gathering darkness at the heart of the white-out, as though departing from reality altogether.

The thin material of her hood drummed against her ears deafeningly so that the banshee howling of the wind seemed to be receding as mysteriously as the light. The whole of her outfit had been designed for ski slopes not polar storms, so that even the agony of the cold was beginning to fade as the deadly numbness of frostbite stole over her. Only the brave, burning strength of her indomitable life force kept her moving and there was very little of it left. She knew this well enough but kept before her mind the one thought – her last thought – that if she stopped moving, she would die. She had no idea where she was going. She had no idea where she was or where she had come from. She was too tired even to be afraid any longer, though fear had kept her going since she had lost contact with Henri. She was moving now only because she was a living thing and some atavistic instinct told her that stillness meant death.

Abruptly, she began to shiver. This was not the gentle trembling of chilled muscles familiar from cold winter mornings, but a bone-deep juddering which came without warning and rooted itself in her most vital organs, sapping the last of her energy at a terrific rate. Only her single ski pole held her erect as she stood helplessly in the grip of it. Only the fact that her right arm was frozen to the fake fur of her hood kept it in place. Unlike the first attack a few minutes ago, this one was fierce enough to cost her part of her tongue and the caps on two teeth before it passed. She should have been in agony but she felt nothing beyond the numbness and the slow calming of the cataclysm within her. A trickle of blood froze, as bright as scarlet nail varnish, on the dull white of her ice-caked chin. She fell forward and her legs took up their stumbling motion again, much more weakly than before.

She had only moments left to live.

It had begun as the simplest of adventures little more than twenty-four hours earlier. As soon as Henri had appeared ready to go up onto the iceberg, with the lifeboat's emergency beacon in his hand, she had been overcome by a desire to accompany him. It was much more than the complex tangle of friendship, suspicion and simple desire she felt for him, it had been something to do with the iceberg itself. She had been 'ashore' with the anchorage teams, but that had only served to put her under the spell of the ice. Something high in this alp of frozen water called to her with a disturbing intensity. Henri was going out to it. She had to go too. It was not something over which she had any control at all, really.

Unlike *Clotho, Atropos* had ski equipment aboard. Ann had no difficulty in kitting herself out with the sort of stuff she felt would be perfect for the adventure. She took skis, poles, a parka with a hood, and waterproof leggings. On her back she strapped a small backpack with some basic survival equipment in it – a silver thermal blanket, a thermos, and one of the hand-held walkie-talkies which would communicate with the bridge from a distance of more than two miles. Henri had one emergency beacon; she took another and slung it round her neck. Henri had a small tent in his backpack, but that just seemed like so much excess baggage to her.

As the afternoon began to think about stretching itself into the long, lingering evening, the pair of them climbed out of a lifeboat and carried the skis, poles and all the rest up the shelving beach to the beginning of the dry ice. Side by side and silently, they kitted up and prepared to set off. They said no farewells and, in fact, none of the busy sailors seemed to notice that they had gone. There was no need for any warnings or injunctions to take care. They were not going far. They were going together. They were going through a clear afternoon which would linger into a bright evening which would give way to a luminous, starlit night with the promise of a fat moon later. They had the walkie-talkie. They each had a beacon and could switch it on so the crew of *Atropos* would have no trouble in finding them should anything untoward happen.

There was no snow, really. No doubt snow had fallen
on the great river of antediluvian ice which had spawned
the berg, and upon the berg itself since it had set sail
onto the Arctic Ocean, but it had either set into the rest
of the solid surface or had blown away like frozen feathers
in the breath of the polar wind. They soon found themselves skiing across a gentle slope of rock-solid ice,
moving up and away from the bustle around the anchorage
point. They were effectively climbing the shallow steps of
a great semi-circular amphitheatre to begin with. The tops
of the steps were flat but only a hundred yards or so wide.
The vertical fronts were drifted slopes, not quite steep
enough to test their technique in skiing uphill. Above the
highest gallery, a gentle ice slope rose like a solid river
flooding round a high, absolutely vertical ice bluff. The
bluff reached out in two towering cliff faces, coming to a
point less than a mile away. They paused at the bottom
of this slope, and looked around themselves. Up ahead of
them, the rise, like the shoulder of a low white hill, led
round the vertical abruptness of the first ice bluff which
rose on their right as though it were the bow of a great
ship sailing southwards and the slope they were about to
climb were a bow wave before it. Their first objective was
to go round the point in the hope that the slope would
continue to rise beyond it, leading them up to the higher
galleries.

Twenty minutes of silent skiing proved their hope to be
well founded. They skirted a jumble of ice boulders at the
foot of the bluff and swung wide until they had a good
view up behind it to the north. Here they paused again,
both looking back over their shoulders at the suddenly
distant *Atropos* and the miniature bustle on her forward
deck. The anchorage points and the stern of the ship were

hidden by the gleaming slope behind them. Then they looked ahead, to the north. Here the slope they had been following climbed up the side of the cliff face of the bluff, which came to a point on their right hand. On their left, the slope fell away until, distantly, it became the foot of another great cliff which stood like a wall in front of them. Behind the slope, somewhere before it became a wide ledge high above, the cliff stretching east to west ahead of them met at right angles with the southward thrust of the bluff. From the ship they had only been able to see the bluff. From here it was possible to see the second, infinitely larger cliff stretching away so massively it might almost have stretched to America itself. And at their feet, reaching up the side of the bluff and to the top of the cliff in a single, unbroken run was the slope of ice they were following upwards. No matter how high the cliffs ahead of them, no matter how massive the feature further west, here it looked like an easy climb to the upper slopes – and to whatever mountainous beauties lay beyond.

'*En avant!*' called Henri suddenly. The merry, indomitable, human cry echoed off the icy walls around them and Ann caught the excitement in his voice. With a great surge of freedom, as though she were escaping the humdrum and entering a world of infinite possibilities, she struck forward, northwards up the new slope. As soon as she did so, the great ship's bow of the ice bluff hid *Atropos* and everyone aboard her from her sight.

As she moved, she felt the freedom buoy her up. Away from *Atropos*, all of her worries and wondering were put into some kind of perspective. The roller-coaster which her emotions had ridden recently now seemed to be a relatively paltry thing. Jamie Curtis's thoughtless words about Nico and Robin, followed so quickly by Nico's

apparent death had set a worm of suspicion gnawing painfully within her. But Nico's rebirth and Robin's almost
girlish glee at Richard's arrival had made her suspicions
seem so childish. And now this new environment, the
simple distance from the claustrophobic little world of
Atropos, made all of her worries seem like a storm in a
teacup. Something more to do with exhaustion and paranoia than reality. As she strove to catch up with Henri,
she was actually laughing at herself.

She would not have been laughing had she had any idea
what effect the same pressure of claustrophobia, exhaustion and paranoia were having on her massive companion.

On this side of the ice bluff, the slope was steeper and
clearly led upwards to the top of an ice cliff which
stretched away to the left like the edge of Conan Doyle's
Lost World. Where that great tectonic mountain had been
fringed with overhanging foliage, this one was edged with
massive icicles. Where those black cliffs had been scalable
only from a rocky point nearby, these blindingly white
ones were easy to reach up the slope Ann and Henri were
now following. As they climbed, however, it soon became
obvious that they would have to keep the west-facing cliff
of the bluff ever closer to their right shoulders as the outer
reaches of the slope on their left fell away more and more
steeply. After half an hour they were effectively on a
ledge, albeit one which was wide enough for them still to
be climbing side by side. Ahead of them, the slope was
steepening, like a child's slide made of sugar icing, up to
the hard edge of the cliffs against the dark blue sky.

'One last push,' called Henri, his voice breathy with the
exercise, but still exultant.

'Are you sure it isn't too steep?'

'No. It'll be easy!'

He pulled ahead and she was content to follow him. Looking up past his hunched shoulder, she saw something she hadn't noticed before. At the high groin where the bluff joined the main cliff, there was a cleft. It looked a little strange, as though an arm did not quite join the shoulder after all.

After that one glance up past him, she looked down and concentrated on keeping her skis in his tracks. She was an accomplished skier, but soon found that her work at Aspen and Cortina d'A was not quite the preparation needed for this. Soon the parallel tramline markings of Henri's ski tracks in the ice drift became herringbone markings. Soon after that, she paused again, her legs threatening to cramp as the muscles down their outer curves cried out, unused to this duck-like form of locomotion. She was breathless and covered in perspiration. Her light-sensitive goggles were beginning to fog up and it suddenly seemed to her that the last of the daylight was fading with unnatural rapidity. On looking up, however, she was given renewed strength by the nearness of their goal and she realised that while she had been concentrating on fitting her skis into his tracks, they had scaled the final section of the slope. The gathering darkness was in fact a shadow from the cliff top above them. Just before her, just above her, Henri was standing, looking ahead. As though wearing leg irons, she moved forward to his side.

If anything, the slope eased off. On their right, very close at hand, the southward reach of west-facing cliff was reduced to little more than a hillock and she saw at once that what she had taken for a cleft was a simple undulation in the snow slope. Ahead, and still above them, the south-facing cliff which reached far away to the west on their left hand was the crest of a low hill, but it still held the skyline as though there was nothing more of the iceberg beyond it. Abruptly, the hard edge of the horizon wavered. Tendrils of smoke reached out towards them only to whisper past just above their heads. The effect was extremely sinister, as though they were being summoned by ghosts. For a moment, the whole of the slope before them seemed to go out of focus and Ann found herself squinting as though she were suddenly short-sighted.

'It's the wind,' called Henri reassuringly. 'Blowing the ice crystals around. Pretty, huh?'

Ann found herself nodding, but she didn't really agree. There was something unsettling suddenly about the alien way in which their surroundings were behaving and all at once she realised how dangerously at risk they might be up here. She opened her mouth to say something, but it was too late. Henri was in motion.

At least she could dispense with the duck walk and the herringbone placing of her skis. That fact, and the fact that, like her friend Robin Mariner, she had a habit of challenging fear head on, made her decide to go for it hard. She even pulled out to the side of his tramline tracks and pushed forward forcefully on her poles to make a bit of a race of it. Henri glanced across at her and crouched forward into a racing stance, meeting her challenge with a grin and a flash of teeth. Side by side, they shot across the top of the ice slope and onto the first part of the undulation. They were both experienced ski racers and used the slope perfectly, pushing hard off the crest and tucking their poles under their arms as they shot across the wrinkle in the terrain. It was not until the slope gathered up ahead of her again that Ann freed the poles and pushed really hard. Like Henri, she was moving very quickly now, and concentrating on clearing the slope first.

Then she was tumbling forward in a wild jumble of wood and steel and blocks of ice. Her ankles felt as though they had both been severely twisted and her right wrist felt broken. It was exactly as though the white slope ahead of her, so much like a wave in every other respect, had broken over her and inundated her in solid foam. The sound, too, brought a breaking wave to mind, for behind the overpowering roaring there was a sibilance as of a great slope of sand sliding away off the edge of a cliff.

She hit solid ground, face down, with stunning force. So hard was the impact, indeed, that it was a moment before she realised, horrifyingly, that she could feel nothing below her thighs. The impact, the confusion of what was happening to her was so overwhelming that for an instant she actually supposed that her legs might have come off at the knee somehow. But then reason began to reassert itself and, as it did so, a hand from heaven seemed to reach down and fasten on the scruff of her neck. With one unceremonious heave, like a kitten pulled up out of a dangerous stream, she was wrenched upwards and almost hurled onto level ground.

Suddenly, there was silence so absolute it echoed. Perhaps she had been struck deaf; it seemed as likely as anything else. Certainly, she seemed to have been struck blind. But she appeared to have got her legs back, at least. She began to move gingerly, checking her wrists and ankles, all of which hurt varyingly. This way she discovered that she still had both her skis and both her poles. She sat up, pulling her hands free of the wrist loops and reached up to lift her ice-clogged goggles up off her blinking eyes. In the overpowering glare of the early evening, Henri loomed over her, his face almost devilish with rage. She jerked back, dazzled eyes spilling tears down her cheeks. Because he was looking at her, she assumed the rage was directed at her. 'What . . .' she began. His expression softened at once. He turned away, she felt him snap her skis free and her ankles felt better at once.

'We have been a little unlucky, I think,' he said quietly. 'Though we are lucky still to be alive.' As he spoke he turned back to wipe the tears off her cheeks and the ice off her goggles. 'Look,' he added when he had finished.

She replaced her goggles and looked down. Such was the magnitude of the shock that she was numbed by it. Coolly, distantly, far too calmly, she looked down at the slope they had just climbed. The top twenty yards of it was gone. The whole of that innocent-looking undulation had collapsed, and she realised that the slight valley in the rolling surface had in fact been a frozen crust covering a deep crevasse.

The top of the bluff of ice whose gently sloping side they had climbed did not join the cliff they were standing on at all. At her feet was a wall of ice which fell to untold depths away on either hand. Then, ten metres distant, as remote as another planet, stood another wall, the rear of the bluff that overlooked *Atropos*'s anchorage. The slope itself now ended in a tumble of snow blocks so steep that it would be death to jump down onto it. The path by which they had climbed up here so easily was gone. There wasn't even any evidence that it had ever existed. They were trapped. There was absolutely no way back along the route they had followed to get up here. 'It was an ice bridge,' said Henri quietly. 'I've heard of them but I've never come across one. I guess we broke it when we skied across it so hard.'

Ann tore her backpack off and ripped it open, reaching in for the walkie-talkie she had been so careful to bring.

But it was no longer there. Her hand reached right through and out of a ragged hole in the bottom of the canvas. The walkie-talkie, the primus and the tins of food were gone. Derisively, only the silver thermal blanket was left. Ann looked down at it, stunned; the loss of the equipment brought home to her the full danger of their situation in a way even the sight of the collapsed ice bridge had failed to do.

'What are we going to do?' Her voice sounded remote in her own ears, like the voice of a stranger.

'Look for another way down. I might risk throwing myself over the edge here and onto the top of that slope way down there but it'd probably kill me. It would certainly kill you. Can you stand?'

'I guess so.' She began to pull herself together and climb to her feet. As soon as she was sure her joints were lightly sprained and nothing more, she put her skis back on. Henri switched his emergency beacon on and stuck it in the cliff top at the point where the ice bridge had collapsed. 'Switch yours on too,' he directed. 'That way they'll be able to find us more easily if we get lost.'

'Won't they get confused between the two of them? I mean it'll be impossible to tell which beacon is us.'

'No,' he said. 'One will be still and the other will be moving. They should be able to tell from that.'

'As long as we *are* moving,' she observed as she pulled the device out of her clothing.

'Face it,' he said. 'If we aren't moving then it probably won't make all that much difference. Now, switch it on.'

She obeyed, and they were off.

They struck east to begin with, as this was the direction which should bring them nearer to the ship and their friends. As she moved forward behind Henri, following

their long shadows along the cliff top, Ann had some
leisure to look around. On their right, the cliff fell away
after a safe distance of level ice wide enough to allow for
the wandering of fatigued feet and the possibility of
dangerous overhangs below them. Beyond the cliff was
the lowering slope of the east side of the bluff, wide
enough at this end to stand like another skyscraper wall
parallel with their own, but plunging as though to a street
between. On their left, observed only in nervous glances
at first as she kept her attention focused on the untrust-
worthy ground at her feet, stretched the rest of the berg.
They were on the rim of a vast plain which sloped away
gently for what looked like many featureless miles before
it gathered itself into what seemed to be a range of ice
mountains on the far horizon. It was difficult to be absolutely sure, because the light was turning pink and this,
combined with the polarisation in her light-sensitive
goggle lenses, made it hard to distinguish ice from cloud
or to judge distances at all.

The ice mountains, if that was what they were, seemed
to come round towards them in a half-circle, the nearer
slopes catching a dazzling rose light from the sun, start-
lingly emphasised by the smoky blue-grey shadows
immediately behind them. The whole scene seemed quite
unreal. Every time she looked at the mountains they
danced like a mirage. Either there was a wind near them,
or there was a strange kind of heat haze or the brightness
was making her eyes water. The place was so contained,
so unique that it seemed to dictate its own sense of scale
and it was impossible to tell whether the nearest wavering
slopes were one mile away or ten. They seemed to get
closer but less real as the two walked on, following their
increasingly monstrous shadows along the edge of the cliff.

When Henri stopped, she collided with him. It was fortunate that he had stopped well back or they might both have plunged over. As it was, they staggered forward a step or two and only their skis held them erect. At any other time, in any other circumstance, this would have been a view to treasure. Now it was almost more than she could bear to look at. They stood, as if on a mountain top, overlooking an infinite vista of seascape. The far horizon was black and the sky reaching up above it slowly surrendered, shade by shade, to the rosy light. Here and there on the lower rim and, once, breathtakingly, higher in the dusky ash-pink, stars glimmered like windows to heaven. In from the low black rim heaved the sea, as ashen as the sky, with no trace about it of green or blue. Like an ocean from another planet, made more outlandish by the cracked crust of ice upon it, like a faded silken banner one shade of amethyst above utter colourlessness, the restless water reached in towards them until what slight colour was left to it vanished under the absolute line of blackness which was the shadow of the cliffs they were standing on. On their right hand and at right angles, immediately in front of them, reaching across to the mauve mountains on their left, the cliffs fell away hundreds of feet, sheer and unclimbable, below them.

Something more than the chill of the arctic night closed its fist round them then, for they began to realise that in this place where even colour seemed forbidden, life could not survive for long.

'What are we going to do now?' Ann had absolutely no idea of her own.

'We're going to find some shelter, then we're going to become very good friends indeed,' answered Henri. He avoided making it sound salacious or schoolboyish because the tone in which he said it was dead and very near defeat. 'We have to get through the night without food and heat, and with nothing but these outfits to keep us warm.' And even as he spoke, a wind came gusting past them which made the ice plain ripple as though it was melting and the ice mountains waver like clouds.

As they plodded doggedly northwards towards the mountains – the only promise of any shelter nearby – the last of the colour faded from the evening. Such was the reflective quality of the terrain around them, the last of the light lingered, seemingly multiplied by the glittering surfaces. They seemed to be walking through a magically luminous place even as the sky above them darkened relentlessly into a fathomless, velvet black. The effect was intensified by the wind which lifted the ice crystals into a series of stratified clouds which caught and held the light around them as though they were under glowing water.

It never really became dark. As the last reflected gleams of the long-vanished sun faded from the glassy slopes, so the first glitter of starlight shone out like the heart of a diamond. The nature of the liquid light carried in the deadly breath of the strengthening wind changed slightly. Ann was too weary, hungry and chilled to appreciate the beauty of what was happening around her, or to take even the briefest opportunity to estimate if what she had heard was true in fact – that one could read a newspaper by starlight in this place. Instead she forced her exhausted legs to push her skis forward one after the other, following Henri across the ice. There was no way for her to measure time. Certainly she had no wish to go through the complicated ritual of consulting the watch which was fastened round her wrist under the sleeve of her thermal vest, which was itself beneath her roll-necked pullover, her heavy woollen raglan, her Puffa and her elasticated parka cuff. Her timescale was reduced to the metronomic movement of her legs. Her eyes, fastened on the ground, soon became almost hypnotised by the whirling ice dust which concealed her feet and skis altogether.

This time when Henri stopped, he stepped to one side and reached out to her as she continued past him like a wind-up toy whose clockwork had not yet quite run down. She was so numb that his grip on her shoulder felt more like a force than a touch but it was enough to stop her and to call her back from whatever deep recess she had withdrawn into. She looked around herself with dazed wonder. As though by magic, just as her eyes tried to come to terms with the sharp hills immediately above her, the moon peeped over the horizon to the south-west.

She did not know it, but she shared a vivid childhood memory with her friend Robin Mariner: the story of the Ice Queen. Although her family had been Italian, she had been told a wide range of fairy stories as a child, like any youngster growing in the States at the time, and the works of Andersen and the brothers Grimm had featured largely in her childish imagination. Now she found herself looking up at the glacial ramparts of the Ice Queen's frozen castle atop the mountain of ice whither she had so feared to be carried from her soft, warm cot. The sight of it chilled her heart until she felt like the Ice Queen herself.

The cold light of the rising moon made the ice bone-white. There was no hint of warmth or softness about the sheer slopes above her. The shadows were stark black and without the hint of velvet in the sky. It was as though they had stepped out of a modern world of warm colour into the steely, gleaming monochrome of a *film noir*. It

was breathtakingly beautiful and utterly, numbingly terrifying at the same time. The slopes stepped up and back like
a massive staircase, stark and sheer; and at the front edge
of each step, a still cascade of icicles plunged down into
great bunches of crystal daggers. It required a shift in her
perception so profound that it actually made her head ache
to realise that some of those glacial daggers must be
twenty feet long.

But Henri was talking to her. She dragged her attention
back to him. '. . . for some kind of shelter. A cave. A deep
overhang. Anything.' The wind battered across the level
plain as he spoke, the renewed force of its blast driving
home the urgency of his words. She nodded and then
hissed as the simple movement tore at the frozen muscles
of her neck.

Side by side, they began to follow the cliff foot, looking
to the right, exhausted eyes probing the white walls bulg-
ing and receding behind the dangerous fringe of icicles.
They resembled the flanks of monstrous animals caught
behind the crystal bars of some huge cage. The wind
boomed and snarled against the surfaces, making strange,
disturbing noises as though the monsters were trying to
break through to consume them. The ice crystals billowed
out on the wind as though giving form to their breath and
the wind itself gathered enough force to make the ice bars
shiver as though the animals were battering against them.
It was more than mere fear of falling ice that made
them walk further and further out from the sinister cliff
foot.

They were lucky to see the cave at all for it had a
narrow opening and seemed to be little more than the
moon-shadow of a particularly thick icicle. Ann's eyes

were fastened on the feline flank of the ice, watching
fascinated as the combination of their movement and its
slow rippling made it seem that the ice was breathing. Her
mind was withdrawing from urgent, agonising reality
again, but she was still concentrating hard enough to notice
that the black band did not move like all the other shadows
had done, and its stillness jerked her awake. She speeded
up and grabbed Henri. He had pulled her the better part
of five metres before he realised she was trying to attract
his attention. '*Oui?*'

His face was fine-drawn. Masked as it was by goggles
and framed with frozen spikes of fake fur from his hood,
it looked other-worldly. In the dead-pale moonlight he
looked ghastly, every bit as white as the ice slopes behind
them; every bit as terrifying as the frozen-hearted characters from her fairy tale nightmares.

'There's an opening, I think . . . something . . .'

'*Alors! C'est vrais?*'

'*Oui*. Yes.'

'*Tu es certain?*'

'Yes!'

'*Bien! En avant.*'

They turned, side by side, and began to work their way
back. Henri was actually stumbling now, in spite of the
fact that his skis were still on tight. Ann, uncertain that
he had actually recognised her during their conversation,
was suddenly struck with worry.

'Henri!' she called urgently to him, but her voice was
lost beneath the thunder of the wind against the cliff.
'*HENRI!*'

He slowed and looked down at her.

'*ARE YOU ALL RIGHT?*' she bellowed.

He shook his head and at first she thought he was saying no, but then she realised he was simply clearing his thoughts.

'Sure,' he bellowed back. And the one word, in English, put her mind at rest.

They found the cave with no difficulty and almost ran towards its fragile hope of salvation. The position of that huge icicle, standing like a stalactite outside the crack, firmly bedded in the overhang above, meant that they had to remove their skis to get close to the opening itself, and then they had to remove their backpacks to get in through it. Henri went first. Ann passed in the equipment, and then followed.

The opening was tiny, just large enough for her to squeeze through, and she wondered how on earth Henri had got in at all. The moon shone directly through the portal and, disturbingly, through the south-facing wall in which it stood, as though the whole wall was made of thick glass. Outlined against the white glow of it, the skis and poles stood above the black bulks of the backpacks. There was not much light in here, but when she took her goggles off, she could see.

Beyond the restricting portal the cave opened out into quite a substantial little room. There was just enough height for them to stand erect and more than enough floor space for them to lie down. The walls were a pale glimmer all around them and the whole aspect of the place was what Ann imagined the inside of a freezer must be like. But out of the wind, it was relatively warm and, for all that it was made of water, it was dry. The floor was covered in a thick drift of ice crystals and the first thing they did was to push them bodily across to the narrow opening and block it as far as they were able. Here the proximity of the icicle proved a blessing for it broke the force of the wind and gave their makeshift sand wall a solid backing which held it firmly until they were satisfied they had excluded all the draughts they could.

They cleared a level area in the middle of the floor which was about the right size and shape to be a double bed. The two of them knelt on either side of it, looking speculatively across at each other, consumed by an almost uncontrollable urge to sleep. 'We can't just lie down fully clothed,' said Henri. 'We'd freeze, either tonight or in the morning when we get out again. We have to get our clothes off and make a bed.'

'But how?'

'Do what I do.'

He reached across and pulled one backpack across to his knees, pulled off his mittens with his teeth to reveal a pair of woollen gloves beneath and tore it open. Out of it he pulled a silver thermal sheet about six feet by six, the sort of thing designed to be wrapped round the shoulders of anyone likely to lose too much heat after running a marathon or getting lost on an iceberg. He spread it out on the ground while she was still tugging an identical piece free of her backpack.

'Leave that a moment,' he ordered, and began to take off his parka. She obeyed and began to follow suit without a second thought. After all they had been through together, it couldn't possibly be some kind of seduction. Although now she thought of it, if Henri still had the energy after the terrors and exertions of the day, then maybe he deserved a little kindness.

The two parkas were laid out on the floor on top of the silver blanket, side by side, lining upwards. Then Henri was sitting clumsily, trying to get his boots unlaced without taking his woollen gloves off. Unexpectedly, he stopped and sat for an instant. 'I'll tell you what,' he said. 'Before we go any further, we'd better think ahead a little. I need to use the john. How about you?'

The light was, perhaps fortunately, not quite bright enough to reveal her vivid, schoolgirl blush. 'Yes, I do too,' she admitted. It had been worrying her increasingly.

'Okay. I'll go first. Up at the back of the cave. Then I'll do some more work on this bed while you follow suit.' He heaved himself up and walked off. A moment or two after he had vanished there was a thump and a grunt of pain. When she called his name there was no reply, but a sound like a distant waterfall assured her he was still all right.

The wait was brief. 'The back of the cave shelves down pretty sharply,' he warned. 'Mind your head.'

'And my feet, by the sound of things,' she quipped tightly.

'No. It'll be frozen solid by now,' he countered. 'You know the old joke about Eskimos pissing ice cubes.'

The back of the cave was as low as he had described. She knelt to loosen her clothing, then turned onto all fours before rocking back carefully into a squat. The combination of Henri's proximity and the incredible cold made things very difficult for her, but the thought of waiting until the cheeks of her bottom got frostbitten finally spurred her into action. She returned to the makeshift bed to find him still wrestling with his laces.

As soon as the boots were off, he tore off his thermal trousers. He shook them and dusted them dry, then folded them over to extend the parkas into a soft, waterproof mattress measuring more than six feet by four. The two Puffas went at the head end as pillows, stuffed with their heavy jeans. They tore off outer pullovers and placed them down at the foot end as extra protection against frostbite. They worked fast and the movement kept the chill at bay in spite of the fact that they were very lightly dressed now. He wore skin-tight white thermal long johns and vest under a brushed cotton lumberjack's shirt with woollen socks and gloves. Her outfit was identical except that she wore a skin-tight roll-necked pullover instead of a shirt. Her emergency beacon hung round her neck and swung as she moved, broadcasting its message unceasingly to a deaf, uncaring world.

'Get your thermal blanket out and put it on top,' he ordered. She was quick to obey and equally quick to throw it over the increasingly inviting-looking bed.

'Get under,' he directed and she rolled under the silver blanket. He rose above her and moved with the deft swing of a fisherman with a net. The canvas of the small tent he had been carrying spread over her to form a second, waterproof, upper layer. She folded the whole lot back and he slid under beside her.

'What about the emergency beacon?' she asked.

'Turn it off. No one's likely to come looking for us tonight. We may need it tomorrow. Keep wearing it, though. The warmth of our bodies will help preserve the batteries.' She obeyed and they lay side by side for an instant. The ice beneath was incredibly hard. She could feel the chill of it burning through the thin layer of clothing beneath them. I'm never going to be able to sleep like this, she thought.

Then his firm, assured hands rolled her over and gathered her to him. One solid thigh slid between hers and his arms wrapped round her, pressing her to him.

She stiffened with suspicion and he chuckled. 'Nothing

personal,' he said, 'but I think you're flattering both of us, honey. This is for body warmth. Nothing more.'

That was the last thing either of them said and as the warmth between them did indeed begin to build, Ann began to drift off into an exhausted doze, sleep kept at bay only by the gnawing hunger in her belly.

Outside, the wind rumbled and thundered. Beneath and all around, the ice grumbled and groaned as though the massive berg were made up of small parts all straining against each other, clashing and rumbling in a bid to break free. Deep in subterranean chambers, air moved with bass rumblings as the water which inhabited the greatest part of the berg forced it in and out of caverns and galleries. Once again the image of prehistoric animals too lightly caged occurred to her and adrenaline joined hunger to keep her wakeful. Her imagination gave a throat to each mysterious, threatening sound, and a body to each throat, the like of which had not been seen on earth since before humankind first learned to walk erect.

She sprang awake some time later. The moonlight had gone but the gently lucent wall at the end of the cave revealed great balls of powerful brightness which it took her a moment to recognise as stars. The night was electrically still, as though frozen in an instant before some terrible cataclysm. The cold was enormous, it had substance and weight. Only the puny warmth kindled by the intertwining of her body with Henri's kept frigid death at bay. But it was not the cold which had awoken her. It was Henri, talking in his sleep.

Several things struck her at once. First, it came as some surprise to discover that he thought, and dreamed, in French. He had a French name, but so did many Canadians. He spoke in a North American English drawl, placeless but unmistakable, and it had never occurred to her that he thought in any other language. She should have been warned, she supposed, when he lapsed into French at the edge of exhaustion earlier.

She was next struck by a sense of mild frustration. Her own French was non-existent. She spoke Italian, but that was all. She found his throaty mumbling, however, almost erotic. Unconsciously, still close to sleep, she stirred against him. Her movement somehow made his dream more vivid and his voice became louder still, echoing strangely in that tiny cave of ice. He was mumbling something about someone called John. Ann half-listened, her mind still on the edge of a fleshly fantasy. She had dreamed of this moment herself, after all. The intertwining of their bodies was like something out of one of those dreams. The fact that they had reached such intimacy innocent of any actual wrongdoing allowed her mind extra freedom, somehow, though lurking powerfully at the back of it was the solid realisation of the danger of their position and the stupidity of indulging something so childish so close to the very real threat of death. She pressed herself against the solid, sculpted contours of his body, the thermal underwear sliding over her skin like warm oil. She wriggled until the uncomfortable lump of the emergency beacon had slid round under her arm. Trapped against their torsos, the points of her breasts were like two tingling pebbles.

Then it occurred to her that if he was dreaming about someone called *John*, things between them might get very complicated indeed. She thought back to his declaration just before Captain Black had interrupted their *tête-à-tête*. She had assumed he was talking about another woman then, but maybe not. And, now she came to think about it, maybe he hadn't even said John at all. His accent was thick and he had been mumbling. He could have been saying Don. Or Sean. Or even Stone.

She just could not think of a woman's name which sounded like the name he had said.

'Are you awake?' His voice came as such a surprise that it made her flinch with shock. No use dissembling after that.

'Yes. Just this minute come to. Any idea of the time?'

He lifted his hand. A spike of breathtaking cold drove down her back under the blanket. 'Six. Time to go. Sounds as though the wind's dropped at any rate.'

'I never thought we'd make it through the night.'

He grunted. 'I wondered myself.' His voice was distant and Ann suspected his mind was still preoccupied with John.

'You need to use the john?' he asked.

She flinched with surprise at his immediate echo of the name he had spoken in his dream, then tried to cover up with levity. 'Are you kidding? I haven't had anything to eat or drink for eighteen hours, why on earth should I need to use the john?'

'That's good,' he observed dryly. 'We seem to have stepped out without any toilet paper in any case. Taking a dump would have been something of a challenge.'

'Don't. I don't even want to think about it.'

'Okay. Let's get dressed and go. It's going to be hard and dangerous even if the weather stays on our side.'

They dressed like children on a chilly morning, pulling their clothing in under the blankets and wrestling their numb, cramped limbs into recalcitrant cloth. It was surprisingly exhausting, and Ann realised with stunning poignancy that she, at least, was growing physically weaker quite quickly. Thank God Henri had had the foresight to pack all their spare clothing into makeshift pillows and feet warmers: at least it was fairly warm and relatively easy to handle. The effort of getting into a pair of frozen jeans, and the shock of the icy cloth, would have killed her on the spot. She had been joking about their lack of nourishment, but she was realising very quickly with each new effort just how hungry and thirsty she actually was. How much the mechanism of her body really did need some solid fuel for both heat and energy. She even thought wistfully about massive, blood-rare T-bone steaks. His voice broke into her thoughts reminding her to switch on the emergency beacon round her neck before she covered it with clothing.

At last they had donned their parkas and stood looking down at the jumble of canvas and silver on the floor. 'Should we pack all this away in our backpacks in case we need it again tonight?' she asked.

When he looked across at her, his face was masked by impenetrable shadow but the tone in his voice told her enough of what the expression would have been. It was every bit as cold as everything else in this Godforsaken place. 'No. We'll never need these again, no matter what happens. If we haven't got back to the others by tonight, then we're never going back. We'll sure as hell be in no position to pitch camp and snuggle down.'

'We'd better get started, then.'

The atmosphere outside crackled with electric tension. The air was preternaturally clear and calm. The stars were huge, hanging low above them like crystal grapes. The sky seemed so close that the interstellar spaces seemed to glow with the reflection of galaxies too distant to be seen and the silent immensity of it was overwhelming. The only sound was the snap of their boots clicking into their ski bindings, a sound as loud as the cocking of a pair of guns, then the whisper of the waxed wood shushing over the solid ice.

They struck back along the route they had come. Time played tricks on them. Yesterday it had seemed far enough coming up here through the storm, but now it seemed further going back through that unnatural stillness. Ann calculated grimly that this was just more evidence of their rapidly deteriorating state. Yesterday conditions had been bad but they had been strong; now conditions were nearly perfect but they were much weaker. Yesterday it had been possible to switch off and retreat far inside herself, following Henri like an automaton. Today she was too hungry and thirsty to do that. And anyway, if they approached the cliffs in the same way as they had approached the mountains, they would probably walk straight over the edge. Wakefulness was all-important, but it made time drag agonisingly.

Long before they reached the cliff edge, Ann found herself watching a shadow gathering in front of her and she soon realised that it was her own shadow. It took a little longer for her to work out that a shadow in front of her must mean that there was light gathering behind her. The realisation that the sky behind her was growing rapidly lighter stopped her dead in her tracks. The only cause of light she could think of was the dawn. And if dawn was breaking behind her then they were in very bad trouble for they must be walking west instead of south.

'Henri,' she said. Her voice was hoarse for her throat was dry, and she spoke in little more than a whisper, but the word in the silence was as loud as a shout. He stopped and together they turned to look behind themselves.

The peaks of the mountains they had just left were outlined in green and yellow fire. In bands of brightness like the strange flames above, blazing acetate, green, yellow, indigo and cherry-red light rose like a strange halo above the jagged crown of the world. The bands were not regular like the even arches of a rainbow, they were struck through with spears of energy which seemed to lance upwards and downwards, making the colours run into each other. As each shaft of energy moved, so waves of crackling sound washed down from the sky over them. Only at the highest edge of the display was there any paling of the powerful iridescence. The sky above and behind was utterly black and here at least the stars were shrunken to a size more familiar to Ann's city-dweller's eyes. She stood and looked at the slow writhing of the stunning colours. The display was the most beautiful thing she had ever seen in her life but all she could think was, *Thank God it's not the dawn; thank God we're not lost after all*. It was as though her death began then; as though it was not dreams that die first but the sense of wonder. Still they stood, side by side, looking north, until the wind began to stir again and Henri grated, '*En avant!*'

The Northern Lights served to guide them south by throwing slowly fading shadows before them at their feet until the dawn itself began to stir. But by that time the wind was much busier and the growing light was increasingly cloaked by flying ice crystals. It was as though the nocturnal respite which had further drained their reserves of energy had refreshed the wind. It doubled and redoubled its ferocity, streaming in from the west, and when they at last found the cliff edge and turned towards the ruined ice bridge, they found themselves walking into the very teeth of it, their remaining energy draining away as quickly as sand in the onslaught of a Saharan khamsin.

They passed the first emergency beacon without Ann noticing they had done so – though by this time she was concentrating on Henri's back so fiercely she would hardly have noticed a giraffe standing there. She realised they must have passed it when Henri turned aside abruptly and back-tracked along a crevasse which crossed their way, and which she had not seen before. It came plunging in from the cliff edge like the black blade of some incredible stiletto. It was not wide, nor was it particularly long, but it was enough to bring disaster. Henri's bulk was difficult enough to see in the fierceness of the driving ice even when she knew he was immediately in front of her ski tips, following a predetermined straight line. Once he turned, her concentration became split between his increasingly vague, ice-camouflaged shoulders and the black edge of the crevasse at her feet. Wisely, he went well past its point before turning left again. Who knew how wide the crevasse really was, beneath deceitful overhangs of ice? Ann followed him grimly, calculating what must be going through his mind and keeping an eye on the ground for any reappearance of telltale black lines on the white.

And then he was gone.

It was as simple and as sudden as that. One minute she knew where he was and the next she did not. One moment he was a ghostly loom in the dervish-dancing white murk in front of her. She looked down at the treacherous ground – it was the briefest of glances and no more. Then, when she looked up again, there was nothing but the white-out in front of her. She did the most natural thing. She speeded up, reasoning that he must simply have drawn ahead. There was no sign of him.

Chilled to the bone with horror, she stopped. 'Henri!' she called, knowing all too well that her voice would be muffled by the cloth over her lower face, that her cry would be whirled away on the banshee wind, that his ears would be deafened in any case by the drumming of his hood against them. But it was all she could think of to do.

'*HENRI!*' Her throat tore and she began to cough. Her chest hurt and for a moment it was as though she was drowning. Only her skis and sticks kept her from falling over. Time passed. She had no idea how much time. Her coughing eased. Her breathing returned to normal. Nothing else happened. The wind did not falter. The white-out did not ease. Henri did not return.

The full horror of her situation hit her then. She was lost and alone. Utterly so. He would not be able to find her, no one would unless they could track her distress beacon. The only people able to do that were on the ship. But no one from the ship was likely to be near; Henri was near but blind in the storm. She was on her own in every way. *Don't panic!* she thought. She actually said the words aloud, strictly, like an adult lecturing a frightened child.

But what was she to do? If she moved, there would be absolutely no chance of Henri finding her when he finally realised they had become separated and he began to retrace his steps. But even that simple manoeuvre would be impossible in these conditions. She had to act on the assumption that Henri was not coming to rescue her.

She had to *act*. To stand here for any length of time meant certain death. She forced herself to take a step forward. Then she stopped again. It was all very well to set off once more, but which way should she go? There was no sign of the crevasse which had caused them to deviate from their clifftop path, but was it still there, like the cliff edge itself had been, under a thin covering of treacherous ice? She drove down with her left ski pole and it went straight through the ground and wedged. She couldn't believe it. Never in her life had so much gone so badly wrong so fast. She was not superstitious – she had often mocked Nico for being so – but this looked like a very unlucky day to her. She jerked on the pole with all her strength, but whatever was holding it beneath the innocent-looking surface of the snow refused to release its grip.

Abruptly she found herself screaming at the top of her voice, swearing at the recalcitrant ski pole hysterically as she wrestled it from side to side with uncontrolled fury. Only when it snapped did she manage to bring herself under some kind of control. Even so, she threw the short end of it away and only when it swung back to hit her on the head did she remember that it was looped round her wrist. Calmer now that the first paroxysm was past, she took the loop off, laid the pole down, transferred the right-hand pole to replace it, crooked her right arm over her face to protect it from the driving ice, and set out on her own.

Once again, time ceased to have very much meaning. At first she was careful to follow some kind of plan in her head. She imagined the simple right angles of her path up the crevasse to a point where her ski pole no longer broke easily through the surface, then left at exactly ninety degrees for a couple of hundred yards – just in case – then exactly ninety degrees left again to take her back towards the original cliff edge. How far away from that cliff she was she had no way of knowing. How long she walked before she realised she had gone astray even from that simple plan she would never know either. Eventually, when the cliff did not materialise, she began to make conscious adjustments, thinking that if she went a little more to the left she must reach it.

But then, all too late, she realised that if she kept going left too soon, she would come round in a full circle long before she reached the cliff edge itself or, worse, strike off in a tangent before the circle was complete to go wandering back across that huge plain which had seemed so like the middle of the Lost World when she first saw it nearly twenty-four hours ago.

And by the time she had worked all that out, she was utterly lost indeed and even the simple plan of finding and following the cliff edge was far beyond anything within her power to do.

Sometime soon after this, she stopped thinking altogether, for thought was just another dangerous burden which might prove too much for her frail, increasingly weak body to carry.

Thought was replaced by sensation but soon, thank heaven, sensation began to grow dull and distant. She no longer felt the stabbing pain of the unremitting cold in her hands and feet nor the ache in ankles and knees as they threatened to seize up with every unrelenting step. She no longer heard the wild sound of the wind beyond the drumming of her hood against her ears. She no longer saw anything in the whirling dance of the ice grains before her eyes, except for the gathering darkness which she refused to recognise as death.

The first time that shivering overtook her she tried to keep moving, but after a step or two it proved to be impossible. Her mind was just active enough to learn from the experience and when she felt the second attack coming

on she had the sense to stop until it passed. Then she
stumbled forward once again into the arms of the waiting darkness.

The darkness achieved a form. Two forms. Two human
forms, shapeless and bundled. As soon as she saw them
she should have stopped but she was too far gone to do
so. She didn't actually recognise them as being real at all.
She continued to walk towards them and was not very
surprised when they simply disappeared. She had no idea
that they had fallen in beside her, invisible beyond the
icedrifts on her goggles. She was too numb to feel the
gentle pressure of their guiding hands, nor the strength of
their uplifting arms when her legs at last gave out.

Some time later the agony of warmth woke her and she
opened her eyes. A woman was watching her. A woman
with long gold hair and steady green eyes; a woman she
had never seen before in her life. 'Colin, she's awake,'
called the woman in English. A giant appeared in the
shadows behind the blonde. He was huge, shaggy, grey-
chinned. He seemed to be stooping so as not to bang his
head on the roof. He loomed towards her, eyes locking
with her own.

'What the . . .' Ann began to say. Then she stopped. The
gulf between where she was now and where she had
been when she was last awake was too much for her
to understand.

'Am I alive?' she asked. She really needed reassurance
on that point, for anything seemed possible.

And the giant laughed, a wild, joyous sound, full of
energy and indomitable humanity. 'Yes,' he answered. 'Yes,
you're alive.'

CHAPTER THIRTY-TWO

Day Twelve

Sunday, 30 May   23:00

Sir William Heritage waited until the camera was off him and then mopped his brow. The girl in make-up had warned him against doing this, but he was uncomfortably aware that he was streaming with perspiration. It was bad enough that he would look exhausted and old; it would be fatal to look sweatily nervous as well. *Face the Press* was a new programme with low ratings broadcast unfashionably late on a Sunday evening, but the chairman of Heritage Mariner had no illusions: everyone who mattered in his business world would be watching or taping this. As he patted the high dome of his forehead dry, he was careful to concentrate on what was going on opposite. John Stonor from the *Sketch* who had given him such a rough ride on Friday, and who had pilloried him and his company on Saturday, was laying out the groundwork of his case. Beside the dapper, slightly smug journalist sat Signor Verdi of CZP, his moustache bristling with carefully presented outrage. Beside them sat another man Sir William had yet to be introduced to.

Beside Sir William sat Maggie DaSilva and she leaned across now to warn him to put his handkerchief away as the interviewer turned back towards him, pulling a long strand of black hair neatly behind her ear, and the red light on camera three lit up again.

'So, Sir William, with the case going against Captain Mariner so strongly, it seems that Heritage Mariner is on the verge of joining that long line of companies currently going to the wall.' She had a soft, almost girlish voice which masked a fierce intelligence.

'That is not the case, Miss Lang. We will be appealing, of course.'

'But you have been directed to settle CZP's outstanding claim in the meantime.'

'That is correct, but the claim is only for the agreed price on a rather elderly vessel, and it will be met out of the insurance Heritage Mariner holds against such contingencies.'

'This is all bullshit,' John Stonor barged in loudly, all journalistic zeal. One of the attractions of the late-night slot was the amount of down-to-earth language that could be used. It gave the show an air of gritty spontaneity which was, in fact, carefully tailored. Stonor was a regular contributor and he knew the ropes well. 'Heritage Mariner is going down. How does it feel to be the captain of the *Titanic*, Sir William?'

'There is no truth in that allegation. As I told you on Friday—'

'Allow me, Sir William,' interjected Maggie. 'You know these allegations are baseless, Mr Stonor. This is nothing but dangerous rumour-mongering.'

'A properly financed company would have nothing to fear.'

'That is simply not the case.'

'There's no smoke without fire!'

'Of course there is, Mr Stonor. It's your job to blow smoke around, usually where there's no fire at all.'

'So you're saying that I haven't uncovered any true facts in this case?'

'In this aspect—'

'What about the terrorist connection?'

'I'll tell you about the terrorist connection,' roared Sir William, and the power of his voice silenced all of them. 'Our ships were searched from stem to stern on the strength of what Mr Stonor told us about the so-called eco-terrorists La Guerre Verte. We found nothing! Why am I not surprised, Mr Stonor? I have no doubt you made them up, just as you make up so many other stories to sell your papers when the truth is not exciting enough! The only real terrorists ever involved in this case were the PLO, and they became involved because Disposoco buried toxic waste in the Lebanese desert without permission, warning or due care and caused countless people to die horribly. Terrorists were the only people with the power to make Disposoco dig up their filth and move it, and they had to threaten the whole company board with execution to make them do it. If it came to a choice between dealing with these terrorists and that company, I know which I'd prefer!'

'It may be true that my colleagues from Disposoco have been forced to live with the threat of terrorist murder,' purred Signor Verdi in reply, 'but I deeply resent your implication.' Sir William opened his mouth to reply but Verdi plunged on, his voice rising to a shout that matched Sir William's own. 'You are the representative of a firm responsible for sinking an unfortunately dangerous cargo

in the middle of the busiest international passenger shipping lanes in the world, near to the most fertile fish breed-
ing grounds on earth, and dangerously close to the most
heavily populated seaboard in America. All this other talk
is persiflage and – what you call it – *hot air* to cover what
you have done! Not CZP, not Disposoco, but you. I tell you
this, Sir Heritage, the courts in London have found your
son guilty of this act. The courts in America will find him
guilty of this act. You will be paying for what has been
done to *Napoli* for the rest of your life and your children
will be paying for the rest of theirs. You are finished. They
are finished. Heritage Mariner is finished. And that is the
truth. *That* is what is real. Not this talk of terrorists.'

Sir William struggled to rise. He was so enraged, he
really feared he might strike the sneering little man, but
Maggie held him in check once more. 'These are more
wild allegations, Signor Verdi. Your threats, made in
public, are actionable and we will be consulting our—'

'More threats, Ms DaSilva?' Harriet Lang's question
stirred things further, as it was calculated to do; this was
excellent television, no matter what else it was. The presenter could see her ratings soaring already. This was the
kind of slanging match which just had to be plastered all
over the front pages of tomorrow's newspapers. She met
John Stonor's gaze and he gave her the ghost of a wink.
The points of her lips stirred in contented complicity.

'*Promises*, Ms Lang. Of more weight than groundless
speculation about actions in the American courts,' Maggie
DaSilva answered firmly, and walked straight into John
Stonor's trap.

John Stonor cultivated an image which he felt to be
appropriate to a successful tabloid newspaper man. He
presented himself as a bluff, honest, rough diamond,

incapable of being put off a just cause by any force under the sun. A pushy, dedicated, almost valiant, slightly common man of the people. Cocky, cheerful and by no means ever too clever for his own good. In fact he had a double first from Oxford where he had been counted one of the most arrogantly intellectual scholarship men of his day. His personal views of life and humanity were slightly to the right of Adolf Hitler and he was never happier than when he was manipulating people. He had perfected a party trick at Oxford which had stood him in very good stead ever since. Before sitting down to dinner, he would deliver to his host or hostess a series of half a dozen sealed envelopes with times written on the front. At the designated moments – which might be minutes or hours apart – the envelopes would be opened and on a piece of paper in each one would be a topic of conversation. As if by magic, it would inevitably be the topic of conversation currently under discussion. Without ever seeming to do so, John Stonor was always able to control what people thought and said.

And he had done it again tonight. Harriet Lang glanced down at her watch. Five minutes to go: John had promised to drop his bombshell now. Monday's front pages would be hers.

'Now that you mention the American courts, Ms Da-Silva,' he purred, 'let me introduce you to Vito Gordino of the American law firm which has just filed a suit against your client in New York on behalf of East Coast Fisheries Incorporated, claiming damages in excess of ten million dollars.'

Sir William erupted to his feet, far beyond even Maggie's control as he saw his life's work crumble before his eyes, all for a combination of chicanery and television ratings. He was too exhausted to see things in perspective and under more pressure than he had handled since the war in the Atlantic. And he was alone. The whole supportive family network of Heritage Mariner was overstretched and near failure when it needed to be at its strongest. Richard and Robin relied upon him absolutely, all the more so since Richard had been effectively convalescent, but they were always careful to ensure he had support. Until now. Richard and Robin were far away and beyond recall. Even Helen Dufour was on her way back to St Petersburg to negotiate shipping rights in and out of the newly liberalised port. Chance had dictated that he should be carrying the full weight all alone just when he needed most support.

He did not see it like that, of course. He saw it as a failure on his part. He thought he was letting them down just at the moment when they most relied upon him. Suddenly the impact of the realisation was like a breaking heart. He swayed there, apoplectic with rage, unable to form the words he needed to rebut the outrageous threat. Maggie DaSilva rose at his side. He saw her in the periphery of his vision, as though she was moving in slow motion.

He realised everyone in the studio was looking at him and distantly he wondered why. His gaze swept over the faces of his enemies: the smooth American, the smirking Italian, the smug newspaperman, the sleek presenter, the merciless camera. He was looking straight into the camera when the agony of his breaking heart clutched the left side of his chest again. He tried to grip his ribs to ease the pain behind them but somehow he couldn't move his left arm. A numbness swept down his whole side and the last thing he felt was his left leg collapsing.

In full view of the camera, before the sleepy editor could cut away, the fine, distinguished, widely beloved old man collapsed under the weight of a massive heart attack.

He would have died there and then if anyone other than Maggie DaSilva had been beside him. She was in action at once, rolling him over and loosening his tie. He was wearing a starched collar and she wrestled with the gold-coloured stud, swearing quietly under her breath. Fortunately, he was a slim man and she was able to get her fingers between the cotton collar and the loose skin of his neck. A wild wrench tore the whole lot wide as far as the crisp white curls on his chest. Her eyes had been as busy as her hands. He was utterly white. His closed eyes were almost blue behind their lids. She pulled his jaw down and moved his tongue. 'Send for an ambulance at once,' she snapped at the stricken group around her. Then, still on camera, she leaned forward to begin mouth-to-mouth resuscitation.

Harriet Lang, shaken but still professional, closed down the show. She kept her comments to a minimum, but there was nothing she could do to minimise the impact of what she realised with sickening clarity would be very damaging indeed. When she and John Stonor had been setting the programme up it had seemed like brilliant television: the fearless exposure of the uncaring side of big business. It was all too obvious now that what they had actually broadcast was the calculated, merciless hounding of a defence-less old man to the edge of death on air. The whole country would be all too well aware that, as she wound things up in close-up, a grim battle to keep her victim alive was going on behind the camera. The effect was finally underlined by the arrival of the company first aid crew in the last second of the broadcast. Behind her

closing platitudes, their urgent directions went out to the
watching nation.

'. . . and next week, the problem of pollution in our
lakes and rivers . . .'

'. . . *Leave him to us now, miss. Get the oxygen in here
quickly, Brian . . .*'

'We'll have Perigrine Prior, Environmental Editor of the
Guardian and representatives from Greenpeace and
Friends of the Earth. Facing them will be . . .'

'. . . *Full pressure now, John. Yes, he's breathing. Got a
pulse? Got the stretcher? Good . . .*'

'. . . So we'll see you then, when we'll all Face the Press
together. Good night.'

'. . . *Lift! That's good. Let's get moving while he's still
got a chance . . .*'

Maggie ran down the corridor beside the stretcher. She
had kicked off her high heels and was running in her
stockinged feet but even so she was having difficulty in
keeping up. Sir William's face still looked terrifyingly
pale, but perhaps it was just in contrast with the black
triangular mouthpiece attached to the oxygen cylinder
lying beside him. Her mind was racing, trying to work
out all the best courses of action and decide which one
she should take first. She was not in shock yet but she
knew it would only be a question of time before she was.
The taste of his mouthwash filled her mouth and the
intimacy of the taste was dangerously poignant.

They stood in silence while the lift whispered downwards. The only sound in the little car was the mechanical
hiss of Sir William's laboured breathing. They came out
into the lobby at a rush, but there the forward impulse of
events came to an abrupt halt. There was no ambulance.

While they waited in the quiet lobby, the first aid team
kept Sir William going, but their body language and the
sounds they made warned Maggie that they were not happy
about the delay. The slim barrister started to shake, just
as she had feared she would, and soon she had to go and
find a chair. All she could think of was the look on Robin's
face when the news got through to *Atropos*. And on Helen
Dufour's face when she landed at St Petersburg to find the
news waiting for her there. Helen and Sir William were
supposed to be thinking of marriage. The French senior
executive would be lucky not to be going to a funeral
instead.

The lift doors opened and a group of people got out.
Maggie glanced up and down again, her dark cheeks burning with rage. It was the group of men and women who
had done this. John Stonor and Harriet Lang, quietly, side
by side, their faces slightly stunned. Signor Verdi had
picked up his sidekick from the trial, the tall lugubrious
Signor Nero of Disposoco. The American lawyer Gordino
walked between them, in intense conversation with them.
She knew what he would be saying well enough: *It's bad
luck the old guy fell ill but remember, your suit is with
his company. Don't weaken; let's go for it.*

She looked away from them through the glass doors.
Out in the dark street, a bright ambulance pulled up. Its
rear section swung wide and two white-coated men hurried
towards the building. The doors opened and the falling
whine of its siren followed the paramedics into reception
like the cry of a dying wolf. Maggie was swept up into
the bustle of things again as they relieved the first aid
men and began rattling off questions to her. Questions she
could not answer for the most part, about medical history
and allergies. Doggedly determined he would not go to

the emergency unit alone, she followed out into the street.

A small crowd had gathered, even at this time on a Sunday night. Maggie hardly noticed them as she rushed forward with Sir William, but something about the way they stirred made her stop and look back. The crowd had reacted to the fact that John Stonor and Harriet Lang had come out. They were obviously famous enough to make the little crowd react in a way that the sight of a dying man on a stretcher had not. Maggie felt like screaming at them. Didn't they care about anything important? She was dangerously close to tears. A motorcycle pulled up behind the line of people. Its pillion passenger swung off and began to walk forward. The driver sat hunched forward with both feet firmly on the ground, helmet and filter mask in profile against the slick brightness of the wet street.

Out through the door behind the television personalities came the other three. The pillion passenger began to push through the little crowd. Maggie's attention switched back to Sir William as the ambulancemen slid his stretcher up into the back of their vehicle.

Everything seemed to Maggie to be happening very slowly now – she was deeply in the grip of shock. The extra time everything was taking gave the images a better opportunity to burn themselves into her memory, but she hardly felt a part of the scene at all.

The pillion passenger walked deliberately across the pavement. There was nothing about the figure to attract her attention except for the sinister anonymity of the black leather and the visored helmet, but something made her look for just that little bit longer. So she, perhaps she alone, saw the right arm come up until the machine-pistol was at shoulder height. John Stonor and Harriet Lang had vanished as soon as they saw the waiting crowd. The three men behind them were hurrying down the steps and were so close to the black-clad figure they could almost have touched the weapon.

Had Maggie been less deep in shock already, she would have acted far more quickly – and would probably have got herself killed in the process. As it was, her first action was to push Sir William's stretcher further into the ambulance as though, having got him this far, he was now her responsibility. Then she opened her mouth and sucked in breath to yell a warning. But her cry of '*Look out!*' was lost in the stutter of the gun and the throaty roar of the revving motorcycle.

The three men danced backwards and their attacker stepped forward after them, still firing. Then the man turned, the smoking gun down at arm's length by his side, and began to walk back. The little crowd beside the ambulance scattered in all directions. A pair of hands grasped Maggie and jerked her up into the ambulance. The doors slammed shut. There was utter silence except for Sir William's wheezing breath and the roar of the motorcycle which rose and began to fade.

'Get us out of here!' yelled someone in the front of the ambulance.

'No! Wait,' yelled the man holding Maggie. 'There's work to do out there!'

He hit the door and dropped to the pavement. Maggie went with him. The motorcycle had gone as though it had never existed, and three almost child-sized figures lay hunched on the steps in the light from the lobby just behind them.

It was as though the blood had always been there and the sad little bodies had simply fallen into it. The ambulanceman reached Verdi first, turning the man over gently, as though he was actually a child. The blue eyes were protuberant and fiercely fixed. The moustache bristled with indignation. There was nothing left of the face below it.

'*Aiuto!*' whispered a voice, and Maggie was on her knees at once, paddling through the blood, trying to work out which of the other two victims might have spoken. It was Signor Nero. She cradled his head in her lap, utterly indifferent to the blood which marked the front of her midnight-blue suit like tar. It was hot against her shock-chilled skin. His soft, sad brown eyes looked up at her out of bruise-dark rings. His lips writhed as he tried to form words. She leaned down to hear. Far, far away, the ambulanceman said to someone, 'No, the other guy's dead as well.'

Nero's breath smelt of garlic and wine and something else she couldn't quite put her finger on. The Italian coughed convulsively and the strange smell got stronger. Of course, it was the smell of blood.

'They kill even the lawyer?' he asked, his voice light as down on the wind.

She nodded, not trusting herself to speak. How recently and how bitterly she had hated this poor man. She felt more soiled by the memory than by his lifeblood.

'The lawyer too.' His voice was infinitely sad.

She looked up. The ambulancemen were standing, watching her. They all knew the wounds were fatal.

'They say,' continued the Disposoco man, his face working to form the words, as though they were the most important thing in the world, and Maggie suddenly, sickeningly knew that 'they' were the murderers on the motorbike. 'They say the case is closed. *In's'allah*. You understand. It is message for us all from the P.L.O. It is their promise from so long ago. *In's'allah*. The case is closed.'

CHAPTER THIRTY-THREE

Day Thirteen

Monday, 31 May   10:00

The three figures came over the low ridge and paused, looking down at the scene of bustling activity below. They all wore thick cold-weather gear of Eskimo manufacture and except for their size they seemed almost identical. The right-hand figure was the tallest, very nearly a giant, in whose mittened hands the ski poles looked like toothpicks. The harness round the immense barrel of his chest reached back to a fully packed sled which, seemingly, he would have had little trouble carrying under one arm. Inuit are a small-framed folk; the clothes he wore would have dressed two of them. Or both of the slighter figures beside him. The left-hand figure stood reed-straight, up past his shoulder, and the central figure, every bit as tall in fact, seemed shorter because it drooped with fatigue. Even so, it was the central figure which moved first, pulling down the covering over the lower part of its face to say, 'Here we are. *Atropos*. Home sweet home.' The noise coming up the wide ice valley towards them was loud enough to require quite a shout, but even so there was no mistaking the voice of Ann Cable.

'I would never have dreamed this could be possible, would you, Colin?' called the second, slighter figure.

The giant simply shook his head, looking down at the hive of activity around the beached ship. Their current position effectively put them at the highest point of the slope of ice which, further down, became Robin's slipway. The height was just enough to give them a panoramic view reaching even over the high bridgehouse with its tall thrust of funnel to reveal the bustle on the forward deck. Here there seemed to be a gaping hole as though a military shell had landed between and immediately forward of the split windlass to leave a rough-edged, round, dark crater. More lengthy inspection, however, revealed that what seemed to be a hole was in fact a dark section of decking, from which a circular object had recently been lifted. No, not circular; bladed. But its fixings had been circular. And the object itself was being raised now, like some massive brass-coloured three-leafed clover. It was being pulled erect by the power of a box-shaped gantry sitting far forward on the deck, seeming to squat like a weightlifter above it.

Clustered in another circle round it stood a group of people whose minuscule size seemed to emphasise the scale of the propeller above them. Five of them standing in a column on each other's shoulders might have reached towards the top of it. Five like the giant looking down on the scene – six or seven of the people actually involved in it. No sooner was the propeller upright than the gantry began to grind back along the deck. Its movement was so slow at first that only the echoing sound of it gave notice that it was moving.

Five hundred feet nearer, the activity was less easy to characterise. A large group of people, arranged on several

levels up a series of makeshift scaffolds, seemed to be
freeing the distorted brother of the propeller on the forward deck. There was no gantry here to squat like a titan
and raise or lower the massive weight. Instead, a strong
hawser, attached at both ends to the capstans on the poop
deck and looped round the hollow-centred propeller, was
lowering it carefully to the ice. The noise was deafening
– the roar of fire from oxyacetylene torches, the bellows
roar of turning capstans, the twang of overstrained ropes.
The insistent, overpowering tintinnabulation of metal
against metal. It sounded like some monstrous blacksmith's forge.

Even Ann, who knew what Robin's plans of action had
been, was astounded by the scale of what was going on.
She could hardly guess what its effect upon Colin and
Kate Ross was, especially as her rescuers had been alone
on their drift ice station on the western coast of this
iceberg for the better part of six months; ever since the
massive craft of ice had been swept out of the Arctic
Ocean and into the Davis Strait, in fact. She had no desire
to linger here, however. She was burning to find out what
had happened to Henri. The unexpected intimacy of their
experience had disturbed her in many ways and the thought
that he might not have made it back alive was incredibly
painful to her. Colin and Kate would have been much
happier simply to have radioed news of her rescue and
given her a couple of days' rest to recover, but something
had made her beg them to bring her back as quickly as
humanly possible. They had not been loath to fall in with
her plans; the thought of doing some socialising was very
welcome to them, even under these rather extreme circumstances.

The three of them rocked forward over the crest of the

slope together and began to slide easily down towards the nearest group of crew members. It was Chief Lethbridge who saw them first. Ann, wearing a pair of Kate's Polaroid sun goggles, saw him much more clearly than he could see her and she was able to discern the fleeting shadows of surprise, shock and suspicion with which he viewed three apparent strangers. She saw him glance up, see them outlined against the bright sky and frown. She saw him check around his men and make sure none of them had strayed up here. She saw him look back up and realise that they were wearing outfits unlike anything *Atropos* could supply. She saw him speak rapidly to a man beside him and then jerk his walkie-talkie up to his lips. As he talked urgently into it, the blacksmith's chorus of sound died down around him so that only the slow grinding from the forward deck remained on the air. It was at this point that she regretted her insistence upon silence; upon this highly dramatic entrance which was already designed in her own mind to form the climax of her next book.

'Suspicious bunch,' growled Colin Ross. Ann still could not get used to the gravelly depth of his speaking voice. He slurred his 'S's slightly, his accent whispering distantly of Scottish ancestry in a way that Richard Mariner's did not.

'Do you think something might have happened?' No more could Ann get used to Kate's calm English tones, more suited to an Oxford professor's garden party than a wilderness of ice.

'They've lost two crew members so far,' said Ann. 'For all I know, they think they've lost two more within the last two days. On top of that, there's someone somewhere aboard who may be trying to kill them all.' Her voice sounded suddenly worried and uncertain even in her own ears. 'That might well make them jumpy.' As she said it, the spectre of Henri's possible death reared up before her again. *Is he dead?* she asked herself once more. *And, if so, what blame do I bear for it?*

Two familiar figures loomed atop the rapidly nearing poop and suddenly Ann found herself tearing back the hood and pulling down the goggles so that they could see her face. 'Henri!' she called exultantly. 'Robin! It's me. I'm all right!'

The silence disappeared at once and the three of them found themselves skiing down into an overwhelming thunder of cheering. A thunder which abruptly came from the ice as well as the assembled throats. The cliff slopes on either hand vibrated and the slope heaved beneath them. Ann went sprawling and the others, more sure-footed than she, had difficulty staying erect. The real thunder silenced the welcome, for it was unexpected and utterly unnerving, like a minor earthquake. Everyone looked up in sudden fear at the glistening upper slopes, but apart from some clouds of crystals which rapidly formed a rainbow above them, nothing else happened. Robin and Henri had disappeared – onto the main deck, no doubt, to see whether the tremor had affected the mobile gantry or its load.

'Icebergs don't have earthquakes, do they?' Ann asked Kate as she struggled to get back onto her feet.

'No. That's just this berg getting to grips with the ice barrier,' said the English woman. Her voice was calm, unruffled, but the white forehead was frowning slightly with concern. 'It'll get worse until one piece of ice decides to give way. Nothing to be concerned about normally, but it looks as though your friends had better get a move on or they *will* have something to worry about.' Colin's massive hand fastened round Ann's upper arm and brought her back to her feet as Robin and Henri reappeared on the after deck and the cheering, mutedly, was resumed.

They already did have something to worry about. It took Ann no time at all to realise that the grim mood, already darkening even before she and Henri went up onto the ice, had darkened further. The welcome she received was joyous; Henri especially seemed nearly tipsy with relief. But Robin was almost perfunctory in her welcome to her miraculously living friend and her quiet rescuers. It was clear that she had something on her mind. 'What is it?' asked Ann as soon as she decently could. 'What's the matter – apart from the obvious?' Her glance took in the ice cliffs and the whole situation of the ship.

'Dead fish. A whole lot of them have just come up to the surface.'

They were on the deck, walking forward past the port side of the bridgehouse. Colin and Kate Ross were just behind them with Henri also in tow. Tea had been sent for and would catch up with them wherever they were. Robin seemed to be drawn and almost febrile with a combination of fatigue and driving power. At first offended by the curtness of the welcome afforded by her captain, Ann was rapidly beginning to see how dangerous Robin thought their situation was; she could hardly have timed her resurrection less well. With the damaged propeller off and the spare one still grinding back up the deck at a snail's place, *Atropos* was highly vulnerable. Another shock like the last one – and Kate had said there would be more, and worse ones – and the ship could all too easily be shaken loose. Ann could imagine the horror of parting lines whipping left and right, of the collapsing galleries astern with men thrown hither and thither as *Atropos* began to slide into the water. They would never get her fixed in time if that happened. They would all have to follow Colin and Kate onto the ice and watch their ship get crushed to death – assuming they themselves survived further violent contact between the barrier and the berg. And then there was the possibility that in the maelstrom one or more canisters of their lethal cargo might burst.

That thought gave an added shock of horror to what Ann saw when Robin took her and her rescuers past the slowly-moving gantry with its giant brass pendulum and past the uncovered circle on the deck onto the forepeak. The prow of the ship, unnaturally deep in the black water because of the angle of the rest of the hull, was surrounded by dead fish floating belly up.

'What killed them?' The rumble of Colin Ross's basso profundo held a distant hint of anger and disgust.

'We have no idea,' answered Robin wearily. 'And we haven't even had a chance to take a sample yet. But I'd give a lot to know.'

'We could tell you,' said Kate, her voice as disapproving as Colin's. 'This sort of thing is in our area of expertise. But we haven't got our equipment.'

'Let's get some up for testing pretty quickly,' suggested Colin. He looked up at the blue sky. 'It won't be long until a gull notices something. Then they'll all be gone in minutes.'

'According to my equipment,' said Henri suddenly, his voice speculative, 'there's radioactivity out here.'

'*What?*' They all swung round to confront him, but

Robin asked the question, her face pale with shock, her eyes wide and dark. 'How do you know? When did you find out?'

'Earlier this morning. I was doing a routine check when I noticed the fish.'

'Why on earth didn't you tell me at once?' snapped Robin.

'It's not much and it's not the cargo.' His voice was flat. His eyes travelled from Robin to Ann and back again. 'There's nothing registering anywhere in any of the holds. Just out here. I think it's the ice.'

'Is that possible?' Ann asked Colin. She had come to respect the opinion of the Rosses on anything to do with ice very quickly indeed.

'Anything is possible,' answered Colin. His face was blank. His gaze lighted on the tall Canadian and it was as cold as the slopes around them. 'Are you saying there is enough radioactivity here to explain all these dead fish?'

'No, I'm not.'

'So I still want a sample so I can find out what did kill them.'

Surprisingly, a sullen silence fell then, as though Henri resented the big man's unthinking assumption of authority. Perhaps he did, thought Ann with a shock. Henri certainly wasn't about to go scurrying off to find a bucket. She suddenly felt deflated, as though the excitement of her arrival back had caused a negative reaction somehow. Or perhaps her brief adventure away and especially her time with Colin and Kate had given her a new perspective on *Atropos* and what was happening aboard her.

The impasse was solved by the arrival of the tea tray. They each took a steaming mug. As the steward turned to go, Robin said, 'Come back with a bucket and some rope at the double, would you, please?'

'Yes, Captain.' The young steward hurried off.

As he vanished back into the bridgehouse, the air was filled with thunder once again.

Robin flinched, looking up at the slopes and then down along her deck to her all too fragile docking lines, but this was no icequake.

With astonishing abruptness, the five of them found themselves at the heart of an overpowering blizzard of screaming white bodies. Thousands of seabirds, a flock seemingly ten times larger than the one which had swept past them in the lifeboat, plunged down out of the sky. The air shook with them and the sea exploded as though an eruption had taken place just below the surface. The five of them turned and ran back towards the bridgehouse, cups of tea flying right and left.

Before they had taken half a dozen steps they were out of the babel of birds. Immediately they turned and looked back. The shrieking cloud of whirring wings and flashing yellow razor bills was settling clear of the forecastle head. The ravenous creatures were plunging down below, tearing the shoal of dead fish to ribbons, grabbing and gulping in a frenzy. The spectacle accorded strangely with the savagery of the setting and added to the sombre atmosphere. They stood silently – any sound would have been lost in any case – and watched. It was only when the young steward came panting up to his captain with a now redundant bucket that the grim spell was broken.

'So much for samples,' said Henri flatly and turned to walk away.

Robin had too much to do to linger and so it was left to Ann to take her guests down to the galley and arrange replacement tea and a warmer welcome. 'They aren't usually so abrupt,' she found herself apologising. 'But you can see what stress we're all under.'

Colin Ross did not suffer fools gladly. He was a man of strong and abrupt character and it was every bit as uncompromising as his profile. Years of work on the ice had chiselled great valleys into the flesh of his face while tanning his skin like leather. His mouth turned down at the corners and the lines which fell from the peaks of his high cheekbones to the outer edges of his square chin paralleled those which plunged from his lip corners. He had had enough of this ship and her crew very soon indeed. He was fascinated to look around it and to meet some of the people Ann had told him about, but Kate and he were neither needed nor particularly welcome here. If the situation should change to demand that the crew go up onto the ice, then the two glaciologists would have a function and a reason for staying. As the current aim was to get *Atropos* and all aboard her as far away from the berg as possible, they had none. What they did have was a camp and important work across the other side of the iceberg. And, suddenly, a reason to do an unexpected series of tests on their ice home to check whether LeFever was right and the iceberg was indeed radioactive.

After they had finished their tea, he was restless to be gone. His mood had more of an effect on Ann than it did on Kate. Ann did not know him well enough to make allowances for his almost rude demeanour. Kate knew his whole manner would undergo an apparently miraculous change the moment his interest or enthusiasm became engaged. She saw all too clearly that their expertise might well be needed yet. She therefore insisted on a conducted tour of the ship and Ann was glad to grant her wish.

They went back up onto the deck just in time to see the gantry arrive back at its furthest point, immediately in front of the bridgehouse. The cab at the front of the folded swan's neck of the crane arm slowly began to move. The propeller was hanging from beneath it. They watched, fascinated, as the cab with its massive burden inched out towards the port side. Such was the weight of the propeller that the whole hull began to tilt beneath their feet and the hawsers holding the ship in place began to hum and spit. 'Stop!' called Colin automatically, but his voice was drowned by a blast on the ship's siren. This was clearly a signal and the crane did indeed stop. Slowly, the ship righted herself and Colin's dark brooding began to lighten. 'She's shifting the ballast to compensate,' he said to himself. Then he swung round to face Ann. 'She's quite an officer, this captain of yours. Mariner. I know the name . . .'

As *Atropos* came upright, Ann was happy enough to tell Colin all she knew about the Mariners. This was more than enough to cover the second extension of the crane and this time the propeller cleared the deck rails and began to disappear over the side. Colin kept his eye on it and seemed to be growing tenser and tenser the further it was lowered. But just as Ann became certain that he was no longer listening to her at all, the siren signalled stop once more. The telltale sound of ballast shifting back again completed the manoeuvre. The weight of the propeller pulled the ship over until the blades settled on the ice. The slow paying out of the crane's cable relieved the ship of its weight and allowed *Atropos* to right herself.

In the still silence after the manoeuvre was completed, Colin, Kate and Ann crossed over to the port side and looked down. The propeller sat safely on the ice with teams of men releasing it from the forward crane and more teams ready to reattach it to the falls of the stores crane on the poop deck. 'She's really thought this through,' observed Colin, and this time there was no disguising the admiration in his voice. Ann caught a glowing glance from Kate which turned into a dazzling smile when their eyes met.

The moment was interrupted in the most unexpected way. The birds, having devoured the dead fish, had mostly disappeared again, but not all had gone. Like scouts left behind by an army, one or two birds lingered, greedy eyes on the lookout for food, tempted by the occasional crust or biscuit from the workers. Those that stayed used the cliff as a kind of eyrie, for it was not as absolute a precipice as it seemed and there were ledges and crannies in plenty for the birds. Just as Colin, Kate and Ann turned away from their contemplation of the propeller, a little feathered body dropped at their feet. It didn't fly in and it didn't land. It fell out of the sky as though it had been shot and hit the green metal of the deck with enough force to bounce. They automatically looked up as though, having snowed a feeding frenzy, it might now start raining corpses. But no. This small body was all there was to see. Colin bent down from his tremendous height and scooped it tenderly into his right hand. He straightened slowly and held it up close to his eyes as though he was short-sighted. 'It's a little auk,' he rumbled. His left hand, rendered almost club-like by the heavy mitten, stroked the little corpse with infinite compassion.

'I didn't know they just dropped dead like that,' said Ann, shocked anew by the relentless savagery of the place.

'They don't,' said Kate. 'Or, if they do, it's very rare.'

'I don't think this little chap died a natural death,' said Colin. 'Look.'

He held the corpse out for Kate's inspection but Ann craned over to see what was to be seen. At first she could make out nothing wrong. Then, as Kate stripped off her mitten and moved the floppy little head on its rubbery, apparently boneless neck, the American journalist saw something which her society had made all too common-place among humans, though it was the first time she had ever seen it in the animal world. The irises of the dead bird's eyes were a bright yellow gold in colour and they glinted in the late morning sunshine like coins. The pupils at their centres were so tiny as to be almost invisible, shrunk to minuscule black dots smaller than pinheads. Ann caught her breath, shook her head and looked again, more closely. 'Well, I'll be damned,' she said.

Colin and Kate Ross exchanged long looks which were suddenly full of suspicion. They glanced around the deck as though someone might overhear their thoughts and add them to a hit list for murder. Ann noticed nothing of this, so struck was she by the state of the dead bird's eyes.

'It looks to me,' she said, 'as though the poor little bastard OD'd.'

Colin placed the tiny corpse in the pocket of his jacket. 'I'll test it when we get back to camp,' he said, his voice as deadpan as his face.

Ann thought he couldn't have understood her American slang. 'OD'd,' she persisted. 'It looks as though he died of a drug overdose.'

'I think the fish died of the overdose,' said Colin Ross quietly, 'and the bird died from eating the fish.'

The three of them looked up at the cliff face and there was not a gull in sight. Ann opened her mouth to say more, but before she could speak, the ship began to tilt once again and the same process by which the propellor had been lowered over the side swung it back aboard hanging from the stores crane behind the bridgehouse. With incredibly delicate precision, the hand at the crane's controls brought the weight exactly onto the line of balance midships, then lowered it out beyond the stern rail so that it could be attached to the main shaft. Once it was resting in place, ready to be skewered and properly attached, Robin called a break for lunch and everyone piled back aboard.

'You know it's a Bank Holiday in England today? Nobody works.'

'Thanks, lady, that's really heartening news,' Lethbridge growled.

Kate Ross stood on the middle level of the scaffolding. The thick ring at the centre of the propellor was being eased over the end of the main shaft. It was an operation requiring the utmost skill and total accuracy. The rods and gears of the variable pitch mechanism, which came up through the centre of the shaft, had to meet up with their counterparts at the bases of the propeller blades projecting in through the circumference of the ring. Each line and cog had to be attached and tested before the big boss was screwed back into place and the ship was relaunched. Kate had quickly decided that Chief Lethbridge and she were two of a kind. She had a dry sense of humour which became more robust under pressure. So did Lethbridge. She liked to use her tongue while concentrating on what her hands were doing. So did he. His expertise was being exercised on making good the engineering components before him. Hers was being exercised on him.

Colin had pointed out with malice aforethought that one of her doctorates was actually in human biology – though she concentrated on sea creatures nowadays – and she was

an able and gifted physician. Ann had backed him up
enthusiastically, innocently, unaware of the deeper dealings
he was engaged in. So instead of discussing with the
captain in her quarters the problems of drugged fish and
dead birds, Kate was checking the scalded flesh of the
chief engineer's face as he was putting the propeller in
place. It was an unhandy arrangement and hardly suited
to the time or the circumstances but both of them were
willing to put up with it. In fact it allowed Lethbridge to
concentrate more fiercely on the task in hand. The simple
act of pulling back his hood in the chill air gave unexpected relief to his scalded cheeks. Kate had not come
equipped with any medicine or ointments of course, but
she was more able than Robin or Henri to make best use
of the medical supplies aboard *Atropos*.

'Yes. There has been trouble with drugs aboard.' Robin's
voice was bitter and she was trying her hardest not to let
this importunate stranger know how much of her irritation
was directed at him. She knew well enough that her presence at the locating of the propeller would be little more
than politic, but she was poignantly aware of how important politics could be on occasion. Lethbridge and his team
would certainly be the better for her presence. They would
work faster. She very much wanted to be afloat and under
power tonight. The icequake this morning had emphasised
all too strongly the danger of staying here another night.

But there was no doubting Colin Ross's genuine concern
nor the fact that he was right to be worried. At the least
conventional moment, just when she needed to concentrate
all her faculties, all her powers of command, on getting
the propeller in place and the hull back in the water, she
was being pulled aside and forced to confront a situation

she had hoped to sweep under the carpet until a less critical moment.

She began to explain the problems which had revolved around Captain Black and Reynolds. Then she added for good measure the problems they had also had with La Guerre Verte. He listened with patience and then nodded. 'No matter where they came from or why they were aboard, it looks as though your drugs were jettisoned last night.'

'I agree. I just can't work out who or why.'

'Either it's someone trying to inflate the market or it's someone who has something of his own to hide. Like your eco-terrorist.'

'Or someone getting rid of a job lot,' said Robin, but she was not really concentrating on the conversation.

Colin knew this and understood why. He had been impressed with the way she had thought things through this morning and he was well aware that she had pressing concerns. Where he might have been irritated to be ignored by a lesser person, Robin's preoccupation was not in the slightest offensive to him. He was all too aware that such a preoccupation was one of his own greatest faults. 'I agree,' he said. 'Your first priority must be to get the hull afloat. You can hold an enquiry into the murder of a couple of hundred fish and birds later.'

'I've held one full enquiry already and searched the ship from stem to stern. We don't have the time to do more at the moment. The American woman John Hennessy seems to have been on *Clotho*.' She paused, and shivered with revulsion at the thought of what Richard had had to deal with. Then she went on, 'But she's not there any more. Any confederate she has aboard here is too well disguised for us to find. And in any case, it would seem pretty stupid for an eco-terrorist to sink a shipload of nuclear waste in the middle of the ocean.'

'So why bring bombs aboard?'

'The only reason I can think of is that the ships would sink in their harbours.'

'Then why tell everybody?'

'As far as I can judge, the story broke the day *after* we were due in dock.'

'I see. But that was days ago and in the meantime nothing has happened. So even if there is someone aboard, they haven't set the bomb after all. That's good thinking.'

'I'm relieved you see things so clearly from my point of view,' she said dryly.

He grinned. It was not a particularly ingratiating grin.

'And drugs in the water are less important than drugs still aboard,' she admitted. 'So I'll worry about the identity and motivation of whoever threw a fortune into the ocean later.' She pulled herself to her feet. 'Please don't think I'm not grateful, Dr Ross, both for bringing Ann back and for bringing this to my attention—'

Her words were drowned beneath a sudden barrage of heavy artillery which seemed to open in the near distance and roar overhead. The whole ship shook and Robin was hurled back into her chair. As soon as it had started it was finished, leaving nothing behind but its echo reverberating between the ice cliffs.

The two of them were in motion at once. Robin pushed through the door and Colin Ross followed. Side by side they reached the after rail on the poop deck and looked down on the scaffolding. Robin expected to see a repeat of the wreckage which had so nearly crippled Richard, but all there was for her to see was a lot of white faces. 'It won't take another one like that, Captain,' said Lethbridge.

The fact that he had said it so loudly in front of the rest
of the crew emphasised the depth of his concern.

'I know, Chief. Let's get the screw in place and get
under way, shall we?'

'Just as soon as we can, Captain.'

'Dr Ross, I think that's all you can do for us at the
moment; we've quite a bit to sort out for ourselves.' Robin
had finally exhausted the meagre store of courtesy she
had left.

'I see that very clearly, Captain. I'll just pop down to
avail myself of an isolation vessel from Mr LeFever so
that I can preserve my dead bird, then I'll take my leave,
if I may. I have a job to do on the far side of the berg
and a camp that won't stand up to these quakes too well.
But remember, we're only an hour away if you need us.'

Kate and Colin Ross turned back at the crest of the slipway
and worked their way down the side of the ice shelf under
the dizzying reach of the cliff. There was a beach here
which seemed to be made of slightly opaque crystal. It
was covered with rocks and boulders, rock pools and sand
drifts like any other beach, but it all seemed to be made
of glass in greater or less densities of opacity and dirt.
All up the cliff foot behind them, bands of earth debris
went back into the ice face itself. When picking up the
isolation vessel for his dead bird, Colin had taken a Geiger
counter and promised to warn the ship if they found any
above-average radioactivity. It ticked away sinisterly every
time the huge glaciologist turned it on, confirming LeFever's findings that the ice was mildly radioactive, in this
bay at least. But there was nothing strong enough to be
dangerous. It might have been a leak from the ship, but
then again it could have been radon from the granite dust

in the dark, dirty debris all around them.

In thoughtful silence, they returned to the crest at the top of the slipway. Here they turned and looked back down at the bustle around *Atropos* for the last time. High on the poop, beside the jack staff with its drooping flag, stood the lone figure of Ann Cable. Sun glinted on the lenses of the binoculars which had followed every step of their little exploration. Kate made an elaborate pantomime gesture, *Nothing to worry about*. Colin raised his right hand in a farewell salute. Then the two of them turned and moved away. Almost immediately they fell into a fast, economical cross-country skier's lope which pulled them over the ice at better than five miles an hour. Neither of them said anything. Both of them were worried about *Atropos* and the people they were leaving aboard her.

Ann Cable lowered the binoculars as soon as the two black figures were gone. No sooner had she done so than Henri joined her at the rail. 'I was never so glad of anything,' he said quietly.

'What?'

'When I realised it was you coming back from the dead with them.'

'They saved my life, Henri. I was dead.'

'Who are they?'

She explained to him what she could remember of the conversations the three of them had had during last night and this morning. The Rosses were marine glaciologists. Experts in the formation and movements of sea ice, including icebergs. Colin was the ice man; Kate was the expert in all the life forms which inhabited the ice and the water surrounding it. They worked in the field for a whole range of business and academic enterprises, as well as for a

government or two. They had a camp on the far side of
the berg from which they had been charting its condition
and progress ever since it had been swept out of the Arctic
Ocean and into the Davis Strait. It was one of the biggest
icebergs to enter the North Atlantic this century, they had
told her; and it was their current project to estimate
whether or not it would be feasible to ride it down into
the shipping lanes and then control its movement further
south. Both Colin and Kate were enthusiastic exponents
of the proposition that icebergs might, some day in the
future, be moved across the oceans and delivered to
drought-stricken areas; they represented hundreds of millions of gallons of fresh water, all of it ice-cold.

'They've both done work at the South Pole too,' Ann
concluded. 'At first it seemed that moving bergs up into
the South Atlantic might be better – much less shipping,
apparently, and far less land. But the winds are too powerful. You'd have to pull a berg three or four times round
the world while you were getting it up from the Antarctic
to South Georgia, say, or New Zealand.' Her voice tailed
away and the pair of them were silent, entranced by the
vision.

They stood on the poop through the rest of that long
afternoon and watched as the articulated blade roots were
painstakingly connected to the variable pitch mechanism.
They joined in the cheering as the great brass blades varied
their angles according to the dictates from the bridge.
They saw the huge boss being rolled into position and
lifted so that it could be screwed back over the giant
thread at the end of the shaft. As the sun began to settle
and the long silken twilight whispered into place, they
watched in wonder as the turbine was started and the
propeller was engaged. With all the care in the world,

the propeller itself was tested. Everyone was aware that the
system was designed to meet hundred of tons of water
resistance; rotating the propeller in the air was extremely
risky. Yet test it they did, and it turned.

At 20:00 hours, a little before full dark, Ann and Henri
were on the bridge with Robin and her watch officers. On
the deck stood the four teams whose function it was to
release the lines little by little so that *Atropos* could be
eased down the slipway and into the water. There was an
air of not very well-concealed jubilation. There had been
no more major icequakes, though they had heard a distant
rumbling on the way up from the deck. Everything seemed
well in place for a second launching of the freighter. Robin
was in radio contact with *Clotho*, or rather Harry Stone
was relaying her messages to Bill Christian who was passing them to Richard, strangely remote on *Atropos*'s sister
ship beyond the barrier to the south. But Robin was too
full of her own concerns to enquire after her husband's
worries. Joe Edwards had driven the gantry on the forward
deck and Errol had operated the stores crane, so it was
inevitable that Sam Larkman should hold the con ready to
steer *Atropos* out of danger as soon as she was in the
water. Henri paced around the airy, spacious wheelhouse,
every nerve alert, able only to see the teams at the split
windlass on the fore deck. Timmins was in close contact
with the men aft. Seconds stretched out unbearably. Robin
at last bustled out of the radio room. 'Ready?' she
snapped.

'All ready, Captain,' answered Timmins at once.

'Right. Easy, all. Let's go.'

'Easy, all,' said Timmins into his walkie-talkie, and the
sound of motors clamoured on the perfect stillness of
the air. Everyone on the bridge, everyone aboard, concen-

trated every bodily power, waiting for that first almost imperceptible movement down the icy slope towards freedom.

It never came.

Timmins's conversations with the teams on the deck came to a halt. With a frown gathering upon her brow, Robin strode across to her first officer and lifted the walkie-talkie out of his nerveless fingers. 'Capstan,' she snapped. 'Mr Hogg, is all slackened off there?'

'All slackened off, Captain,' came Hogg's distinct reply.

'Windlass. Chief, is it all slackened there too?'

'Affirmative, Captain,' came Lethbridge's reply. 'All slackened off and we're still sitting here.'

Robin stood silently with the walkie-talkie hissing in her numb fingers. It was Timmins who put their predicament into words. 'We're stuck!' he said bitterly. '*Stuck!* We're frozen into the fucking ice and we're not going anywhere at all!'

CHAPTER THIRTY-FOUR

Day Thirteen

Monday, 31 May   20:00

Richard stood on the ruined prow of *Clotho* facing north as the last light drained out of the day. Ahead of him, seemingly scant yards away, rose a wall of ice nearly fifteen metres high. Behind that wall, the ice gathered itself up in a long, continuous sweep until it attained a crest. Then it plunged away steeply into half a mile or so of low ridges. Beyond these lay he knew not what: the ice was too dangerous to allow further explorations, and the fog from the berg was sweeping over the barrier now, so that it was impossible to make out the northern reaches. He had tramped across every inch of the solid ice during the last two days but he could find absolutely no way through it either for his ship or for himself.

His mind was not concentrated on the view, however, but upon a mental picture of what was going on beyond it. He was wound up so tight he felt as though he might explode. All through the day he had been fed snippets of news about the situation on *Atropos*. The survival of Ann Cable – he had seen tears in Nico's eyes as the first officer reported it; the fitting of the propeller; the preparations to relaunch the ship. He was far past the point of praying that everything would go well. He had come down here, driven by some superstitious instinct, as though he could affect things by the force of his will, if he could only come close enough.

As he stood and watched his mental picture of the activity on *Atropos*, the whole cliff seemed to jump out of focus and a small avalanche of loose debris thundered down into the restless gulf between the ship and the barrier. He slammed back to reality with such force it almost winded him. An overwhelming sound, so deep as to be a force of nature, a throbbing sensed with the soles of the feet and the back of the throat and the trembling of the tearful eyes rather than the ears rolled over him. He clutched at the twisted railing and held himself upright by sheer effort of will.

The movement of the iceberg and the violence of its contact with the ice barrier were intensifying. His last direct contact with Robin had informed him of her concern about the icequakes she was experiencing on the berg itself but these were as nothing compared with what seemed to be happening to the barrier. It was because the ridge of ice was so much less massive than the berg itself, he supposed, that it seemed to be reacting to the collision so much more fiercely. He had spent the last day hoping that the southward pressure of the berg might cause the barrier to snap before *Atropos* was trapped and crushed, but instead, the barrier was beginning to show signs of moving slowly southward while the berg ground inexorably eastwards along its northern shore. And this was the situation guaranteed to do most damage to the ship and the beloved woman who commanded her.

They had been lucky that the weather had been so calm during the last few days, but there was no doubt that it was deteriorating more rapidly now. Deteriorating in every way, he thought grimly. It was a mercy that he had agreed to be the communications centre, for there was an increasing amount of bad news he was filtering out of the information he was passing northwards. He had the detailed weather forecast which Robin had not had the time to collect from the widening circle of stations and ships around and to the north-west of them. It was bad and threatening to get worse. There was another storm about to boil over out of Hudson Bay and come thundering down to push the iceberg even harder southwards with gale- and storm-force winds from the north-west. That storm was due within twenty-four hours.

His distress signals had at last roused some promise of aid. An icebreaker was on its way up from Boston, but it was a slow sailer and showed no real prospect of arriving much before the foul weather.

The quality of the information coming in from Heritage House had dropped alarmingly since Sir William had been rushed into hospital. Inevitably. Helen Dufour was stuck in St Petersburg and there was no one with their finger as firmly on the pulse as the old man's had been.

He had been up since Audrey had called through from the twenty-four-hour desk at Crewfinders and put Maggie DaSilva on the line. That had been at midnight last night and he had spent the intervening hours agonising over whether or not to pass on the news to Robin. He knew that she would find it difficult to forgive him for his twenty hours of silence while her beloved father lay in intensive care without even the benefit of her prayers. She was a strong woman, an unflinching personality. In any other circumstance he would not have hesitated, but he felt she was simply under too much stress at the moment to have another care loaded onto her shoulders.

Thinking of her in these terms brought a grim smile to his thin lips. It showed how tired and worried he was himself and how long it had been since they had been together. The vision of her as being frail, bowed down by worry and reliant on his manly protection was a romantic fiction of the most self-indulgent chauvinist kind. But the fact that he knew she was strong and utterly competent made no real difference. He still could not bring himself to break the news of Sir William's heart attack to her. On the other hand, she would hear about it soon enough if Harry Stone ever got the leisure to tune one of his radios into any of the news services.

The walkie-talkie in his pocket buzzed. He put the icy earpiece under his hood and answered. 'Yes?'

'I'm getting a message through from *Atropos*, Captain.'

'Yes, Nico?'

'They're slackening off the shore lines now. They hope to be in the water in a few minutes.'

'Is it Captain Mariner speaking?'

'No. She's on the bridge. Harry Stone's relaying—'

There came a sudden, hissing silence.

The last of the twilight was trembling on the edge of darkness. The sky was low and pale, like a sere sheet stretched up towards the Pole, billowing gently in a high northerly wind which didn't seem to reach into the still air down here. It was too thin to be cloud. It was more like a skim of ice on the surface of a darkening pond. Richard looked up at it, his mind miles away, concentrating on the hissing silence on the radio link. The stillness was absolute. The chill seemed solid, gathered in as though the very air was freezing to glass around him. He had a sudden, ridiculous vision of the sister ships frozen together, like flies in amber, like mammoths in the permafrost, to be discovered in a block of solid, crystalline air sometime in the future. All of them, like the frozen corpses of Franklin's ill-fated expedition through the Northwest Passage.

His moment of black thought proved strangely prophetic. Nico's voice came back almost at once. 'It's no good. It's no good, Captain. *Atropos* is stuck fast. Frozen in the ice.' Nico tried manfully to hide the shock and horror in his voice. He failed.

Richard felt stunned and sickened. He walked across to the twisted rail and looked northwards. He moved slowly as though he was wading through deep water, mind racing, lost in thought. It was strange. He felt closer to Robin out here but he was of course further out of contact. Perhaps he was avoiding direct contact because of the news about her father. Distance was easier to handle than lies or evasions.

He drove his fist onto the railing and the sound echoed strangely in the dull, dead air of the gathering night. He felt so helpless. He was by no means an indecisive man. He was used to making decisions and taking action. But everything seemed to be slipping away from him somehow. Nothing he did seemed to make things any better. Every hope that things would improve was just a prelude to things getting worse. He found himself thinking back to the drive from Cold Fell to Seascale less than a fortnight ago when Robin was just about to take over command of *Clotho*. He had felt helpless then; felt as though fate was working against him even before things had gone from bad to worse. But even then he could never have imagined how desperate things would become, and so quickly. He had lost his court case and stood to lose his company. He might well have lost his father-in-law, partner and friend, and now he stood to lose the last of what he cared about most deeply: his ships and his beloved wife. There seemed nothing left for him to look forward to except doom, disaster and death.

He pressed the walkie-talkie to his lips. 'I'm coming back up to—' His voice died away. He frowned. He walked forward as far as the steepening cant of the deck would allow him to go.

'Captain?' came Nico's voice urgently in his ear.

He paid no attention to it; hardly heard it, in fact.

'Richard?'

The whole pale plane of the sky was behaving very strangely indeed. What new horror was this? Were those dark patterns clouds? Was this a storm coming unexpectedly and early? Were those pale patches some kind of electrical activity? What was going on here?

'Richard?'

It was vaguely familiar. What he could see; what it meant. As though in a dream he could feel himself cudgelling his brain, searching through the massive volume of knowledge he held in his capacious memory, seeking through everything he knew about dangerous conditions at sea.

On the sky above his head a kind of picture was forming. The picture showed a bar of white, stretching from horizon to horizon on either hand. There was blackness above him but it had an edge, sharp and well defined against the white. It reached away on either hand before plunging in along a straight black line to a bright shape which seemed to stand like a star immediately above his head. As he looked further up towards the Pole, the edge of the blackness defined a contra-edge of whiteness. But it was not a blank whiteness, it seemed to be ridged and contoured like the underside of a great cloud lit from below at sunset. Except that this could not be happening. There were no clouds up there, only that pale skim of icy air. Even further towards the northern horizon, the ridged and shadowed white gave way to black again. Black which swooped in from the east, reached southwards towards him across that strange white roof, then ended abruptly as the white cut due north again. In the angle of this, lay another bright shape, the exact double of the one immediately above his head.

'Richard! Captain!' Nico came panting up. 'Are you all right? When you didn't answer, I—' And his voice too trailed away mid-sentence. 'What is it?' he whispered, looking up.

'It's the ice blink. Ice blink! My God, I—' Richard stood, straining his eyes to take in every detail of what was drawn across the sky. 'How's your memory for pictures, Nico?'

'Is good.'

'Right. Remember what you see up there because we're going to try and draw it out in detail.'

'But what is it?'

'It's a *chart*!'

'Is what?'

'Ice blink. It's a kind of mirage caused by the cold air and the light. Keep looking; it won't last long. It's an exact reflection of everything for ten miles or so ahead of us. The black is water. The white is ice. The ripples are pressure ridges, so pay particular attention to them. The bright shape above our head is *Clotho*. The bright shape over there is *Atropos*. God Almighty, she's so *close*!'

'Is upside down.'

'I know. That's why it'll be difficult to remember accurately . . . It's fading.'

'Yes. Is going very fast now.'

'Right. We should be able to draw up a good chart, though. We can doublecheck scale against the last set of satellite pictures Bill Heritage faxed over. We can really get the problem measured up at last. God, I wish that icebreaker was nearer. *Atropos* looked so clear, so close. Did you see?'

'*Si, Capitan. Veni, vidi.*'

'*Vici!*' Richard finished the Latin quotation and gave a bark of laughter. 'I came, I saw, I *conquered*.' Julius Caesar's famous observation seemed to give him new strength as they hurried along the deck.

Richard erupted onto the bridge with Nico puffing in tow. Tearing off his cold-weather gear before the overwhelming warmth of the contrast with the frigid outside suffocated him, Richard strode across to the chart table and pulled out some plain white paper, size A3, and some pencils. 'Come on, Nico,' he ordered. 'Get it down while it's fresh in your mind. Bill!' he called through to the radio shack without taking breath. 'Get *Atropos* for me.'

Side by side, the two of them began to sketch what they had seen on the sky above their heads. They had laid down a confident outline each before Bill called through.

Richard hadn't really expected to talk to Robin but she was there on the far end. 'Are you going to go any further tonight?' he asked, feeling himself filling with calm and supportiveness, supposing that that would be of most use to her now. He heard his voice becoming gentle, reliable. The very tone said, *Lean on me*.

'I can't. The ballast is frozen so I can't move it. We're going to try lifting the spare propeller. The weight of it rolled her over when we were working this afternoon. It may roll her free now before the crane breaks but I don't hold any great hopes for it.'

He strained to hear more detail. Did she sound tired? Depressed? Defeated?

'So, what do you plan to do?'

He had read or heard somewhere – from the Samaritans, perhaps, or on one of the management courses he had attended years ago – that you should always talk positively; always leave the person on the far end with something positive to do or to look forward to.

'If raising the propeller doesn't work, I'll have to leave it for tonight. I haven't got enough lights to illuminate the whole site. I've got the deck lights, of course, but I would really need a good supply of arc lights to light up the whole slipway. In the morning, I'll pile everything that will burn along her sides and set fire to it. I can't heat the holds, the bunkerage or the ballast, and turning up the central heating in the bridgehouse won't be any good. Can you think of anything else to do?'

'No. That's a good plan. The bulk of the heat will go up but the metal should conduct enough warmth downwards to break things free. Are you going to re-tighten the shore lines before you go into action?'

'Good idea. I hadn't thought of that. We'll still need to have a controlled slide down.'

He thought: *Is there any chance that heated metal will crack like glass when it hits below-freezing water?* He said nothing, his mind a racing turmoil of what he dared say to her and what he had to avoid telling her. Her voice had remained level – no doubt her bridge was as busy as his and elementary leadership dictated that she sound confident and give nothing away.

'In the meantime,' he said, filling his voice with positive vibrations, 'we've had a bit of luck here. Nico and I saw the ice blink tonight and it showed us pretty clearly all the details of the ice between *Clotho* and *Atropos*. We're just sketching things out now. We're going to balance things up with the faxes Bill sent in yesterday and get it all to scale.'

'Has Daddy sent any new faxes in?'

'No. Nothing. It's a Bank Holiday—' He knew that this fact would make no difference at Crewfinders or at Heritage Mariner. Local considerations, even national ones, never did. There were too many vessels in too many seas and oceans all over the world.

She knew it too. 'He must be up at Cold Fell with the twins—'

For the first time he did hear hesitancy in her voice and it wrenched his heart with unexpected force. She knew that her father would not dream of taking a holiday while his ships and his family were in such dire straits. For the first time in their relationship he felt that he was lying to her.

It hurt.

'Well,' he prevaricated, 'when we get the chart of the ice barrier drawn we'll be able to help you more effectively from this end. We're expecting an icebreaker here some time within the next twenty-four hours. They'll have explosives aboard so we can blast our way through even if we can't break our way through. Once we've broken this barrier, you'll be out of trouble.' He tried to make it sound positive, bracing. The facts were indisputable. It was the timing that was crucial.

She knew that. 'Any weather reports we should know
about?'

He couldn't lie any more. 'There may be a storm
coming down from the north-west within the next twenty-
four hours.'

'I'd better get busy early in the morning, then. That's
our most exposed quarter. If we're still here when it hits
then we're dead.'

'Right then. We'll get this new chart drawn up here,
and you get sorted out with what you want to chuck over
the side and set fire to tomorrow morning over there. We'll
be back in contact later. Okay?'

'Right.'

It was hardly a satisfactory conversation but it was the
best he could do. He felt that she had been preoccupied.
Understandably, after all. They never made unnecessary
demands on one another. They were both so busy that
demands seemed unfair. In fact, in their relationship up to
the Gulf War and the birth of the twins there had been
little need for great demands on either side. But things
were different now. Richard was wise enough to know that
giving could become mechanical and relationships could
well be defined by what people were willing to demand
from each other rather than what they were willing to give
to each other. Was it Joseph Conrad the novelist who had
said, 'A man is defined not by what he can overcome but
by what can overcome him'? If not, it should have been;
and the same was true of relationships, he supposed. How
much you loved your partner was sometimes measured by
what you were willing to demand from them. Except that,
right now he felt that he wasn't giving Robin as much as
she had a right to expect from him: he wasn't giving her
the whole truth.

'Right,' he said to Nico as he came back into the wheelhouse. 'How are you doing there?'

'Not bad, I think.' The Italian held up the sketch and Richard crossed towards him, frowning as he began to concentrate.

Two hours later they had the scale drawing finished. The ice blink enabled them to match up the southern shore of the ice barrier with the absolute outline on the faxes Sir William had sent to them. It also allowed them to draw in the pressure ridges in the ice itself and to detail the northern shoreline which had up until now been concealed by the fog surrounding the iceberg itself.

The detail was at once frustrating and illuminating. It showed how narrow the ice barrier was at this point. The high ridge in front of *Clotho* was the only major feature separating the two ships. The full width of less than a mile at this point seemed to be largely composed of slush. Only that frozen wave of ice fifty feet high, unknown metres deep and a quarter of a mile wide really stood between them. On this side loomed the cliff against which *Clotho*'s bows were knocking. On the far side, beyond the long, smooth slope, the slushy ridges which had defeated Richard's exploration northwards simply petered out into a wide bay and the open ocean, with *Atropos* sitting on the iceberg just to the north of it, swinging round and south as the mass of ice moved inexorably. Even faced with soft slush at first, it was only a question of time before the marooned ship became caught between the jaws of solid ice. And as the storm in the north-west began to draw nearer, so the time *Atropos* had left to live grew ever shorter.

Suddenly Bill Christian shoved his head out into the wheelhouse. 'I've an incoming for you,' he said.

'*Atropos*? Heritage House?' Richard began to pull himself erect.

'No. Another vessel. *Northern Lights* out of Boston. Johnny should have her on visual if he goes out to full range—'

'Got her,' chimed in Sullivan. 'Just in range. Coming up fast.'

Excitement boiled up within him. Out of Boston! he thought. It had to be the icebreaker.

'I'll come through and talk to her at once,' he said. Then he turned to Nico and patted him on the shoulder. The gesture was one of excitement, almost of victory. He only just managed to stop the pat from becoming a boisterous thump. 'This is more like it, eh, Nico?'

He pressed the microphone to his mouth and tried to control the excitement in his voice. 'Hello, *Northern Lights*? This is *Clotho*, over.'

The contact was unexpectedly loud and clear. 'Hello, *Clotho*. This is *Northern Lights*.'

'Good evening, *Northern Lights*. You are very welcome. You have made very good time from Boston. Can you give me an ETA at our present position?'

'We'll be with you before first light, *Clotho* but—'

'Excellent. We will reverse out of the lead we have opened and let you in first. You will need more than simple icebreaking equipment, though. I hope you are well supplied with high explosives. We have quite a cliff here—'

'Explosives? We have no explosives aboard, *Clotho*. Why should we have explosives aboard?'

'Excuse me, but aren't you an icebreaker? We were expecting an icebreaker.'

'Sorry to disappoint you, *Clotho*. No, we are not an

icebreaker. We are a cruise ship. We are under charter to several major news networks and agencies. We are bringing a wide range of leading media personnel to witness your dilemma and to report it worldwide. In fact I have several people here who would like to interview Captain Richard Mariner over the radio link. Is that acceptable, *Clotho*? . . .

'I say again, is that acceptable, *Clotho*? . . .

'Hello, *Clotho*? Are you receiving me? Over? . . .

'*Clotho*? Come in, *Clotho*—'

CHAPTER THIRTY-FIVE

The Last Day

Tuesday, 1 June   00:00

The storm broke out of Hudson Bay at midnight. It was
a hybrid, caught between two seasons and given two identi-
ties. It was the last storm of winter and the first of summer.
It carried into the Labrador Sea all the worst aspects of
each season in the near-Arctic. In broad human terms it
might have been called almost schizophrenic. It was gener-
ated by the failing weight of the frigid air over the Pole
and it sucked into its wicked gyre warm winds from the
Canadian midwest where day temperatures were reaching
a humid 20 degrees Celsius in Saskatchewan, Manitoba
and Ontario. The towering clouds along its front lines
carried thunder, hail and rain. The winds which whipped
it into its frenzied drive to the east were edged with ice
but warm at their hearts, and all the more dangerous
for that.

The tracks of the previous storms had been dictated by
the ridge of high pressure lying down the centre of Greenland, but during the calm, clear, final days of May this
had dissipated and so the track of this new storm lay

straight across the north of the Labrador Sea. In the still
airs it found when it got there, however, it spread its
tentacles southward like an octopus laid out on the shore.
Most of the warm, wet, storm-force winds which preceded
it swung in from the north-west and because it had so
much room to spread out, they reached far down into the
North Atlantic.

The first thing that the storm front encountered after it
had swept across the low-lying, lake strewn, north-pointing
peninsula of Quebec and Labrador, and spread a little
devastation down as far as the Avalon Peninsula in Newfoundland, was the open sea. Most of the pack ice had
been pushed down into a large icefield lying further to the
south. The warmth of the clear, calm weather had made
the icefield thin. Only the berg and the barrier retained
any solidity, and they were currently engaged in a mutual
destruction which the storm was shortly to abet.

In the open waters to the north of the icefield, the winds
found room enough to release a high storm swell which
they pushed before themselves with relentless force down
to the thin icefield. Under the teeming downpour of warm
Canadian rain it began to melt rapidly. Only the pressure
of the light winds and strong currents had held the floes
together and now the waves tore them apart. For the first
time in nine chill months the wide surface of the Davis
Strait heaved into crests and troughs. The shock ran south
and east at an incredible speed, sucked into the stillness
and calm. And everything it found before it was sun-
dered and scattered by the power of the waves and the
force of those warm, wet winds.

'That's it,' said Robin, closing down the meeting at last.
'I can't think of anything else we need to prepare, check

or doublecheck. We're ready for the morning. Let's turn in. We've all earned a good night's sleep.' She looked round at her officers, then added dryly, 'But three hours will have to suffice.' Automatically she went to throw down her notes onto her day-room table, but she stopped herself just in time. Like every other non-essential combustible fitment, it had gone to fuel the fires they would be placing along the sides of the ship and igniting at first light in the hope that the heat would melt *Atropos* free of the murderous clutches of the ice.

'Anything else?' She looked round the circle of exhausted faces, then glanced across at the clock which now stood beside the phone on the floor in the corner. Just coming up for 02:00. Three hours was about right. They all had more work to do in the first light of dawn to get the wreckage of the furniture along the ship's sides and soaked with paraffin and petrol ready to be ignited as early as practically possible. It was only the darkness which held them helpless at the moment. They would have to be up at five, dressed, fed, organised and ready to start at first light just after seven.

Three hours for the rest of them. Not for her. She still had work to do. Thank God she could trust Richard to give her a short digest of anything it was imperative for her to know; dealing with all the radio messages she might expect to be incoming in these circumstances would have taken her the rest of the night. As everybody stood up and stumbled out, she crossed to the phone and called up to the radio room. 'Harry? Get *Clotho* for me, would you? There are some things I need to check.'

'Yes, Captain. And I'll want a word with you too. I've had time to check with some weather stations.'

Just the way he said it made her answer tartly, 'More

bad news. Oh, good!' Then she hung up.

Henri LeFever was last to leave and it looked as though he had something he wanted to say to her, but she really didn't have the time. She pushed past him almost rudely and ran across to the lift. It was waiting at her deck level and she was in and powering upwards before he even crossed the corridor.

'Tell me about the weather.'

'There's a storm coming. It's not a bad one, but it could be tricky. It's warm and wet. Looks as though it's breaking up the ice in front of it and pushing our way anything that won't break or melt.'

'Great!'

'In the meantime—' He handed her the handset and left. She put on the headphones and collapsed into the chair. She could imagine Richard with his headphones on too, hunching forward over the microphone. He was probably as exhausted as she was but he would have waited up. She was suddenly flooded with warmth for him so poignant that tears filled her eyes and there was a sob in her voice as she pressed the transmit button.

'Richard?'

'Hello, darling. Nothing but bad news, I'm afraid.'

'Start with the weather. When's the storm due?'

'Harry getting bored with waiting for us to tell him everything? He's a good man, but I wish he'd obey orders. He—'

'He what?'

'Nothing. About that storm. It will probably be here by noon. It broke out of Hudson Bay at midnight and it looks as though its centre is travelling south at about thirty miles an hour, but the fronts are moving much faster than that. We should see conditions deteriorating from dawn.'

'What will conditions be like at the height?'

'Storm-force winds, thunder, rain. High seas, they reckon, but I don't think we'll see those. The winds and rain are melting the ice up towards the Davis Strait.'

'Is this going to help us? Is *our* ice going to melt?'

'No such luck. Apparently you know someone called Colin Ross? Amazing man. I've had him on all afternoon. He wanted to tell you he got back to camp safely and he'll be looking at the auk tomorrow first thing.'

'Okay, thanks. I never had any doubt he would get back safely. What did he tell you about the ice?'

'The storm will break up and melt sea ice and floes. It will damage and begin the disintegration of the icefield to the north of you but it won't do anything at all to the berg or the barrier except make them more dangerous. They are both too big to be melted by the warm winds or the rain but the berg especially will be moved quite powerfully by winds coming in from that quarter. You should notice some more lively movement quite soon. Did he tell you there's an outside chance the whole iceberg will tilt over? He says it's big but it isn't all that stable. It's definitely swinging round much more rapidly now. Looks as if the whole trap will swing closed really quickly after lunch tomorrow.'

'We'll be floating by then.'

'If you're not, you'll have to abandon ship. If the iceberg is unstable, then you'll have find some way across the barrier to us.'

'We'll talk about that at the time.'

'Robin! You can't be stubborn over this. If you can't free her, you must abandon her. Promise.'

'Don't be silly, Richard. I'll make that decision nearer the time. I don't propose to try and then give up if it doesn't all go smoothly at once. I'll be trying to get her free until there is absolutely no way of helping her any more. Anyone who is useless to me will be sent to safety at the best moment. But I myself and anyone I need will be here trying to get her off the ice right until the bitter end.'

'Of course.' He took several deep breaths. She could hear him and it irritated her almost as much as his over-concern was beginning to. 'I know you will. All I'm saying is that you must be careful. And leave a way out for yourself.'

'Of course I will. I'm not suicidal. Now, what other news is there?'

'We've a new arrival. The *Northern Lights*. At first I thought she was that icebreaker Bill started out of Boston, but no. She's a cruise liner, if you please, hired by the press who want some good photographs. And some good interviews. I've been talking to them all afternoon and evening.'

'I thought Daddy was supposed to be doing all that.'

'These aren't London journalists,' he explained quickly. 'Most of them are from New York. And they want live interviews, and pictures too. They want to see us all go down on live TV.' He gave a dry, ambiguous laugh. 'If you had a TV set over there you could watch the broadcasts. I've been on the six o'clock news and the seven o'clock. Voice only, over an old photograph from some magazine or newspaper. And the nine, ten and midnight news. They keep on at me all the time, but I only give them the same story. I sound confident but concerned, if you see what I mean. I hope I can keep it up if things get much worse.'

'And they're right there with you?'

'I won't let any on board, though there hasn't been much pressure yet. They arrived at the end of the lead I opened in the southern ice at about twenty-two hundred and they aren't too happy in small boats in the dark. They'll get really restless at first light, I expect. But I'll deal with that then.'

'Right. Good. Anything else?'

'You're going to put the plan into action as agreed at first light?'

'Yes. I have everything that will burn ready to go.'

'Okay. That's about it, then. I've talked to Nurse Janet directly for once. The three of them were in Heritage House for a visit. The twins are fine. She said they were sending their love but it sounded to me as though they were having a battle royal.'

'Good. I've been thinking. I'm not going to keep much of a bridge watch tonight, but I'll get Harry Stone to go through the airwaves with a fine-toothed comb. I want a close eye kept on that storm.'

'We'll be doing that. Let him get some rest. It'll be a hard day tomorrow no matter what—'

'No. He's got to stay on duty anyway, even if just to be here if you come through suddenly. He's my watch for the night and I might as well make full use of him. Even tied up like this, I insist that at least one officer keeps watch at all times. We still don't know what's really going on with these Green War people. Tonight it's Harry's turn. Even if he just listens to the BBC World News it'll be better than nothing.'

There was a silence so absolute that she thought the signal between the sister ships had been broken somehow. Then Richard came on again and he sounded incredibly tired, as though he had aged a century a second since they last talked. As soon as she heard the change in his tone she knew he had been hiding something bad from her.

'Robin. Darling. I'm afraid I have some other news. I wouldn't have worried you with it but Harry's bound to hear about it if he gets a news station and ... Well, it's about your father. Bill's in hospital, I'm afraid, and he's asked me to tell you ...'

Colin Ross could make do with four hours' sleep and Kate was used to him getting up in the middle of the night. This was especially true when they were wintering north or south of sixty degrees, as they had been recently; the nights could last for months. It was no great surprise to her, therefore, when she awoke at four in the morning to see him hunched over his work table examining the dead auk.

She dozed off again.

They had a large hut, like the winter quarters of Inuit, the Eskimo people they knew so well. It was just big enough for the two of them to live and work in, but small and light enough to be easily transportable. It was strong enough to withstand the worst the high Arctic could throw at it, but flexible enough to bend with changing conditions. It was filled with high-tech aids, but nothing too bulky or complex to be packed up and moved quickly. This was a drift ice station designed for thinnish ice. It was an efficient living and working environment but it had no permanence about it at all. If the section of the iceberg it was pitched on broke free and floated away, they would, in theory, be able to pack up, move out and get themselves back to the main berg within the daylight hours, and still have enough time to re-erect the hut and cook dinner for themselves. It was something they had never had to do –

and never wanted to do. But, for all its impermanence, it
was home to Kate. She loved it and she loved sharing
it with Colin.

Except that Robin Mariner had found time to show her
photographs of the most enchanting twins . . . As she drifted off, Kate wondered whether Robin had shown the picture to Colin. He was much more baby-minded than she
was.

'Kate! *Kate!* Wake up.' Colin was shaking her and she
was indeed waking up very quickly indeed.

'What is it?'

'You have to look at this. I can't make head or tail of
it. Come along. I'm only a humble glaciologist. I think I
need a biologist for this.'

'Is it that damned bird?'

'Well, yes and no.'

The inside of the hut was surprisingly warm. She was
sleeping in a baggy old jogging outfit so she simply swept
her hair back, stepped into the broken-backed trainers she
used as slippers and slopped across to his work bench.
The dead auk was pinned out in his meticulous manner,
like a dissection in a biology exam. Under the lights it
gleamed unnaturally brightly – all blacks and pinks, blues
and reds. She wasn't really ready for this at this time in
the morning. Its little chest was as wide as its wings
and the stomach bag had been lifted out and opened by
its side. The contents of the stomach consisted of three-
quarters of a surprisingly large fish – some kind of whiting
by the look of things though it was difficult to be sure
without a head to examine. The fish had been as efficiently
autopsied as the bird. It too was open and it was obvious
that the head would have been placed above the ragged
ribs, if there had been one. She guessed some other bird

had stolen it. Beside the half filleted fish lay another
stomach and a partially-presented package of stomach contents. Brightly coloured gelatine pill cases; glistening white
powder, looking like wet salt. A small but solid ball of
putty-like material perhaps the same size as a chilli bean,
with something pale pink inserted into it. As Kate looked
closer, her stomach sinking, Colin fastidiously used the
point of his scalpel to turn the putty ball towards the lights.
There was no doubt about it: the pink thing embedded in
it was the end of someone's finger.

Henri LeFever jumped as though he had heard Kate Ross's
cry of distress across seven silent miles of ice. Apart from
Harry Stone in the radio shack, Henri was the only person
left awake aboard. He knew this because he had just
finished checking. He had watched Robin go up to the
shack and come down again in tears. He had seen her go
into her cabin and he had listened outside the door while
she sobbed herself to sleep. Then he had prowled the
corridors, happy that Ann was too tired to seek him out.
He had listened as she too had sunk into restless, mumbling sleep. He was desperately tired himself, but he had
to finish the job. He had to get rid of the rest of it now
so that no one would ever know for certain how close he
and Jeanne had come this time to destroying the sister
ships. So that he could be free to carry on her war in
another place at another time. Her Green War.
    The thought of her haunted him. At times he thought
she haunted him. He never doubted that she was dead.
They had selected her hiding place very carefully. He had
been back in Canada, waiting aboard *Atropos*, when she
must have gone aboard the British ship, and he knew
she would have hidden in the crane cab on the gantry, as

agreed. It had taxed all his self-control to the very edge of madness not to show the cataclysmic reaction he had felt when he had seen the whole gantry whirled away to destruction, and something deep within him had told him she was gone too. She began to inhabit his dreams immediately and he knew he often woke up with her name on his lips. He was half convinced she had saved him on the berg by guiding him to the ice fall and giving him the courage to slide down it to safety.

But he was so tired. He felt so lost and alone that at times he suspected he was going mad. He wasn't sure what was real any more. He didn't really care, except that the thought of her still drove him, that and the knowledge that she would want him to fight on. *Atropos* looked as though she was lost in any case so he could stop worrying about her. Days after *Clotho* was due to have blown up in Sept Isles she was still afloat on the far side of the ice barrier, so Jeanne had not set the explosives there as planned either. The plan had been so elegant. Jeanne had been so beautiful. Well, they were both gone now. Tears filled his bright blue eyes.

He did not have the expertise to set the bomb. That had always been her job. That was why their plan had turned upon getting her across from *Clotho* to *Atropos* when the ships passed each other off Cape Farewell. Everything he had done aboard this ship had been designed to enable his wife to reach that rendezvous on time – in spite of the delays, the weather, the drug-addicted captain, the drug-dealing officers and the mutinous crew. And the increasingly inquisitive Ann Cable. The demonstrations and the unexpected delay in sailing had slowed them down. The storm conditions had moved them along faster than anticipated, however, and they had soon more than made up the lost time. The damage to the engine had been done to slow them down again but it had gone further than he had expected, and he had found himself undoing his work by nursing the engineers back to health so that the ship could be moved again.

The death of Reynolds had arisen from the near certainty that he must have seen something of the detonators Henri had concealed within that cable conduit. But he had moved almost everything out of there now, along with the Semtex which Captain Black had discovered in the swimming pool. He should have chucked the old man's body over the side along with the drugs and the bomb-making equipment. If there was no bomb-maker, there would be no bomb. The Semtex was expensive and increasingly hard to come by, but it was an unnecessary risk to his security to keep it aboard. He had been going to dispose of the blocks hidden in the empty swimming pool when he had found the old captain frozen in among them. Trying to hide his body had revealed the Wide Boy's stash of drugs.

Like Richard Mariner – though Henri had no way of knowing this fact – he believed all his good luck was gone and only bad luck was left. How else could one explain what he had been forced to do? Chopping off the captain's fingers so that he could relieve him of the explosives he was holding so tightly had been even more disturbing than disposing of the Wide Boy. And even when he did get rid of the drugs and the first part of the explosives, it had poisoned the fish all around the boat and the dead fish poisoned the birds!

But now he had to get rid of all the rest. This idea of setting fires along the sides of the ship looked like a long shot to him but, in spite of the fact that Jeanne had told him how safe it was until properly detonated, he still

feared that the rest of the explosives would go off by
accident as an unexpected part of the captain's plan in the
morning. Especially as the cable conduit where they were
now hidden ran along the line where the metal would get
the hottest. Jeanne and he had been happy to think of
these carriers of filth soiling their own nests in Sept Isles
and Seascale when explosive retribution finally came, but
to allow the canisters of nuclear waste to be blown open
and then dropped into the ocean here was out of the
question. Jeanne would certainly haunt him to his grave if
he allowed such a thing. And she would be right to do
so, for it would be a betrayal of their love even more
faithless than if he had slept with Ann Cable.

This thought was further emphasised in his mind ten
minutes later by the letters. Jeanne's letters, safely sealed
in a waterproof container, were the first thing he saw when
he opened the cable conduit, the last of his hiding places.
Here he kept the small things. The timers, the detonators,
the letters. He would never know about her final letter to
him, her final declaration of her love, but he had many
others which traced the history of their passionate, deadly
relationship since the first time they had met up in the
tundra of north Quebec where he had been hunting and
she had been on an exercise with the US Army. At first
he had thought she was an American man. Only later
had he discovered the truth: that she was French Canadian-
born like him and, in spite of her deadly training, a sensitive, compassionate, passionate woman.

The letters were all that were left of her now. It would
break his heart to destroy them, but he knew all too well
that as things stood they were just one more proof of his
guilt. One more way in which the snoopers with whom
he was surrounded might find the truth and slow him

down; maybe even stop him altogether. No. Like the rest
of this stuff, they would go over the side and only the fish
would read them through to the end of time. The thought
of it brought tears to his eyes. He felt them trickling chilly
down his face. Better that the fish should read them than
Ann Cable. He remembered all too clearly what she had
said about having a suspicious mind and the impact her
words had had on him. From that moment in Don Taylor's
cabin he had been watching her.

Of all the ways he had thought of to control what the
reporter thought and did, only two seemed feasible: to
seduce her or to murder her. Murder seemed the most
likely option if she came much closer. And he hoped it
would be as neat and simple an affair as releasing the
Wide Boy's safety harness in the storm. But he doubted
it would be quite as easy as that, somehow. That was why
he had listened so assiduously outside her door until she
had fallen asleep. Perhaps he should have killed her up
on the ice. The thought had occurred to him, but Fate had
intervened. Ah well, *c'est la vie*. Or, more correctly, *c'est
la guerre*.

They set off just before first light and as they skied eastwards across the ice they saw the dawn come up. They
saw it first from the top of a low ridge which nevertheless
gave them a long view down a considerable slope, with
the ice mountains distant on their left. What they saw was
a wide horizon burning with incredible brightness in a
long, thin line. The line seemed to stretch from the reaches
of the barrier in the south to the Pole itself, hidden behind
the mountains in the north. Below it, the ice appeared to
be a simple shelf, grey more than white, with only the
topmost crests of any irregularity catching fire from the

light. Above it was solid blackness. Featureless, apparently utterly still, like a gallery of darkest coal. It had weight, oppressive power. It crushed down physically as well as mentally with tremendous force and even the giant figure of Colin Ross seemed bowed by the weight of it. Silently, they moved forward into that strange world, apparently inverted, where the sky was solid, heavy and dark, and the ground was light-flecked and bright, as though made of clouds.

As time went by, the narrow band of brightness became the merest crack in the gathering darkness, snuffed out beneath the awesome weight of the coal-face sky. Then it was as though they were skiing forward between two great surfaces closing together upon them like a narrowing gallery deep in a mine.

There was utter silence all around them. Even the thunderous grinding of the berg against the barrier had paused. There was no wind yet, though the state of the sky made it all too plain there soon would be. There was no sense of calm, however. Neither figure hurrying so urgently forward was even slightly fooled by this brief armistice in the war of the elements. The atmosphere was electric, and would have been so even had they not been so concerned about the news they carried with them. Everyone had to be removed from *Atropos* at the earliest opportunity. They should go over the barrier for preference, but onto the berg if need be. Robin Mariner was going to need all the help she could get. That much would have been obvious even had the weather been clear and the forecast good. They had discussed at some length as they were preparing to come out which of the ships they should warn about what they had discovered. A moment's thought made them realise that direct communication with *Atropos* might be

overheard by whoever was involved with this and so might
do more harm than good. They had promised to use
Richard Mariner on *Clotho* as their first point of contact
in any case. But when they had tried, it had proved frustrat-
ingly impossible to get through to *Clotho* at all, and so
they had set out without warning anyone of their discovery
or their intentions. Or of their fears.

As they topped the last crest and looked down on the
ship, it seemed that they were already far too late. Right
along her whole length *Atropos* was ablaze.

Sam Larkman had the hands of a wet nurse when it came
to dealing with machinery. He had moved the propeller
yesterday, when *Atropos* had rocked sideways under its
weight, and he was in charge of it this morning when
the ship was stuck fast. Errol was sitting beside him on the
bench seat in the crane's cab, the walkie-talkie pressed to
his face, keeping up a constant dialogue with Robin on
the bridge and the officers overseeing the long banks of
flame. Sam was effectively working blind, by feel. The
swan's neck of the crane was extended fully and rotated
to the port side so that it projected over the port railings.
The falls were tight round the broken propeller, and
stretching with the gathering stress of trying to lift it. Sam
knew what was happening by the mystic way that forces
could transfer news of themselves through inanimate
objects. He could see nothing except the walls of smoke
which were painted across the window pane in front of
him.

'It's coming up,' Sam told Errol.

'Okay. No movement of the hull though.'

'I know. I'll hold it there. It's maybe a metre up off the
ice. I don't want to go swinging it around any.'

'Captain, Sam says the propeller's about a metre off the ice,' Errol reported into the walkie-talkie, then he was overcome by convulsive coughing as the acrid smoke began to seep into the cab.

On the bridge, Robin said, 'Tell him to hold it there, Errol. It's at its optimum position. Mr Hogg, how're the port-side crew doing?'

'Catch twenty-two, Captain,' said Hogg's voice lugubriously. 'The more the flames catch hold here, the more the ice melts and soaks the wood. It's nowhere near as hot as we need it. Is the ballast melting at least?'

'Chief?' asked Robin, her voice tense with strain. 'Any joy with the pumps? Is the ballast melting yet?'

'Nothing yet, Captain. I daren't go to full pressure, though. If they suck too hard on solid ice, they'll just break down altogether.'

'I know. We'll just have to wait and hope.'

'Captain? This is Walt Hogg.'

'Yes?'

'It's those people from yesterday. People called Ross.'

'What about them?'

'They're just coming down the slipway now.'

'Keep them there with you. There's no way for them to come aboard at the moment until we move down the slope or until the fires die down.'

'Yes, Captain. Oh. One other thing.'

'Yes?' She tried to keep the irritation out of her voice but she failed. The strain was really starting to get to her.

'I don't know if you'd noticed, Captain, but it's snowing.'

Richard stood on the port bridge wing of *Clotho* looking north. Behind him, through the open door into the wheel-house, he could hear Bill Christian's courteous repetition,

'No, I'm sorry the captain is too busy to speak to you just at the moment. No, I'm afraid it will be impossible for him to call you back. No, I'm afraid you cannot come aboard just at the moment. Yes, madam, I do know who you are and yes, I do realise you have come a long way and I *do* know how close you are but . . .'

It had been going on since before first light. Richard was wild with frustration. What the good people of the press didn't seem to realise just at the moment was that their overwhelming attempts to communicate with him were making it impossible for him to communicate with anyone else. With Robin, for instance. And he particularly wanted to talk to her. The binoculars crushed freezingly under the overhanging jut of his frowning brows showed him the distant column of smoke climbing up the still air in the distance. It was a thick column and would have been plain to see – for all that it was just a darker shade of grey than the rest of the scene before him – even had he not known exactly where to look. The press on *Northern Lights* had seen it too, with the result that the traffic Bill was having to deal with had redoubled.

As Richard looked steadfastly northwards, the column of smoke was suddenly no longer all there was to see. One moment the view was quite clear, the next, as though it had always been there, caught in the act of swirling between the black sky and the dull grey ice, a great blizzard of fat white snowflakes confronted him. And, as the first of them brushed down his face like the kiss of a dozen slugs and he realised not only how big they were but how wet, he saw the distant dark column jerk, writhe and explode into tatters in the air, so that even before he felt it on the chilled skin of his face, he knew that the wind had arrived.

*   *   *

'It's no good, Captain,' yelled Yasser Timmins. 'The wind's getting the flames up but the snow's just damping them down again. We got to give it up. It's getting pretty bad out here and if we don't get moving it'll be too late.'

Hogg was in command of the fires along the port side in the relative shelter of the cliff, but Timmins and his men were on the starboard, out on the more exposed side, where the sudden squally wind was roaring down the funnel of the slipway from the roiling black north-west. Even as he spoke, jamming the walkie-talkie against the thin material of his hood to hear Robin's reply, another gust swept down upon him and the billowing brightness of the long flames before him was lost in an impenetrable fog of large, wet snowflakes. He staggered, trying to keep his feet.

Robin seemed to be whispering to him from a long way away. 'Okay. Come back aboard.'

He turned. The two figures of their visitors still stood at the back of the ship, halfway between his team and Hogg's. He gestured to them to go up and they understood. The scaffolding around the new propeller had been left in place precisely for this reason. It was dispensable if the ship moved down the slipway, but if she did not, then it was an easy, safe route on and off. The plan now was that they go aboard, join the teams which were already told off, changed, ready and waiting to abandon, then come out onto the ice and go for safety. If these Ross people knew their way around, then they could take the lead. Otherwise, it would be LeFever, who had at least proved he knew his way around an iceberg, and the Cable woman who had proved she was lucky, if nothing else. Robin hadn't told Timmins what she proposed to do herself. In fact, she hadn't told anyone. Timmins wondered if she actually knew what she was going to do now.

He saw the last of his team up and went round the stern to make sure that Hogg and his men knew what was going on. They were halfway down the ship's length, near the propeller which Larkman in the crane seemed still to be trying to move. No chance of that now, thought Timmins, and he put his walkie-talkie to his lips again. 'Walt? Walt, can you hear me?'

As he spoke, another gust of wind took him and he staggered forward a couple of steps before leaning back into the fierce blast of it. But even as he regained some kind of stability, at once he lost it again. This time it was not the wind which was in violent motion. It was the ice. The whole berg heaved and rolled. On the far side of the high ice mountains, the power of the storm had arrived and the whole floating massif answered its implacable force.

The sound was incredible. It overpowered Timmins and came close to deafening him. He was actually thrown into the air as he had been when the lead had opened up beneath him and he thought for an awful moment that he was falling into another ice cave. But when he landed it was on solid ground. Solid, but heaving and twisting in the most terrifying manner. *The scaffolding*! he thought, and had the presence of mind to scrabble away up the slope. And the scaffolding did in fact fall – or some of it at least. The sound of its collapse was drowned in the thunder of heaving, grinding ice.

But at last the noise began to quieten and the motion began to ease and Timmins could scramble into a sitting position. He just had time to notice that the main steps had survived and the figures clinging precariously to them all seemed to be all right when the rumbling started once again. Timmins spread himself out like a starfish, expecting the ground to heave again. But it remained firm. This time it was the sky which was falling in.

'*Avalanche*!' yelled Errol into his walkie-talkie, but there was so much noise going on that he doubted the captain heard him. He and Sam had a grandstand view of it. Indeed, they seemed to be in the middle of it. The whole cliff side was in motion scant yards in front of the window of the gantry's cab. It did not curl over and cascade like a breaking wave; it seemed to start about the middle of the slope and settle down along a vertical plane, what had once been a whole wall of ice breaking into individual blocks and sliding almost tiredly down against the ship. Everything that the men could see was sliding downwards. Everything level with them, everything below them and, most terrifyingly of all, everything above them as well. Their whole world, everything they could see, was tearing itself to pieces and sliding down around their ears.

The cab jerked and both of them were flung off the seat. Errol rolled forward to smash his head against the toughened glass. As he did so, a black snake came whipping upwards against the thin pane as though trying to break in at him. There was the sound of a massive gong, struck once and instantly muffled. He yelled at the top of his voice and jerked back into Sam's strong arms. 'What was that?'

'The rope. The propeller's gone!'

The fact that they could hear what they were saying suddenly struck them. They looked up. Everything was still. Silent.

Safe again. For the time being.

Robin was out through the port bridge wing door as soon as the avalanche stopped. She ran out into a brighter world where the overhang above her head now lay beneath her feet. The wall of the cliff, which had been so sheer and so close, was now a gentler slope further back at its crest, but piled against the ship's side at its foot. The air was full of ice dust. Not snow, but frozen water dust mixed with enough real dust to crunch between her teeth. She skidded over the liberal sprinkling of it on the deck beneath her feet and fetched up against the forward rail, looking down, scarcely able to believe the change a few seconds had brought about. Where there had been fire, there was ice. Where there had been a propeller, there was now a slope. Where there had been Walter Hogg and his team, there was nothing. Nothing at all.

'We got to dig in, Mr Timmins. We got to look at least.'

'They're dead, O'Brien. I saw it all. The propeller came down on top of them and then the fucking mountain came down on *it*! They're gone, believe me, all of them. And if we don't get a move on, we'll all be joining them.'

The walkie-talkie squawked and he answered it in the same brutal, panicky tone he had used on the crewman.

Robin didn't even notice. 'Timmins! How many are left down there?'

'All of my team. None of Hogg's.'

'My God . . .'

'I saw it all quite clearly, Captain. They went under. The propeller came down on them. All that ice pinned them down as it came up against the side of the ship. And the old girl didn't move an inch. Not an inch, Captain.'

'I know. I would have felt—'

'I think we got to give it up now. I think we got to get onto the ice and look for safety.'

'I know.' And she was gone.

But O'Brien was still there, pulling at his sleeve. 'It

was impossible to see. You couldn't have seen that much, Timmins. We got to dig. We got to look. There may be somebody still alive.'

'Well, fuck them, O'Brien,' screamed the terrified officer. 'And fuck you too.'

Colin and Kate found Robin still on the bridge wing and the three of them looked at each other in desperate silence. Then Robin said, 'I know. We've just run out of time.'

'The scaffolding at the back's still standing,' said Colin. 'You can still get everyone down it if you're quick. Then Kate and I can get them all across the barrier. It'll be risky but possible. Then with luck we can get them onto *Clotho*.'

She was nodding at once. 'There's another ship there now, a cruise liner. They should have room aboard her too.'

'Right. Let's do it.'

Robin nodded again. 'Right, Joe. Sound "Abandon Ship".'

The big crewman hit the alarm. It was a prearranged signal and, as with lifeboat drill, everyone knew exactly what to do. The silent ship suddenly filled with bustle as two crews – what was left of them – prepared to go down onto the ice.

They heard Harry Stone's voice trying to break through to Bill Christian with the news.

'At least that lurch has made that bit easier at any rate,' observed Kate suddenly.

'What do you mean?' Robin still sounded preoccupied.

'Well, take a look for yourself.'

Robin crossed to the inmost edge of the bridge wing and looked south. The bay was gone. The slipway led down to little more than a puddle. There was a wall of ice cutting right across *Atropos*'s bows. That last lurch had swung the iceberg round through nearly forty-five degrees and it was now grinding up against the hard ice of the barrier. Robin had been so preoccupied with the avalanche that she simply hadn't realised. Even had she been able to launch her ship, there was nowhere much for it to go any more.

Nevertheless, under the astonished eyes of the ice experts, Robin suddenly strode into the wheelhouse and pressed the tannoy button. 'This is the captain,' she said quietly. 'Leave the ship in the way we have discussed and be prepared to follow Mr and Mrs Ross across the ice barrier. Before you go, however, I have two things to request. Firstly, Chief Engineer, please leave the alternators running. I still want power. Secondly, would any volunteers to stay aboard report to me on the bridge at once. We have a team of men buried out here and I'm not going anywhere until we've tried to dig them out. Good luck the rest of you; good luck and God speed.'

CHAPTER THIRTY-SIX

The Last Day

Tuesday, 1 June   12:00

'*What*!' said Richard, simply awed. 'She's doing what?'

'She's down there now, sir, digging them out,' answered Harry Stone distantly. 'She's got a team of volunteers with her. Dr Ross has stayed as well. If they find anyone alive she'll almost certainly be needed. If they don't, then she can lead us all across the barrier after her husband and the rest of the crew.'

'Just let me get this clear, Harry. The captain won't leave until she's found these men or some proof of their death. In the meantime everyone else has abandoned and is on their way across the barrier led by Mr Ross?'

'That's it, sir.'

'So who's still there?'

'Me, the captain, Dr Ross. Miss Cable. The three general purpose seamen, Larkman, Edwards and Jones. Chief Lethbridge and Don Taylor are here too. The chief's looking after the engineering sections but Don's down on the ice.'

'Is that enough? It doesn't sound many.'

'They're digging off the top of the pile, trying to uncover the propeller. The idea is to reattach the falls from the crane and pull it upright again. The missing men are underneath it. As soon as I've finished this contact, I'll be gone. I'll leave the channel open and go down to help them.'

'But what if we need to contact you?'

'I'll send one of the others up – whoever needs a rest most. Not so much for your benefit, though, but to keep in contact with the people on the ice until they get within walkie-talkie range of you.'

'Why didn't they bring a radio from a lifeboat?'

'Too heavy to be worth it. The ice barrier looks as though it's beginning to come apart under the pressure from the berg. It's changing in nature this side, at any rate. It seems to be getting narrower as the berg pushes the thin stuff at the edge out of the way but it's also that much more dangerous to walk on. Why carry a heavy radio? Who's going to come when you call in any case? They've got walkie-talkies if they need help from us and to warn you when they're on their way in. That's all they really need.'

'Okay. I won't hold you up any more. Good luck over there. Give my love to my wife.'

'Who?' asked Harry. He looked at the radio with a frown, wondering for a moment who Richard Mariner was talking about. He had stopped thinking about her as even being a woman, let alone a wife. She was the captain, and the best chance of survival they had. He broke the contact, set the radio and got up. He wanted to get down onto the ice as quickly as he could. They needed able-bodied diggers down there.

He ran down the internal stairway rather than using the lift because he wasn't about to rely on the power under these circumstances even with the chief in the engine room. He paused on the threshold of the bulkhead door out onto the main deck to readjust his cold-weather gear. He settled his gloves on tight and pulled his hood up. Then he stepped out onto the deck and stopped. The first snow-laden squall had passed. There was a quieter wind out here now. It was less blustery but much more forceful; it was gathering strength even as he paused, his senses suddenly alert. It was exactly the kind of wind that would drive the berg against the barrier with unremitting force. And it was full of huge, wet, warm drops of rain.

The pressure between the berg and the barrier was building to its most intense. The forces involved in driving the two rock-solid pieces of ice together were gargantuan and growing in strength. The northward thrust of the Gulf Stream had released forces in the water which even now were pushing the barrier north with all the force of hundreds of millions of tons of moving ocean while the wind was driving the iceberg south with equal, perhaps even greater, strength. The effect of all this power was to ensure that any ice on either contestant that had been flat or thin was twisted and buckled until it had broken away or folded up against the solid central sections. On the one hand, this meant the crew who had just abandoned *Atropos* had a shorter distance to travel; on the other hand, it made that passage very dangerous indeed.

They were strung out over a quarter of a mile – on this terrain, plenty of room for the stragglers to be completely invisible to the leaders. The stragglers in this case were Timmins, O'Brien, Symes and LeFever. They were still on top of the first ice ridge and able to look back at *Atropos* when the rain swept over them. Three of them were already grumbling bitterly. With yet another cross to bear, they actually began to whine. Only LeFever paused, all too aware of the danger this new element could bring to the situation. He looked back, but the bows-on loom of *Atropos* was growing vague already, even though all her lights were on, lost behind the grey curtains of rain. He looked down at the three men in front of him. His job was to act as back marker, but he reckoned the rain changed that. He'd better go and talk to Ross, he thought. Lengthening his stride to the sure-footed lope he had perfected in the tundra of Quebec and on the shores of Antarctica, he pulled past the sorry-looking group of crewmen and began to overtake the rest.

'Now where's he going so goddamned quickly?' asked Timmins bitterly, but neither of the other two had an answer or the energy to speculate. Ahead of them, a long undulation had been concertinaed into a steep slope by the pressure of the ice. Down it straggled a line of hunched figures like dirty raindrops running down a grubby windowpane. Some moved singly; some coagulated in little groups. All spread out at the bottom of the slope onto a grey puddle of people as something made them hesitate before they defied gravity and began to drag themselves up the long, slick back of the next slope.

Fighting to keep his footing and his dignity in front of the two crewmen, Timmins trudged on down the slippery slope. He bitterly regretted his earlier panic and his decision to come across the ice rather than staying and looking for Walter Hogg. He regretted it particularly because O'Brien had been right. He had not had a clear view of the accident at all. He had lied, hoping to ensure that no one asked him to waste time looking for survivors when all he wanted to do was get out of that trap and over the ice barrier to some kind of safety. In actual fact there was every likelihood that someone might have survived; all he had seen with any clarity was the damaged propeller falling against the ship's side like some huge lean-to, and then the ice falling over the top of it. Anyone getting under the shelter of the broad brass blades probably would have had a fighting chance.

What kind of a man was he, who gave up like that and left his friends to die so that he could get away himself? he wondered bitterly. Normal. That was what. An average guy. No better than anyone else, sure. But no worse either. For all his fine words, O'Brien hadn't volunteered to stay behind and dig for the fat son of a bitch and his men. Like he had said. Fuck Hogg. Fuck them all.

In his dark brown study, he never realised he was beginning to fall behind. When he reached the bottom of the slope, he was effectively alone. Most of the rest of the crew were struggling up towards the crest of the next rise. Only O'Brien and Symes were anywhere near. As everyone else had done, he stopped and looked down at his feet. The lowest curve of the ice-valley floor had fractured under the folding pressure of the berg behind them. The two edges of the ice had split apart to reveal a lead of black water. It was not wide. Nor was it even particularly dangerous if care was taken in crossing it, but it exerted its own sinister power. Water had no right to be as unfathomably black as that. The break in the ice was so sheer, the edges of it folded back under such pressure, that there was not even a gleam of submerged paleness to relieve the awful fascination of it. It was utterly, mesmerisingly malignant. The rain gusted over it, the downpour heavy enough to make it foam and spit evilly. Timmins jumped back a little, looking down in something akin to horror.

He was the only one so far who had approached the lead alone and, without the support and simple distraction of a companion or two, he fell more absolutely under its spell. He was still standing, alone, on the edge of it when the iceberg towering behind him moved again. It did not move far, no more than a metre or two, adjusting its position against the barrier like a wrestler trying for a throw. It was enough. Timmins's feet shot out from beneath him and he suddenly found himself sitting on the edge of the ice with his feet dangling in the water. *Stupid bastard*! he thought, and went to get up. He put his hands on either side of his hips, palms down and fingers spread against the wet surface. As soon as he put any weight on them they lost their purchase and slipped. He sat down even harder and his skinny buttocks slid forward nearly a foot. The silent black water flooded into his boots, jerking him down yet further, and reached for his crotch. The shock was enough to knock the breath out of him. He was suddenly overpoweringly aware of how thin the ice was and how deep the ocean. He looked up in increasing panic. Almost everyone else had gone. Only two last figures lingered on the crest of the next ridge looking back at the iceberg. '*Hey*!' he shouted. 'O'Brien!' He wasn't quite panicking yet, largely because this didn't actually seem real.

The force of his shout made him lose his grip on the ice altogether and he slid right into the water. Where he had been leaning back like a reluctant bather on the edge of a pool, suddenly he was reaching forward, arms spread wide against the steep heave of the ice ahead, the slippery edge of it under his armpits. Cold lanced into him along with shock and uncontrollable terror. He went wild, scrabbling with his hands against the ice, searching for any kind of handhold at all, screaming as he did so at the top of his voice, 'O'Brien! Help me, O'Brien!' The edge of the ice caught him bruisingly under the chin and he bit his tongue but he didn't stop shouting for an instant.

Only when the black water slapped him in the mouth and choked him into silence and resignation did he stop, look up and listen. O'Brien hadn't moved a muscle. He was still up there, looking down at the helpless, drowning man. Their eyes met for an instant and the last thing Timmins heard before his head slid into the black, black water was the big New Yorker's mocking, terrible, echoing answer, 'Fuck you, Yasser.'

'So,' said LeFever. 'Why did you come back?'

They were on the top of the central ridge now, side by side, watching the line of exhausted men toiling up over the top. Behind them, the huge berg loomed, seemingly closer still, shrouded in the driving rain, its upper reaches lost in the low, roiling clouds. The wind was pulling ghastly rags and banners of icy spray off its mountainous shoulders where they loomed above the invisible *Atropos*. In front of them lay the wider, shallower slopes down towards the flat ice plain at whose heart stood *Clotho* with the cruise liner beyond her. Both ships were blazing with light and it was possible to see the bustle of preparation to receive them on the ice. Colin Ross had already spoken to Richard on the walkie-talkie so he knew they were coming in.

This was hardly a time for social chit-chat, but Colin reckoned he and LeFever had done a good job getting everyone safely here and he was prepared to be indulgent.

'The bird,' he said. 'The bird brought us back.'

'The dead auk?'

'Yes. I autopsied it and found a fish inside.'

'Big deal. So?'

'When I autopsied the fish, I found it was full of drugs.'

'I thought we'd already concluded that it would be. That's how both the fish and the bird died.'

'There was more. Semtex.'

There was the tiniest of silences and then Henri said, 'I wouldn't have thought even a drugged up fish would eat something like Semtex.'

'You're right. It wouldn't. It was eating part of a human finger. The flesh seems to have been buried in the Semtex.'

This time the silence was longer and Colin thought his companion must be thinking with wonderment, as he had done himself, about the mentality of someone who could chop off fingers and chuck them overboard with whatever they had been clutching.

This wasn't quite what Henri was thinking, of course. He turned away to look back towards the distant ship. There was nothing to see but a ghostly glow of brightness from her lights, refracting in the cliffs above the anchorage, illuminating the dull grey sheets of rain and the long streamers of wind-driven spray reaching out from the berg towards them. 'That's incredible,' whispered the French Canadian.

'Not really. Whoever threw it overboard must have been working on the assumption that it would all go straight down to the bottom of the ocean, but I don't think it really went very deep at all. That slipway, and the gallery around it, projects out pretty far beneath the surface. Remember, there's far more of an iceberg under water than there is up above it. The fish I autopsied was a top swimmer, a shallow feeder. I don't think that stuff's gone very deep at all. I think there's about twenty feet of water clear beneath *Atropos*'s bow. Then there's a shelf of ice. And that's where all that stuff is lying. Well, the bits of it the fish haven't eaten.'

'You mean you think it's all still *there*?'

'Has to be. How else could the fish have got so much of the stuff?'

'In twenty feet,' breathed Henri. He was thinking, not of the Semtex or even the detonators, but the letters. Jeanne's letters.

'Very much less than that now, of course. The barrier's closed across the bay and the berg's tilted back. It's all probably piled along the shoreline, if you know where to look.'

They were still standing there in silence when Symes came panting up, pale and shocked-looking. 'Mr Timmins is gone,' he said. 'I didn't see nothing, but O'Brien says he thought he heard him calling. There's nothing to see back there. No one left behind us. He's gone.'

The two tall men looked at each other for an instant. 'You go on,' said Henri, quietly and decisively. 'The others may need you. I'll go back.' He turned, but Colin's hand fell on his shoulder.

'If he's in trouble, you might need to give him this.' He passed Henri a hip flask. 'It's brandy. French cognac. The best I could get: Hennessy.'

The tremor which killed Timmins also had its effect on Robin. Her team were working at the top of the slope of ice blocks hard against the ship's side. The blocks were of different sizes, varying from the rough dimensions of half a brick up to those of a large tea chest. None of them were so square that they sat on each other with any firmness. They all had rough, rounded edges and they would all roll if pushed hard enough from the correct angle. The slope above the angle of the propeller was quite steep and the avalanche had actually left a kind of valley between the ship and the cliff. Spades pushed the topmost blocks down the slope quite easily at first but inevitably the more they moved, the harder the work became.

Robin had been there from the start. As soon as the rest of the crew departed, she had been busy getting the equipment they needed and putting it to work. Kate Ross worked silently at her side. The doctor had no idea when her skills might be called upon and needed to be there at all times, and she was not the kind of person to stand idly by when others had their sleeves rolled up.

Sam, Errol and Joe were a team within a team. While the others were primarily concerned to uncover the propeller and to discover whether there was anyone alive beneath it, the three seamen were concerned to find the ends of the broken falls. It was their mission to get these uncovered and reattached to the falls dangling from the crane itself. If the propeller could be craned back upright, or even partially so, the task of looking under it would be quickly and efficiently achieved. Don Taylor and Harry Stone were working further down the slope. As the ice from the topmost sections came down to them, they moved it further down, and, when they could, they prepared the ground for the arrival of more.

Ann Cable was the first person to go up and keep an eye on the radio. She had remained with the ship in the pursuit of her next book. Her bravery was of a different type to that of the others. She was slightly shamed by it, by the self-serving nature of it. The others were working primarily, perhaps absolutely, for the wellbeing of the men they were trying to save. Ann knew all too well that her own part in this drama had another, more commercial, aspect. She had decided to stay on in the location which would be the most fitting climax for the book she was working on. And she felt slightly cheapened by her commercial calculations. This made her unusually malleable, especially when Robin gave her direct orders. She was in the radio room, therefore, when the tremor hit.

Robin was at the top of the pile, hard up against the black side of her ship. She was working with a kind of contained rage. Most of her anger was directed at herself. Had Richard been doing what she was doing, even had he been in charge of the stranded ship as she was, she would have found it very difficult to forgive him. She was very well aware of the danger she was in but at the same time she could see no way in which she could possibly act in a different manner. Even though she had been captain of this ship for only a short time, she was nevertheless the captain. She hardly knew the missing men, and what she did know she didn't much like, but she owed them her duty. Someone had to look for them and there was no one else to do it. She had had to ask for volunteers and by the same token she had to lead them once they had volunteered. Desperate husbands, sick fathers, potentially motherless children counted as nothing against that absolute, professional, commitment. But she could not shake off the feeling that this was an unnecessary, almost self-indulgent act. It was too dangerous. She was risking more lives in the faint hope that someone down there might still be breathing. Almost certain death bet on a very long shot indeed. It was simply stupid. It seemed to verge on weakness. Was it weakness or strength? Inspired leadership or utter ineptness?

She had always preferred Shackleton to Scott: in their

drive for the Pole, Shackleton had killed no one and Scott had killed damn near everyone. But Scott seemed to be the greater hero, so who could say who was right?

She was quite certain, however, that if everyone here now were to die when the berg moved again, she would be seen as some bloody silly woman trying to prove a point about sexual equality. Which maybe she was.

These thoughts did nothing to dampen her burning rage or to alleviate the sheer bloody misery of digging in a huge pile of ice in a deeply sub-zero environment during a rain storm. Her legs were bruised from ankle to groin from slipping and smashing too sharp bones against too sharp ice edges. The effort of the gruelling physical work was making her feel more sick than anything since morning sickness. The strain of holding her feet firmly on the slick, slippery surfaces made the insides of her thighs throb as though she had been horseback riding for a week. Her back ached with that exquisite agony which carrying the twins in her womb had brought. Her hands were blistered and bleeding in her gloves and she was dying for a pee. Despite the exercises recommended by the midwife and *accoucheur*, her pelvic floor was not what it once had been.

The cliffs lurched upright again. *Atropos* was thrown to one side. The slope beneath her slid away. She was hurled forward and delivered a kind of head butt to the unforgiving side of her ship. She hit the metal so hard she actually heard it ringing. Then, face down and not a little dazed, she found herself slithering downwards, feeling with exquisite, agonising clarity every rolling edge and angle of ice beneath her on her shins and knees, hip bones and elbows, breasts and belly and bladder. She opened her mouth and screamed at the top of her lungs.

It never occurred to Sam Larkman that his captain was yelling with anything other than perfectly understandable rage and frustration. He was lent a greater stability than she enjoyed because he had been holding onto the fall from the crane when the iceberg moved. Although his feet seemed to be dancing over the rolling participants of yet another avalanche, his left hand was clasped round the steady rope with a grip like iron. He was able and willing, therefore, to reach into the sudden waterfall of ice and pluck out his captain like a drowning puppy by the scruff of her neck. He hung there for a moment as the whole world seemed to waver and reform itself, with the weight of his own body – and hers – painfully twisting the joint of his left shoulder.

Something slapped Robin in the face and she caught at it without further thought. She was still holding it when things calmed down again. The overpowering rumbling sound died down until she could hear simple speech. 'That's wonderful,' she heard Sam saying. 'That's wonderful, Captain.' At first she had no idea what he was talking about, but then she opened her eyes and realised that she was hanging on to the end of a rope. The lower end of a broken rope. 'That's just what we need, Captain,' said Sam, his voice full of cheerful wonderment.

While the crane operators effectively tied a massive reef knot in the broken fall, Robin surveyed the scene. The tiny readjustment of the iceberg had done more in a few seconds than they had been able to do with all their work so far. The cliff face behind them had dropped a few more ice boulders, but nothing major. The slope against the side of *Atropos* had not proved to be so firm, however. It had settled substantially and, as well as the rope, the downward movement had revealed the top of the propeller itself.

Robin allowed herself a tight smile of satisfaction. This was good luck. Perhaps the whole situation was beginning to turn round.

No sooner had the thought leaped into her mind than her walkie-talkie squawked. 'Captain here,' she answered at once.

'Robin, it's Ann. Have you seen the ice barrier?'

'What do you mean?'

'It's moved again. Look for yourself.'

With her tiny glimmer of hope dying stillborn in her breast, she walked down to the bow of her ship and looked beyond its black side, southwards across the ice.

There was no water visible any longer except that pouring from the black sky. The bay which had been at the foot of the slipway was gone and might never have existed. The ice of the barrier lay piled in pressure ridges across the whole horizon in front of her and she noticed inconsequentially that it was a different colour to the ice of the berg. And that fact, too, suddenly added to her disquiet, for she could see all too clearly that the last movement had closed in the hillsides which had formed the right arm of the bay. The hawsers which had held the hull so safely in place when she had reversed *Atropos* up the slipway all those weary hours ago now hung slackly on either hand, swinging in the grip of the driving, dangerous wind. One more movement like that and her command would be gripped between jaws of ice like a bone in the mouth of a rabid dog. And the thunder of the wind against the side of her streaming hood warned her that it was only a matter of time before that movement happened.

'Damn you!' she shouted at the ice, and it mockingly echoed her words of condemnation, making them a threat of its own: *damn you! Damn you! DAMN YOU!*

* * *

At first Henri thought the ghostly voice ringing in ice was damning him; his grip on reality was so loose now that he wouldn't have been surprised if it really had been doing so. He could hardly believe what luck was doing to him now. The sequence of events which had forced him to ever more desperate action over the last few days seemed set to destroy him as relentlessly as the storm had destroyed Jeanne. How could he risk leaving the letters lying on the shoreline of the berg where Robin Mariner and the rest were busily digging? The drugs and the explosives might well be gone now, but there was no guarantee. They were all in dull-coloured bundles and would be difficult to tell from the rubble around them. The detonators, however, were in bright coloured packages, guaranteed to catch the eye in that dull grey wilderness, and it was in among the detonators that the letters would be lying. He simply could not take the risk. When he found them – if he did so – he would have to think of some excuse to rejoin the crew on *Atropos*.

The lead which had swallowed Timmins had closed and he crossed it without ever knowing that the dead first officer was floating just beneath him. He was, of course, making no real effort to look for the missing man and this fact added yet another little weight of guilt to his weary soul. So that when the ice cliff on his right, the last one, overlooking the beached hull of *Atropos*, called out to him that he was damned, he wasn't much surprised.

He paused, looking down on the scene, trying to come to terms with the changes which had overtaken the situation even during his relatively short absence. The whole slipway seemed to have tilted away from him by several degrees – an effect enhanced by the fact that the ice cliff now sloped back at a slightly gentler incline and the overhang was gone. As Colin Ross had said, the water of the bay had gone and the grey moraine which had been the shore line where he and the glaciologists had taken radio-activity readings was now part of the lower slope. The bow of the ship, which had been in apparently fathomless black water, now sat high and dry. Not absolutely dry, of course: the downpour was thickening almost to the intensity of a fog. Water was running everywhere, adding the sounds of a deluge to the roaring of the ice around him. There was no hope of him being able to see even the bright detonators from this distance. He would have to go right up to the ship. What he would do if anyone was watching from the bridge and came down to find out what he was up to he simply did not know. Kill them, almost certainly. It was too late now for anything else.

As he slid down the back of the ridge, the first clap of thunder echoed in the ice chambers beside him like the beginning of the end of the world.

Richard and Colin Ross stood side by side on the bridge of *Clotho*. Nico sat in the watchkeeper's chair but he was neither on watch nor at ease. All three men were looking northwards in silence. Each one of them had a woman beyond the barrier; each one of them knew how great the danger was becoming. The only sounds in the great, broad wheelhouse were the driving of the rain and the swish of the wipers across the clearview. From their position they were able to see a vista created exclusively of deep and darkening grey. The chronometer above the wheel itself stood at 14:00 local time but it might as well have been after sunset. The sky was still the colour of coal, pressing down with terrible, absolute weight upon the dull, streaming shoulders of the granite berg. And the mountainous berg itself sat heavily on the slate breadth of the ice barrier which glittered and gleamed dangerously in what little light there was, like a deadly rock at the tide line, waiting to send the unwary foot slipping and sliding to its doom.

Everyone was in off the ice now, tucked up snugly aboard *Northern Lights*, all with so many hair-raising stories to tell that for once the radio was silent while the American media people avidly interviewed them instead of Richard. Only Colin Ross had come aboard *Clotho*, for he and Richard had communed at length over radio and walkie-talkie and the huge glaciologist knew that the captain was desperate to take further action while there was still time to influence events. He had only been on the bridge for the briefest moment, and his clothing was still dripping on the floor as he strove to take in the view which the added height of *Clotho*'s bridgehouse afforded him.

The silence was broken, not by any word from either of them, but by a column of dazzling brightness which connected the sky to the top of the distant ice mountains. Almost immediately, thunder boomed through the waiting *Clotho*. 'That just shows you how close the berg actually is,' mused Richard quietly. He had never lost the childhood habit of counting the seconds between lightning flash and thunder roll and the unexpectedly low number he had reached genuinely surprised him. 'Is the barrier melting, do you think?'

'Hardly,' answered the glaciologist. 'But it's certainly getting narrower. The berg has pushed all the thinner outcrops to the north of the central ridge out of the way, that's all.' He looked down at the map Richard and Nico had drawn using the ice blink. 'All of this has gone now, I'd say.' His broad right hand, big as a bear's paw in its mitten, swept across the whole of the northern plane. 'The berg is hard up against the central ridge. The ridge itself has closed off the anchorage and the angle it's sitting at seems to be closing the sides of the bay together. You'll have lost your ship within the hour and if they don't get off the berg soon, they'll all be in very bad trouble.'

'Do you want to go back and help them?'

'I want to talk to Kate first. I'm not going to hang around here if they need me but I'm not going charging back across there without warning them.'

'Bill,' called Richard through into the radio room, 'get *Atropos* for me, would you?'

But before his order could be carried out, the walkie-talkie on the arm of Nico's chair buzzed. He picked it up and switched it on.

Ann Cable's excited voice filled the room. 'They're still alive! My God, they're still alive!'

'Ann,' said Nico, 'is that you? *Ann*?'

Colin exchanged a look with Richard which was suddenly full of hope. In her excitement, the American reporter had contacted them by walkie-talkie instead of by radio. And it had worked. She had got through.

The ships were within walkie-talkie range of each other.

There was nothing there. Ross had sent him back for nothing! Henri raged among the ice blocks along the old shoreline and down along the slick, running slipway to what had once been a submarine ridge where the rain was gathering in pools and puddles which were already freezing over. Nothing! He had been foolish to come. He was stupid to stay longer. There was no trace of anything incriminating, and the team of men and women working up on the rubble by the ship's side showed no sign of coming down here at all. And if they didn't, no one else would, that was for certain.

He would give up and go to join them. He would go back across the barrier and away to safety with them, and they would never know the truth. Unless he joined another crew and completed his mission, of course.

He turned and began to climb the slope towards the high bow of the ship. Walking up this way, he could see what they were doing up there quite clearly, for all that the impenetrable downpour still effectively hid him from their sight. The crane was still extended at its fullest reach and someone had reattached the fall. As Henri walked up towards the ship, he could see that the crane was being used to lift the propeller back from its position against *Atropo*'s side and, as it did so, the ice rubble was sliding back as well. The team involved in the rescue were all looking down into the gap which must slowly be opening between the black metal and the bright brass. Certainly, none of them was looking his way. Idly, Henri began to speculate, like a child playing hide and seek, how close he could creep up behind them before they realised he was there.

When he fell over he thought he had simply lost his footing; it was only when the whole slipway began to jump and heave beneath him that he realised what was going on. The sound overwhelmed him. It seemed to be much more terrible down here on the surface of the ice itself. He did not realise that the increased power of what he was hearing – though in fact the experience went well past anything he had ever thought of as *hearing* – was a combination of noise and echo. The submarine ledges of both barrier and berg which had been grinding against each other down the black fathoms beneath were tearing each other apart as the next great thunder squall powered into the north-west quarter of the berg. The berg heaved

up and then thrust itself massively downwards and hard
ice clapped thunderously against hard ice. The caves
within the spine of the ice barrier took up the sound and
doubled then redoubled it. This was a quake which made
all the other movements so far seem little more than tre-
mors. It was only the fact that all the loose ice on the
cliff had already come down in the original avalanche that
stopped *Atropos* being buried.

But Henri knew nothing about any of this. All he knew
was that the ice of the slipway leaped up and smacked
him in the face. Then he was drowning in a cacophony
of sound so overpowering that he could not catch his
breath. Literally. Every time he tried to breathe back in
the breath which the first impact had knocked out of
him, the overpowering throbbing which was moving
through the air caught in his throat and lungs and the
shaking became so terrible that it seemed to him that his
very heart would be broken loose within him.

But at last the agony began to ease. The icequake was
passing. Water washed up around him and he hurled himself up onto his knees with wild, mad strength, only to
remain there as though he was praying.

As, indeed, he may have been. For *Atropos* was grinding
down the slipway towards him like doom, and gathering
speed as she moved.

Sam Larkman's magic hands tickled the controls of the
crane's lifting mechanism. The propeller lifted back fractionally, opening a slim black mouth between the side of
the ship and the bright, bent brass blade. Robin danced
on the sliding, settling slope of ice and called, 'Hold it,
Sam!' into her walkie-talkie.

In the sudden silence, someone deep and distant called,

'Light! I see light!' And the words came from the bottom of that black pit.

'Ann,' said Robin into the cold little handset, 'there's someone still alive down there. Tell *Clotho* we have survivors.' She snapped off the radio and flung herself down on her knees. 'Walt?' she bellowed, and Walter Hogg's disbelieving voice came back up at her.

'*Captain*?'

'Hang on for a moment. We'll soon have you out. How many are there down there?'

'Three. The whole team. There's a kind of a cave. We—'

'Any of you hurt?'

'Few bruises . . .'

'Okay. We'll try and open things up a bit more then we'll send down a rope.'

Robin looked up at Kate. Thank God she wouldn't be needed after all. Not as a doctor at any rate. They would still need a guide across the barrier though. 'We need a rope, maybe a ladder,' Robin snapped and Kate automatically sprang to obey, but in fact Robin was talking to Don Taylor. The two of them went off together, however, leaving Robin and Joe Edwards side by side on the top of the ice fall.

Robin put her walkie-talkie to her lips again. 'Right, Sam, let's try that again. Very, very gently.'

The fall creaked and the propeller blade stirred once again. The ice blocks began to tumble back, the majority of them falling at an angle dictated by the slope down towards the cliff and the slope of the slipway down towards where the sea had been.

Robin moved round to the up-slope section of the jumbled pile, looking for a new position of vantage. The action saved her life.

Suddenly all hell was let loose and her world was brought as close to destruction as was Henri LeFever's. Her pain was less than his because she was further from the echoing cliffs of the ice barrier. But he was on solid ground and she was on a tumbling jumble of rock-hard boulders. Her feet flew out from under her and she felt herself tumbling backwards. She had fallen down the long staircase at Cold Fell on the night of her twelfth birthday and now, of all times, she remembered her father saying to her, 'If that happens again, roll yourself up into a ball. Much the safest thing.'

It had seemed good advice then. It seemed good advice now. Her last conscious thought for an unknown length of time was that she should get her knees up by her nose and hug them for all she was worth.

She came to lying flat on her back on a lumpy pile of ice with the cliffs on her left looking down the slipway. In front of her, towering over her but thankfully leaning back away from her, was the propeller.

She sat up so suddenly that she slid a little down the slope towards the dazed, dazzled bunch of men she had stayed here to save. They were looking around themselves with about as much intelligence as a bunch of lice on a suddenly upturned log.

The ice beside her moved and she jumped. But it was only Joe. 'It swung round, Captain. The propeller fell back and swung right round.' He moved his shaking hands to show something moving through ninety degrees like an opening door. She looked up, and saw with simple wonderment that there was smoke pouring from the underside of Sam Larkman's crane. Distantly, she hoped that he and Errol weren't getting roasted up there. Then she looked back at Joe Edwards.

He was screaming words so loudly that the veins were

knotting on his forehead below the grey crew cut. And she could only just hear him.

She looked right, awed by understanding. What he had described to her could only have taken place under one set of conditions.

It could only have happened if *Atropos* had moved. And, judging from the overwhelming rumbling sound that was going on around them, the ship was moving still.

'She's moving. My God, she's moving!' There was absolute, utter terror in Ann Cable's voice and it was reflected in the expressions of horror on the faces of the three men aboard *Clotho*, who were listening to her.

'Ann! Who else is on there with you? *Who else is aboard*?'

'No one. I'm on my—'

The walkie-talkie went dead.

Clotho's bridge was no longer a silent place and there was more than the echo of Ann's words disturbing the atmosphere. The ice wall in front of the ship was going wild. Although all of them had had proofs aplenty of its solidity, as they looked at it now they might well have been forgiven for doubting their experiences or their memories. For the whole barrier seemed to be twisting as though the entire length of its great grey flank was the back of a great grey serpent. The grinding thunder was shot through with sharp reports as though there was lightning crackling down all around them. For the first time in many days, the battered ship was stirring as waves rolled beneath her keel. The flat plain of ice at whose heart she lay like a dagger point seemed to be rippling. Everything they could see, hear and feel was in violent, terrifying motion.

Colin looked down at Richard, but he was paying no

attention to his guest; he was on the telephone to the chief engineer and his hand on the engine room telegraph was emphasising his words as he screamed over the thunderous sounds, '*FULL ASTERN. FULL ASTERN. FULL ASTERN*!'

The hawsers on *Atropos*'s port quarter had gone, along with their anchorage points in the avalanche. The two remaining on her starboard had been slackened by the movement of the right-hand reach of the ice. So it was that she gained so much speed on her slide down the slipway before they tightened once again. They pulled her round to the starboard until the single, thread-thin fall from Sam Larkman's crane, anchored still to the great weight of the propeller, snagged in spite of the fact that he had hit the release button before he and Errol abandoned the cab, and managed to bring her up short. But not for any great length of time.

Robin was in action most quickly. It was the frayed end of the broken hawser hanging from *Atropos*'s port quarter which prompted her, because it swung in from the black overhang of the poop which was suddenly right above her, moved by a momentum which the still hull no longer possessed, and nearly took her head off.

'Quick!' she bellowed, with the full power of her quarterdeck voice. 'Get aboard! *GET ABOARD*!'

Ann's estimation that she was alone aboard was mercifully inaccurate, because even as Robin gave her bellowed command, Don Taylor thrust his head over the railing far, far above and shouted, 'Look out below!'

Even as his words reached her, so did the reason for shouting them: the end of the spare Jacob's ladder.

She caught it at once and yelled to the others, '*Get aboard*!'

Joe was quickest to obey and she stood back to let him pass, still holding the bottom rung. '*HOGG! FOR CHRIST'S SAKE! MOVE*!' The ladder, as sensitive as a fishing line, joined her left hand to the deck of her command and warned her all too vividly that *Atropos* was not sitting quite as still as she seemed to be.

Ann Cable, pale as a ghost, was waiting at the top of the ladder when at last Robin scrambled over the rail onto *Atropos*'s poop. She paused for a moment beside Ann. 'We won't be sitting still for long,' she said. 'The others will be loosening the hawsers when I tell them. You stay in charge of the ladder here. We may need it later so I don't want to lose it. If it snags on anything, though, you just pull this line and it will go over the side.'

Ann nodded dumbly and Robin rushed up onto her bridge. The ship was still trembling on the very edge of stasis when she got up there and started calculating the odds. That last movement of the ice had opened the bay in front of them only a little. Across the whole prospect in front of her, there still stood that mocking cliff of ice which was the backbone of the barrier. If she told the crewmen at the stern to loosen the hawsers, she would only run her command down into that solid wall of dirty grey. If she didn't issue the order, the jaws of ice already holding onto the sides of *Atropos* would crush the life out of her the next time the iceberg stirred.

In a frenzy of desperation she looked back at that solid, unforgiving, immovable cliff of ice, and at the second she did so, the very centre of it, exactly in front of her, immediately before the sleek head of *Atropos*'s forecastle though a mile and more distant from it, exploded into a column of fire.

The waves of power from that explosion, washing over *Atropos* as inevitably as waves on the open ocean, rattled the windows, shook the superstructure, and started the ship's wild slide again.

Ann Cable stood rigidly on the poop deck. She was still trying to come to terms with the depths of terror she had plumbed when she believed she had been on the sliding ship alone. She was a strong woman, and basically self-reliant, and yet, at the bottom of that pit of despair, with the deck trembling terrifyingly beneath her feet and the cold angularity of the walkie-talkie pressed to her lips hard enough to bring blood into her mouth, the fact that she had been talking to Nico really made a difference. Only Don Taylor's utterly unexpected arrival at the door of the radio room had made her break contact and ever since she had done so, she had regretted it. Standing on the poop deck of *Atropos*, feeling her straining to be gone down the slipway no matter what might await her at the bottom of it, made Ann all too well aware that she had not been playing fair with her gentle, witty, understanding, genuinely macho Neapolitan lover. *Son of a bitch,* she thought. *How I miss the son of a bitch.*

She felt the deck begin to stir beneath her feet. She heard a distant rumble of thunder and looked up at the low, black sky.

And *Atropos* was in motion.

It was slow to begin with, a kind of gathering of inertia as she began to grind down the slope again. Ann was held rigid by the lingering power of the shock of her terror, distanced from the current scene, which might well have terrified her even more.

As the foot of the ladder swept past the pile of ice blocks behind the sprawl of the propeller which was no longer attached to the fall from Sam's crane, it jerked and she looked down over the edge of the poop. Someone was climbing upwards.

At first she had no idea who it was. The hood of the cold-weather gear hid the face absolutely from her sight. She frowned, wondering whether this was some kind of hallucination brought on by the terror she had felt.

But then the figure looked up, and it was Henri.

She ran to the rail, the better to look down at him. What was he doing here? Why wasn't he safely aboard one of the other ships?

What was going on?

He was near the top of the ladder when he looked up and saw her there. He grinned, and the flash of his teeth turned her knees to water.

'What on earth are you doing?' she called down to him.

'I've brought you a present,' he called exultantly. 'See. It's cognac. The best: Hennessy.'

That one word brought it all into focus for her, suddenly and utterly unexpectedly. Hennessy.

That was the name of the terrorist woman who worked for La Guerre Verte. Joan Hennessy.

She had seen the poster and all the information which had come in from Heritage House. It had seemed to her that Joan Hennessy was a New York Irish name – belonging to someone like O'Brien.

But now she understood.

Cognac Hennessy. It was a French name, belonging to someone who was French Canadian, perhaps. And the given name, Joan. Like Joan of Arc, it would be Jeanne in French. *Jeanne*. Sounding, in oddly accented French Canadian, so much like *John*.

She was jerked back to that cave in the iceberg's mountains when he had mumbled the name in his sleep and she had wondered if he was gay. It was as simple, as unavoidable, as that.

She looked down. He saw the accusation in her eyes.

She saw the admission of guilt in his.

At once he started climbing again with feverish, febrile speed. She stood there as though turned to stone, watching him as he swarmed up towards her. Her mind was a whirl of revelation. Of the two people closest to her aboard, she had trusted the wrong one and suspected the wrong one. Robin would never do anything underhand, she realised; not with Nico, not with anyone. And Henri had never done anything honest. She thought of his attempt at seduction, of her childish suspicions about his sexual orientation. How stupid she had been. How he must have laughed at her. Well, he wasn't laughing now.

And she pulled the line Robin had shown her with all the strength at her command and let the ladder fall free.

'*FULL AHEAD, FLANK SPEED*!' Richard was under such stress that his voice rose beyond a shout again. *Clotho* had just swept out of the lead into the open sea beside the *Northern Lights*. Her reverse thrust was cancelled and, even as she swept backwards, stern wave foaming under her counter, so the blades of the great propeller were reversed to drive her forward once again. Richard watched narrow-eyed as the knot meter began to click up out of reverse. He had every intention of throwing his vessel as hard as he could against the central ridge of the ice barrier. The Maier-form icebreaker bow lifted as the great Rolls-Royce engines thundered up to full power. The edge of the ice swept away in front of the ship as she reversed out of the lead, then hesitated and began to race back towards the ship as the course went back on itself.

Colin and Richard both rocked onto the balls of their feet as *Clotho*'s momentum also reversed. She seemed to hover for an instant, the water heaving behind her like a big surf behind a surfboard. Colin actually took a step forward as though the deck were on a steeper slant than it was.

Clotho gathered way into the black water of the lead. Richard took the helm himself and held the line as the vessel began to speed up the mile's length between the floating fields of ice. The pair of RB211 turbine engines delivered so much power that the freighter took off more quickly than a speedboat. She came majestically up to full speed, the knot meter in the bridgehouse clicking relentlessly through twenty knots, twenty-five and thirty.

'We're going to hit very hard indeed,' Richard warned as the ice skimmed past on either side. He wasn't speaking particularly loudly, but his words carried across the wheelhouse as though he had been shouting at full voice.

It seemed to him in those moments as he prepared to throw it all away that he had nothing important left to lose. His company was effectively lost. His personal possessions were tied up with the finances of the lost company. The only things he cared about were lost: his ships. The only people, too, apart from his children: his father-in-law in intensive care and his beloved wife trapped at death's door. Posterity would write him off as just another self-destructive failure. But, in the final analysis, at least he would be going out with a bang, not a whimper.

Running his ship at full speed up against the ice ridge seemed to be a futile gesture, but any gesture would be better than none. It was self-indulgent, as any borderline

suicide always was. But it was worth making, he calculated. It would be remembered, and perhaps the reason for
making it, and even the love which had caused it, would
be remembered too.

Clotho was moving at thirty-five knots when she hit the
ice. Her bow was riding high and it lifted out of the water
and rode across the narrow area of flat ice which lay
before the fifty-foot cliff.

The ruined forecastle head was still moving at full speed
when it hit the solid ice.

The water in the first hold was frozen and the weight
of it was hurled forward by the impact, to tear through
the front of the ship. It weighed several hundred tons and
it was travelling at nearly forty miles an hour. Likewise,
the men on the bridge and in the engine room were hurled
hither and yon, tumbling about the place like puppets. And
that was lucky, especially for the men up on the bridge.

The ice from the hold and the ice from the cliff came
together with tremendous force. And sandwiched between
them was Jeanne Hennessy's bomb. The bomb had been
designed by the explosives expert to spread its power as
widely as possible. The effect of the ice from the hold,
however, was to force the whole power of the bomb forwards into the ice ridge. A huge column of ice exploded
up and out, to the sides and over the barrier. Massive shock
waves from the explosion sped at light speed through the
ice barrier and were, if anything, amplified in the echoing
caves beyond the crest.

The impact of the ship and the bomb came together just
as the full force of the berg was pushing back, with the
power of the thunder squall behind it, and the effect was
devastating. The backbone of the ice barrier was broken
as completely as a neck severed by the headsman's axe.

At once the westward section of the barrier began to swing southwards, borne against the breast of the triumphant iceberg. The eastern section of the barrier, still gripped by the northward pressure of that offspring of the Gulf Stream, began to swing back up towards the coast of Greenland which had given it birth.

And while *Clotho*, her forward quarter blown to smithereens, rolled sideways onto the solid section of the ice barrier over which her ruined bow had lifted her, so *Atropos* her sister thundered down off the edge of the icy slipway into the clear deep water of the North Atlantic Ocean, into the channel opened up for her through the cold heart of the barrier, relaunched, reborn, resurrected after all.

CHAPTER THIRTY-SEVEN

Independence Day

Sunday, 4 July   12:00

The consultant had completed his round of the private rooms and Bill Heritage had decided it was time he got organised for when the youngsters came to pick him up. All he had to do, really, was to dress himself and then finish packing his weekend case with the basic necessities and the hospital treats he had been surrounded by during the last weeks since his heart by-pass operation.

He could have called for one of the private nurses to do it for him with no more than the press of a bedside button. But he retained the independence of mind traditional in men late of the navy. He could do his own darning; he had done his own ironing on more occasions than he cared to remember; he was more than capable of doing his own packing. As soon as he had managed to get his trousers on.

He was a very lucky man, they informed him. He was lucky that Maggie DaSilva had known what to do and had done it so quickly; that the studio had maintained such an expert and well-equipped first aid team; that the ambulance had arrived so quickly; that he had suffered no brain damage during the attack; that it was possible to repair the damage short term; that it had proved possible to correct it so effectively long term.

He didn't feel all that lucky; perhaps that was why they made a point of emphasising his good fortune to him so often.

He felt that he had let Robin and Richard down; that he had let Heritage Mariner down; that he had let Helen down; and, in the final analysis, that he had let himself down.

If he wasn't retired, then he ought to be. How could anyone trust the running of a major company to a man who got out of breath while buttoning up his trousers? He shrugged his braces over the shoulders of his pyjama jacket with more than accustomed resignation and reached for the cashmere polo-necked pullover he preferred to wear on Sundays after he had been to church. His hair surrendered to the flats of his palms; he would brush it later.

He crossed to the window on the sill of which were piled a collection of papers, books and magazines. He paused before he collected the pile together, looking downwards, struck as always by the view. The Thames flowed by as brown as toffee, seeming to wash the wall beneath his feet. On his right hand, the span of Westminster Bridge stepped across the river. If he looked up, his face and that of Big Ben seemed to be about level and not very far apart.

The riverside balconies of the Palace of Westminster stood out over the dark water opposite and his room was high enough for him to gaze down on them, remembering functions he had attended there with friends and colleagues in both Houses of Parliament, the Commons and the Lords.

He looked down to gather up the pile of printed matter and was struck again by the picture of an exploding ship and the headline which accompanied it: TERRORIST BOMB SAVES SISTER SHIPS.

It was an old paper, the better part of a month out of date, but it was the first thing he had been conscious of seeing when he had come out of the anaesthetic after his operation, and he knew he would keep it for ever.

He would probably keep all of them which day by day had given the world the story of how the bomb in the bows of *Clotho* had exploded on impact with the ice barrier and so released *Atropos* from the lethal clutches of the iceberg. How *Clotho*, apparently fatally damaged, had remained wedged on the ice with her bows clear of the water until simple repairs could be effected and then how *Atropos* had towed her sister ship to Frederiksdal in Greenland, the nearest safe port.

It was a story which seemed to have caught the popular imagination on both sides of the Atlantic, and in among the correspondence which accompanied the printed matter was a letter from Ann Cable informing him that he could expect a typescript of her new book *The Sister Ships*, based on her experiences aboard *Atropos*, to confirm his part in the whole adventure.

There was the gentlest tapping on his door and he swung round to see Helen Dufour standing there. The tall woman swept across the room towards him and he enfolded her in a huge bear hug. Usually she complained that he crushed the life out of her, her Provençal chic being something which did not react well to his bluff northern gallantries. This morning she answered his grip with possessive fierceness and indeed it was he who broke away first. His ribs were still a little tender after the rough treatment they had received during his operation.

'How did it go?' he asked gruffly.

'St Petersburg? Fine. It's all sewn up. When we have the ships, they will have the cargo. The same as Archangel and Murmansk.'

'You've been working so hard, my darling.'

'We all have. But the worst is over now. Things started looking up when the insurers agreed that *Clotho*'s damage definitely came from a terrorist bomb and they would meet the salvage and repair bills in full. The Russian deal is just icing on the cake now. I think we can all take a well-earned holiday.'

Another knock came at the door and there was Maggie DaSilva partially obscured behind a massive bunch of flowers.

'Matron says you're going home,' she said accusingly. 'What shall I do with these?'

Sir William smiled at her, as indulgent as a father with a favourite daughter. 'We'll think of something,' he rumbled. 'To what do I owe the pleasure? You've never struck me as a Sunday morning girl.'

'I'm only up this early because I haven't been to bed yet,' she countered. 'I've been out on the town with the most gorgeous New York attorney. I think he's trying to tempt me into going West with him.'

'Well, you think it through carefully,' warned Sir William and the kindly concern in his tone elicited a wide grin from her.

'Oddly enough, I didn't come for paternal advice,' she purred. 'I have a little news for you. Apparently the word has gone out forcefully, even in the Big Apple. The people who killed the Italians outside the TV studio have said that no one will be allowed to profit from the *Napoli* affair. Anyone else who goes ambulance-chasing like the late Vito Gordino can expect to meet the same fate as he did. So that just leaves the US government. And they will only take action if our appeal fails; and if *Napoli* proves to be doing damage within their legitimate area of jurisdiction. Either way, Heritage Mariner is off the hook for the time being.'

He nodded at her, a lump in his throat forbidding speech.

Into the silence which lay between them came the sound of approaching mayhem. Maggie put the flowers down. 'If that's who I think it is then I'm off,' she said. 'You pay me handsome fees and Richard buys me stunning dinners, but nothing will induce me to play with the twins when I've had no sleep for thirty-six hours.' And she was gone like a sorceress leaving only a whiff of Obsession.

'Did you see Maggie?' asked Helen an instant later as Robin struggled through the door swinging William by his reins.

'Maggie DaSilva? No. Has she been in already . . .' The Obsession hit her nostrils. 'Oh,' she said. 'I see what you mean. No, we haven't seen her. Is she avoiding us?'

'She's avoiding some of you,' said the French woman dryly.

Mary burst in next, seemingly dragging Richard by main force. 'All ready?' he asked. 'Whew! What's that smell? Helen?'

'No,' chided Robin lovingly. 'Helen's a Chanel girl, like me. That's Maggie.'

'Is it? What did she want so early?'

'She wanted to tell me some good news,' said Sir William. 'I'll tell you more about it on the way home.'

'Great,' said Richard. 'Mary, sit down. *Sit*! Good girl. Now, let me get that suitcase.'

'Helen says we can all take a holiday,' said Sir William,

gathering together his bits and pieces. 'And Maggie's news means we do have the breathing space, if we want it. I think you two should get away.'

Richard nodded soberly. 'I think you're right, Bill. We've put a good, reliable senior management structure in place more quickly than I'd have thought possible in the time. It's going to take a load off all of us.'

'Excellent! Helen and I will be going to Grimaud. What about you four?'

'We've been thinking about it. Haven't decided yet.'

'We're supposed to be teaching the twins to ski, but it's the wrong time of the year unless we go to Australia,' said Richard.

'Spare me,' shuddered Robin. 'No more ice. Please!'

'Well, I've got to get used to it anyway,' said Richard defensively.

'What's he talking about?' asked Sir William.

Richard zipped up the case and hefted it as though it weighed nothing at all. He remained quite pointedly silent.

'Well?' asked Sir William.

Robin answered. 'Oh, he's got himself mixed up in this scheme to deliver a bit of ice, that's all.'

Sir William looked across at his son-in-law with total incomprehension.

Richard burst into laughter. 'Deliver a bit of ice,' he echoed. Then his eyes met Sir William's, and he explained, 'It's Colin Ross and me. We're going to try and tow an iceberg from the Arctic to the Congo.'

ACKNOWLEDGEMENTS

Two weeks before the Long Vacation, when I had planned to start writing *The Bomb Ship*, I went blind in my right eye. My thanks must therefore start with the ophthalmic department of the Kent and Sussex Hospital in Tunbridge Wells who diagnosed the precise nature of the problem. More especially, I must express my deepest gratitude to the Eye Department at St Thomas's Hospital in London, particularly to Mr Chignell and his team who performed the emergency surgery to save my sight; and to the matron, sisters and nurses in the Royal Eye Ward who nursed me for a week afterwards.

At this point I must therefore say thank you to my brother Simon and his flatmate, Clive, who took me in until a bed at St Thomas's could be found for me.

It was at St Thomas's that I met Errol, Sam and Joe and I thank them for allowing me to include them in the story – my only regret being that I lost some of the notes made of conversations with these extraordinary characters and therefore have changed names and missed out one beloved motorcycle.

I am pleased and grateful to thank my colleagues at The Wildernesse School who, at the busiest time of the academic year, shouldered my responsibilities along with their own. I thank all those colleagues who took lessons for me. I owe my deepest thanks to Hilary Burdett who ran the English department, to Beverly Butler who ran the Sixth Form (or the Post–16 Provision, as we must now call it) and to the Senior Management team who shared the rest of my responsibilities – to Steve Guest, David Flint, Stuart McTavish and headmaster Ron Herbert.

The research for *The Bomb Ship* is based on a wide range of material. The situation and some of the characters are drawn from my earlier novel *Killer*. I revisited much of the original research material, including the diaries of Captain Scott and *South* by Ernest Shackleton. The more recent material fundamental to the work includes the writings of Tristan Jones, Robert Swann and Ranulph Fiennes. Pictures as well as words were particularly important in Bryan and Cherry Alexander's *The Eskimos* and, for the berg itself, Reinhold Messner's *Die Alpen*. Even as I write this, Sir Ranulph has just completed his epic journey across Antarctica for charity. I hope it is not too presumptuous to offer him my most sincere congratulations on a truly historic feat.

As ever, I must thank Stanfords the map makers of 12–14 Long Acre, London, for their help. This time I promised to mention Paul Hart. Especially, I must thank Kelvin Hughes, ships suppliers of 145 Minories, London, who supplied hard-to-get charts of the Davis Strait and the Arctic Pilot for the region.

Finally and most warmly of all, I must thank Richard

Atchley. Not only did he advise me in great detail about the legal aspects of the story, guiding me round the chambers and courts in question, but he also added a crucial amount of maritime experience and, perhaps most importantly from my point of view, a portion of that cheerfully boundless enthusiasm with which he approaches everything he does.

More Terrifying Fiction from Headline:

DAVID MARTIN

LIE TO ME

THE MOST COMPELLING NOVEL OF SUSPENSE
SINCE *THE SILENCE OF THE LAMBS*

'A rip-roaring read, a novel that grabs you from the
first sentence and, like the best horror tale,
becomes both compelling and terrifying, daring
you to read to the end' *Washington Post*

LIE TO ME

The violent death of a multimillionaire. A maniac on
the loose.

LIE TO ME

An enigmatic, sensual widow. A cop who can't be
lied to.

LIE TO ME

Two kidnapped children. Four horrific murders.

LIE TO ME

A shocking secret. An explosive climax.

'Gothic in its grisliness, disturbingly
persuasive . . . a master writer' *Los Angeles Times*

'A novel rich in complications and deft character
studies' *San Francisco Chronicle*

FICTION/THRILLER   0 7472 3507 4

More Thrilling Fiction from Headline:

—— JONELLEN HECKLER ——
CIRCUMSTANCES UNKNOWN

SHE'S ALREADY LOST HER HUSBAND.
NOW HER CHILD IS AT RISK...

It was supposed to be the perfect family holiday:
Tim and Deena Reuschel in a magical cottage up
in the mountains with their five-year-old son Jon.
But the idyll ends in nightmare when Tim's body
is found washed up on the river bank. Despite
the circumstances, Deena refuses to accept that
the tragedy was an accident and when her
suspicions are casually dismissed by the police,
she begins her own exploration of Tim's past,
searching for connections to her husband's death.

But someone else is taking a close interest in
Deena's investigation. Someone whose twisted
obsessions are focussed on the young woman and
her precious son. And with every clue she
manages to uncover, Deena brings herself and
Jon closer and closer to mortal danger...

'A superb mystery thriller' *Woman and Home*

'A suspense tale that draws the reader in from the
first line' Mary Higgins Clark

'Chilling suspense as the killer's psychotic
personality steadily deteriorates' *Publishers Weekly*

FICTION/THRILLER   0 7472 4133 3

More Thrilling Fiction from Headline:

PHILIP CAVENEY
SPEAK NO EVIL

THE LATE-NIGHT WHISPER
FROM HELL...

Radio presenter Tom Prince hosts the graveyard slot: the after-midnight phone-in programme for Manchester's *Metrosound*. Despite a broken marriage, he now finds personal happiness with a caring girlfriend and his seven-year-old son Danny. Otherwise Tom is stuck in a rut...and about to be hurtled out of it with terrifying momentum.

It begins with just another late-night call, from a man who talks in a strange whisper. But this one claims he has committed a murder, and is standing over his victim's corpse.

Thus begins a chilling nightly dialogue between Tom and 'the Whisperer'. Badgered by police intent on tracing the killer, Tom reluctantly keeps the line open, while the gruesome deaths continue. And as his audience constantly grows, he suddenly finds himself a celebrity.

Though Tom himself is the focus of this terrifying bloodlust, his child and his girlfriend are soon exposed to extreme danger – never knowing from which dark shadow the next surprise blow will fall.

And as he begins to understand the full horror of the Whisperer's psychosis, Tom realises that his success may cost them all too high a price.

FICTION/THRILLER   0 7472 4045 0

A selection of bestsellers
from Headline

GONE	Kit Craig	£4.99 □
QUILLER SOLITAIRE	Adam Hall	£4.99 □
NOTHING BUT THE TRUTH	Robert Hillstrom	£4.99 □
FALSE PROPHET	Faye Kellerman	£4.99 □
THE DOOR TO DECEMBER	Dean Koontz	£5.99 □
BRING ME CHILDREN	David Martin	£4.99 □
COMPELLING EVIDENCE	Steve Martini	£5.99 □
SLEEPING DOGS	Thomas Perry	£4.99 □
CHILDREN OF THE NIGHT	Dan Simmons	£4.99 □
CAPITAL CRIMES	Richard Smitten	£4.99 □
JUDGEMENT CALL	Suzy Wetlaufer	£5.99 □

All Headline books are available at your local bookshop or newsagent, or can be ordered direct from the publisher. Just tick the titles you want and fill in the form below. Prices and availability subject to change without notice.

Headline Book Publishing PLC, Cash Sales Department, Bookpoint, 39 Milton Park, Abingdon, OXON, OX14 4TD, UK. If you have a credit card you may order by telephone — 0235 831700.

Please enclose a cheque or postal order made payable to Bookpoint Ltd to the value of the cover price and allow the following for postage and packing:

UK & BFPO: £1.00 for the first book, 50p for the second book and 30p for each additional book ordered up to a maximum charge of £3.00.

OVERSEAS & EIRE: £2.00 for the first book, £1.00 for the second book and 50p for each additional book.

Name ....

Address ....

....

....

If you would prefer to pay by credit card, please complete:
Please debit my Visa/Access/Diner's Card/American Express (delete as applicable) card no:

Signature ....Expiry Date ....